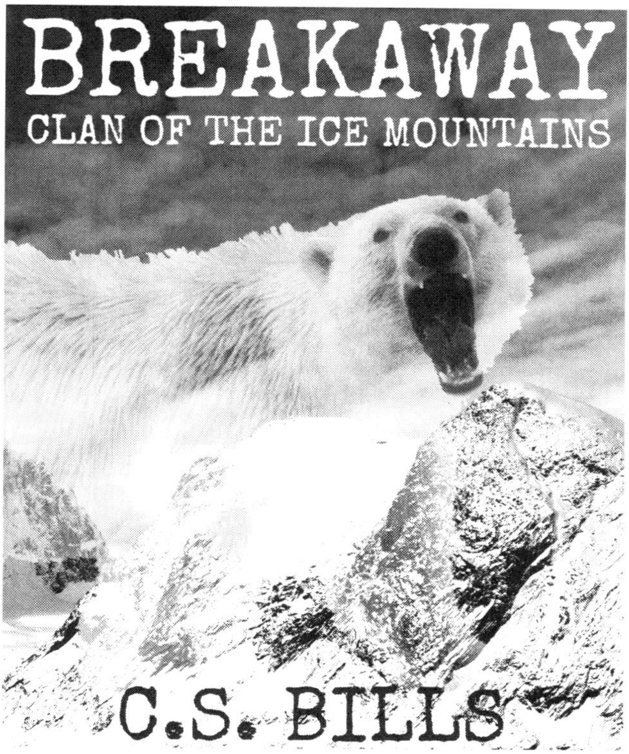

Clan of the Ice Mountains
Book One: Breakaway

C. S. Bills

Highest Hope Publishing LLC

Copyright

ISBN 13 ~ 978-1481079143

 Cover and print formatting by Jeff Bennington. Edited by Bethany Eicher. Published by Highest Hope Publishing LLC.

Dedication:

To my students at Hahn Intermediate School:

You are amazing!

About the Author:

C.S. Bills has taught reading and writing to middle grade students for many years. Her home is surrounded by acres of Michigan meadows, woods, and wetlands. There, she says, it's easy to imagine prehistoric hunters and gatherers living exciting lives of adventure and romance. As darkness falls, she has often "almost seen" the shadows of Attu's people moving among the trees.

Visit csbills.com to learn more about Attu and Rika's world and to catch previews of upcoming books in the *Clan of the Ice Mountains* series. Find tips on how to write adventure stories and explore the "Fun Fan Feedback" section. Use the email link to ask a question or leave a comment.

Acknowledgements

Thanks to Jackie, my dear sister, for being a super supporter all the way. Thanks to my beta readers, especially Valorie, Yvonne, and Deb. And thanks, Mark. You are the best life buddy a gal could ever ask for. Your support of my every endeavor, including my writing, has enabled me to get out there, stay out there, and succeed!

Many thanks to Bethany Eicher, my editor, who got her hands on my manuscript and worked magic. Her ideas and exacting digital "red pen" are an indispensible combo.

Bethany has an MFA in creative writing and teaches college English. She has done freelance editing and writing for publishing houses and independent authors and now runs Clarity and Grace Editing; she can be reached at ClarityAndGraceEditing@gmail.com.

Cover and book formatting by Jeff Bennington from 'The Writing Bomb' and @TweetTheBook Thanks, Jeff! Your work is awesome!

Prologue

Cloudless sky laced with stars met the endless expanse of ice on the horizon, then stretched itself up into an infinite black. The sparkling pinpricks of light beckoned to the twelve men and women who sat below, each on a large rock flattened and polished by countless generations of those who had sat as they sat now, mountains to their backs, rotting ice over an endless ocean stretching out before them.

Motionless since the sun disappeared below the horizon, they stared out over the ocean's Expanse, each seeming to see something that was not there, something important, something dangerous.

Now the wind, warm and carrying the scent of open water, whipped around them, blowing hair out of hoods and jangling the ornaments on the sticks positioned across their laps, long implements of gnarled wood decorated with shells, feathers, and curiously carved dangling charms. Theirs was the only movement, the only sound.

Until one of the watchers spoke.

"I have finally found the one from the Ice Mountain Clan who will heed the call," the man said, and he turned, grunting as his old bones complained about sitting still for so long. The female watcher beside him turned as well, her fiercely red hair gleaming dark in the starlight, flashing occasionally like fire in the light of the rising moon.

The two faced each other; the rest, seemingly oblivious, continued to stare out over the ice. This would be the last clan called, if their plans worked out as all hoped. The other clans were already well on their way to safety.

"So, most Ancient One, who will it be?" the red-haired woman asked, pulling her hood up over her flaming hair and tucking her bare hands more firmly into the long sleeves of the woven outer garment she wore. “Their leader? Or his brother?”

“Neither,” said the first, and pulled a strand of long white hair back into his cloak. He fixed his eyes on the woman, and she caught a twinkle of amusement in their blue depths. “It is the young hunter, the son of the one who can no longer lead, who has heard the Call. He is restless. He will listen. He will come.”

“But how can he do this thing?” The red-headed woman protested. “Why will the clan follow such a young hunter?”

“Because he has the Gift,” replied the first. “And their healer is believed to be the embodiment of Shuantuan. She also has the Gift. She will encourage him. Others will listen to her.”

The female watcher turned back toward the Expanse, her eyes unfocused, her head tilted, as if she were listening to something. Then she nodded, slightly at first then more earnestly.

“Yes, it will be so,” she agreed. “But the dangers… they are so many, and his chance to succeed, so small.”

“I have tried all others who could lead more easily. None will listen. It must be him. We must cause him to find help, when he needs it,” the blue-eyed watcher said. “And I know just who to send to our young hunter. Together, they will bring two clans to us, if the Great Spirit wills it, before it is too late.”

“Who?”

“The young woman of the Great Expanse clan. She has dreamed, and although she does not yet believe, she will when the time is right.”

“Perhaps. But you see what they will face, do you not, oh Ancient One? Disaster on the ice, attacks from both animal and man, and worst of all, betrayal by one of their own. Their clans seem bent on destroying themselves. Certainly their chances of success are slim?”

"You are right, Young One," the blue-eyed Ancient agreed. "Do you sense another choice?"

The woman's shoulders sagged. "No," she answered, her voice edged with both reluctance and resignation.

"Then let us do this now. We must travel soon, back to the Rock and its safety. We have many days of journeying ahead of us to reach the final place of Guidance."

The blue-eyed man stood and threw his hood back. White hair blew behind him as he faced the now gale-force wind coming off the ice, warm on his face.

"The time has come!" The man shouted above the wind, and shaking the long stick in front of him, he began to chant. The others on the rock stirred at his words. They stood as well and each chanted. They called the clans, called to the people scattered across the great Expanse of melting ice to race for the safety of land and be saved.

BREAKAWAY

Clan of the Ice Mountains

C.S. Bills

Chapter 1

Attu and Suka strode across the vast expanse of hardened snow over ice, a bitter wind cutting through their fur-lined miks and hoods. They were cold and tired, but the hunt had been good and two large snow otters hung across Attu's pack and one across Suka's.

"I'm not taking one of your otters, so quit trying to give it to me." Suka scowled and walked faster. "It won't make a difference, anyway."

Suka tightened his hood against the cold and the glaring sunlight reflecting off the flat endless white around them.

"I'm just saying-"

"My father isn't like yours, even though they're brothers," Suka said, thrusting his spear butt out before him, testing the ice as he walked. "Haven't you figured that out by now? I could come home with ten snow otters and still whatever game Kinak gets will be better, just because he's the oldest son. It's always been that way. 'Kinak the broad shouldered, Kinak the wise. Suka the weak, Suka the stupid one.' Nothing I do changes how my father feels about me."

Attu shook his head, sorry for his cousin. Ubantu, Attu's father, was so different from his younger brother, Moolnik, Suka's father. *It's hard to believe we're part of the same family...*

Suka picked up his pace. He was long-legged for a Nuvik, narrow in the body and tall for his age. Like Attu, he wore bone goggles, slitted to keep out the constant glare of the ice around them, carved to fit snugly against his dusky skin around deep set brown eyes. The long trim on Suka's parka hood hid his round face with its high cheek bones and flat wide nose, but Attu didn't have to see Suka's face to tell his cousin was angry as he strode toward the distant dark rocks that jutted up behind a thin strip of grey and tumbled ice.

"Careful," Attu said. "We're nearing the shore."

Suka and Attu struck the ice in front of them with every step, using the butt of their spears. No Nuvik walked on the Expanse anymore without testing ahead. Full of death traps set by Attuanin, the Spirit of the Deep, the thin ice waited for them to take one wrong step and plunge into the frigid water beneath. In their heavy fur clothing, they would sink like stones.

"Do you think the stories about Attuanin are true?" Suka asked, as the young hunters approached the rocky outcropping of land.

"My father says more hunters have been lost since you and I were born than ever before. Attuanin must need men for his water kingdom," Attu replied.

Lomkut and Shrantik, two hunters from their clan, had fallen through the ice and drowned within the last twenty moons. They'd left women and children behind. Some of those were near starving now. The clan women shared the meat from their own hunters, but there was never enough.

"It wouldn't be such a loss for my family if I fell through the ice," Suka grumbled. "But since your father's accident six moons ago, with his injured leg-"

"That's why I'm careful," Attu interrupted. He paused, listening to the sounds of the ice. Satisfied, he moved on.

Attu had been named after Attuanin, but he didn't think that would keep him safer on the ice than anyone else. In his two hundredth moon, at his final naming ceremony, Attu's name had been changed from Neetook, which meant "quiet one," because he was almost as good as his father at sneaking up on game without a sound, to the name of the water spirit, Attuanin, the greatest of all hunters.

His father, Ubantu, had braided Attu's black hair down his back in the single braid worn by men, chopping the bottom off below the rawhide tie, and setting that hair aside to be burned at the ceremony. His mother, Yural, rubbed grease into his upper body until his bronze skin shone, careful not to touch his upper arms with their still healing clan tattoos, the ice mountain for his clan on his right arm, and the down facing line under the flat ice of the Expanse, the symbol for Attuanin, on the other. It rippled over his left bicep whenever he flexed his arm.

Mother smeared blood from Attu's latest kill on her weathered palm and pressed it over Attu's heart. Meavu, his little sister, did the same, although Father had to lift her up to make her tall enough to reach. She placed her small blood-stained hand over the imprint of her mother's on Attu's chest. Thus Yural and Meavu were bound to Attu and he to them, sworn to hunt for his mother and sister until the day he took a woman of his own.

Attu stood amongst the clan, stripped to the waist, the bloody handprints on his chest, his body gleaming in the light of the nuknuk lamps, while all around him the clan danced. Elder Nuanu, the clan's healer and spiritual leader, spoke the words and shook the bone rattle. And then he was a man, a hunter, Attuanin.

"You must call him Attu. It is profane to call someone their full spirit name," Attu's mother had scolded Meavu when she danced around the shelter later that night, smiling and singing, "Attuanin, mighty hunter, my brother, Attuanin."

Attu heard a soft groaning sound, and both hunters froze. But no crack raced across the ice.

Attu looked to Suka.

"I think it's safe," Suka said, and as if to prove it, he forced his spear butt roughly into the ice in front of him, testing his next step. Suka's spear plunged through the ice, and his weight threw him forward after it.

"No!" yelled Attu, and he grabbed for Suka, latched onto the snow otter tied to Suka's pack, and pulled.

Attu yanked Suka backward several steps, dragging him by the snow otter. Then both turned and ran away from the rotted ice, opening up a space between them for added safety. Once on solid ice, the two hunters stopped running and looked back.

A hole just big enough to drop a man through, Attu thought as he gazed toward the place where Suka had almost fallen through the ice.

"It's an old nuknuk breathing hole," Attu said as he walked back to where Suka now stood, far away from the hole. The huge seal-like animals were the main meat of the Nuvik, and their fat was burned in long soft stone bowls, the nuknuk lamps that lit and heated every Nuvik snow house or hide shelter.

"That hole in the ice was almost my grave," Suka whispered after a moment. "Thank you." He clasped Attu in a fierce embrace.

"Just trying to save a good snow otter," Attu teased. He pulled away from his cousin and punched his arm.

"You just about strangled me with it." Suka grinned back. His eyes were mere slits in his face as he tried to join in the joking, but Attu could still see his fear.

They stood still, breathing slowly, until Attu stopped hearing his blood pounding in his ears.

"Guess we go the long way," Attu said.

He turned and walked east of the broken ice, carefully avoiding the cracks around the hole.

Suka followed, walking slowly as he checked the ice.

"We shouldn't have been talking about Attuanin and his traps," Suka said after they'd walked another spear throw's distance. "Talking, or even thinking about something bad that could happen, sometimes makes it happen. That's what Elder Nuanu says."

"She should know."

Attu adjusted his pack across his back again. The snow otters were heavy. Their dark bodies dangled the length of his torso, and their tails almost touched the ice behind him as he walked.

"Let's think about how delicious these snow otters will taste instead," Attu said. "I'm thinking of my favorite part, the livers, sliced thin, warmed over the nuknuk lamp, but still bloody."

Suka's stomach growled loudly in response. "You sound like the women talking about how to prepare the meat."

"Your stomach seems to like it," Attu teased. When his own stomach growled too, he patted it gently. "Soon, soon," he crooned.

Suka chuckled.

A few more steps and they reached the large rock that marked the boundary between the Expanse and the safety of solid land.

Just beyond the rock, Attu and Suka paused for a moment, enjoying the ground under their feet. They shifted their spears to carry them loosely, spear point forward, and set off down the rocky shoreline path toward home.

"Don't say anything about what happened," Suka demanded as they walked.

"I won't. My mother worries too, every time I go hunting-"

"It's not that," Suka interrupted. "I don't want my father to know. If he finds out I almost fell through an old nuknuk hole, he'll yell at me for the next moon."

"Oh." *Twenty-eight days of being yelled at by Moolnik?* Attu shuddered at the thought. *I'd tell my father everything, and he'd grab me up in a strong hug and thank the spirits for saving me...*

Attu decided to change the subject. "Do you think Elder Tovut is still angry with me?"

"You did argue with him in front of everyone," Suka said. "Why'd you do that?"

"Because he keeps telling those stories about the Great Frozen melting, and I just got tired of it. It scares Meavu, and it's nonsense. I wanted him to stop."

Suka stood in the middle of the path. Clearing his throat and leaning in toward Attu, he deepened his voice and spoke as if he were addressing a clan meeting. "It has always been cold on the Expanse, where we hunt. The sea has always been frozen. That is why it is called the Great Frozen. Water is always frozen on the surface; everyone knows that. Why tell such stories, Elder Tovut? Do you enjoy scaring the children?"

"Was it that bad?" Attu asked. Suka had repeated what Attu had said three nights ago when he'd confronted Elder Tovut, the clan's oldest and most revered member, in front of the whole clan gathered in the great snow house.

"Yes," Suka replied. "Worse, actually. Didn't you hear your mother hissing at you? You're going to go hungry if you keep talking that way to an elder in front of her."

Attu shot a glance at Suka as they started walking again. Suka was shaking his head mournfully. Once the game was given to the women, it became theirs to do with as they saw fit, but Attu couldn't believe his mother would let him go hungry when he was the one who brought the meat home. Yural was a kind woman, generous to all and a devoted mother.

Had Suka's mother ever refused to feed him because she was mad at him? Mother had seemed angry the night I challenged Elder Tovut, but I still ate the next day. Besides, Elder Tovut's stories are not new. I've been hearing them since I was small. It's just that Elder Tovut has begun telling them as if they are true, not stories at all. That's what made me angry enough to confront the frail old man, elder or not.

"The Nuvikuan-na, the land of our people, has seemed to us to always be a land of cold, with the Great Frozen and its frigid waters below the ice, and the Great Expanse, the top of that ice and the sky above, where we live," Elder Tovut said. "We hunt the snow otter and the nuknuk, make our homes on the small rock outcroppings, gather the mussels, and light the lamps at night. Here we are born and live and die, each his eight hundred moons or so, if the spirits allow. Most go the way of the Between much sooner. More generations than we can count have lived this way, without seeing the Great Frozen melt and become water on the surface once again. But the Warming comes."

Elder Tovut had paused, looking at each of them sitting in the large gathering snow house, his dark eyes like two polished beads beneath his deep lid folds. "It is part of the cycle of the Nuvikuan-na," he continued, "and we must heed this cycle or die. We must remember, or all the clans will perish. I'm the oldest of this clan, and it was told to me by my father's father, whose father told him, and his father before him. It is a sacred trust to be told. It is my duty to make you see the truth of what I say."

The old man cleared his throat. His breath sounded ragged in his thin chest. Elder Tovut's skin looked sallow in the light of the lamps, and the shadow he cast against the curving walls of the snow house seemed more like a child's than a man's. But as he spoke his voice became stronger, and his words caused the hair on Attu's neck to rise.

"The Cold is coming to an end. The Warming is coming once again to Nuvikuan-na. Soon I will travel to the Between, and the trystas will change me into a star and hook me on their spear of light. They will hurl me into the great bowl of the sky. After I am gone, the cracks in the Great Frozen will become larger. You'll begin to see open water, like that in the cooking skins, where once there was only ice."

Elder Tovut coughed. One of the women brought him a bowl of warm drink. He took it but did not drink from it.

"And," he repeated, "the Great Frozen will stay open water, just like the water in this bowl." He held up the bowl in his veined hands, misshapen from years of exposure to the frigid elements. "It will not freeze again for countless generations until the Warming ends and the Cooling comes, finally bringing the Cold again."

A child began to cry. Many of the clan shook their heads in disbelief…

"Attu."

Attu realized he'd let his thoughts wander. He looked at Suka. "What?" Attu asked.

"What do you think about Elder Tovut's stories?" Suka asked. His voice sounded anxious.

"Whether or not I believe in the Warming, and I don't," Attu said, "we still need to leave this place, and soon. We were lucky with this last hunt, but the game has grown scarce. We must move on before we starve."

"But do we have to go as far south as Elder Tovut says?" Suka asked. "He said we have to cross over strange mountains to a new land, to keep us from drowning when the Great Frozen melts and the water rises."

"I don't think we have to do that. I think Elder Tovut is starting to slip Between already. His stories are crazy."

Suka grasped the stone amulet hanging around his neck and spoke a word of protection over himself. "He seems so feeble…"

"I know," Attu said. For a moment, he felt guilty for thinking of Elder Tovut as an old man no longer in his right mind, instead of the wise elder of Attu's childhood.

Attu struck a loose piece of rock with his spear butt. It skittered over the rocks and ice toward the nearest hill.

"Stories or not, we must head south soon. We can't go north, because that's where we came from. The game won't have recovered there yet-"

"But not as far south as Elder Tovut says?"

"No, just far enough to find game. That's all."

Suka placed his mik over his slitted bone goggles, shielding his eyes even more from the sun's glare. He looked down the windswept shoreline of jumbled rocks and gravel with hills of ice rising behind it. "We're almost there," he announced.

At the thought of a meal soon, Attu began the slow loping gait that would cover ground quickly but not make him sweat. Suka matched strides with Attu like they had since they were children.

Rounding the last bend, they saw the settlement ahead, a sprawling group of snow houses, mounds of white resting among bright patches of sunlight and shadow cast from the hills behind them.

"Race you," Suka shouted, and he took off across the packed snow toward their dwellings on the far side of the settlement.

The snow otters weighed Attu down too much for him to beat the longer-legged Suka. *He knows that,* Attu thought. *Why does Suka always have to make a competition out of something he knows he will win?*

Suddenly, Suka stopped. He turned back to Attu.

"Something's wrong," he said.

Attu looked around him. Suka was right. This time of day the settlement should be noisy with children playing, people working outside, and the smell of cooking meat filling the air.

But instead, there was no one outside at all. And it was deathly quiet.

Chapter 2

"Elder Tovut has gone Between," Meavu whispered into Attu's ear as he scooped his little sister up with his free arm upon entering his family's snow house. She was getting too big for him to pick up easily, but she wrapped her legs around him now so he could hold her, leaning into him, her two dark braids falling on both sides of his face. "Father hasn't spoken to me since he was told, and Mother has been checking all our clothing, furs, and cooking tools, getting us ready to move south. The men have decided it's time."

Meavu placed her mik covered hands on either side of Attu's face, drawing him even closer to her own, so he was looking directly into her bright dark eyes. "I should be excited," she continued, her voice still low, "because I don't remember the last time we moved; I was still a poolik, riding in Mother's hood."

Meavu shook her head, and a few strands of thick black hair escaped her braids, curling at the sides of her round face.

"I know it is the way of our people. It's time to move. But I'm scared, Attu..." and Meavu slid her arms around Attu's neck and clung there.

"Kip, scared?" Attu teased.

"The people are afraid to go," she breathed into his ear, in case speaking their fear aloud might make the situation worse. "I heard Moolnik talking with Mother about it. He's been talking with everyone. Some want to go right away, as Elder Tovut said to do. Some want to stay to follow ritual for his burial. No one seems to know what to do. And Moolnik is in the middle of it all, stirring up trouble. Father said, 'Even though he's my brother, Moolnik's name fits him. He's a troublemaker, stirring up any evil he can find with his stinging words.'

"Mother said, 'Quiet now, Ubantu, or the Moolnikuan will hear you speak so of your brother and then we WILL have trouble. The men follow Moolnik now because he is strong, an excellent hunter, and the father of three sons, two of them grown hunters for our clan. His tongue is quick and his temper quicker, but the men seem to admire him for it. They don't know him like you do. They don't see the danger in following such a hothead.' Father agreed with her. That's why I'm scared."

Attu hugged Meavu and set her back down on her feet. "Don't worry, little Kip. I'll talk to Father."

Attu felt his blood quicken at the thought of leaving soon.

"When is the stone gathering?" Attu asked.

"Next sun."

"Where are Father and Mother now?"

"Father's with the other men, trying to decide on plans for the move now that Elder Tovut has passed. Mother's seeing to the preparation of Elder Tovut's body."

Attu, suddenly feeling weighed down by the news of Elder Tovut passing Between, realized he was still shouldering his pack and his kill. He slipped his pack onto one of the sleeping platforms.

"Oh, what a good hunt you've had!" Meavu removed her miks and clasped her hands together.

"And new miks for you, just in time for the move."

Twin bits of red appeared on Meavu's pale cheeks. She'd accidently sliced a hole in her miks with her ullik knife just a few days ago. But she didn't scold Attu for his teasing now, just as she hadn't scolded him earlier for calling her Kip, the sound newborn nuknuks made crying to their mothers. Instead, Meavu reached out her hands, palms up, and said, "May the spirits of the snow otters be thanked for the offering of their bodies to you, mighty hunter of the Nuvikuan." With her mother gone, Meavu had stepped into her place as the woman, accepting meat from her hunter.

Attu inclined his head to his sister and replied, "Indeed may they be thanked, and live again in the body of another to grow and be given to our people yet again." He smiled as he carefully handed the large otters to his sister and watched her struggle under their weight. Still, she maintained her dignity in this ritual display of roles and most important exchange between the hunter and his family. She turned and, straining to lift them, carefully set the otters onto the cooking slab.

Attu left as Meavu began the ritual of the preparation of food. He heard her clear high voice chanting to the spirits of the otters as she dripped a few drops of water into each snow otter's mouth, giving them a drink to send their spirits on their way in comfort, before she began slicing her ullik knife down the front legs of the one closest to her. Attu knew they'd eat well tonight, and that thought brought him pride. He was the hunter, and he'd done well. And Meavu, his little sister, was growing up.

Attu entered the snow house of his father's younger brother, Moolnik, and sat on the edge of the sleeping platform where his face was in shadow. The six older men, led by Moolnik, were talking in low voices, gathered around the nuknuk lamp in the center of the snow house. Attu could see the cords in his father's neck bulging.

For two moons, Father couldn't walk; he still can't hunt. Meanwhile, Moolnik, being the next oldest hunter and the leader's brother, has smoothly stepped into his place. Too easily, too quickly.

Moolnik was making slashing motions with his hand against the mik on his other hand as if by doing so he could convince the others of his opinion.

"We must wait," Moolnik said. "We must not anger the trystas by leaving Elder Tovut's body before the next moon. We must not disrespect our elder in that way."

"I agree with you," Attu's father said. "But remember, Elder Tovut told us during the storytelling a few days ago that we need to leave immediately."

"This is true," one of the other hunters said, and all heads nodded except for Moolnik's.

"Elder Tovut was a very old man," Moolnik replied, his lips curling into a sneer as he spoke. "We should not listen to one whose spirit was perhaps already on its journey before his body followed a few days later."

Moolnik leaned back, his sneer turning into a grin as he nodded his head slightly, inviting the others to join him.

Attu moved forward and placed himself in the group, his shoulder touching his father's. Once sitting in the circle of men, Attu gestured with his right hand, placing it palm down before him as if to warm it at the lamp. The men grew quiet.

"Speak, my son," his father said.

"All here know my great respect for Elder Tovut, may his spirit soar on the spear of the trysta into the night sky and become a bright star in the heavens," Attu began. "I believe Elder Tovut spoke the truth about our need to leave now. I see the hollows in my sister's cheeks, and I know she is not getting enough meat. I'm sure it's the same with your women and children. The game has grown scarce. I believe we must go now while we are still strong enough to travel."

Several men nodded their heads, paused, then looked toward Moolnik.

Always now they defer to Moolnik. Can't these men think for themselves? Attu thought.

"If we do not respect the spirits and stay," Moolnik argued, "disaster will follow us, and we will all die. We must stay and guard Elder Tovut's grave for the full time ritual dictates."

The other men popped their lips, a sharp sound of agreement. Only Attu's father remained silent.

After a moment, the men began talking again, working out the details of guarding Elder Tovut's body from the evil spirits until the next full moon. Attu felt himself flush with anger. Motioning with his head in a quick sideways gesture the hunters used, a signal he was leaving, he crawled out of Moolnik's snow house and headed for Elder Tovut's.

Attu slipped into Elder Tovut's snow house, bending to walk through the entrance tunnel and up the steep incline, pausing where the tunnel turned to the right before opening up into the snow house. He heard the women before he saw them, the eight adult women of the clan working around the body of Elder Tovut, wrapping every inch of him with soft skins cut into strips like bandages. Elder Tovut's face was creased with the traditional painted signs of a departed one. On his right cheek the sign for his clan, Ice Mountains, and on the left, the jagged zigzag sign for Tovuttuan, the spirit of the ice cliffs themselves.

"Are you going to ask for entrance, Attu, mighty hunter, or are you just going to crouch there all day like a Moolnikuan spirit waiting to play a nasty trick on us?"

"I bring no evil," Attu spoke to gain entrance.

"We'll see about that," was Elder Nuanu's terse reply.

"Attu, you're back," his mother said, and Attu heard the relief in her voice.

"Yes, Mother, and two snow otters have given up their spirits for our cooking skins," he replied.

"I must go," his mother said and began to rise.

"Meavu has taken the meat," Attu explained. "When I left she'd already begun preparations. And yes, Mother," Attu added when he saw his mother's dark eyes widen in sudden alarm, "she followed all ritual. She's no longer a little girl, but knows her duties."

His mother knelt back down again and resumed her wrapping of Elder Tovut's left leg, a hint of a smile brightening her round face.

"A good girl," several of the women said, their lips popping slightly as they spoke the compliment. "You've done well, Yural."

Attu's mother lowered her gaze, but Attu could see she was beaming with pride.

Attu approached Elder Nuanu, who was sitting cradling her man's head as if he were merely sleeping.

"I know what you are going to say," Elder Nuanu began.

Attu sat down beside her and waited for her to continue.

"I've already tried persuading Moolnik and the others to leave immediately after my man's burial. Your father understands. The other men do not. These women here…" and she waved her arms at the other women present with a gesture that seemed half anger and half resignation, "assure me they cannot change the minds of their men. Their men are like tooth fish grabbing at the bait and not letting go, even when dragged out onto the ice to freeze."

Her voice was harsh, but once the words had passed her lips, Elder Nuanu seemed to draw into herself, weariness and sorrow carving new lines into her already creased face. She looked almost as old as the man whose head and shoulders she cradled, even though Attu knew she'd been Elder Tovut's second wife, much younger than the ancient elder.

Elder Nuanu looked at Attu, understanding and resignation clearly evident on her face now. "Those men will wait," she said, "even if it means all our deaths."

The snow house was silent. Elder Nuanu slumped down, her hand caressing the brow of her dead man.

Yural shook her head, a quick movement, and full of determination. "We must rely on our hunters until the next full moon, Attu. I know you will do your part to keep us in meat until we can go."

Attu's stomach clenched. *There's hardly any game left for the taking here. How will we keep our families strong enough so we can leave when it's time?*

After a moment, Elder Nuanu pursed her lips in agreement with Yural and sighed. "I'll ask the spirits of shallow water to draw the animals and fish," she said, as if she had read Attu's mind. "It's all I can do."

"Thank you, Elder Nuanu, embodiment of Shuantuan," Attu said. Still needing to know the answer to one question, he placed his hand out, palm down.

"Speak, Attu," his mother said.

"What did Elder Tovut say before his spirit left his body?"

Attu asked this question reverently, for even though he had argued with the elder before leaving on his latest hunt, Attu had had great respect for Elder Tovut.

A hush came over the snow house again as the other women stopped wrapping Elder Tovut's body and leaned in to hear what Elder Nuanu would say.

"First, my man spoke for my ears alone," Elder Nuanu began, and paused as a single tear rolled down her wrinkled cheek. She touched the body of Elder Tovut tenderly, her fingertips gliding over his grey hair.

Taking a breath, she continued. "Then he said, 'When Attu comes to ask you what I said, tell him if he does not believe in the Warming and the need for haste, our clan will be lost. Attu must stay strong, so he can lead the people to safety, that all may survive the great breaking. When the separation occurs, Attu must prevail, along with the one who will bear his sons and daughters. He is the hope of our people. Tell him he must not give up this hope.'"

Attu sat silent, and when the pressure of the other women's eyes on him became too much, he shut his own. *People will perish without me? A great breaking? The one who will bear my sons and daughters? Do not give up hope? What did all of this mean?*

"Attu," Elder Nuanu said. "I know you are shocked to hear that Elder Tovut's last words were for you, rather than for the leader of our clan as we would expect. But these events will come to pass. I've seen this truth, also. You will save our people. You must."

As Elder Nuanu spoke, a great weight seemed to fall on Attu, the weight of his whole clan, as if all their bodies suddenly rested on his shoulders, he straining under the load.

"How can this be?" He asked Elder Nuanu. "I'm just a young hunter. I'm not an Elder. I'm not yet a father of strong sons and daughters. I'm just Attu."

"The spirits do not call a leader who is worthy in his own eyes," Elder Nuanu said. "They call the one who is willing to listen and to sacrifice for his clan. You are that man, Attu, Mighty Hunter. The spirits have chosen you. Move forward with what you know to do. And pray it will be enough for us all."

Chapter 3

Elder Tovut had been given to the hills. The men danced the burial dance and took turns guarding the mound of rocks that covered his body, keeping the evil spirits away by their ritual chanting.

Attu had been a young boy the last time he'd stood with his father guarding a body, learning the rituals of protection. That night had seemed a never-ending time of bitter cold. This night, in comparison, seemed mild. Attu wondered. *Could a Warming time be coming? Had Nuvikuan-na been growing warmer over time, so gradually as to be missed by the generations of the Nuvik who lived out their lives upon the Great Expanse? And now, had Nuvikuan-na finally reached some invisible turning point? Had the Warming begun?*

~ • ~

"Suka, Yupik, you're with me," Moolnik said. "Head out!" Without waiting for anyone to follow, Moolnik walked off the land they had called home for so long, and out over the Expanse upon the Great Frozen.

Suka looked at Attu, an apology in his eyes.

Attu shrugged and gathered his things, placing himself in the middle line of the clan as they headed across the ice to the south. The sun seemed warm for this early in the morning, the ice under him crunched in an odd way. He watched and listened as he walked along, wary of the changes in the surface of the ice and in the weather.

"Moolnik was furious when he heard Elder Tovut spoke of you and not him as the leader of our clan," Yural reminded her son as the two of them walked along. "Don't be surprised if he tries to slight you in every way, including not allowing you to lead with your cousin."

"I know," Attu said. Suka had told him how Moolnik had ranted at both him and Kinak because Elder Tovut had spoken no words about them.

"As if it were somehow our fault," Suka had said. "The only good thing about it was that this time he was yelling at Kinak, too."

As they walked along, Attu turned his thoughts away from Moolnik and worked instead to remember the last time his clan had moved. Then, they'd simply trekked across the Expanse unconcerned, people moving from one group to another, chatting and calling to the children who ran back and forth amongst them all, playing. The Great Frozen had always been solid ice beneath them back then, as secure as walking on the rocky outcroppings where they built their homes. Attu had been one of the children, laughing and running…

Now, the clan walked in three lines, each person in the tracks of one of the lead hunters, distributing their combined weight of people and belongings over a much larger area. They walked in silence, listening for the sudden moan of splitting or rotten ice. And although no one spoke of it for fear it might happen if they did, all knew that by dividing the group and putting a spear throw between them, and by carefully parceling out the supplies each person carried, if one group fell through the ice, the rest would have a greater chance of survival.

Moolnik led at a grueling pace and continued long after the clan needed to stop and rest. Moolnik was out to prove his strength, to contrast it with his brother Ubantu's weakness since his accident.

Again. Attu was furious with Moolnik. First they'd stayed too long to fulfill the ritual for Elder Tovut because Moolnik had insisted on it, and now, on the ice, Moolnik had decided to push the clan at a brutal pace.

Frustrated, Attu hit a chunk of loose ice with his spear butt, sending it skittering across the Great Frozen.

Meavu looked back at him and started to smile, but then frowned. Attu knew she'd hoped he was being playful, but she'd seen anger brewing on his face instead. Meavu turned back and continued trudging ahead. By the slump of her shoulders, Attu knew Meavu was growing more tired with every step, and it fueled his anger.

Attu wished Suka wasn't leading with his father. Suka must know they were going too fast, but suggesting they slow down for the sake of the women and children would only anger Moolnik, and he would ridicule Suka for suggesting it. Yupik, the other hunter leading with them, followed Moolnik like a nuknuk pup after its mother. He'd never question Moolnik's orders. They trudged on.

Attu felt the tension in the clan increase as they moved over the ice, falling further and further behind the leaders. Once, Attu saw Suka stop, turning to look at the rest of the group, now at least twenty long spear throws behind them. Attu thought he heard him shout something to Moolnik, but Moolnik didn't pause for a step, nor did he turn around to acknowledge Suka or look behind him at the floundering clan.

It was hard to tell from that distance across the glaring ice, but Attu thought he saw Suka shake his head before picking up Moolnik's pace again. Attu was proud of Suka if he had indeed tried to slow his father down.

Finally, Moolnik called a halt when the sun was at its highest point in the sky, shining directly in their faces as they headed south. Someone saw Moolnik's raised hand and signaled for the others, who stopped where they stood, slinging off their packs and sitting on them. The women grabbed food pouches and began feeding the children. Moolnik, Suka, and Yupik were forced to walk back to the clan for food.

The women of the clan have their own ways of getting even. Attu watched Tulnu hand Moolnik a small slice of dried meat. Moolnik growled at her, but she turned away as if she hadn't heard him.

"My father is crazy," Suka whispered between bites of dried meat as he stood beside Attu. "Look at our people." Suka waved his hand across the group of red-cheeked women and children, their parka hoods thrown back, their hair damp with sweat.

"Even the littlest child knows sweat is a killer on the Expanse," Attu agreed. "Soon we'll have people with chills and headaches from their spirits not getting enough water. No one can drink enough with all this sweating, and it's so warm-"

"Evil spirits will attack the weak as they chill again," Suka interrupted. "I know. But my father won't slow his pace."

Suka grabbed up his pack where he'd flung it on the ground moments before. "I'm going to see if Kinak can talk some sense into him."

Moolnik thought his first born son was as wise as an elder, and his second son was a fool. "Moolnik is the fool," Attu muttered to himself, careful to keep his voice low.

Looking toward his own father, Attu saw the strain on Ubantu's face. His father shook his head, one long slow swing, emphasizing his own low opinion of his brother's actions.

Attu walked over to his parents and Meavu and flung down his pack of rolled furs and supplies. He took the dried meat his mother offered him and slipped his hand into his parka for his water skin. He watched as the other women adjusted their children's slitted goggles and handed out more food. Meavu sat down heavily on the furs Attu had been carrying and, leaning back against them, pulled her parka hood down over her face to block out the sunlight. She fell asleep almost immediately.

Attu and his mother exchanged glances. It was only halfway through the first day and already Meavu was exhausted. *How is she going to be able to walk the many days it will take to reach the next land to the South?*

Yural clasped her spirit necklace in her hand, and Attu saw her lips forming a silent plea to her name spirit, Yuralria, one of the trystas of protection who dwelled in the Between. Protection trystas entered the women's bodies through ritual dances, bringing their power of safety into the here and now. They were crucial to the wellbeing of every clan.

Her prayer finished, Yural turned her attention to her man.

"Ubantu, you cannot take your turn at the lead. Your leg-"

"My leg is fine."

"But you're already limping; your ankle aches, I know. One of the other hunters can take your place. You can-"

"It is not your place to say, woman," Ubantu interrupted her again with a downward thrust of his right hand, chopping off any further discussion. Ubantu turned his back on Attu's mother and silently chewed on the leathery piece of dried snow otter she'd given him.

Attu knew his father was worried about taking his place as the lead hunter after their rest. The wind had picked up, and Ubantu would be heading directly into its teeth, with no one ahead of him to block its strength.

He knows he's not strong enough to lead in this wind for half a sun as Moolnik has done, Attu thought, *especially at such a grueling pace. But not leading will show weakness. And father has had to give up so much because of his injury. Moolnik has taken charge and the others have let him. No one else seems to want the responsibility to lead but Moolnik. The other hunters see him as the natural leader if his older brother cannot. And Father has not objected.*

For as long as Attu could remember, it had been this way between Ubantu and Moolnik. His father tried to get along with his brother, but Moolnik refused to see that Ubantu only wanted their life-long rivalry to end.

Once, when Moolnik had sworn at Ubantu and stalked out of their snow house, Attu had grown frustrated with his father's constant placating of his younger brother.

"Why does he hate you so?" Attu had asked.

Instead of answering, his father had grabbed his fishing tools and left.

Once his father had gone, Attu turned to his mother, who'd been busy doing woman's work in the shadows, away from the men's argument. "Why, mother?" Attu pleaded. "I need to know."

Attu's mother moved to the heat of the nuknuk lamp and patting the fur beside her, motioned for him to sit. She placed her hands on her spirit necklace and took in a deep breath.

"Your father's father, your grandfather, was a cruel and violent man," she began. "He played favorites between his oldest son, Ubantu, and Moolnik, his younger brother. Through no fault of Ubantu's, Moolnik grew to hate him, and Ubantu's father fueled that jealousy with his taunting and teasing." Yural shivered. "I remember your grandfather. He was vile. He hit his sons. He hit his woman."

Yural stared into the flame of the nuknuk lamp, silent for a long time. Attu sensed her story was not finished however, so he too remained quiet.

"When Moolnik was young, he had many dreams," Yural finally said. "He desired to become a shaman of the clan. But his father laughed at him and called him weak. Still, Moolnik dreamed, and many of his dreams did come to pass. Only his father could not see he was special, born to lead the clan in the way of the spirits. He named him Moolnikuan when Moolnik became a hunter, just to spite him. Who would name their child after a trickster spirit of evil omens and trouble? But your grandfather laughed in the face of the spirits."

Yural clutched her amulet even tighter, her lips moving in silent prayer before continuing. "One night Moolnik had a dream his father died of an evil mussel spirit. He told Elder Nuanu, who had become the clan's healer by then. When Elder Nuanu warned your grandfather, he beat Moolnik and told him never to speak of his dreams again. Then he demanded his woman feed him mussels as often as she could find them, just to prove he was not afraid and to belittle his son. She was sent out day after day to hunt mussels until there were few good ones to be found. She grew weak from her searching, and Moolnik grew sullen and withdrawn. He was close to his mother, and it hurt him to see her mistreated. He blamed himself, your father said, even though it was not Moolnik's fault his father was such a cruel man.

"When your father was only twenty moons older than you are now," his mother continued, "your grandfather did die from eating a bad mussel. The evil spirit in it caused him much pain and fever before he passed into the Between. Elder Nuanu did everything she could, but still, he died. Many said it was his own fault for beating his woman and sons and treating the spirits with disdain. Once he was gone, we all hoped the two brothers could be reconciled."

"You knew Father then?" Attu knew his mother had come from the Ice Wind clan. He didn't realize his mother and father had been paired so young.

"Yes. We'd been bonded just the moon before. Your grandfather had acted horribly at the celebration, taunting Moolnik about how he'd never find a woman like his brother because he was a weak dreamer. He called him lazy and stupid, and said no woman would ever have him. Moolnik was furious, but he said nothing. If he tried to defend himself, his father would shame him even more. Moolnik knew we were all embarrassed for him, which made it worse."

Yural reached out and adjusted the long horizontal wick in the soft stone bowl of fat, making it burn brighter. Attu saw her face, grave in the light of the lamp, before she sat back in the shadows of the snow house again.

"Within the next moon, your grandfather was dead. I know your grandmother tried to intervene in the argument. I saw her bruised face and black eye later, although she tried to hide it from me. But I've always wondered… Your grandmother was a skilled woman. Even with mussels hard to find, to make such a grave mistake and serve her husband evil spirit mussels…"

Had Moolnik's dream been prophetic after all? Or had Moolnik's dream simply given his grandmother the means to murder her abusive man, thus "fulfilling the prophecy?"

Attu's flesh crawled at the thought.

But she hadn't been able to stop the rivalry between her sons. And instead of learning from his painful past, Moolnik had repeated his father's crime on his own two sons.

Coming out of his thoughts, Attu realized his mother was watching him now, a pleading look on her face. He knew she wanted him to convince his father not to take his place in the front, not to expose himself to further ridicule by his brother. She was asking the impossible.

What am I supposed to do? He shrugged at her in reply.

Yural seemed to sink into herself at his response, becoming lost in the thick parka she wore, with its tiny bone decorations dangling from sinew strings, its message stones, and its long fur ruff. His mother's face had aged since his father's accident; fine lines crossed her forehead now that even sleep did not erase.

Checking to see his father was still turned away from them, Attu held up one hand, placing it on his forehead, signaling to her that he would think of something. His mother understood, and she pulled herself up, pushed her dark braids laced with new grey more securely into her hood, and began bustling about the piles of belongings.

Yural pulled a wide nuknuk carry strap from a pouch in one of their bags. She walked over to her man and knelt before him. Ubantu turned toward her, and Attu saw the look that flashed between them. The warmth of their love shone clearly.

Slipping off Ubantu's foot mik, Yural skillfully wrapped Ubantu's lower leg and foot in the stabilizing nuknuk skin. The wrap would allow him to walk on the twisted joint with less pain. She slipped the foot mik back on and rubbed his knee gently.

Seeing the two of them supporting each other again gave Attu an idea. He approached his father. "May I lead with you, Father?"

"Are you willing to lead in the way of the true Nuvik, with thoughts of the safety of others always before you and thoughts of your own self left behind for others to determine?"

Attu looked down, for fear his surprise would show on his face. His father had practically admitted he thought his brother a poor example of a Nuvik male.

"Attu?" His father spoke as he held up a hand to gain Attu's full attention again.

"Yes?"

"I would be honored to have my son lead with me," Ubantu said. "I will inform Moolnik."

His father rose slowly, and only slightly favoring his crippled leg, he walked straight-backed to where his brother was sitting with a group of hunters.

The sun was about to touch the horizon when Ubantu, with Attu on his right and Kinak on his left, decided to end the journey for the day. They'd taken one more break, much needed by the women and children, and as far as Attu could figure, had covered about half the distance Moolnik had forced them to travel earlier. The smaller children were being carried now, and the other youngsters were barely putting one foot in front of the other.

Ubantu motioned for the clan to stop. Moolnik ordered them to set up camp. People began to chatter as packs were flung down, and women began pulling out the necessary supplies to set up skin tents for the long night ahead.

Attu, still off to the side, was about to begin walking back to help set up camp when suddenly a groan like a woman about to give birth rose up from the ice in front of him.

"Run!" he screamed, and waving his arms, he ran back toward the group. "Run!" he yelled again and began flailing his spear in the air to draw attention to himself.

Ubantu saw his son and in one fluid motion, reached out with his right hand to grab Meavu and his left to grab the most important pack, the one containing their food and nuknuk fat lamp. Attu heard him cry, "Yural, this way," and his mother launched herself after her man, grabbing up the remaining pack, a roll of skins for tent-making wrapped around furs for sleeping. The others, seeing Ubantu running as if he had two strong legs, his woman following on his heels, grabbed up their packs and ran also.

Behind him, Attu heard a large crack spreading. From the direction of the sound, he could tell it was moving out from his left to his right, which meant they had a chance. It was not going to open along the direction they were running, so if they could run fast enough, and it didn't spread too quickly…

A movement to Attu's right caught his attention, and he turned his head to see Elder Nuanu struggling to keep up with the group, her overly-large pack of potions and other healing items weighing her down, slowing her down.

She's not going to make it, Attu thought. He turned to see a dark strip of unfrozen water roiling as huge pieces of the ice they had just walked on fell in massive chunks into the ever-widening chasm. Attu couldn't believe how large the crack was, like nothing he had ever seen before.

"Moolnik!" Attu hollered. Moolnik was also at the back of the group, running to catch up with the others who had already run far ahead of him. *What had he been doing, that he hadn't begun to run sooner?* Attu thought briefly, but then he realized Moolnik, in his efforts to catch up, had just passed Elder Nuanu, who moments before had slipped and fallen under the weight of her pack. Moolnik hadn't seen her.

"Elder Nuanu, she's behind you!" Attu yelled at Moolnik, waving and pointing at the old woman as he began veering toward them both.

Moolnik hesitated. Attu saw it. He hesitated, just for a heartbeat, then continued running, as if he had not heard Attu. Attu knew for certain that Moolnik had heard him and had chosen to leave their Elder Nuanu, the healer of the clan, the embodiment of Shuantuan, behind to die.

Rage swept over Attu, and he ran toward Elder Nuanu, a war-like cry escaping his lips as he forced all his strength into his legs. Almost immediately, it seemed, he was at her side. With one strong arm, he grabbed up both Elder Nuanu's pack and her with it, for the two seemed stuck together like fish glue. He threw Elder Nuanu with her pack over his shoulder and heard the rush of breath as her slight body hit his back, knocking the wind out of her.

Elder Nuanu still seemed able to clutch onto his parka, and she did so fiercely; he could feel her bony fingers as she clung to him, while she relaxed the rest of her body so she rode with him instead of banging like a dead snow otter across his back, slowing him down.

Attu glanced over his other shoulder as he ran and saw a widening gulf of black churning water just a few spear lengths behind him.

"I'm not falling into your trap, not today, mighty Attuanin," Attu growled and redoubling his efforts, he ran like he'd never run before, out across the Expanse. He caught up with the rest of the clan, and soon they were running together, like a storm front of blowing snow, out across the ice, away from the deadly spreading open water.

Attu's lungs were on fire and his legs began to feel as heavy as the rocks on the hillside where the body of Elder Tovut lay. A moment later, the huge crack stopped expanding, but the clan continued running until the crack became distant, its huge ice chunks floating in the unfrozen water in the growing gloom of the eastern sky. Then, as if of one mind, the people stopped.

Attu set Elder Nuanu down gently, embarrassed at the way he'd hauled her to safety like a dead nuknuk pup flung across his back. She slumped to the ground and was immediately surrounded by the other women of the clan, who popped their lips in amazement at her rescue and half-carried her to a pile of furs.

Attu continued staring after the women until he felt a touch on his shoulder.

"You… have saved… the clan," his father said between gasps as he tried to catch his breath.

"I did what you taught me to do, Father, no more. Do you think Elder Nuanu will be all right?"

"She is… as tough as… old dried meat." His father smiled as he continued to huff great breaths of air. "She will… be fine."

Attu felt his face flush as he saw the pride on his father's face. He looked away.

Moolnik stood a few feet behind Attu's father, among the group of exhausted hunters. Before he could stop himself, Attu let his eyes meet Moolnik's, the truth evident in them. Moolnik's eyes widened as he realized Attu had not been fooled. Attu continued to look steadily at Moolnik, daring him to look away first.

Moolnik's face grew increasingly ashen in the fading light. Suddenly, he turned away and began rummaging through his pack as if nothing had happened between them. *But it has,* Attu thought. *He knows I know he is a coward. What will he do about it?*

"What's wrong, Attu?" His father said, concern in his voice as he looked at his son.

"Nothing, Father," Attu replied, forcing a smile. "Nothing at all."

This is not my father's problem. It is a problem of honor between two hunters. I will never forget what Moolnik did, and someday...

"It's growing dark," his father said, looking off toward the south and west where the sun had already set. The fire-color was fading from the sky.

"Are we far enough away from the open water?" Attu asked.

"Who knows? No one's ever seen anything like this before," His father replied. "But our people can't run any farther."

Attu agreed. He was too tired to even consider trying to move any farther away from possible danger tonight. He grabbed a hide and handed it to Ubantu, who was setting up their shelter.

As they worked, Attu noticed hands reaching for amulets and spirit necklaces as the men and women, even in their exhausted state, worked quickly in the gloom of twilight to erect tents and get under cover before the long frigid night set in. Nuknuk lamps soon glimmered within the shelters, giving off much needed heat, and mothers spread out packs with furs on top to provide sleeping spaces for their families above the icy surface of the Great Frozen.

The Great Frozen, Attu thought as he started drifting off to sleep a short while later, comfortable in his raised bed of furs. *So much for trusting that it will stay that way...* and with the sudden realization that he was, right now, resting on top of ice that could no longer be trusted to remain secure underneath him, Attu's whole body stiffened in sudden fear.

He lay for ages, his breath quick and shallow, as his mind created all sorts of imaginary scenarios of falling into the unfrozen water, down into the depths, down to Attuanin's kingdom, never to return. His fear held until the sheer exhaustion of the day and of his flight across the ice with Elder Nuanu on his back forced his mind to shut down as his body demanded rest. But his dreams turned into nightmares, as one watery crack opened after another, and his body fell into them, down and down…

Chapter 4

It took three days to get around the open water. The morning after the crack had forced them to flee for their lives, the clan began the long trek around the huge expanse of water and floating ice hunks. The hunters decided to head east around the water, since that was the direction they'd need to head eventually.

"Perhaps some time can be saved by this choice," Elder Nuanu said as she walked behind Attu and Meavu on the second day of their journey. A fresh wind blew at their backs, making it easier to walk. Loose snow raced across their foot miks, and the edge of the eastern horizon was hazy with its blowing. North of them, the open water gleamed in the distance whenever the wind lessened, and its moving ice chunks seemed to float either on water or on the layer of drifting snow when the wind blew. Both seemed equally impossible.

Attu pulled his eyes away from the floating chunks and glanced over his shoulder at Elder Nuanu. *She seems fine after her rescue. She is tough, like Father said.*

Elder Nuanu began humming.

"What song is that, Elder Nuanu?" Meavu asked. "I haven't heard it before."

Elder Nuanu nodded at Meavu but continued to hum softly for a few more moments.

"I think I've got it now," Elder Nuanu said and tucking a loose grey braid back into her parka hood, she pulled the hood back slightly so they could hear her better.

"Listen," she said, and Elder Nuanu began to sing, her high voice carrying in the stillness of the cold air.

"Skim the water, slip and slide
In my skin boat I glide, I glide,
Huna, Hina, see it glide.
Past the ice hills
Past the frozen boats of ice.
See them on the water floating
Do not glide too close!
Skim the water, slip and slide
My skin boat glides, it glides.
Huna, Hina, Huna, He-ee, see it glide!"

Elder Nuanu paused, looking to the left horizon, where indeed the floating ice did look like hills in the distance, slowly moving.

"I always thought that song of my grandmother's was nonsense." Elder Nuanu shook her head. "Now, I'm not so sure."

"What are *skin boats*?" Attu asked. "What could glide on the water with a person in it and not sink? Is it some sort of magic, something of the spirit world?"

"Grandmother said that in the time of the last Warming, before the Cooling came to Nuvikuan-na again and the People began to walk north and west across the Great Frozen, the world had much unfrozen water. A man could sit in a skin boat, which was like a skin-covered pack frame, only two or three spear lengths long, made of the bones of the giant whale fish."

"But, Elder Nuanu," Attu protested, "the whale fish is a spirit creature. It's not real."

"I'm simply telling you what my grandmother told me," Elder Nuanu replied. "The skin boat was made of giant whale fish bone and covered with nuknuk skin. The skin was made watertight the same way we make our water pouches, by sealing the seams with fat."

"An old woman's tale, an old woman's song," Attu said. "It's not real."

"I know, Attu. That's what the clan thought whenever she told her tales."

Elder Nuanu stared out at the open water with its large masses of floating ice moving along in the wind. "And until the sun before this one, I thought such an expanse of open water could not exist, either. But, there it is."

She motioned with her mik toward the expanse of dark water in the distance. The wind had calmed so it was now reflecting the blue of the sky above them.

"Maybe giant whale fishes are real, too, and they live down in the deep water, and not in the Between," Meavu whispered. She had stopped walking and was looking down, as if she could see through the ice to the watery depths below. She looked terrified.

Attu knew Meavu had suddenly realized the Great Frozen was no longer the secure place she'd always thought it was. *I know that feeling,* he thought, as he remembered his own fear the night before.

"Perhaps there are giant whale fishes under us, right now," Meavu continued, her voice rising with her growing hysteria, "and they will crash through the ice and-"

"Nonsense, Kip," Attu interrupted her. "It's all just stories." He couldn't stand to see his sister so afraid.

"You're right, Attu, I suppose," Elder Nuanu said. She was watching Meavu closely as she spoke. "Nothing but stories and songs to entertain children. That's all."

"Attu!" Yural called from many spear lengths ahead of them. "Are you all right?"

Attu looked ahead and realized they'd fallen behind the rest.

"We're fine!" Attu shouted back, and Attu, Elder Nuanu, and Meavu picked up their pace.

But until the sun before this one, I thought such an expanse of open water could not exist, either...

Try as he might to think of other things, Elder Nuanu's words kept echoing in Attu's mind, long after their conversation had ended.

~ • ~

The days began to blur together. The weather grew a bit warmer, and the ice under their feet often felt grainy, like small pebbles on the edge of windswept land. The clan moved forward with even greater caution now, watching the signs of changing weather and temperature, monitoring the ice under their feet as they walked. One day Ubantu was first to notice a change in the clouds, and the clan got their tents erected just as the first stinging ice fell. As the storm rolled by, Attu, Suka, and some of the other young hunters spent the afternoon playing games in one of the tents as if they were children again. But most of the days were long treks, wearying travel over the flat ice in the never-ending glare of the sun slanting through deep blue sky.

~ • ~

"I've never seen this many nuknuk holes this far from land," Attu's father said as the two of them walked carefully amid the several holes within sight, searching for one that looked most recently used. They were hunting ahead of the clan, and Attu's father had just marked another thin patch of ice near an old nuknuk hole with one of his message stones and string.

Attu looked down at his own parka. Every Nuvik carried message stones and hide strings. The stones and strings, when set into a small hunk of ice, communicated with other clan members. The message depended on the type of stones used and how the strings were connected to them. Attu had marked so many areas of danger with his round stones in the last few days he had run out and started using flat time stones instead. The clan would understand and avoid these areas of thin ice.

Attu could see by the gleam in his father's eyes that dangerous as it was, he was enjoying being out on the ice again with his spear in hand. The coiled rope attached to it bounced as Ubantu walked.

"The ice is so thin here," Attu said. He sidestepped an area that his spear butt had tested as weak. "It should be much thicker. We're still a day's journey from that ridge of rock we've been walking toward."

Attu adjusted his slitted goggles and looked out over the ice toward the land they were headed for, a dark outcropping barely visible on the horizon.

"I'm beginning to think we should believe Elder Tovut-"

Ubantu motioned with his hand and Attu froze. His father stared at a hole, larger than the rest, a few spear lengths away and off to one side. A bubble broke on the surface. A nuknuk had just raised its snout above the water line to take in a breath, and might still be hovering just below.

Moving soundlessly across the ice, Attu's father inched his way closer to the hole, careful to keep his shadow from crossing over the water as he drew near its edge. He slipped into a crablike crouch as he moved still closer. Attu marveled at how his father could move with such stealth even with a bad leg. The walking his father had been forced to do seemed to be strengthening it. Almost without realizing it, Ubantu had become a hunter again. Attu's breath quickened. He balanced himself, ready to run to his father's aid if he speared game.

Ubantu stopped so close to the edge of the hole Attu feared his father might crack the ice and fall in. But Attu kept silent. Ubantu raised his spear so slowly the motion was virtually undetectable.

Attu knew that herein lay the real power his father had as a hunter: his patience.

Time passed. Attu's legs began to grow cold and his fingers numb, but he didn't move. He knew the nuknuk below could see the darkness of his shape through the ice in this bright sunlight, and any movement he made would sound below.

Ubantu held his spear close to his ear, the point aimed at the hole before him, as motionless as the hunks of ice that surrounded him and the rocks far to the distance behind him. Ubantu had become part of the light and shadow of this landscape, and Attu could no longer detect any motion of breathing in the long fur around Ubantu's parka hood near his mouth. Ubantu had slipped his goggles off, and his eyes were mere slits in his face, steady, blinking only rarely. It was as if his spirit had left his body behind, and it had frozen there.

Attu, like most of his people, could sense when another living creature was near. But somehow his father could make even his spirit blend into the wind and the sky and the ice as if he were part of the Expanse itself. Attu was sure a returning nuknuk wouldn't be able to sense his father's presence.

Suddenly, Attu saw the tip of a nuknuk's snout break the surface of the water just as Ubantu's spear flashed out. The barbed bone hook at the end bit solidly into the flesh of the animal, and Attu ran forward, catching at the rope his father was pulling in. Both of them heard the crack of ice as the nuknuk was pulled from the water, and instinctively they fell flat on their stomachs to distribute the weight of their bodies over a larger area. But they did not let go of the rope. Instead they pulled, scrabbling backward at the same time.

The ice held. The nuknuk thrashed about as they drew the massive flippered animal forward and away from the hole. As they did, the cracks expanded, flaring out like the wavering lights that often danced in the sky on clear cold nights.

Once they'd pulled the creature far enough away from the hole, Attu's father stood, and taking the heavy bone club he carried at his waist, he struck the animal dead with a single blow to the head. Then he reached out his hand to Attu, pulled him up, and thumped him on the back. Attu gripped his father and pounded him as well. The smile on Ubantu's face lit up Attu's, and the two stood grinning foolishly at each other as the blood from the huge animal's spear wound reddened the ice.

Remembering his duty to the rituals, Ubantu knelt beside the nuknuk. "Thank you, mighty one of the water, for giving us your flesh to eat," he said. "May your spirit find its place again in the body of another nuknuk, and may you grow strong once more to father many kips and increase your kind. See I have killed you quickly and with mercy. Your life will be used to sustain the lives of many. For this we give you thanks."

Standing up once again, Ubantu worked his spear out of the body of the nuknuk where he had struck it in the neck, behind its large curved tusks. He carefully coiled the rope attached to the spear and fastened it to the weapon mid-shaft. He grinned at Attu once again, then glancing over Attu's shoulder he said, "We won't need to haul our meat to the women after all. Look!"

Attu turned and saw the rest of the clan, clearly visible and walking towards them. "There will be feasting tonight!" Attu exclaimed, and his stomach growled so loudly in response that Ubantu struck his good leg with his mik and roared with laughter.

As if he'd never been injured. How happy Father's success at the hunt will make Mother and Meavu, Attu thought as the two of them began to drag the weighty animal further away from the nuknuk hole, toward a good area of ice upon which they could make camp.

Chapter 5

Now there was no lack of nuknuk flesh to fuel the people and fat to fuel their lamps. Over the next moon, the hunters speared at least one nuknuk every day, and the whole clan began to look healthier than Attu had ever seen them. Meavu's cheeks were round and flushed with strength. The food had played a big part in it, Attu knew, but also the journey, he decided. Walking all day instead of sitting in the stale air of the snow houses seemed to help even the older clan members feel strong once again. Still, the children benefited most of all, running and playing whenever the hunters stopped on the rocky bits of land that also seemed to occur more frequently as they traveled farther and farther south and east. The cries of delighted children at their games cheered everyone.

~ • ~

The clan left one of the larger land areas behind them at the end of their second moon of travel south, and for once, Attu was not in the lead with the other hunters, but walking between his mother and sister. He had awoken at first light with his head filled with dreams, strange dreams, and he told his father he needed to stay behind, to sort out what he'd experienced while in the Between of sleep and dreaming.

Now, as Attu walked, he thought about the dreams. In one, a snow mound had risen up and chased him, suddenly possessing teeth and claws, as if it were alive. He'd woken up in a sweat of fear from that dream, only to fall asleep again and dream of the icy open water of the chasm they'd left behind on the second day of their journey.

The clan hadn't encountered another one, even with the thinning ice, and most of the men believed it was a mystery that wouldn't be repeated. Attu didn't know what to think. But the chasm had found him in his dream, and like the mound of ice, it had opened behind him, chasing him, and when he turned, he'd seen a young woman on the other side. His heart lurched. She was going to be lost to him forever, separated by the growing expanse of open water…

He'd cried out then, and awoken tangled in his sleeping skins, blood pounding in his ears.

What did it all mean? He wondered as he walked. *Is it just my fear of the unknown land ahead wrestling with my spirit in the Between, or are these dreams something more, omens of some kind? How can I tell the difference?*

"Attu. Attu, my son."

Attu realized his mother was speaking to him. Yural's voice held an edge of concern. "Attu, what's troubling you? You were so far away just now; I was worried for your spirit."

Attu stopped walking and turned to look down at his mother. *When did I grow so tall?* He wondered as Yural reached up and touched his cheek with her strong bare hand, a rare gesture of affection in the cold of the Expanse.

Attu grasped his mother's hand in his mik. "You will freeze," he said, but released his grip on her reluctantly.

Sometimes I wish I were younger once again, when Mother used to treat me gently as she does Meavu, and not as a hunter. He sighed. "I've had dreams," he said, answering her question.

"And they have disturbed you?"

"Yes."

"Why?"

"Because," Attu said as he looked at his mother's concerned face, "I can't tell if they are my own fears or omens I should heed."

"What does your spirit say?" Yural asked.

"It's not that simple, Mother," Attu protested.

Seeing they were falling behind the rest, the two began walking again.

"Elder Nuanu said you'd save the clan, Attu. Remember that." Yural's voice was proud.

"But I warned the clan of the break in the ice; I've fulfilled that prophecy," Attu said.

"And that you will also lead," his mother continued. "Elder Nuanu said you were to lead. Not just warn the people once-"

"I know," Attu interrupted. He'd wanted to be done with Elder Tovut's prophecy, for it had weighed heavily on his spirit from the moment Elder Nuanu had spoken it. He'd almost convinced himself that his warning the clan of the ice crack had fulfilled all Elder Nuanu had said he must do, even though he knew it didn't.

Mother is right. My spirit still feels heavy with responsibility for the others, more than my share. I've been pretending it's over. I've been trying to forget the rest... about leading, about not giving up hope, and especially about "the one who will bear my sons and daughters..."

Attu felt his face redden at the thought. He couldn't take a woman from his own clan, but occasionally clans did meet, and men quickly found their women among the other clans then. Sometimes men went searching alone, stealing women from other clans.

That is not the true Nuvik way. I would only take a woman if she were willing, and never in secret or with violence. Someday, will a woman truly want me?

Yural interrupted his thoughts, putting into words what he'd been trying to deny for the last many suns. "We're not yet at the end of our journey. You will be called to lead us still, Attu, I'm sure of it. You must be vigilant to all knowledge, whether it comes to you by your senses, or by a dream, or by some other means."

Yural's dark eyes glistened in her tanned face, browned by the constant exposure to the sun's light and reflection off the ice.

Attu studied Yural. He'd never seen his mother look so healthy, so strong, and it filled his heart with joy that his father, too, was doing so well. *So far, this journey, rather than being a terrible hardship, has been a good thing for all of us, once we escaped the chasm of open water that first threatened to kill us all before we had barely made a start on our journey...*

"Do you hear me, mighty hunter, son of my own flesh?" Yural asked.

Attu realized he'd been lost in his thoughts yet again. *What's wrong with me, lately?* He wondered as he felt his face growing red.

"Oh, I know. You're thinking about the woman who will bear your children." His mother laughed and poked her mik into his chest, a broad smile on her face.

Attu felt his face grow even redder still. "I hear and understand, Mother. And I haven't been thinking about THAT part of the prophecy," he lied. "My spirit says to beware and to heed these warnings for all of us. You're right. It's what my spirit says they are."

"Then you must heed them." Her smile vanished. "Do you want to tell me about your dreams?"

"I can tell you about one." He wasn't ready to talk to anyone about chasms as if he were a small child fighting his fear of the spirits and trystas of the Between after hearing their tales. And he certainly wasn't ready to talk about a young woman calling to him from across the open water, one who seemed to have his heart, at least in the dream. But it seemed right to tell his mother about the mound of snow that had come alive.

"What do you think it means?" He asked his mother when he finished describing the dream.

"My spirit says it's a warning for sure, but of what, I do not know. You will tell Elder Nuanu and your father?"

"I must lead next, will you tell them for me?" Attu felt uncomfortable sharing his dreams, especially with Elder Nuanu. His mother seemed to understand.

"I will tell them both, my son. And soon you will tell us the other?"

"Yes, but not now."

"When you're ready, I'll listen," his mother said, and seeing Meavu far ahead of the others, called out, "Meavu, you are too far ahead, come back."

She grabbed Attu's parka sleeve. "Speak to her, Attu; she'll listen to you. Meavu wanders further and further ahead and behind the group. She should take more care to stay with the others."

Attu nodded. He was reluctant to hinder his sister's new freedom. He loved seeing her race first in front of, then behind the others, noticing everything, stopping to examine first this shard of ice she could see through and then this speckled stone, thrown up as the ice formed near the edge of the outcroppings. She'd run back and share these things with Attu then off she would go again. Meavu was always on the move, but was careful to stay on the path she knew others had traveled safely.

Attu marveled at the change in his sister since those first days when she'd scarcely been able to walk the day's distance. Still, it was dangerous, Attu knew, to separate too far from the group. Look what had almost happened to Elder Nuanu. He'd speak with Meavu and urge her to stay closer. Later. She was running towards them now, and he didn't want to reward her obedience with sternness.

As Meavu reached them, Attu swooped her up in his arms and she squealed with delight.

Yural frowned.

~ • ~

Moolnik and his brother were disagreeing again. They sat whispering near one of the nuknuk lamps in the darkness of Ubantu's skin tent. Moolnik occasionally jabbed the air with his hand, trying to make Ubantu see things his way. Attu pretended to concentrate on sharpening the bone points of his spear in the light of the second lamp he was sharing with his mother and sister. They were working to patch one of Ubantu's miks with new hide and were huddled close to the lamp to see their stitching. Attu strained to catch the hunters' words. His mother and sister were talking too, however, and it was hard to hear over their voices.

"He will need another pair soon," Yural said to Meavu. "I will let you make them, Meavu, if you'd like."

"Yes, Mother," Meavu replied. She bent her head over her work.

Attu knew Meavu was not fond of sewing the tough hides used for miks. Cutting the pattern wasn't difficult, a bone knife or sharp cutting stone would do the job, but poking small holes in the hide for stitching required both strength and precision. The holes had to be just big enough, not too big, and placed exactly, close to the edge of the hide. It was easy to ruin a mik if you weren't careful because making the holes required a strong thrust of sharp bone. The double stitching necessary required strength, also. Meavu would have to pull it tightly enough to make it impervious to the cold, using sinew thread to stitch the pieces together in the proper shape.

"I say we should stay," Moolnik's voice cut through the air, and everyone but his father jumped. Attu almost cut himself with his sharpening stone. He felt his spirit stir within him.

"We need to continue to head south, my brother," his father replied, reaching out to touch Moolnik's shoulder, his voice deep in the sudden silence after his brother's outburst.

"There's no reason to continue," Moolnik argued, pulling back from Ubantu. "The land we're approaching is very large; you saw it, almost a day's walk in length, plenty of space for us all, and the game here is plentiful. Why should we continue past this place?"

"I'm seeing the signs, as you are," Ubantu replied. "The Warming-"

For a moment Moolnik looked away, his face tense. Then he shook his head. He looked determined. "Others will see as I do," Moolnik said as he stood abruptly and strode to the door of the tent. There, he suddenly paused. "Do not trust in dreams and the words of those who listen to spirits. Did you not learn that lesson, brother, when we were young? It brings nothing but pain and trouble. I'm surprised you have not told your son to keep his dreams to himself before he embarrasses our whole family." Moolnik glared at Attu, disdain on his face, before he walked away, leaving the tent flap loose behind him.

Yural quickly moved to tie the hide door closed, stopping the cold wind from entering their shelter. She turned from the door flap and faced Ubantu, a question in her eyes.

"I don't know, Yural. I don't know what to do," his father said, and Attu heard the weariness in Ubantu's voice. "You did the right thing, Attu, to tell us of your dream. Do not listen to him, my son. He cannot forget his own past long enough to see the present clearly. I can't convince Moolnik we need to keep moving. He doesn't believe what Elder Nuanu says, that when she was this far south before, as a young girl, it was much as it was at our last settlement, not like this, with the warmer weather, the thin ice, the bountiful game so easy to take. If he won't face the facts around him, why should we think he might trust in the warning of a dream?"

"Perhaps the others will see the truth and not choose to stay on the next land with Moolnik."

"Perhaps," Ubantu replied, but Attu knew his father didn't believe this. "If I think we need to keep moving, Moolnik will oppose me, just to see if he can gain his way over mine."

"Even if it means the death of all of us?" his mother snapped. Attu had never seen her so angry.

Meavu rose and slipped her arms around her father, hugging herself to his side and snuggling under his arm when he reached out to enfold her. The nuknuk lamp sputtered in the silence. Attu felt the rise of the Moolnikuan spirits, and he shivered. Right now, they would be racing from tent to tent as Moolnik stirred up trouble, again.

But what can I do? The whole clan knows now that I was warned of something coming. They do not believe, even with what Elder Tovut said before he died. I'm just a young hunter in their eyes, even if I did save the clan by warning them of the crack in the Great Frozen.

Increased holes in the ice, the sun warmer every day and higher in the sky. A sense of foreboding, niggling at me like my dreams are haunting me. Nuvikuan-na, the habitation of my people, is changing, the sky above, the water below no longer clearly divided by ice. Now, we need not drill holes at all to fish, for the nuknuk holes are not freezing over immediately, sometimes not even after darkness falls. The nights seem to be growing shorter, the suns longer. The ice crunches oddly under my feet, the wind feels wrong. The color of the sky, it seems less blue, sometimes hazy, odd. All these changes fill me with a sense of both unease and anticipation. I feel like when a fish touches my line, as well as like when a storm is coming and I'm far from shelter.

Attu's spirit was singing in his blood, "Prepare, prepare," but he didn't know how. *What new danger is coming? What did the snow mound chasing me mean? And the woman across the crack in the ice?*

Attu turned back to his spear sharpening, gritting his teeth on the words he desired to speak, and allowing himself to only think them, instead.

Why doesn't Father take the leadership back now that he's once again strong in his body, hunting with the rest as if he were never injured? Why must it be our mother who speaks the truth while he just sits there and lets his brother have his way?

Attu felt ashamed of his father's passivity, and he didn't like that feeling. Long after Moolnik had gone and his mother had shortened the nuknuk lamp wick so they could sleep in the semi-darkness of its warming light, Attu's thoughts kept biting at the corners of his mind like tooth fish fingerlings with their sharp teeth.

Chapter 6

The clan neared the large land mass late the following sun. Moolnik was leading again, and he soon left the rest of the clan behind in his eagerness to gain land. Attu was certain he would try to convince the hunters to stay there.

Attu grumbled as he walked, watching Moolnik and the other two lead hunters drawing further and further ahead of the group. It was warm again, and many of the people walked with their parka hoods thrown back. *It all feels wrong.*

Attu turned to see where Meavu was, for although she'd been running back and forth between the hunters and the clan for most of the morning, she'd fallen behind a while ago, studying some hummocks of ice, which had somehow been pushed up out of the Expanse and into buckling mounds. The mounds must have been there for some time, because wind and weather had rounded them.

Meavu knew better than to go off the sure path the hunters had followed, so she was at least a spear throw from the mounds, but they were interesting to look at, with their shadowy bulk on the otherwise flat ice field of the Great Frozen. Sure enough, as Attu looked back, he saw Meavu standing on the path several spear throws behind the rest of the clan, apparently captivated by the sight of the mounds.

"Meavu," he called to his sister. "You are falling too far behind. Come back!"

Meavu turned toward him, and he saw she was not alone. She was holding the hand of Shunut, Moolnik's youngest son, who was little more than a toddler. Attu was surprised to see him so far from his mother, but Meavu was a favorite of Shunut's and he liked to chase after her.

"I'm coming," Meavu called. "Shunut is too big for me to carry and he's growing tired."

"I'll wait for you, but hurry," Attu said.

A small niggling began in Attu's mind, a hint of a worry. Something was not right with the scene before him. It seemed oddly familiar. Attu shifted his weight, balancing his spear automatically in his throwing hand, getting ready. *But for what? Why are the hairs on the back of my neck rising? What's wrong?*

Attu scanned the horizon, listened hard. Nothing. No sound of ice cracking, no movement other than Meavu walking with little Shunut back toward the group. They were only a couple of spear throws away, when suddenly, one of the smaller ice mounds, which had been partially hidden by the others, moved. It detached itself from the ground and rose up. Attu saw four legs, a head, and wicked black claws as the mound leaped toward Meavu and Shunut, a spray of snow flying off it as it ran.

"Meavu!" Attu shouted, and grabbing his spear tightly, he raced toward his sister and little cousin.

Shunut, sensing the movement behind him, turned. The wall of white was coming at him, claws ripping into the ice. Shunut screamed.

Meavu turned as the beast roared, and Attu knew she saw the mouthful of dagger-like yellow teeth that showed as the white mound leaped across the ground, bellowing. It was huge, and still it moved fast.

Meavu did not scream. She grabbed Shunut up like he was a light pack and began to run toward Attu. But it was obvious they could not outrun the beast. And even if they did, where could they hide? There was no place safe from such a monster…

Attu raced toward the animal, for that must be what it was, a white wall of fur, with claws and teeth, just like he'd dreamed it would be. It was real, not a spirit, and if it was real he could kill it. He had to. His spear alone was not going to stop the beast, however; this Attu knew instinctively. It was far too large to be killed with one spear, but he kept running and pulled his knife from his belt also, glad he had worked the evening before to sharpen both his weapons.

Attu had almost reached his sister when the monster swept one massive paw as it ran, knocking Shunut out of Meavu's grip. She fell backward in the snow, clutching her shoulder where she had been struck. Shunut tumbled across the ice and came to a stop. He lay there, unmoving.

The animal turned toward Shunut, and Attu knew this would be his only chance. He screamed a cry to give him strength, a cry from his very spirit, a cry of defiance toward this mad monster, and with his cry, he plunged his spear into the side of the creature where he guessed its heart to be.

The beast roared in pain. Turning to face Attu, it reared up on its hind legs, easily twice Attu's height. His spear dangled from its side where a large red stain was growing against the white fur.

Attu leaped to the other side of the animal, drawing it away from the children. It swatted at him, roaring and rearing again and again as Attu barely kept out of its reach. Then it dropped to all fours and lunged. Attu dodged to the left, escaping the black curving claws as they flashed across his face. But the blow struck his shoulder. He felt his parka tear, and the force of the swiping paw spun him off balance. He fell, but leaped up again, his hands now red from the bloody snow.

The beast should be tiring, but even though blood spouted from its side, it came at Attu again, roaring and raging. It was too close. He was going to die. He was going to be caught in the grip of that dripping mouth of teeth as long as his fingers, and he was going to be ripped to pieces.

Suddenly, a stillness came over Attu. It was as if his spirit left his body, rising above the fight, and he looked down at himself, facing this monster with only a knife in his hand. And he knew what to do.

His spirit slammed back into his body as Attu leaped at the monster, catching it by surprise. Its claws raked the air where Attu had been standing just a moment before. Attu reached up, as high as he could, and as the creature came down on him, he sliced his knife across the animal's throat, not just once, but three quick slashes, each one carving deeper into the beast's neck. Blood spewed from the animal's throat and the massive beast fell on him like a huge fur-covered boulder. Attu was swept under its body as the creature took one last swipe at him, and his back exploded in fire as vicious claws tore through his flesh. Then, nothing…

~ • ~

Attu awoke to a sharp pain radiating up his back diagonally from his hip to his shoulder. He was lying on his stomach, but when he struggled to sit up, pain shot across his back. A cool hand eased him back onto the furs he was lying on and gently held him there. Attu took in a few shallow breaths to stop his rising nausea. The pain was overwhelming, but as he concentrated on breathing, the hot fire of it eased a bit, and he could think. He could feel the hand on his shoulder, and it steadied him, helped him to endure the pain.

Attu looked up, expecting to see his mother, Yural, resting her hand against him. Instead, he was surprised to see a girl about his own age, kneeling next to him, one hand firmly held against his uninjured shoulder, the other resting on a pouch in her lap.

Her skin was dark, and yet her eyes were light, almost the color of a new hide, light brown flecked with gold, large for a Nuvik and slanted upwards, with brows that slanted up as well. They made her look mischievous. She was wearing her hair loose, not braided, and its velvety blackness fell across her face as she leaned toward him, continuing to press her cool hand on him. He suddenly felt his nakedness under the furs covering his lower body. He looked away, feeling his face redden.

"You must not try to get up again," the girl said. "I have to treat the bear wounds on your back or you will get the fever."

She reached into the small pouch she was holding, pulled out a gooey brown paste and rubbed it on Attu's back. The paste stung as it touched open flesh, and it was all Attu could do not to cry out. This was what had awoken him. He wished he'd stayed unconscious.

"I know. It hurts."

That was his mother's voice, and he raised his head enough to see her looking at him from behind the strange girl. Yural's lips were a tight line in her face, her arms clenched across her body.

"Rika says the salve will heal you, will pull out the bad spirits that cause the fever. She's a healer."

Attu couldn't tell if his mother was trying to reassure him or herself with this knowledge.

"Meavu?" he managed to ask, his throat so dry he could hardly speak. "Shunut?"

"They're safe," his mother said. "Meavu's shoulder is bruised, and Shunut has a large bump on his head, but he's come back from the Between. You saved them both."

"And the beast?"

"Dead. I-"

"The 'beast' as you call it," Rika interrupted his mother, "was an Ice Bear." She shook her head. "Now, lay back and be quiet. I must finish tending your wounds."

Attu rested his head on the furs. He must be hearing things. The ice bear was a spirit being, like trystas. It did not exist in the world of the living…

Rika began the gentle motion of salve spreading again. Attu peeked at her through half-closed eyes. Her face was impassive, her touch gentle, but still he felt a fine sheen of sweat break out across his upper lip and forehead as he forced himself to endure the pain of her ministrations without flinching away. Each touch was agony.

This can't be happening, Attu thought. *It's not real. I'm probably dreaming. Mother is tending my wounds and I'm dreaming it is this girl, this Rika, instead.*

Or, he thought, *perhaps my spirit has left my body. Perhaps I'm dead. No, that doesn't make any sense, for Mother is here. I'm just confused, that's all… the pain… ice bear… this strange girl… like a dream… but the pain is real, and if that wasn't an ice bear, then what was that monster?*

Attu's head was pounding in rhythm with the pain throbbing in his back. He couldn't think. He gave up trying.

"He is brave," the girl named Rika said to his mother, and Attu tried to listen again, to hear this girl's words. It was as if he were listening from another room, however, the pain dulling his ears. The girl seemed bold, as if Attu were not lying right there in front of her as she spoke. He wanted to be angry with her for hurting him, and when she touched a new part of his back it was all he could do to hold still.

"He has always been strong," Attu heard his mother reply while he struggled against the pain that smeared across his back, flaring with each stroke of Rika's hand as she rubbed still more of the goo into his raw flesh. The two women continued speaking over him as if he were a small child. He wanted them to stop. And the pain… he desperately needed that to stop…

Attu took in a breath to steady himself, as a hunter must. The salve was spicy, and the whole shelter was filling with the smell. Attu's eyes watered from the pungency, and he buried his face in the furs to protect them.

"Just one more," Rika said, her voice like soft wind now, wind across newly fallen snow. "This is the deepest one, and will have to be stitched, but I must clean it with the salve first. Do you want a bone to bite on?"

Attu realized she must be looking at him, and he raised his head again. She was gazing at him, calmly waiting for his reply. Her message was clear. *Here comes the real pain,* as if what he'd been feeling before was just the preparation before the true test.

She will finish the cleansing, no matter how painful it is for me, Attu thought. *Who is this girl, that my mother trusts her over Elder Nuanu to heal me?* He studied her. *She is so confident in her healing she's able to sit there, knowing her treatment is excruciating, yet she proceeds to discuss the pain she's causing me with my mother as if she were considering how best to cook a stew.*

No matter who she was or how painful this last cleansing was going to be, it had to be done, Attu realized. He felt sick.

"Finish," he said, and quickly shoved his fist into his mouth as Rika spread another glob of salve into his back. It felt like she was cutting him again, like the beast had done. The shelter began to spin, and Attu cried out, biting down on his own knuckles in agony as everything went black.

~ • ~

"You should have used the bone," Rika said, a hint of teasing in her voice as she took Attu's hand in her own.

"How long have I been in the Between?" Attu asked, as he looked at the hand Rika was holding. His teeth had penetrated the flesh, and she was spreading more of the spicy salve on it by the light of a nuknuk lamp.

"One night, one day, and now it is the second night," Rika replied.

Lit from behind by the lamp, Rika's face was deep in shadow; only her hair, outlining her form, shimmered around her as she moved, and the dark strands caught the light. The rest fell loose across her face as if she were trying to hide herself behind it.

Rika finished spreading the salve and taking a soft hide, bandaged his hand in a few deft movements.

"Next time I will," Attu said.

"Will what?" Rika asked. She looked into his eyes.

Attu realized his hand was still in hers as he gazed at her in return, and before she could remove her hand from his he gripped it, wincing a bit from the pain, but holding on to her still.

"Your hand," Rika protested.

"I'll take your advice," Attu said, trying not to smile. "Next time. I'll bite the bone instead."

Rika laughed and pulled her hand away.

He let her go.

"Do you think you can sit up now?" Rika asked. "You need to eat."

Pain flared across Attu's back as he struggled to sit up, but he was ravenous, and the nausea caused by moving seemed to be overridden by his hunger. He watched Rika scoop up some nuknuk meat from a stone platter over the lamp onto a bone plate and arrange a few thin slices of raw tooth fish on the side. He reached out to grasp the plate, wincing as his back protested the movement.

Rika turned away again to fetch him a small pouch of water. "You need to eat and drink as much as you can," she said as she sat down beside him on the furs. "You haven't eaten in days, and the meat will give you strength to heal."

"And the fever?" Attu asked through a mouthful of nuknuk meat.

"It never came," Rika replied. "I think we got the fever spirits out in time. You'll be fine."

Attu grimaced as a wave of pain spasmed through his shoulders when he lifted the water pouch to his lips.

"In a moon or so," Rika added. She stared at him with interest while he ate. "Is it true what they are saying about your dream? That you dreamed about a mound of snow attacking you before the ice bear went after your sister and cousin?"

"Yes. I didn't know what the beast was, in the dream. Where I come from there are no ice bears. I thought it was a spirit warning, not a warning of something real, about to happen."

"That makes sense. Ice bears only live where there is ample game, and from what your mother tells me, far to the west and north there would not be enough meat for such large hunters as the ice bear. They also need some areas of ice thin enough for them to break through easily. They also swim, hunting nuknuks under the ice. They couldn't do that where the ice is frozen thick everywhere."

Attu nodded. It did make sense. He shuddered as he thought of that huge beast falling on him…

"Have you dreamed before?" Rika asked him, interrupting his thoughts. "Other warnings, other-"

Attu's mother opened the tent flap. She rushed in when she saw Attu sitting up, eating.

"This is good," she declared, and placed her palm on Attu's forehead. "It's cool," she said, as if she needed to reassure herself that Attu was indeed healing without having to fight the spirits of burning flesh.

"We got the salve on and the wounds stitched up in time," Rika said softly. "And your pleas to Yuralria were answered."

"Yes, they were." Yural nodded and added, her voice now strained as she spoke, "Paven wants you."

"Thank you," Rika said. She jumped up, slipped into her fur parka, and was gone before Attu could even say goodbye.

"Who is Paven?" Attu asked. "And who's Rika? Where did they come from? Are there more, a clan? Do they live on the land we were headed toward when the ice bear attacked us?" His mind tumbled with questions.

His mother put up a hand to silence him. "You've just had your first meal after many days. You need to lie down now and rest, let the strength from the meat begin healing your body. We can talk about Rika and her clan later."

Attu started to protest but yawned instead. He was tired, and he was no longer hungry, even though food remained on his plate. Attu allowed his mother to take it from him and to help him ease down onto the furs again. He groaned with pain as the stitches Rika had sewn into his back pulled. He thought of Rika, her sharp bone needle entering his flesh, and was grateful he had passed out before she'd stitched his wounds. Attu shuddered, thinking of the pain he would have had to endure.

Yural, looking concerned, carefully covered him with another fur. "Once you've rested more, we'll talk, and I'll answer all your questions," his mother reassured him. "Meavu wants to see you; Suka and the others do too, but I've told them they must wait. Your father will come in and sit with you soon. Rest now."

The last thing Attu felt before he slipped into sleep was his mother's cool hand brushing loose hair away from his forehead.

Chapter 7

Attu awoke to the sounds of many men arguing outside the shelter. He started to roll over onto his back, but a sharp stab of pain stopped him, and he remembered his wounds and rolled carefully to his uninjured side to sit up.

Sunlight lit the interior of the tent through the open flap. Attu saw many foot miks of men who were standing just a few feet from the tent's opening.

"I'm not leaving this land!"

Attu recognized Moolnik's voice.

"We've traveled a great distance, and Elder Nuanu is sure this is the place where our clan has stayed before. I walked up to the heights and found at least three burial sites, all with our clan's marking etched into the stone slabs. That's proof enough for me. It's our land, and we're staying on it."

"Don't be a fool, man," another voice said. Attu didn't recognize the man speaking, *but he must not realize Moolnik has a quick temper or he wouldn't be speaking to him like that.*

Sparks of light shot around Attu's vision as he struggled to pull himself up by one of the tent poles. He gained his feet and stayed upright, breathing quickly until his head cleared. Ignoring the cold, Attu stepped to the door of the tent.

Attu couldn't believe what he saw. There were at least twenty men gathered before the shelters. He recognized the six lead hunters of his own clan, his father among them, as well as Suka and his brother Kinak and the other younger hunters, all standing to one side. Moolnik was in the front as usual. They had their weapons balanced in their hands, as they challenged a larger group of hunters, all strangers to Attu, who also stood with raised spears. The man who had apparently been the one to call Moolnik a fool stood in front, his weapon also at the ready.

"So, I'm a fool?" Moolnik said, his voice suddenly quiet as he glared at the other hunter. Moolnik began to move forward.

"Wait, brother," Ubantu said, and Attu watched as his father grabbed Moolnik's shoulder and tried to pull him away from the stranger.

Moolnik's going to get our hunters killed, and for what? What are they fighting about?

"I said," the stranger continued, as if Moolnik hadn't threatened him, "that if you stay you are a fool. You are welcome to this land. We are leaving. We have lost two children, one woman, and two hunters to the ice bears in a single attack. You almost lost three of your clan, if it hadn't been for your strong young hunter, fast on his feet and quick of mind."

The stranger gestured toward Attu's shelter, turning as he did, and a look of surprise crossed his face when he saw Attu standing in the doorway, bare to the waist in the freezing cold.

Attu stared back at the man's face. Clearly he'd been attacked by something himself, by the looks of his scars. The hunter had two deep lines across his face, from forehead to chin and possibly down onto his neck and chest, Attu realized, but the man's parka hid any further scarring. The skin around the scars was puckered in places, as if the wound had not healed easily.

Attu knew this man had been attacked by an ice bear. Only an ice bear's claws could have torn the man's face like that. The memory of the ice bear's huge claws swiping at him just a few days ago caused Attu's knees to weaken at the sight.

The hunter smiled at him, or gave what appeared to be an attempt at a smile. He bared his teeth and the left side of his lips went up, but the right side no longer seemed able to move, and his eyelid stayed half-shut on that side of his face as well. Attu looked away, embarrassed to be caught staring.

The man moved away from Moolnik, as if a battle had not been seconds away from erupting between the two groups. He walked toward Attu, and when he reached him, thrust his hand up in the sign of greeting. Attu noticed, however, that his spear never left its ready position in his other hand.

"I am Paven, leader of the Great Frozen clan," he said, and Attu returned the greeting, letting go of the tent and holding up both hands. He winced at the pain his movement caused. "I am Attu, son of Ubantu and Yural and brother of Meavu, Ice Mountain Clan."

Attu slowly lowered his hands and reached for the shelter's door pole to steady himself. The objects around him spun.

"Attu," his mother cried suddenly, and in a flurry of parka fur, Yural was beside him, trying to push him back into the tent. "It's too soon for you to be up. You invite the spirits of fever to come upon you, my son." And ignoring Paven, she pushed at him again.

"I'm all right, Mother," Attu said, embarrassed by his mother's actions in front of this clan leader. "Get me my parka," he ordered her, a bit too loudly.

Yural, suddenly realizing what she was doing, stopped trying to get Attu back into the shelter. "Yes, my son," she said quietly, and brushed past him, returning in a moment with his over shirt and parka, which she proceeded to help him put on in front of everyone.

Attu tried to ignore the men who now surrounded their shelter. He thought he saw an amused look flick across Paven's face, but it was hard to tell with the man's scars. *Surely he must think me a child, being ordered about by my mother,* Attu thought, and he was tempted to scold Yural in front of the men, put her in her place. But, he didn't. She was his mother, after all.

Attu struggled into his clothing, forcing himself not to let out a cry when the weight of his heavy fur parka settled on his wounded back, pulling at the stitches and sending tremors down his arms.

Attu glanced into his mother's eyes, and his anger vanished at the look of love and concern he saw there. "Thank you, Mother," he said to Yural and briefly touched her shoulder as she stepped away.

"A mighty hunter and a good son," Paven remarked, and Attu flashed a look at him. He saw no sarcasm in the man's scarred face. Looking past him for a moment, Attu saw Moolnik scowl and his father smile. Suka, standing a bit behind his father, gave Attu a broad wink.

"You are a strong one," Paven said, and he held out an arm for Attu. "Walk with me, and we will talk of ice bears and swap stories of how we both survived killing one."

Turning away from the cluster of angry men, Paven steered Attu out across the rocky edge of the land they were camped on.

Attu looked back to see Moolnik kick a loose stone and stomp away with his sons, a few other hunters following behind him. Men on the other side wandered away as well. Ubantu didn't follow the other men, but limped slowly toward the shelter and Yural.

"Don't be concerned, young hunter," Paven said as Attu turned back. "We'll not come to blows over land, not this time. My clan isn't staying on this trysta-forsaken place any longer. It's the dwelling of the ice bears, and there's no question they are the strongest among us. Their claim will not be taken from them. Eventually Moolnik will see this truth, hopefully before any of your clan are killed."

Attu said nothing. He wanted to tell Paven that Moolnik was a stubborn fool and would probably not leave until several of his clan had died, victims of the ice bears. All Moolnik could see was the plentiful supply of nuknuks. That was, of course, what the ice bears saw as well. As hunters they would require large amounts of meat to sustain themselves. And to the ice bears, Attu's clan was simply more game, easier to catch and kill than the nuknuks because the humans couldn't escape under the ice. *Except here, the ice bears can get under the ice also, it's so thin everywhere. What if they chased hunters onto thin ice, just to let them fall through and kill them under water?*

Attu shuddered at the thought of ice bears hunting and feasting on his people. At the same time, he felt the old frustration toward Moolnik's rivalry with his father rising up in his spirit. Right now he was so weak he couldn't possibly confront Moolnik if his father wouldn't, and no one else in their clan would even try. It shamed Attu to think his people would follow such a leader. *How has it come to this? What is it about Moolnik that others seem drawn to him? And why hasn't my father done something about his brother? It's as if Moolnik has some spirit power over them all.*

Meanwhile I can barely lift my arms, let alone wield a weapon. What if I don't heal? What if I don't grow strong enough to hunt again?

Attu was exhausted just from the short distance the two of them had walked. He glanced at Paven, but the man seemed set on getting them as far away from camp as possible. Rounding a bend in the rocky path, Paven motioned to a large rock a spear throw ahead of them. "You can sit there, and we'll talk," he said.

Attu headed for the rock. When he reached it, he sat down heavily, wincing at the pain the movement caused.

"I've been told how you got your wounds, my young hunter, but I'd be glad to hear the story from you, if you're ready to tell it."

Attu stared at the rocky ground in front of him. He didn't want to think about the attack, but flashes of the fight came unbidden, flooding his mind as his thoughts turned to where he had refused to let them go until now. Against his will, it was as if he were there again, and he reeled with the terror of the attack. His heart began to race, his face broke out in a sweat, and he felt like he was going to throw up…

The claws were coming for him, the teeth. The monster was huge. Surely it was going to kill him this time. Attu felt the ice bear's claws rip open his back again as he sliced into the bear's throat. He felt the blood of the bear pour over his bare hand and his own blood flow down his body as if his back were bare also. The pain, the pain...

Attu felt a strong hand grabbing him by his good shoulder. "Steady now, Attu," he heard Paven say. "You're having a Remembering. Take in a deep breath."

A what? Attu breathed. The man had said to breathe. But *there was the bear again, coming at him. He saw the claws, the teeth, and in the distance he heard Shunut scream, over and over again... he screamed and screamed...*

"Attu!" Paven shouted, and Attu's head snapped back as Paven struck him across the face with his mik.

"What… why did you strike me?" Attu asked, his mind still reeling with the memory of the attack.

"You were screaming," Paven said.

"I was?"

"Yes. Rika told me you hadn't spoken a word of the attack after coming back from Between. I brought you away from the others so the first time the Remembering grabbed at your mind, I'd be here to help you."

"It was so real…" Attu shook his head, his mind still trying to make sense of how strong the memory had been, how it had consumed him, torn at him, much like the bear had done. He had felt lost in its grip. *Did the bear somehow enter my mind? Is it going to attack me from inside my head now whenever it wants to?* He groaned at the thought.

Paven knelt beside the rock, his eyes even with Attu's. "No one in either of our clans has ever survived an ice bear attack except for me, and now you. They don't know the horror of facing those claws, those teeth." Paven grasped Attu's shoulder again as Attu began to tremble.

Attu realized the Remembering was trying to take him again, and he worked to concentrate on what Paven was saying and not on the memory. It was difficult, but he willed himself to put the memory aside and to focus on Paven instead.

"Good," Paven said, as if he were aware Attu had just won a small battle of will against memory. "You're strong of mind as well as body, and your spirit won't let you be lost in the world of Remembering."

"I didn't know…" Attu's voice trailed off. He couldn't think. *I want to tell Paven how horrible it was. I had no idea a person could relive an event with such detail, such feeling, as to be lost in it as if it were happening over and over again…*

"Now, you will recount the ice bear's attack," Paven commanded. "Every day you will tell it to me, until the power of the spirit of the ice bear is weakened by the telling, and his spirit can no longer attack your mind."

"I don't want to talk about it," Attu said, his voice shaking as he tried to stand up, to end this conversation.

"You must and you will!" Paven declared. He pushed Attu back down on the rock as he himself stood up again.

Attu gritted his teeth against the pain and his anger.

"I will not allow such a strong young hunter as you, Attu, to be lost to the spirit of the ice bear," Paven continued, his hand slicing the air in front of him to cut off all argument.

"I won't," Attu yelled back, his temper erupting. "You are not even of my clan, how can you force me to speak of something I don't wish to talk about?"

"You will!" Paven shouted.

"No!"

Attu pushed himself up again and tried to stand as straight and proud as he could. This time, Paven didn't try to stop him. It took every last bit of energy he had, but Attu turned, determined to walk away, no matter how weak he felt. He wouldn't allow this strange hunter to order him to do anything. But Attu's head was spinning and he couldn't walk. He gritted his teeth in frustration, which just made his head hurt more.

He forced himself to relax his jaw, taking in a deep breath before placing his hand against the rock to steady himself. *I'll rest here a moment, then leave,* Attu told himself, even though he knew he didn't have the strength to return on his own.

"Attu," Paven's voice was suddenly calm.

Attu felt Paven take a step closer to him, but Attu didn't move.

"This is not a matter of who is stronger, who is leader," Paven said, his voice almost a whisper in Attu's ear. "It is a matter of survival."

Attu turned to face Paven again. He knew only his pride was keeping him on his feet. Attu began to sway.

"Here, sit beside me, Attu. There's room on the rock for both of us." Paven sat down on one side of the rock.

It's either sit down or fall down, Attu thought. He collapsed on the other side of the rock, took in a breath, and tried to ignore his trembling legs.

"My woman used to tell me," Paven began again, "that if I would talk like the wind that blows gently from the south, she could hear me much better than when I spoke like the biting north wind, all bluster and ice." Paven shook his head. "She was right. She always was."

Attu stayed silent. His head was pounding, and he wanted to lie down. He had no idea how he was going to walk back to the shelter. He just wanted Paven to leave him alone. But that didn't seem to be what the clan leader had in mind.

"Four of us were attacked that day," Paven began.

Attu shuddered and pulled his mind back from the image of teeth and the sound of flesh tearing that Paven's words had triggered. He didn't want to hear Paven's story. Not now.

Paven glanced at him, and apparently satisfied he wasn't going to try to get up again, he continued. "We had traveled farther south than our clan had ever gone, searching for game. We, too, thought the ice bear was only a spirit. When it rose up among the snowy boulders at the edge of the land, we were so shocked none of us reacted fast enough. The bear killed the first man instantly. Broke his neck with one paw. The second took longer. Two of us survived: myself, and Rovek, a young hunter who had raced to my side when he saw the others go down. A braver hunter I have never known, until now…"

Paven paused and studied Attu.

"Didn't you say you and I are the only ones to have survived an ice bear attack?"

Paven continued. "There is more. We killed the bear. I was wounded much as you see now, mostly my face, neck, and chest. Rovek was bitten on his leg. The bear picked him up and shook him like a nuknuk shakes a fish before it dropped Rovek and fell over dead from blood loss."

Why is he telling me this? Attu thought. *To impress me? I don't care. So he survived. So did I. So, apparently, did this hunter, Rovek. Just let me go back to my shelter and sleep…*

"Afterward, I began to have horrible times Between, dreaming of the attack over and over again," Paven continued. "When I'd awake, my woman would do like her clan had always done with dreams; she'd make me tell the dream, each part, and she would release the dream back to the spirit world of Between, from where it had come."

Paven looked off into the distance, his eyes growing vague in their staring.

Attu wondered if Paven was getting lost in the Remembering himself, but after a few moments Paven cleared his throat and spit off to the side of the rock before he spoke again.

"The dream Remembering began to fade. I no longer saw the attack so strongly in my waking times, either. I healed. Rovek did not."

What happened to Rovek? Attu wondered. He looked at Paven, sure the question was in his eyes.

"Rovek refused to speak of the attack. He grew quieter every day, lost in the Remembering. A moon went by, then two. His young woman was beside herself with worry. She came to me, telling me of his terror in the night, of his temper, how he was beginning to act as if the ice bear's spirit were living inside him now, instead of going into the Between until the time for it to be born into another ice bear's body. It was as if the ice bear's spirit had chosen to take over Rovek's body instead."

Attu shuddered at the thought.

"One night, Rovek came to my shelter. He was angry. He attacked me. I saw the spirit of the ice bear in his eyes, as clearly as I see you before me now… and I… was… afraid."

Attu stared at Paven. No hunter EVER admitted to fear. NEVER. *Paven must have been truly terrified, and he wants there to be no doubt in my mind about the seriousness of his fight with Rovek.*

"What happened?" Attu asked, both dreading to hear and needing the answer. "Did you kill Rovek?"

"No. I tried to reason with him," Paven said. "He struck me across the face, just like the ice bear had. The pain made me pass to the Between of sleep, and when I awoke, both he and his young woman, who was expecting their first child, were gone. Their snow house showed signs of a struggle, and both of them had disappeared. A hunter found their bodies two days later at the base of a cliff near our camp. We left that accursed place, moved back north and out of the ice bears' territory."

"And you believe the spirit of the ice bear killed them?"

"Yes."

Attu shook with fear now. *Will I be overtaken by the bear spirit?* He thought. *Has the Remembering already begun to take hold of me?* He looked at Paven, knowing his fear must show. He didn't care anymore.

"My woman was right," Paven said. "The ice bear has a unique spirit. Strong. It continues to fight after the bear's body is dead. If a hunter kills its body, the spirit of the bear will attack that hunter's mind, taking it over through dreaming or through the Remembering. That's why you must tell me your Remembering over and over again until the ice bear's spirit stops trying to gain its hold on you. Then you will simply remember the event like any bad memory. The ice bear's spirit will no longer have power over you. It will be forced to go to the Between, where it should have gone immediately after its death."

"I understand," Attu said. He was suddenly grateful to this man, this scar-faced clan leader, who was willing to be honest with a young hunter about his own fear, so he, Attu, could avoid what had happened to Rovek.

"Thank you, Clan leader Paven, mightiest hunter of the Great Frozen Clan," Attu said and attempted to stand again, to honor

Paven as he should, but his knees buckled under him, and he sat back down, grunting at the pain the jolt cost him.

"Here, mighty hunter, Attu, hunter for the Ice Mountain Clan." Paven stood up and held out his arm for Attu to grasp. Attu heard the humor in Paven's voice, but didn't take offense. He just wanted to get back to the warmth of the shelter and his soft fur bed. His mind was reeling from what Paven had told him, and he'd have to think about it some more. But for now, he wanted nothing more than to lie down and rest. The two made their way slowly back toward camp, Attu leaning heavily on Paven.

Rika rounded a corner in the trail, running toward them. Attu noticed Rika was wearing her hair braided in two braids like the women of his clan now, and the long shining strands bounced on her chest as she ran. Her cheeks were flushed as she reached them.

"Father, Attu should not be walking this far his first day back on his feet," she scolded as she rushed to Attu's other side to help support him as he walked. She grabbed Attu's arm, near his injured shoulder, and an involuntary yelp escaped Attu's lips.

"Sorry," Rika said to Attu.

He managed a smile at her as his thoughts took over again. *Paven is Rika's father?* Now it all made sense to him. She had known how to treat the ice bear wounds, had known how much pain Attu was in, and she must have either been old enough when her own father had been attacked to remember Rovek and the tragedy of the young couple's deaths, or her father had warned her about the ice bear's mind attacks. *And she did ask me about my dreams...*

As Rika walked beside them, Attu tried to move a bit faster and to appear not to be leaning so much on Paven for support. He didn't want Rika to see him looking so helpless.

Paven glanced at him, and Attu saw the curiosity in Paven's eyes at his sudden show of strength.

"Run ahead and prepare some hot drink and meat for Attu, daughter," Paven said. "I can get him back to his shelter on my own."

"Yes, Father," Rika said, and glancing at Attu one more time, turned and darted back down the path to Attu's shelter.

"Rika is a strong-willed stubborn girl, but she seems eager to obey my wishes today," Paven said.

When Rika was out of sight, Attu slumped heavily against Paven again. He realized Paven was studying him, but the man said nothing. Attu concentrated on walking, feeling weaker with every step.

"Let's hope she's as obedient a woman to her new man," Paven added after they had walked a spear's throw further. He glanced at Attu, who was no longer even attempting to appear stronger than he felt.

"Rika?" Attu asked, surprised. "Surely she's too young to take a man."

"She's to be joined to Banek at the next full moon," Paven answered. "And may the trystas shine on their union. Banek will need it. She's as obstinate as her mother was." He looked at Attu again, his expression unreadable.

Attu said nothing as he worked out what Paven had said, his mind as slow as his body was weak. *Obviously Paven's woman has gone Between. Why was Paven letting his daughter take a man when she was so young, especially if she was the only woman of his household now? Maybe she has a sister. I'll have to ask Mother. Right now I can't think about anything but sleep. Some food, too,* Attu thought, as his stomach rumbled. *Food and sleep.*

Attu pretended he didn't care about anything else as he struggled toward the shelter, even as his mind flowed back to scenes of Rika by the fire, Rika smiling, even Rika, her healer's impassive expression, as she asked him if he was ready to face the pain of cleansing his deepest wounds. He barely knew the girl. *Why should I care if she's going to be another man's woman soon?*

Attu shook his head slightly, so as not to hurt his back, and concentrated on the task at hand, getting back to his warm shelter and fur bed.

Chapter 8

Paven came by Attu's shelter for the next several days. He sat quietly across from Attu or walked slowly with him down the rocky path where land met the ice of the Great Frozen, and Attu told of his attack, over and over again. At first, the telling made him sick. His head pounded and he felt like throwing up, especially when he got to the part where the bear had raked his back with its claws. With her claws, actually. Paven told Attu the fourth day that the bear had been a female. Attu shuddered at this thought. That meant she wasn't the largest of her kind. Males would be even bigger.

"We think she has two almost-grown cubs," Paven said as the two of them settled back on the furs in Attu's shelter.

Attu's mother handed them each a bowl of ice bear stew.

"Thank you, Yural," Paven said, and Yural ducked her head and withdrew from the tent.

As Attu looked down at the bowl of rich stew in his hands, he realized he didn't feel sick as he had the first few times after the retelling. Instead, he was just hungry. *My body is healing, and my mind is winning the fight with the ice bear spirit,* Attu thought as he moved to get more comfortable on the furs. His back was still painful, but it also itched. He knew that was a good sign of healing.

"You have only seen the area of land along the ice where we walk each day," Paven said. "You know there are low hills near the edge of the land with a steep ridge of ice and boulders dividing the whole length from north to south, right to the edge of the Great

Frozen. Last sun, my hunters discovered tracks in the snow on the west side of that ridge, south of our camp here on the east side. We think another small group of bears is living there, hunting that side of the Great Frozen."

Attu's mind was still grappling with the fact that the ice bear who attacked him really existed in the Here and Now. He'd always thought of the ice bear as a one-of-a-kind being of the Between. Not a whole race of beings in his world.

"Ice bears are usually solitary," Paven explained. "They hunt a large territory. But the game here is so plentiful they seem to be willing to share."

"And now we're here, like a nuknuk sunning spot, all gathered together in one place, ready to be feasted on," Attu muttered.

"That's what I've been trying to tell Moolnik," Paven said. "It's dangerous to stay here. But Moolnik is a stubborn man. Rika tells me you dreamed of the ice bear before it attacked?"

"Yes, but I didn't know what it was in the dream."

"But when the time came, you reacted in part because you sensed something wrong?"

"It was as if I saw the dream before me again, coming true."

"Which gave you the courage to react quickly."

"Yes, I guess it did. I hadn't considered that before, but you're right."

"Beware of dreams, Attu," Paven warned. "Do not trust them. Dreams are tricky, sometimes showing us what we want, sometimes what we fear, and rarely something important to come, like your dream. Many of us have dreamed. I act only on what I see in the Here and Now, with my own two eyes. I would not be taking my people through ice bear territory if I wasn't convinced the Warming is real and the Great Frozen is melting. Some of my elders say I have waited too long to make this journey, that we will all die on the way. They are wrong. We will make it."

~ • ~

Later that day, Suka came by Attu's shelter for the first time since the attack. He threw himself down across from Attu and tossed a pouch into Attu's lap.

"What's this?" Attu asked, holding up the pouch. The contents clinked together, making an unusual tinkling sound.

Suka scowled and grabbed the pouch back from Attu. He loosened the hide drawstring on the bag and pulled out a large necklace of ice bear teeth and claws. Attu cringed at the sight of the massive black curving claws and sharp yellow teeth alternating on a rawhide string. Suka dangled it in front of Attu, his face now a mask of stone.

When Attu didn't reach for it, Suka dropped it on the fur between them. "Your mother has been given the hide of the ice bear and its meat. Small necklaces have been made for Shunut and Meavu. The rest of the teeth and claws are in this pouch."

Suka tossed the pouch on top of the necklace. "They make good tools and weapons, my father says. Both can be sharpened to a point like bone, but much stronger."

"Would you like some?" Attu asked. He began to reach for the pouch to give away as many of the teeth and claws as he could. Attu didn't want anything to do with those wicked instruments, and his only thought was to get rid of them.

"Do I want some?" Suka suddenly yelled at him, half rising to his feet in his anger.

Attu winced. "What?" *Why was Suka so angry?*

"Do you know how much grief your killing that ice bear has brought me?" Suka shouted at him. "My father has been throwing himself around our shelter, lashing out at all of us, just because of you and your trysta-forsaken ice bear."

"It's not my fault," Attu protested. "Your father-"

"Not your fault?" Suka sneered. "Of course it's not your fault. You can't help it if you just got lucky and were in the right place at the right time. It's not your fault that Shunut won't take his necklace off and tells the story about how you saved his life from the awful monster to anyone who will listen…"

Suka's voice drifted off as suddenly as it had erupted, and he sat back down on the furs across from Attu. "Why couldn't it have been me?" He asked, looking pleadingly at Attu for some answer he must know Attu didn't have. "Why couldn't I have been the hero for once?"

Attu felt himself growing angry at Suka's childishness, to wish for such a horrific experience to have been his, rather than Attu's. "Yeah," Attu replied, his own voice rising. "Then you could have these slashes across your back that will leave you scarred for life, and terrible Rememberings you have to relive over and over again. And," he added sarcastically, poking at the pouch between them, "you would get your own tooth and claw necklace and some extras."

"And the respect of my father, maybe, just for once, and of everyone else, too," Suka retorted. "That's what I'm talking about. I'm trying to make you understand."

Suka rubbed his hand across his eyes, his own weariness now apparent to Attu. "Every person in both clans is talking about you," Suka said. "Don't you know that?"

Suka slumped where he sat, a defeated look on his face.

Attu didn't know what to say. He'd had no idea he was the talk of both clans. He'd been moving as little as possible because of the pain of his injury, sleeping both day and night, and he hadn't been outside the shelter for more than his brief walks with Paven each day to tell his Rememberings. They'd always walked away from camp for that. His mother and father hadn't allowed anyone into the shelter since the attack except for Meavu, Paven, and of course Rika, who tended his wounds twice a day. None of them had mentioned it. Elder Nuanu had stopped in briefly a couple of times to check on Rika's work, but she'd been strangely quiet lately. Suka's words were a shock to Attu.

"I didn't know," Attu said, his voice a mere whisper.

Suka looked at Attu like he didn't want to believe him.

"I didn't know," Attu repeated. He looked at Suka and his heart sank. Suka's face had gone stony again.

Not knowing what else to say, the two young hunters sat in silence for a while. Then, with a quick sideways motion of his head, Suka got up and walked out of the shelter, leaving the flap open to toss in the wind.

Attu sat alone in the rapidly cooling shelter, his thoughts in turmoil. Killing the ice bear had caused a rift between him and Suka as impossible to fathom as the cracking ice and open water the clan had run from at the beginning of their journey. The clans rested on solid ground now, but Attu had never felt so vulnerable, as if he still walked alone on rotten ice.

He stuffed the necklace and pouch into his pack, his fingers trembling when he touched the smooth cool sharpness. His back ached just from remembering those teeth and claws. Wearing them was unthinkable. *Why hadn't it been Suka? I'd gladly have changed places with you, cousin.*

But would Suka have been able to kill the ice bear? Or would the bear have killed him? And maybe Shunut and Meavu as well? Attu shuddered at the thought, realizing he would never know. The spirits had placed him in the bear's path, and he'd done what he had to do. No more.

~ • ~

Several evenings later, Attu's family gathered in the shelter around the nuknuk lamp after another meal of ice bear. They'd shared the meal with Paven, Rika, and her little brother Rovek, named after the young hunter who had died. Rika had no sisters, older or younger, and once Ubantu had discovered that Paven's woman had gone Between, he had asked Yural to invite them to their shelter to eat the evening meal. Several days had gone by before Yural had finally asked them, at Ubantu's insistence. Attu thought it odd, since his mother normally loved to entertain others.

Paven came into the shelter as dusk fell, and before Ubantu had the chance to invite him, Paven took the best seat, the one furthest away from the drafty door flap. Rika and Rovek hardly spoke, keeping their eyes down and flinching when Paven ordered them to sit, motioning to their places as if they might somehow forget the obvious, that Rika would sit with the women and Rovek with the men. Ubantu frowned, but said nothing.

Paven ate heartily, but did not thank Yural for the food, as was customary of a guest. It seemed like Paven expected to have the right to be there, as if once he walked into their shelter, it became his. Attu didn't like it. This was a side of Paven he hadn't seen before. In his own way, Attu realized, Paven was as arrogant as Moolnik. *Was this why his mother had been reluctant to invite him?*

After eating, Attu sat in the light of the nuknuk lamps, listening to Ubantu and Paven discuss the need to move south as soon as possible. The two men were working to convince Moolnik and the other hunters that the two clans should travel south together, but neither man thought their chances were good.

"Moolnik doesn't listen to me," Ubantu said, his voice strangely harsh.

"That is unfortunate, for you are the older brother," Paven replied.

Moolnik hates Paven because even our own hunters seem to prefer him as a leader, Attu remembered his father saying the day before. Attu noticed his father seemed to follow Paven as well, listening to him, taking his advice, and urging others to do the same.

Tonight, however, Ubantu seemed different. Sullen and angry, much like Moolnik.

Why doesn't he step up and lead our clan himself, instead of relying on Paven to do it for him? Is he still feeling less than a leader because of his old injury? Why is he so out of sorts tonight?

It seemed to Attu that although his father's leg rarely pained him or slowed him down anymore, he still acted as if he weren't the strong hunter from before the accident. Attu understood how difficult it might be for his father to get his confidence back after his injury. Since the bear's attack, Attu worried constantly about whether or not he'd get his full range of arm motion back, his strength to throw the spear, to carry the heavy animals home after the hunt, and to walk the long distances over the Great Frozen.

Meanwhile Moolnik seems to spend all his time trying to convince himself of his own greatness, when I know better... Flashes of memory flooded into Attu's mind: Elder Nuanu falling; Moolnik turning and seeing; Moolnik pretending he did not see; Attu exchanging a knowing look with Moolnik. Moolnik being forced to look away.

Attu glanced up from his own thoughts as Meavu and Rovek began giggling and wrestling on the furs. The two were playing a game of Bones. Small bones with markings on one side were tossed in the air and lost or won depending on which side landed facing up. It was a fast moving, simple game, and the two were obviously having fun with it. Attu smiled.

Rika and his mother were sewing by the light of the second nuknuk lamp, sitting so close to the flame to see their stitching that Attu worried their braids might catch fire. Rika's mother had died when she was about Meavu's age, according to his mother, but she seemed to still have been taught the women's skills. Attu wondered who had taught her the healing ones.

Rika glanced up and Attu caught her eyes. Instead of looking away as most girls would, she continued to look at him, her eyebrows arched up as if to dare him, her gold-flecked eyes twinkling. He found himself looking away first, frustrated by his shyness. He turned back to listen to the men again, but he could no longer concentrate on what they were saying.

"Would you like more algae drink?"

Attu jumped. Rika was beside him, her hand clasping the steaming bowl of the hot blue drink, a strong smelling beverage made from algae that grew on the rocks at the shoreline.

"No thank you," Attu said. He was annoyed Rika had been able to sneak up on him, even in the closeness of the shelter.

"I'll take some, daughter," Paven said.

Rika tensed as she stepped over and handed Paven the bowl, her eyes lowered. She slipped back to her seat beside Yural as silently as she had approached.

"Have you noticed how much more of the algae there is here than on the islands to the north?"

Ubantu looked surprised. This was women's talk, about the small types of gathering foods. It wasn't hunter's work. He looked to Yural, who remained silent.

"There's much more of the blue algae along the shoreline here, growing in great clumps along the rocks. Also, rock moss. Elder Nuanu sends women out each day to gather both and to dry them." Paven looked at Ubantu.

"Elder Nuanu is a wise woman, a good leader of women," Ubantu said. His words were halting.

"My hunters have been happy to watch out for the women of both clans as they gather." Paven smiled at Yural as he spoke. She ducked her head and continued sewing.

"Oh," Ubantu said. His father had apparently not realized that Paven's hunters guarded the women of both clans as they gathered the algae on the shore, or the rock moss, which was rare on the other lands, but here seemed to grow abundantly in any sunny sheltered spot up in the hills.

The women went almost every day to gather, for both algae and moss could be dried and carried easily. Being stuck near the shelters, Attu had overheard the women discussing who would be foraging each day. Paven had chosen two hunters to do the guarding. One of them had no woman. There'd been much giggling involved, and a few hot arguments over whose turn it was.

"Oh," Ubantu said again, in a drawn out breath almost like a sigh. He was looking at Paven, who was still eyeing Yural. Attu suddenly felt afraid, but he couldn't figure out why. The moment passed.

"Elder Nuanu is instructing the women to stay ready to move and to gather what they can," Paven said, suddenly turning back to Ubantu. He grinned at Attu's father. Ubantu did not smile back.

Attu wondered if Rika went off into the low hills to gather with the other women. Thinking of the possible danger to her, Attu glanced toward Rika. She was watching him again, but she flashed him a look of annoyance as their eyes met, and looked away first this time, suddenly giving all her concentration to the work in her hands.

"Rock moss is not all that's been gathered," Paven said, glancing again in the direction of the women, and bringing Attu's attention back to the conversation. "My brother's son, Topulek, has asked permission to become Pashua's man."

Attu's father grunted. "That makes two now, to be taken and given at the next full moon."

"Yes, an even exchange, one hunter from my clan, and one from yours."

"Who from our clan?" Attu asked.

"Kinak," his father said. "He has asked for Suanu."

"Kinak?" Attu was surprised. *Another thing for Moolnik to taunt Suka with, the bonding of his older brother, just like his own father had done to Moolnik.* In spite of their recent argument, Attu felt sorry for Suka.

Paven said, "Now that you're feeling better, Attu, you must come and walk our camp. Perhaps a twinkling eye may catch yours." Paven chuckled. Ubantu and Yural exchanged looks, but did not laugh.

Attu felt his cheeks grow hot, and he picked up his knife, suddenly interested in checking its sharpness. Out of the corner of his eye he noticed Rika was sewing furiously. She pulled her sinew thread so hard through the furs it snapped.

"Here, let me help you with that," Yural said, and the two women examined the break.

Paven had said Rika would be given at the next full moon as well, to the man Banek, Attu thought. *Yet she sits there looking boldly at me. Women.* He turned his attention back to his sharpening. The conversation seemed to die out after that, and Paven left soon after, Rika and Rovek following behind him out into the darkness of the Nuvik night.

~ • ~

"Mother is afraid of Paven," Meavu told him the next day. The two of them were sitting in the shelter. Mother had gone gathering, and Father fishing.

"She heard he's looking for a new woman. Mother is beautiful, strong, and an excellent keeper of our fire. He might try to take her."

"Paven? You don't know what you're talking about, little Kip," Attu said. "Paven has helped me fight the ice bear's spirit. He's a friend, not an enemy."

"Don't believe me then," Meavu said, her lower lip full in her pouting face. "Watch Father. He knows. Watch Rika. She's nervous around her father, also."

That much was true. Even though Attu had never seen any reason for it, he knew Rika watched her father closely, always. She acted as if she felt unsafe around him. He remembered the tenseness in the shelter last night, the feeling of fear he had suddenly experienced. Attu wondered.

Meavu got up from her spot on the furs and knelt in front of Attu, taking his face in her hands as if she were little once again and wanted his full attention. Her hands were soft on his cheeks, but her eyes appeared ancient in her face, not the eyes of a child at all, but of one as wise as Elder Nuanu. "I speak the truth, Attu," Meavu said. "Paven is not a true leader. He does not treat his women as precious."

Attu knew in his spirit his little sister was speaking the wisdom of the women of her clan, as true as the spirits that surrounded them all.

Meavu turned away and busied herself in straightening the furs, much as his mother did. Attu pondered her words for a long time afterward. Was the Paven he knew on their walks together the real Paven? Or was he as Meavu had said? Perhaps he was somehow both, and if so, Attu must remember to be wary of Paven, no matter how much help Attu had received from him.

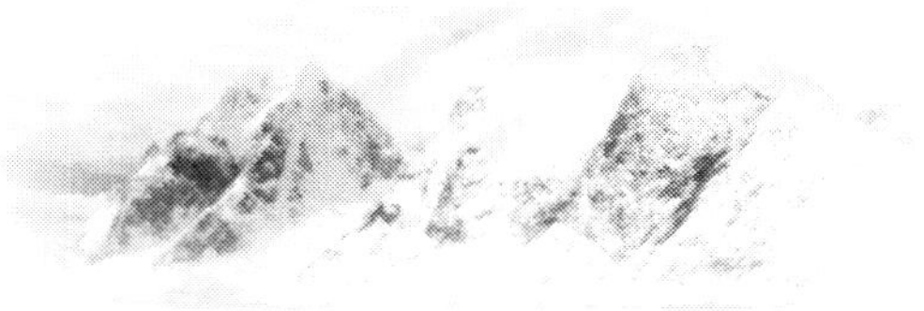

Chapter 9

Late the next night, Attu overheard his father and Moolnik as they sat talking in the shelter.

"More game?" Ubantu asked Moolnik. "Why, my brother?"

"Tomorrow will be a good day to hunt," Moolnik replied. "This is our home now. Why not?"

"We can't stay here, you must see that!" Ubantu hissed, trying to stay quiet but clearly upset.

"Have you seen an ice bear since the attack?" Moolnik asked. "No, I know you haven't. No one has, because there are no more. Your son was lucky enough to have the last bear fall on his knife. We're safe now."

Attu almost growled at such an outrageous remark. Leave it to Moolnik to act as if Attu's bravery had been a lucky accident. But Attu didn't want the two men to know he was listening to their conversation in the shadows of the shelter instead of sleeping, so he stayed quiet.

"But the tracks Paven's hunters have seen-" his father began.

"Are just a trick to get us to leave," Moolnik sneered. "Don't you see it, brother? They want this land for themselves, so they're trying to convince us to leave. They will leave too, but once we're out of sight of each other, they'll turn back and take this great hunting place for their own."

Moolnik sighed, as if he were trying to explain something to a small child. "You're too trusting, Ubantu. You always have been."

"No, you're the one who doesn't see the truth. You only see what you want to see, hear only what you want to hear."

"Then why do the others follow me instead of you now?" Moolnik said, pointedly looking at the brace of nuknuk skin Ubantu wore over his mik to strengthen his ankle.

"Because you tell them what they want to hear, instead of what is true. That's why."

"You just better watch yourself, brother, or that schemer Paven will steal what's most precious to you."

Attu saw Moolnik gesture with his head toward Yural's sleeping form.

"You go too far, Moolnik. Get out!"

Ubantu jumped to his feet, his fists clenched to his sides, his face livid in the light of the lamp.

Moolnik laughed as he left the shelter.

Attu's father collapsed back onto the furs once he was alone, cradling his head in his hands.

Attu buried his face in his sleeping furs. *Even Moolnik knew Paven might try to take my mother. How could I have been so blind?*

~ • ~

The weather was so warm Attu threw his parka hood back as he walked. The sun shone on the ice and low hills near the edge of the land as he traveled in the direction of the Great Frozen camp instead of his usual route the opposite way. Attu looked at the sky. Far above, a few thin clouds ran fast to the east. *As if even they feel the need to hurry to safety.*

He had dreamed again last night of the crack in the ice, of the woman calling to him, and something more, something about ridges of rock on either side of him, something through which he must travel. But it made no sense, and he awoke in the middle of it.

Beware of dreams, Paven had said. Dreams bring only pain and trouble, Moolnik had said. Listen to your dreams, heed them, his mother had said. Elder Nuanu had not said a word to him about his dream coming true. That seemed the most unsettling of all.

What should I believe?

Attu had felt anxious that morning and decided to take Paven up on his offer to visit the camp, not to look for a woman, but because he needed to get his mind off things and he was curious about these new people. He was feeling strong enough to walk further away from his own shelter.

As he walked, Attu noticed that on this southern edge, where the water met the land, there were several areas of unfrozen water, patches many spear lengths long and at least a foot wide, water gleaming and lapping at the rocks of the shore.

What if the Great Frozen were to melt and we got trapped on this land? Eventually the game would run out…

Attu lengthened his stride, pushing himself to exercise his legs. He wanted to be ready to leave. His clan needed to leave. But again today, Moolnik and several other hunters from their clan had left the camp to hunt nuknuks, even though they didn't need the meat.

"You're too late," Rika said as Attu walked between the Great Frozen Clan shelters a little while later.

"What?" Attu asked. He'd been busy studying the hunters, most of who were sitting outside their shelters, sharpening weapons in the bright sunlight. *Too bright,* Attu's mind warned him, but he pushed the thought back. He'd already learned a new way to get a better tip on his spear point with the dark rock slivers this clan used. He had negotiated a trade of one of his bear claws for a small sack full of the sharpening rocks from the hunter who had shown him the technique. Now he was walking further into the camp, wondering what else he might learn from these people.

"You're too late to find a woman," Rika said, her eyes daring Attu to find fault with her boldness. "There are only two available women in our clan and only one is young. A hunter from yours has already laid claim to her. So you might as well just turn around and walk back, lazy hunter who brings back no game."

Attu stood there, his mouth open like a dead fish as Rika stomped off, her braids tossing behind her as she went.

What's gotten her spirit swirling? Attu thought as he tried to figure out what had just happened.

"Don't bother trying to understand Rika," a new voice said, and Attu turned to see a man, older than Attu but younger than his father, sitting on a pack and sharpening fine-looking spear points. "Rika's moods are like the wind at the heights of the hills, strong and always changing direction."

The man looked up from his work, putting down his spear and standing in greeting. Attu was surprised to see he had thick dark hair growing on his face. Attu had only seen one man in his life with a beard, a lone hunter who'd joined their camp for a few days. That man had claimed to come from far to the south. Did this man?

Raising both hands in greeting, the man stepped forward. "I am Banek, son of Rallod, hunter of the Tooth Fish clan. And you must be Attu."

Attu returned the greeting.

"I'm glad to see you're up and walking," Banek said. "To survive an ice bear attack is an amazing feat."

"I was just protecting my sister and cousin," Attu replied.

"And humble, too," Banek said. "Come. Sit."

Banek slid sideways on his pack, giving room for Attu to sit beside him.

"So, tell me, what's it like to fight an ice bear?" Banek asked. "We have rock bears where I come from, but they're only the size of a large man, and two hunters can usually kill one without serious injury. Ice bears, now that's a whole different fight!" Banek grinned at Attu, as if he would welcome the chance to fight an ice bear.

Attu shuddered. He didn't want to speak of the attack, but he was also curious about this man who had won Paven's approval and laid claim to Rika.

"Until I saw the hill of white rise up and move, saw its teeth and claws, I thought ice bears existed only in the Between," Attu said in a round-about way of answering without going into detail. "And now you say there are rock bears also?"

"Yes," Banek replied. "Rock bears are gray like the rocks where they shelter. They fish for tooth fish near the shore by chipping holes in the ice with their great forepaws and dabbling their claws into the water to attract the fish."

"They put their paws in the water, like bait?" Attu was astonished. *How clever of the bears, but tooth fish teeth are dangerous.*

"They actually let the fish bite their claws," Banek said, drawing his eyebrows together at the wonder of it. "Then they drag the tooth fish out. You know how tooth fish won't let go, once they grab onto something."

"Yes, I know," Attu said, pushing up one sleeve to show Banek the scar on his left forearm where a tooth fish had bitten him.

"Me too," Banek said, and he rolled up his right sleeve to show a similar mark. "It's like an extra clan tattoo for my people. By the time we're grown, everyone has at least one. Some, if they're slow to learn the fish's ways, more." They both laughed.

"So, consider yourself a member of my clan," Banek added, and he turned and gave Attu a rough thump on his back, right over his deepest wound.

Tears sprang to Attu's eyes from the pain, but he didn't cry out. *Did Banek forget my injury, or is he somehow testing me?*

But Banek seemed not to notice Attu's pain.

He must have forgotten, Attu decided. He was curious to know more about Banek. "How did you happen to come so many moons north and west alone? To hunt?"

"For a woman," Banek grinned. "And Paven has given me Rika in exchange for leading his clan back the way I came. I have never seen the great land to the south and east of our clan's territory, but I believe it exists. Our storytellers also speak of it. It will be a great adventure to see it for myself."

Banek abruptly stood and gathered his sharpening tools. "See you at the ritual of gift giving?"

So Banek and Rika would be joined then, at the full moon.

"I'll be there." He wasn't looking forward to watching Banek and Rika being given to each other. The man seemed too old for her, but Attu knew this was often the way of his people. The older, experienced hunter would make a better provider, the younger woman a healthy mother. Still, Rika was being given to him as payment. Had she been given a choice? It all seemed wrong.

"We are not to be joined this moon," Banek said after a moment, clearing his throat and looking away, across the Great Frozen. "Paven has asked for a few more moons to have his daughter with him."

Attu could see the frustration in Banek's eyes and tried to ignore the lifting of his own mood at the information.

"She is young yet; there is time," Banek continued. "She'll be mine soon enough. Then she'll settle down, not be so bold. Paven has been too easy on her since his woman passed to the Between."

Attu felt his stomach clench at Banek's words. He sensed no caring for Rika in Banek's voice at all, just the same eagerness he had expressed when wanting to hear about the ice bear attack and exploring new places. *Why would Paven allow this rough hunter to have his daughter?*

Attu walked home, wishing things were back to the way they'd been just a few moons ago, the clan safe on their own land, no threat of ice bears, no more than the usual arguments between Moolnik and his father, *and no gold-flecked eyes of a girl promised to another man haunting my dreams*

Chapter 10

"Hold still," Rika said. Attu was lying face down on his furs, his bare back bathed in the sunlight streaming in through the open door of the shelter. Rika was removing his stitches.

"You're a terrible nuisance," Rika said, and she slapped the back of Attu's head playfully. "Now hold still, and I mean it."

A sharp sting as Rika cut and pulled another stitch out caused Attu to flinch again. Rika's hand slipped, and Attu felt a small pain in his back near where the stitches were being removed. "Now you've done it," Rika exclaimed. "You made me knick you with my cutting bone."

"Me?" Attu protested. "You're the healer here. Watch your tools."

"Treating you is like trying to remove stitches on a squirming poolik," Rika scolded.

"I can't help it; they sting," Attu said. He was frustrated by this girl, who thought she could order him around by day, just because she was a healer, then proceeded to give him meaningful glances in the evening, like she was free to do so and not spoken for by Banek.

Every day she'd come by, check his wounds, re-clean them as needed, and rewrap his torso in fresh hide bandages. She'd put a poultice on a couple of places that had started weeping, to prevent the spirit of fever from attacking him. Yet she was often rough in her treatment of him, especially since the day he had visited her people's camp. Attu didn't like it. Still, he had healed quickly.

"Attu?" Rika's voice was suddenly soft.

"Yes?"

"Have you had any more dreams?"

"Why?"

"I just wondered." She pulled another stitch.

Attu tried hard not to move. "Yes, I have. But I can't talk about them."

"Oh."

Another stitch. *Ouch.* But Attu held steady.

"I, too, have dreamed."

"You have? Can you tell me about them?" Attu tensed, his stitches forgotten.

"The dreams are confusing. It's not so much what I see in them. That keeps changing. Once it was ice surrounded by water."

Attu held his breath. *Has Rika dreamed the same dream as me?*

"Another time it was as if I were floating under the stars. It's what I hear each time that stays the same, that bothers me."

"What do you hear?"

Rika didn't answer, just pulled another stitch.

Attu jumped.

"Hold still, I said," Rika exclaimed. "I can't believe how much you're wiggling now, when not too many suns ago, your back was slashed open and bleeding, and you held perfectly still while I cleansed your wounds."

"Yes, and most of that time I was Between from the pain," Attu grimaced at the remembering.

Rika pulled at another stitch, a deep one, but Attu held himself still.

"What do you hear, Rika?" He asked again as she settled back into the routine of cutting and pulling out stitches in his upper back, where it wasn't as tender.

"I hear a voice, a man's voice, as if calling over a great distance. He says, 'When others would show judgment, you must show mercy. If you do this all will live. If you do not, all will die.' The voice is powerful, Attu, and it scares me."

"And what do your elders say about your dreams? What does your father say?"

"I have told no one about them, until now I've told you. My father would laugh at me. 'Show mercy?' He would scoff. To him, showing mercy is showing weakness."

"So why tell me?"

"I thought," Rika replied softly, "because you have also dreamed and it came true, you might understand."

"I do." Attu turned his head, so he could see Rika. She looked frightened. Something deep inside him stirred with compassion for her. He continued carefully, wanting to reassure her. "I know most people will not believe your dreams until they come true. Then for a while, they might. But it doesn't last. I've been trying to help my father convince Moolnik to leave this land and continue south and east to the great land beyond that our Elder Tovut told us we must reach, but Moolnik won't listen to us, like he refused to listen to Elder Tovut when he was alive, or Elder Nuanu now. He thinks men who believe in dreams are weak. Your father said dreams are dangerous and usually just our own imaginations, needs, or fears. Our leaders no longer believe in the power of dreams as our ancestors did. So I think you are doing the right thing to keep your dreams to yourself. And you must decide for yourself whether or not to trust in them, follow them."

"Do you trust in them, Attu? Your dreams? Do you believe?"

"I don't know. But the ice bear did attack."

Rika sighed then turned back to cutting out Attu's stitches again. A few moments passed in silence, then Rika pulled a deep stitch and Attu jerked.

"Just hold still!" Rika seemed to have lost all patience with him.

Attu gritted his teeth and tried not to move. "Show mercy," he said in a beggar's voice.

Rika laughed, "It's only justice for you, hunter who cries out like his wound is mortal when it's only a scratch."

"Ouch. Your tongue is sharper than your tools, Poosha."

"Who told you my old name?" Rika slapped his leg, hard.

Before being named Rika, after Rikakuan, the healing trysta spirit of fresh air after a snow, Attu had found out from Rika's little brother that she had been called Poosha, which meant "strong mouth." It meant she always had something to say about how things should be done, even when her advice hadn't been sought.

Attu grinned now at the thought. Rika had recovered quickly from her fear and gotten bossy again. *Poosha, this girl was.* His words had helped.

Attu jumped yet again as another stinging pull of a sinew stitch sent the flesh on his back quivering.

"You have to hold still," Rika exclaimed. "This is going to take forever if you don't." She let out a sigh of frustration mingled with annoyance.

Suddenly, before Attu could take in a breath to protest, Rika threw her leg over his backside and Attu found himself pushed deeper into the furs. Rika was sitting on him, low, below the edge of his wounds, her legs on either side of his back, knees pushing in to steady him.

"Rika," he breathed, too shocked to say anything else.

"Be quiet, mighty hunter," Rika said, "and let me concentrate on getting these stitches out without your back ripping open again. Men…" the last word was a mere whisper as Rika bent to her task, Attu now firmly held in place.

What will this crazy girl do next?

Attu lay as still as death while Rika breathed on his back, her face inches from his skin, concentrating on clipping and removing each small stitch. She seemed oblivious to the fact that she was sitting on him, her warm legs embracing his sides.

Rika moved slightly to get a better view of the stitches near his shoulder. Her braid brushed lightly across his side, and a sigh escaped Attu's lips. Rika didn't seem to notice; she was so intent on her task. Attu waited for her to be done, trying to push his mind away from thoughts he should not be having. It didn't work. Rika was beautiful, with her light eyes and curving brows, her bossy ways and her healing hands. And she was being given to another. It made him feel sick, not unlike how he felt about the bear attack. He hated that feeling.

"There, all done," Rika said. But she made no move to climb off him. Instead, she patted his back, tracing her hand along the lines of his rapidly healing wound tracks, most now new scars. "You need to begin using your muscles, throwing your spear, so your back does not become rigid with the scarring," Rika said softly. Still she sat there, stroking his back. Nuvikuan-na itself seemed to stand still.

"Rika," Attu whispered.

"Yes?" Rika said, as if lost in thought and only half paying attention to him.

"Do you want Banek for your man?" Attu hadn't meant to say it. But he had to know how Rika felt. Banek was a strong hunter. He was probably exactly what Rika would want. *He is certainly more hunter than me, a wounded boy-man,* Attu thought.

Rika went still.

Attu waited.

"Oh," she finally breathed. "Oh, no… I didn't mean…" and she scrambled to her feet, grabbed up her pouch, and was gone from the shelter in an instant.

~ • ~

Two days later, the gift giving ritual was held in the light of the full moon. The two young couples were given to each other along with an exchange of gifts. There was dancing and feasting. Attu sulked in a corner of the huge shelter that had been erected between the two camps, watching Rika dancing with the younger children. He refused to join in with them. He was not a child.

Attu's healing back gave him the excuse not to participate when the group gathered around the large sewn skins that would make up each new couple's shelter. First one couple and then the second sat wrapped in each other's arms on the new skins, which were lifted up quickly by at least twenty pairs of hands, causing the couple to be tossed into the air, falling back down onto the skins that were held off the ground to cushion their fall. The process was repeated several times, while everyone hooted and called out to the young pairs.

Attu noticed Suka worked his way around the skins so he could stand near Rika for the second tossing. Suka spoke to Rika, leaning in to make himself heard. Rika laughed and flashed Suka a smile. Suka glanced back at Attu, as if making sure he saw.

Always trying to show me up, Attu thought. *Be careful, Suka.*

Suka leaned in to say something else to Rika, but he never got the chance. Banek appeared at Rika's side and with a shove, pushed Suka so hard he fell backwards into the rest of the jostling crowd. Banek scowled at Rika and took Suka's place hanging onto the skins. Rika grew still, her face now a mask. Attu's heart skipped a beat, and he balled his fists in frustration. No one else seemed to notice as Suka got up and walked away into the night.

Everyone else laughed and grinned as the second couple, Kinak and Suanu, clung tightly to each other, tumbling together on the skins. They didn't pull apart when the tossing was over, but stayed wrapped in each other's arms. The other men whistled their approval amid the women's lip popping. Jokes about how soon a baby would follow such a good tossing became the main topic of conversation for the rest of the evening as the men set up the two new shelters, one in each camp, a bit off to the side for privacy, but close enough for safety. Attu walked over to help the men set up Kinak and Suanu's shelter, hoping to see Suka, but he hadn't returned. Moolnik had kept up such a tirade of insults towards his second son all evening that Attu didn't blame Suka for staying hidden somewhere. He was tired of the whole thing himself and headed back toward his own shelter as each clan's women said a tearful goodbye to the young woman leaving to join her man.

Attu could not fall asleep until late that night. When he did, he dreamed of the young woman crying out to him for help, across a rapidly spreading dark chasm of water. And this time she had Rika's golden eyes.

~ • ~

Paven's clan left two days later. A group of his hunters had seen a young ice bear roaming along the edges of the camp, and Paven would take no more chances with the safety of his people. Attu stood with his family, watching the other clan traverse across the flat ice of the Great Frozen, *in the direction we should be heading,* Attu thought. *South and east.*

Attu knew he was well enough to travel, and for a while he had considered talking with his father, of asking him to speak with Paven, to try to convince him to let him, Attu, speak for Rika, not Banek. But his people needed him now more than ever with Moolnik set on staying on this ice bear-infested land. And Attu didn't know how Rika felt. He couldn't ask her, not after she had run from him. He had his pride. So he said nothing.

Attu stood on the edge of the land until the whole Great Frozen clan was only shadows on the horizon. Everyone else had long since turned and walked back to camp, leaving Attu alone. He had hoped

Rika would turn to look back at him, see him, give the sign of farewell, safe hunting. But she hadn't looked back. Not even once.

Attu picked up some small loose rocks and began bouncing them across the ice. He couldn't believe Rika was gone. He threw harder, ignoring the pain that stretching his back muscles caused. Let his wounds rip open again. What did he care?

Rika hadn't even come to say goodbye. She'd sent her little brother with a small pouch of ointment. "Rika says to use this for the next moon, to keep the scars soft and help the rest of the healing," Rovek had said. The child had run off before Attu had a chance to reply.

"I'm the fool," Attu grumbled to himself. "She's just a girl."

"Attu!"

Attu turned and saw Meavu running toward him, her ice bear necklace jangling. Since it had been given to her, she'd never taken it off. He smiled.

"Mother says to come," Meavu said, and she put her arm in his and began pulling him up the small slope toward the camp. "She's cooking the last of the ice bear meat, rare, over the nuknuk lamps. And there is rock moss, enough for everyone!" Meavu beamed at him. "Come!"

"I'm coming, Kip," Attu said. "Don't pull me so hard." He was hungry. And ice bear meat was greasy and smoky. It was the best meat any of the clan had ever eaten. *Almost worth a few scars,* Attu thought. *Almost.*

They headed back toward camp. Yet, at the thought of eating the ice bear meat, Attu felt uneasy. Moolnik was impulsive, a reactor, not a planner. Would he place guards around the camp as Paven had done, or would he simply ignore the threat of the ice bears and send his men out to hunt nuknuks, leaving the women and children behind, defenseless?

Attu's stomach knotted at the thought. *I must speak with Father about this,* he decided, and hurried even faster, causing Meavu to jog beside him to keep up.

"You sure must be hungry," Meavu said.

"Race you," Attu replied, and the two of them ran back to camp.

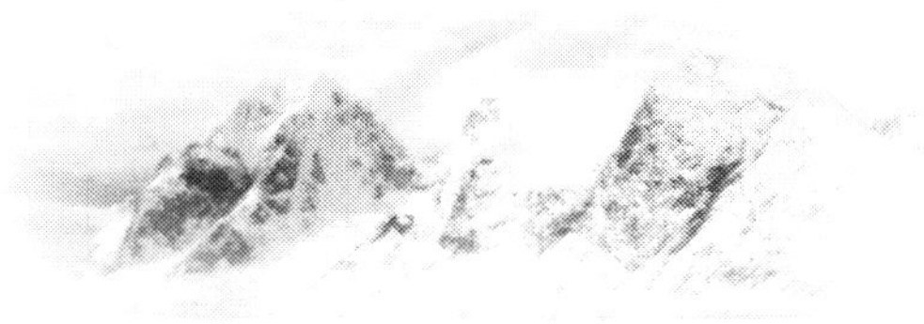

Chapter 11

The following day, Attu climbed up into the rocky hills, high above the camp. At the top, along the ridge of the land where the snow blew off the flat surfaces, he could see both sides of the outcropping they were camped on, sloping down to meet the Great Frozen. It was quiet up here, away from the noise of the camp. Attu needed to be alone today so he could think, could figure out some way he could convince his father to take back leadership of the clan.

Ubantu had made no move to regain the allegiance of the other hunters, who had now grown used to following Moolnik. Most of them liked Moolnik's loud and brash manner, so unlike Ubantu's quieter ways. They thought Moolnik decisive and confident, Attu knew. Moolnik was careful not to allow the others to see his true cowardly nature.

But strange as it was to Attu, Moolnik still seemed to need his brother's approval and constantly sought it, even as he remained jealous of him, just as Suka was jealous of Kinak. Perhaps Ubantu could use Moolnik's need for approval in some way. Still, whenever Ubantu refused to go along with Moolnik's schemes, they argued.

Just yesterday, Attu had decided to try to influence the other hunters on his own. He began by speaking with Kinak and Yupik again about the need to move south. They'd laughed at him. The other hunters wanted to hear him tell of the ice bear attack, which he refused to do, but they didn't want to listen to him explain why the clan needed to begin moving south and east again, like Paven's clan had done. Attu brought up the subject with the rest of the hunters, and they all grew uneasy, looking over their shoulders for signs of Moolnik.

"Why are you afraid?" Attu challenged them. "Moolnik is not an ice bear. He's just a man." But at his words, the other hunters turned away, their faces cold.

No matter how angry Moolnik gets, Father must take the lead hunter's place again, so we can get off this land before it's too late, Attu reasoned with himself for the hundredth time. *The other hunters are like Moolnik, only seeing the rich game here. They must see the changes in the Expanse; every Nuvik hunter watches the weather signs constantly. But they choose to believe it will stay like it is now, no warmer. They are afraid to go out on the ice again. So am I. But if we wait, we will all be trapped here.*

But so far, his arguments had not caused even his own father to do anything other than wait with the rest of them. *And for what?* His people needed to travel beyond the Expanse, away from the ice bears and onto the large land to the south and east. And they needed to go NOW.

Attu thought about the ice bear, and how something he had been taught to believe was a spirit of the Between had proven to be real. He wondered how many other stories were also real, not tales at all, but important information passed down the generations for his people to remember when they would need the knowledge again. He thought of the whale fish and trembled to think it, too, might be real. Whale fishes didn't seem possible, but Attu remembered Elder Nuanu's words, "…until the sun before this one, I thought such an expanse of open water could not exist, either…"

Attu thought about the nuknuk holes that didn't refreeze for days, and the way the blue green algae and rock moss flourished here in such large quantities. Every sign pointed to the warming of Nuvikuan-na and the need to get to the large land mass Elder Tovut had spoken of, before they were trapped on land like this one, big enough to camp on, but too small to live on for the countless generations they might be confined to its small dry space. And that would be IF the water did not rise any more, like Elder Tovut had said it would.

Attu felt a fear stronger than his fear of the ice bears rising up in him as he thought about his family being trapped on an ever-shrinking spot of land while the water rose around them. The prophecy Elder Tovut had spoken said that he, Attu, was to lead his people to safety. Yet here he was, still recovering from massive wounds, and no other hunters would listen to his advice. *But if I can somehow convince my father to lead...*

Attu's thoughts continued to roll back on themselves as he looked down toward the shore where the clan's camp was set up. In some places, the strips of unfrozen water were almost a spear length wide, edging around the land where the sun warmed the dark-rock shoreline.

Attu sighed. *One more sign that Elder Tovut was right.*

As he began to head down the slope again, toward camp, Attu noticed two women walking away from camp, gathering blue algae along the shoreline. Attu knew they must be Yupik's woman, Taunu, and their daughter Inung because of the bold pattern of colorful fur on the backs of their parkas. All the women created unique designs for parkas, and Attu had walked behind the other clan members so long on the journey, he knew every pattern.

And of course they have no hunters guarding them, Attu thought.

Attu was looking down at the women, judging the distance between him and them, figuring out the best path to take down the steep hill, when he saw an ice bear edging its way behind some snow-covered mounds that butted against the shoreline. Attu could see the bear from this height, but he knew the women couldn't.

Attu bolted down the hill, cupping his hands and shouting a warning as he ran. He knew the women couldn't hear him from this distance, but someone in the camp might. As he ran, Attu's feet got ahead of him and he began sliding, using his miks to steady himself as he slid down the loose rocks. Twice he almost lost control, but he recovered by allowing his body to slam into larger rocks to slow himself down.

Slewing around a boulder, Attu cried out again, and this time, two hunters, Moolnik and Yupik, looked up from the edge of camp where they'd been standing. Attu knew a cloud of rock dust was rising behind him, and he yelled again when he saw them turn in his direction. Attu forced himself to a stop, jumped up on the nearest rock, and pointed toward the place where the women were gathering.

The men raced toward the women, spears at the ready. But they had far to run, and the bear was coming around the mounds. Attu held his bruised sides, steadying himself on his rock perch, and tried to catch his breath, so he could make it the rest of the way down the steep slope. He'd veered off the easier path, and he realized now as he stood there he was trapped. He couldn't go down any further this way, but would have to climb back up and take the path the others had worn over the last two moons. He couldn't reach the women in time, either way. Attu watched in agony as the bear rounded the mound heading for its prey.

Moolnik and Yupik were yelling as they ran; Attu could hear their voices carried to him on the wind. Taunu and Inung must have heard as well because they looked up from their gathering and saw the bear, and Attu heard their combined screams as they dropped their pouches and began running toward the hunters.

The bear broke into a charge. In two leaps, it had covered the ground between itself and the women, and as the bear leaped again, Attu saw a huge paw catch Taunu, throwing her sideways against the mounds. She did not get up again. Inung continued to run until she neared the hunters. She slowed, as if to throw herself into her father Yupik's arms, but suddenly veered off and began running again, streaking past the hunters toward camp. Attu knew Yupik would have yelled to his daughter to run for safety. Her fear would give her enough speed to make it.

Moolnik and Yupik slowed as they neared the bear that, ignoring the two hunters, was beginning to drag the limp Taunu back the way it had come. Attu's stomach sickened at the sight of the bear, Taunu's arm in its massive jaws. He watched as Yupik launched himself at the bear's back. The bear dropped Taunu and reared up on its hind legs.

It was huge.

Yupik somehow hung on and began climbing up the bear's back, stabbing as he went, using the two knives he always carried. Blood darkened the bear's white fur as it spun and roared, trying to shake Yupik off. It flailed wildly in the air over its head with its huge paws, but couldn't seem to reach behind itself far enough to grab Yupik.

That man has a demon spirit, Attu thought as Yupik clung to the bear and stabbed it, first with one knife, then the other. He continued to climb up its massive shoulders, using the embedded knives as handholds, stabbing, climbing, and stabbing again. Reaching the bear's head, Yupik ducked a swing of claws and with a mighty thrust, stabbed the bear in the face. It screamed and swung a massive paw. Yupik was so high up on its back now that the ice bear got a grip on him with its huge claws, and with one swipe, Yupik was torn from the bear's back and thrown to the side. The bear dropped to all fours and screamed again, a high pitched keen of fury as it ground its paws into its own face, blood spewing as it shook its head. Attu saw something fly off.

One of Yupik's knives, Attu realized. *It must have been imbedded in the bear's eye.*

The ice bear turned, rising up on its hind feet again. It WAS a giant, taller than twice a man's height plus the length of an arm. As Attu watched, the bear let out a roar, towering over Moolnik, who stood frozen in place. The bear roared and roared down at Moolnik and Attu could see the yellow teeth in the gaping red mouth. The hills shook in echo to the roar, and Attu trembled.

The bear ·shook its head again, and dropping to all fours, it turned away from Moolnik and headed back toward the mounds, slowly, leaving a trail of blood behind it. Attu stood as still as Moolnik. He couldn't believe the bear had left without attacking Moolnik. Yupik must have injured it severely. Perhaps being attacked from behind had scared it. Perhaps Yupik's raw fury had made the bear hesitant to attack Moolnik. But for whatever reason, Attu watched as the ice bear disappeared behind the mounds again.

The rest of the clan swarmed out over the shoreline to help the injured Taunu and Yupik. Attu turned and started the climb back up to the path, feeling as weary now as if he'd been Yupik, attacking the bear. He wondered if Taunu was dead, and how badly Yupik was injured. Whatever the outcome, Moolnik would have to see reason now and leave this land before someone else got attacked. Attu's hands shook as he grabbed for handholds among the rocks, his back aching from the effort of climbing back up to the path that led to camp.

Chapter 12

Attu hurried into camp on legs that felt like rubbery hides. All he could think of now was how good it would feel to sink into his soft fur bed and sleep, but first he needed to find out how Taunu and Yupik were. The clan would've taken them to Elder Nuanu's. He hurried through the camp toward her shelter, passing the hunters talking in loud voices.

One voice caught Attu's attention. Moolnik's. Lies were pouring out Moolnik's mouth as he retold "his" version of the attack. *To hear him tell it,* Attu thought as he slowed down, *Moolnik was the hero who chased off the bear, not Yupik, when the truth is Moolnik stood there too terrified to do a thing to stop the bear. It's as if Moolnik has a spirit of trickery within him. Others listen to him and believe, no matter what the truth is.*

Furious, Attu picked up his pace, wincing with the strain of trying to walk faster, but needing to put some distance between himself and Moolnik.

"Wait, Attu!" Suka called after him.

Attu stopped and turned, looking back at Suka.

"What did you see?" Suka asked. His shouted question caused the group to become quiet as the hunters, including Moolnik, stopped talking to hear what Attu would say.

Attu looked past Suka and glared at Moolnik instead, letting every bit of his anger and disrespect for the elder show on his face.

"Enough," Attu replied. "I saw enough."

Ignoring the calls of the others to return and tell what he'd witnessed, Attu turned and headed toward Elder Nuanu's shelter again. He heard footsteps behind him, and recognizing his father's slight limping gait, Attu slowed, allowing his father to catch up.

"Attu, what's wrong?" Ubantu asked.

"Not here," Attu hissed. "I'll tell you, Father; I will tell you everything, but we need to go where others can't hear."

Attu picked up his pace again, but caught his foot on a stone. He stumbled, almost falling in his weariness.

Attu flinched in pain as his father grabbed his injured shoulder to stop his fall. Attu's back was screaming at him, and he was afraid he'd ripped open the deepest wound again.

"Are you hurt?" his father asked.

"My back."

Ubantu grunted and carefully steadied Attu at his elbow, hurrying him toward their shelter. "Let your mother tend your back," his father said. "I'll check on Taunu and Yupik again. You need to lie down."

"Tonight, my son," his father said as he slipped back out of the shelter once Attu was settled in, his mother gathering up her supplies to treat his back. "We'll talk tonight."

Attu saw Yural look anxiously between the two of them, but she said nothing as she worked to carefully remove Attu's inner fur vest.

It was late evening, and although the darkness gave the illusion of privacy, still Ubantu walked around camp, checking to make sure everyone else was in their shelters, except for the two hunters Moolnik had instructed, after the attack, to walk the perimeter of the clan's camp watching for ice bears.

"Now he seems to have an interest in keeping us safe," Attu said to his father as Ubantu returned and told him of the guards Moolnik had posted.

"It's hard to continue to ignore the spirit of Death when it rears up in your face with slashing claws and sharp teeth," his father said.

You don't know how right you are about that, Father.

"But why did you stare at Moolnik with such hatred? What happened?"

Attu poured out his story to Ubantu, from the very beginning. Much of what he spoke of, his father already knew: how he believed Moolnik was not a good leader, not caring for his people, usurping Ubantu's right to lead past when his injury had healed. Ubantu listened without comment, occasionally nodding his head.

It feels good to tell my father everything, Attu realized, as some of the weight of the frustration he'd been carrying began to lift from his shoulders.

Gaining courage by his father's acceptance of what he'd said so far, Attu told Ubantu about Elder Nuanu and how Moolnik had left her, and what had really happened with the ice bear attacking Taunu, how Yupik had climbed the bear's back with his double knives while Moolnik just stood, apparently too terrified to move. He told how angry it had made him to hear Moolnik lie to cover up his own cowardice, and how frustrated Attu was to have to follow such a leader as Moolnik.

"I can't do it anymore, Father," Attu finished, suddenly weary of it all.

"I knew Moolnik was irresponsible and a jealous braggart set on making himself more than he should be, but this…" Ubantu gazed at the nuknuk lamp's steady flame, his eyes thoughtful.

Attu let out his breath with relief. *He knows I wouldn't lie to him, or stretch the truth to make Moolnik look worse than he is.*

Too tired to remain sitting, Attu stretched out on his bed furs. He'd slept some, but he was still weary. Yural had put more salve on his back, and no wounds had reopened, but his back and sides still hurt.

Attu's mother had gone to Elder Nuanu's as soon as she'd re-bandaged Attu's back and he was resting. Yupik had suffered only one gash across the back of his head, not too deep, and would recover, Elder Nuanu said. His mother had taken some of Rika's salve over to the healer's shelter.

Taunu's arm had been nearly ripped from her body. No amount of healer's salve would help such a wound.

Attu was almost asleep before his father spoke again.

"We must stay until Taunu either passes Between or recovers enough to travel." Ubantu shifted his sitting position, easing his crippled leg. "Then, we will travel toward the land Elder Tovut spoke of again, with or without Moolnik."

"And the others?" Attu whispered. "Will they come with us?"

"I do not know," Ubantu said. "We must try to convince them all, even Moolnik. Perhaps now that he felt the hot breath of an ice bear on his neck, he will see reason."

Fear rose in Attu at the possibility of having to leave part of the clan behind. Even as much as he hated Moolnik, still it wasn't right to divide their clan. It was dangerous for everyone. *And what of Elder Tovut's prophecy? How can I lead a clan to safety when I'm no longer a part of it?* Attu didn't want to lead, but Elder Nuanu had insisted it would come to pass, and she'd never been wrong in her predictions.

Attu, now no longer sleepy, lay awake long into the night, falling asleep only to dream again of the girl on the other side of the chasm of open water. There was no doubt. It was Rika. He called after her in the dream, even as it unfolded, even as he saw the logic in the dream as he was dreaming it. Rika was unreachable, unattainable, as if a large body of water did indeed separate them. Yet still, he heard his own voice, crying out to her that he was coming. After that, he dreamed again of a journey between two ridges of rocks, but all was hazy around him. In the distance he heard a voice. Was it Rika's? She was calling, "I must show mercy; I must show mercy." Then it all faded to darkness, and he found himself floating somehow as if in one of those skin boats Elder Nuanu had spoken of. He floated along in the darkness, water surrounding him, stars above. And he was not afraid.

Attu awoke the next morning wondering about the dreams of ridges and floating on the water. They made no sense to him, so he put them aside in his mind and considered the dream of Rika. *Did the spirits give me the dream of Rika before I met her, just to help me see she could never be mine?* He'd wanted her for his woman, Attu had to admit to himself, as crazy as that sounded. He'd barely become a hunter, and then she'd shown up, tipping his world on edge like ice tilting under his feet just before plunging him into the freezing cold water underneath. She'd been there when he needed her, after the bear attack, with her healing hands and her insolent ways. And then she was gone.

"And you need to stop thinking about her, calling after her in your spirit like a nuknuk pup crying for its mother," Attu mumbled to himself.

"What did you say?" asked Meavu, who was still rubbing the sleep of Between out of her eyes.

"Your father has gone to see Elder Nuanu," Attu's mother said, thinking Meavu had been speaking to her. "Taunu hasn't woken since the attack." Yural sighed. "Elder Nuanu says there's not much hope."

Yural waved Attu out of his bed, moving in behind him to straighten his sleeping furs. Attu knew his mother was trying to keep herself busy in her worry. Their shelter had never been as neat as when his father had first been injured.

"Did Father say what else he was doing this day?" Attu asked as he grabbed a large hunk of dried nuknuk and shoved it in his mouth before his mother could scold him for taking her food without asking her.

"He's going to talk to Moolnik and the other hunters about leaving," Yural said. She continued to scurry around the small shelter, like the little whirlwinds that pick up old snow and spin it in the air.

Attu knew he needed to get out of her way for a while. And he needed to get out of camp. He was still furious with Moolnik. It wouldn't be good for the others to see his anger, not today, when his father would be trying to influence the other clan members to leave against Moolnik's wishes.

It will take more than one ice bear attack to get Moolnik to leave this prime hunting ground, Attu thought. *He will not be easily persuaded, if Father can make him see reason at all. It hadn't worked before, even with Paven and the other entire clan working to convince Moolnik.*

"I'm going fishing," Attu announced.

"Alone?" his mother asked, her eyes widening in fear.

"I'll stay close to camp, along the shoreline, and away from the rocks on the other side," Attu assured her. "It will be all right, Mother." He reached out and touched her arm. "Besides, wouldn't tooth fish stew be good to eat tonight?"

"Don't brag about game that's not in the pot yet," his mother scolded him. She smiled. "Tooth fish stew does sound good. I never thought I'd say this," and she lowered her voice to a whisper so the spirits of the animals couldn't hear her but Meavu and Attu still could, "I've actually grown tired of eating nuknuk." Attu's mother giggled like a young woman who has said something bold to her hunter, as she turned away, busying herself with cleaning the already spotless shelter.

Attu grinned at Meavu, who smiled back. He grabbed up his fishing pouch, with its ball of thin line, bone hooks and dried mussels for bait, and his knife and spear. He grabbed another piece of dried nuknuk, dodged his mother's playful slap at his hand full of meat, and headed out to the south end of the land to fish at the shoreline.

The next day, Taunu died.

Chapter 13

"She lost too much blood," Elder Nuanu told Attu as the two of them sat in Elder Nuanu's shelter. "Her spirit couldn't remain in the body without the life force of blood to sustain it."

Yupik lay snoring in the corner of the shelter, his sharp breathing punctuated by occasional murmuring and twitching.

"I think he's dreaming of the ice bear attack," Attu said. "He may need the Remembering."

"Yupik is healing," Elder Nuanu said, "but the wound on the back of his head required many stitches, and his eyes now see only darkness. He didn't even notice when the body of his woman was moved to his brother's shelter for burial preparation. His spirit is with us still, but it's not strong, and I'm concerned for him."

"What did Moolnik say when he saw Yupik?"

"That mighty leader has not seen fit to visit this wounded hunter, or to confer with this clan's healer." Elder Nuanu gazed into Attu's eyes, her formal tone giving away her true feelings while her face remained impassive.

Attu was shocked, but he worked to hide his reaction. "Father has decided we'll travel south, with or without Moolnik and those following him, as soon as Yupik is able and Taunu's body is buried in the proper manner for a woman of the clan."

Women's bodies were guarded, but only for three days. Because they weren't hunters in the Here and Now, their spirits didn't need to be guarded until the trystas could spear them into the heavens to light up the night sky for the clan. Women became part of the Between, where they could continue to guide their families as long as those family members followed the rituals of the clan.

That's why it was so important to follow ritual. In the Between, women were the hunters, hunting out evil and destroying it before it could destroy their families. Men, with their spirits in stronger bodies, hunted in the Here and Now. When they passed to the Between, they kept the fires of the stars, like giant nuknuk lamps in the sky. Women kept the fires in the Here and Now because their bodies were weaker, and became the hunters, the protectors, in the Between, once their spirits were freed to fight and protect as fiercely as the men did in the Here and Now. Thus the cycle of hunter and protected fire-keeper was complete for both men and women.

"Attu?" Elder Nuanu interrupted Attu's thoughts.

"Yes?"

"Tell your father I will come with him, whether Moolnik comes or not. My man was right. The Warming Time is coming, and I won't spend the rest of my few remaining moons trapped on this land with water all around, while my people slowly starve to death."

"Thank you, Elder Nuanu." Attu smiled at the old woman, jumped up, and headed back to his family's shelter.

This news will help Father persuade many to come with us.

~ • ~

Later the next day, Attu heard sudden shouting, voices raised in either anger or fear, he couldn't tell which. Grabbing his spear from its place beside the door of the shelter, Attu left his half-finished bowl of tooth fish stew and raced toward the noise coming from the middle of camp. He scanned ahead as he ran, looking for signs that a bear was attacking. *Would an ice bear be so bold as to come right into the center of camp?* Attu could hear a man's voice, and now a woman's, then several women. *What was happening?*

Rounding the corner of a shelter, Attu was almost knocked to the ground as his father threw out his arm to stop Attu from taking another step.

"It's Moolnik and Elder Nuanu," his father hissed. "Moolnik found out Elder Nuanu said she will come with us."

Attu saw the entire clan gathered in a loose circle around Moolnik and Elder Nuanu, who were hurling insults at each other. Most of the women were standing behind Elder Nuanu, including Attu's mother with Meavu by her side. Attu would have chuckled at Meavu's pretending to be an adult, but the look on her face showed Attu this was not play to Meavu. She was furious.

Moolnik, with Kinak and Suka flanking him a few feet back, stood facing Elder Nuanu. The other men were staying off to the side, as Ubantu was. Attu took all this in at a glance as he turned his full attention to the arguing pair.

"And you are a fool, Moolnik, the son of a trysta grasped by a tooth fish," Elder Nuanu spat. Attu cringed at her lewd insult.

"And you are a bag of bones in a body soon to go Between," Moolnik yelled. "I can hardly wait to guard your grave."

The women of the clan collectively drew in sharp breaths, frowning in disapproval of Moolnik's daring to show such disrespect to an elder who would be even more powerful in death than she already was in life.

"What is it going to take to get you to see what's right in front of your eyes?" Elder Nuanu continued, undaunted by Moolnik's remark. "Three people died in Paven's clan. Taunu has died, and Yupik is slow to recover. His sight is still impaired. And yet-"

"And yet we are here, eating better than the clan has ever eaten before, rich in the meat of the nuknuk and tooth fish." Moolnik took a threatening step closer to Elder Nuanu. "When have you ever seen the children so chubby, the women's cheeks so round, the men so strong?"

"Like fat nuknuks, waiting to be an ice bear's meal," Elder Nuanu replied as she rolled her eyes at Moolnik. Then her voice softened, became persuasive. "That's not the point, Moolnik. This is not a competition you must win against your older brother. Your father is long dead and his cruel ways died with him."

"Don't you dare speak of my father like that!" Moolnik spat.

"I will speak of him, Moolnik. Can't you see? It's as if he still lives inside your head, jeering you, poking at your spirit to fight your brother. Ubantu is not your enemy. He just wants what is best for this clan. So do I. We must keep traveling south and east, before it's too late, before this land is surrounded by water. The nuknuks will leave, for they need the ice, the cold, and perhaps the tooth fish as well. None of us knows for sure."

"That's right, YOU don't know, Elder Nuanu," Moolnik said, his tone derisive as he leered at the old woman. "You listened to your man and you believed every word he said. You trusted in the words of an old man, slipping into the Between, an old man who for all we know was simply repeating the lies told him by his grandfather. Both our fathers would have laughed at him."

Moolnik turned to go, but Elder Nuanu took a step forward, closing the gap between them. She grabbed Moolnik's shoulder, and he spun back around.

"Don't you touch me, woman," he growled.

"And don't you turn your back on an elder," Elder Nuanu shot back at him. "This is no longer about what my man Tovut said." She paused, and Attu saw her back straighten as she pushed forward with her argument. "I do believe he spoke the truth, but this is now about the facts we see. It's warmer here than it should be; plants grow in abundance where they should be sparse. Water forms at the edge of the shoreline every day the sun shines, and there SHOULD NOT BE so many nuknuks."

Elder Nuanu shook her head. "Where are they coming from? Are they coming from the south, because the ice there is now no longer able to bear their weight, so they must travel farther north to find places upon which they can rest?"

Sighing, Elder Nuanu looked off for a moment to the southeast. All eyes followed hers as she called quietly upon the trystas of safe travel, "Oh, keep the ice firm until we can pass over, spirits who can…"

Attu looked at his people. Elder Nuanu had done what all of his father's persuasion hadn't been able to do. She'd spoken out the fear that had been smoldering in the hearts of Attu's clan for the last moon. This place was wrong. It was all wrong. They needed to leave, to travel toward the great land Elder Tovut had said awaited them, as fast as possible, before it was too late.

"What do you know of hunting, of the ways of the nuknuk?" Moolnik said, pulling himself up to his full height and leaning forward so that he towered over Elder Nuanu like an ice bear over its prey.

Oh no, Attu thought. *Moolnik is going to be the "mighty leader of hunters" now. He didn't hear a thing Elder Nuanu said, except that she tried to tell him about hunting.* That wasn't done amongst the people. Women didn't advise men on the hunt. Attu could see Moolnik was ready to upbraid her.

Beside him, Ubantu tensed. Attu knew his father hated it when his brother acted so arrogantly, as if he alone knew what was right and wrong to do.

W*hy does he just stand here?* Attu thought. *He does nothing to stop his brother. Again.*

"When the hunter cannot see to catch the game, all go hungry," Elder Nuanu replied. "I speak the truth. You'll let us all die here. All you see is the game in front of you; you cannot see the danger lurking behind it. You cannot even see the danger when it breathes down your neck and you are too terrified to move."

"How dare you-" Moolnik began, but Elder Nuanu slashed her hand down across her body, silencing Moolnik by her man's gesture that meant be quiet, or I will silence you by cutting your throat.

The whole clan grew deathly still.

"I know what really happened with Taunu and Yupik. He told me as he lay bleeding on the furs of my shelter, the shelter you haven't even entered since the attack."

Several hunters popped their lips at this announcement. Their leader hadn't even gone to the side of his injured hunter? That was unthinkable. A few men stepped back from Moolnik even further.

"You're afraid to continue," Elder Nuanu said. She glared up at Moolnik now, as Healer, and as the Elder who commanded respect by her mere presence, and all could see the warrior spirit growing within her even now, ready to be released to the Between.

She will be unstoppable, Attu thought.

In a dangerously soft voice, almost crooning, Elder Nuanu said, "You know the words of my man are true, and you're afraid to continue the necessary journey to the great land beyond the Expanse. You did nothing to protect us from the ice bears, just as you did not see the crack coming as we began our journey, and when you did, you chose not to come back for me, but ran to save your own life, instead." Elder Nuanu glanced at Attu. "You forced a young hunter to do what our leader SHOULD have done but could not."

Moolnik looked like he was going to speak again, but Elder Nuanu held up her hand, palm toward him.

Attu saw Moolnik cringe. He took a step backward.

"Swear, Moolnik," Elder Nuanu commanded, her voice now so strong, Attu felt it in his very bones. "Swear on your spirit, on its journey to the heavens after you go Between, that you did not see me when the chasm opened; you did not hear Attu's cry, and you did not know you were leaving me behind to die."

Moolnik stood silent, a guilty child before the fierceness of this Elder, this woman of truth.

"This is your leader," Elder Nuanu said, her voice raised for all to hear. "Obey him if you will. Stay here and die."

She raised her hands toward the sky, and turned. "Or follow Attu, who leads with the wisdom of his father behind him, the bravery of one who saves the weak, and the courage of one who faces death, even death by an ice bear, and still he protects. He is a true Nuvik, sacrificing for his people. He has dreamed and it has come to pass. What more must you see to believe him, whom my man has proclaimed will be the one to save us, and who has already proven his worth to us in saving us all from the chasm? I have made my choice. I will follow Attu. Make yours. There is not much time. It may already be too late."

Elder Nuanu turned and disappeared inside her shelter.

Moolnik threw himself out of the center of the group, his face flaming. "Dreams, sacrifice, how can you believe in such foolishness, such weakness?" He yelled toward Elder Nuanu's tent as he lurched toward his own shelter, followed closely by Kinak. Suka hesitated, turning toward Attu, a look of utter despair etched into his face. He turned back, rushing after his father and brother to catch up with them.

Attu stood frozen to the spot. *It is as if Moolnik truly has a Moolnikuan spirit within him, tricking him, as if the spirit his father named him for is trying to take him over. How else could he not see what needs to be done to save us? And so many have been fooled by him. Is that Moolnik's own cunning? Or an evil spirit within him?*

The rest of the clan broke into noisy chatter, milling around Elder Nuanu's shelter, talking amongst themselves.

"Time to organize," Ubantu said quietly to Attu. "What do we do first?"

Attu couldn't believe that after such a shocking display of anger and truth telling, so humiliating for Moolnik, that his father could calmly face what had transpired and begin planning.

"You have known these things about Moolnik for a long time, my son. Now the rest need a chance to consider what they've heard today. Our people know the truth when they hear it, and…" Attu's father paused, the corners of his mouth lifting slightly, before he continued. "If it looks like a dead tooth fish and smells like a dead tooth fish…"

"…it must be a dead tooth fish," Attu finished the old saying without pause.

Ubantu put his arm around Attu's shoulders. For the first time since his injury, the added weight didn't hurt Attu's back.

"Moolnik put his pride before the hunt too many times, and the game scattered," Attu's father said. "He did it to hide the fear of being less than others. My father corrupted his spirit by not allowing him to travel his true path and saying that to be a dreamer, a shaman, was weakness and lies. The abuse he suffered at the hands of my father has ruined him. Only jealousy resides in his heart of cowardice now. There is no room within him for true leadership. I have known this must be true since you told me what happened with Elder Nuanu. Now, give the others some time to see it, too."

Ubantu drew Attu off to the side. "And now we must watch my brother as if he were a wounded ice bear, for Elder Nuanu's shaming him has made him dangerous to us all. She has dropped the stone upon his honor that will cause all the other stones to fall off his pile."

Attu nodded. Moolnik wouldn't let his public humiliation go without revenge. His father was right. Moolnik would never be the same after this day. Attu shivered at the thought.

Attu glanced at his father, and a look of understanding flowed between them. *I am not alone,* Attu realized. *The people are now on my side. Elder Nuanu has made it so.* He felt a sudden rush of affection for the wise old woman.

"What's next, mighty leader of the Ice Mountain Clan?" Attu's father said, dropping his arm from around Attu's shoulders and standing in front of him to await Attu's orders. Ubantu's voice was a bit teasing, but Attu heard the pride in it as well.

"I'm not the leader of these people, Father, you are," Attu said. "No matter what Elder Nuanu would like to think."

Ubantu put his hand up to protest, but Attu continued. "I will lead with you, Father. We'll lead together. We'll be strong together for our clan."

Ubantu smiled, a wide strong smile that filled Attu with warmth. "We need to pack for the journey my son," he said, "and fast."

"Like Elder Nuanu said," Attu added, "we must pray it's not already too late."

Chapter 14

The clan left two days later. The sky edged with the pink of dawn as each family readied to begin traveling again. Shelters came down. Men strapped on packs made heavy with large hide bundles of extra meat and fish. Women carried rock moss tied into packets with sinew and thrown across the top of their packs, and even small children carried pouches of the dried blue algae.

Those who were ready scouted the shoreline for a safe place to step out onto the Great Frozen. Attu went with them, anxious that no one fall into icy shallow water with the surface of the ice so thin near this southern edge of the shoreline. Eventually they chose a path out onto the ice from midway up the land where the ice was thicker.

It won't be long before no one will be able to get off this land, Attu thought as he looked at the precariously thin ice that now surrounded the entire southern end.

He walked back toward the camp, leaving three families at the shoreline waiting for his return with the rest. Attu wasn't sure about Moolnik and his family, however. The hunter hadn't spoken to anyone since Elder Nuanu had shamed him. Suka had been avoiding Attu as well. When Attu had left for his first trip to the shoreline, Moolnik's shelter had still remained untouched, his camping area eerily quiet. Attu didn't know what Moolnik had decided, but from what he could see, his uncle had made no move to get ready to leave.

How can we leave Suka, Kinak, his new woman Suanu, Shunut, and Tulnu behind? But Attu knew they would stay with Moolnik if he refused to leave.

Rounding the low hills, Attu came back in sight of camp.

Moolnik stood stubbornly in front of his shelter, his silent presence menacing and bitter. The other hunters ignored him as they made their final preparations. None were willing to risk their lives or their families to another ice bear attack. Moolnik was alone now, only his shelter still standing.

Moolnik's woman, Tulnu, came out of their shelter, and seeing that they were the only ones left, she cried out in a shrill keen like one might call out for the dead. Tulnu threw herself down in front of Moolnik and wailed, tearing at her hair and her parka, throwing the bits of hair and fur and bone she ripped off into the air, screaming and howling with a voice that sent shivers down Attu's spine.

The rest of the clan watched in horror as Tulnu began scratching her face, and bloody lines appeared on her cheeks. Attu stood open-mouthed. He had never seen a woman crazy with grief like this. Tulnu began biting at herself, tearing bits of her parka fur off with her teeth and moaning, rocking back and forth, clutching her body like she was dying of a bad mussel spirit.

Moolnik stood for several more moments, stonily watching his woman in her agony, until suddenly, apparently unable to bear his wife's fierce grieving over the loss of her clan, Moolnik shouted at her to be quiet and began taking down the hides on the outside of the structure.

Tulnu immediately fell silent. She rose up out of the pile of torn fur bits and parka ornaments that surrounded her and rushed inside the shelter, coming out a few moments later, pack on her back and holding little Shunut's hand. Kinak and Suka came out next, packs at the ready, and began helping their father dismantle the shelter.

"Allow him to save some of his pride, my son," Ubantu said, reaching down to pick up his own large pack. Attu realized he had been staring, and lowering his gaze, picked up the pack he had dropped in his amazement at the sight of Tulnu. He positioned it on his back for travel.

"We go," Attu said and turning away from Moolnik's half-dismantled shelter, walked away from it and toward the shoreline. The others followed.

Attu hated Moolnik, but he knew that leaving Moolnik and his family behind would have meant death for them all. A good leader kept his people together, no matter what. Attu couldn't help but smile as he walked out on the ice, leading the group slowly so Moolnik and his family could catch up.

Tulnu had known Moolnik would come all along, Attu realized as he continued to think about what he'd seen, and how Tulnu had readied everything except for taking down the shelter, in spite of Moolnik apparently insisting they were staying.

Attu shook his head at the wisdom of that woman, who knew how to get Moolnik to do what she needed him to do, pride or not. Later, Moolnik would say he'd had no choice but to come because Tulnu would've died of grief if he hadn't, then haunted him from the Between. The whole clan had seen the wildness of her pain. No one would contradict him.

Elder Nuanu walked up beside Attu, both about a spear's length from Ubantu. The ice seemed thicker here, just a short distance from the shoreline, almost as if it had been pushed together. They'd decided it was safe to remain closer for a while.

Attu was surprised at Elder Nuanu's boldness, walking in front with the lead hunters. She began calling out to the spirits for safe travel on the ice, sprinkling small bits of a dark substance from her hand onto the Great Frozen behind them.

Attu didn't understand the ways of this Elder, this embodiment of Shuantuan, the greatest trysta of all, living in the body of only one woman of all the clans at a time, protecting and guarding that clan above all others as a reward for their following all necessary rituals with true hearts. It was a great honor to have her among them. She made him feel safer as she walked in the lead with them, reaching out into the Between of the spirit world for guidance and help.

Perhaps that's the most important task Elder Nuanu does, Attu thought. *Her knowledge of the rituals and her confidence in interacting with the Between spirits makes the clan feel protected. Whether what she does works or not, still we feel better because she does it. Is that what it truly means to be Shuantuan?*

Attu decided to ask his father about this later, when they had a private moment. Now, he needed to make amends with Elder Nuanu. Just because Moolnik hadn't asked Elder Nuanu to perform rituals of travel didn't mean there weren't any. Obviously that's what Elder Nuanu was trying to show him.

"Elder Nuanu, please forgive me for not asking you if there were rituals you needed to perform before we set out again," Attu said. He lowered his head.

"I accept your apology," Elder Nuanu replied. "You did not know that a journey across unfamiliar ice requires rituals. You have only traveled the established route of our clan, the circle we travel from land to land to find new game. First south, then east, then north and west again, the territory of the Ice Mountain Clan as it has been for generations. I have traveled the entire route twice. And your father, once."

She shot Ubantu a look. "But you should have known. Didn't Elder Tovut teach you this?"

Ubantu hung his head. "Please remind us of what is required, Elder Nuanu."

"There are rituals for beginning and ending each day, as well as for good resting at mid-sun," Elder Nuanu explained. Attu caught the hint of a smile in her voice at putting Ubantu in his place.

"Would you please perform these rituals from now on, Elder Nuanu, healer of our clan and embodiment of Shuantuan?" Attu asked in the formal manner of one requesting such an important task be done by a woman of Elder Nuanu's status.

"As you wish, Mighty Hunter and Leader of the Ice Mountain Clan, Attu," Elder Nuanu said, her voice now serious.

S*he means to make me see myself as leader.* Attu winced.

Elder Nuanu cleared her throat as they continued walking. Changing the subject, she said, "Moolnik is a tooth fish, biting just to bite. This time he bit himself."

"Sooner or later, the tooth fish bites us all," Attu replied.

"That is true, young hunter," Elder Nuanu agreed.

So now, when she wants to give me advice, I'm suddenly 'young hunter' again, Attu thought.

"Still," Elder Nuanu interrupted Attu's thoughts, "only a fool puts his arm near a tooth fish's mouth."

Attu agreed with Elder Nuanu's warning to be careful around Moolnik. Glancing down at her, Attu saw Elder Nuanu wink at Ubantu, who had moved up to walk alongside Attu as well. All seemed forgiven between these old friends.

"I have warned him also, Elder Nuanu," Ubantu said. "Attu isn't the only one who must watch himself. You must also be wary."

"I'm old meat, too tough to get a grip on, even by a tooth fish," Elder Nuanu laughed.

"Don't be too sure of that," Attu's father said. "I know my brother. He won't forget what you said, how you shamed him with the truth in front of the whole clan."

The three walked on in silence. Attu shivered. *Were the restless Moolnikuan spirits already at work helping Moolnik seek revenge?*

The clan struck out south and east, in the same direction Paven had taken his Great Frozen Clan days before. The sun shone directly in their faces as they walked. Attu adjusted his bone goggles against the ice glare and turned his thoughts to the journey ahead as the day grew brighter. He was anxious to make as much distance as possible this sun, but he also knew the people would tire more easily again until they regained their traveling stamina.

Elder Nuanu fell back with the women, and Attu's father moved away from him, putting a safer distance between them. After a while, Ubantu moved closer to Attu again as they walked, calling so he could be heard, "I think we need to position two hunters at the back of the clan to watch for ice bears."

"Suka and Kinak?"

"Yes, that's a good choice. They're still near the back anyway."

Will my cousins do what we tell them to do? Attu wondered. *Or will they be as stubborn as their father, Moolnik?*

"Now's a good time to find out where their loyalties lie," Ubantu said, as if reading Attu's thoughts. "I'll walk back and tell them."

Attu nodded, relieved not to have to do it himself.

A while later, Ubantu returned, a bit out of breath from working his way back to the lead, but smiling.

"They agreed," he said.

"Good."

"And Suka said to tell you this traveling pace is good for his mother and Shunut, not too fast."

Attu nodded. *Is he acknowledging my wisdom to lead, over his father's? Was that the meaning hidden behind those words?* Attu hoped so. If he had been Suka, he'd have a hard time following the orders of someone his own age, even if Elder Nuanu insisted on it, let alone someone who'd been a part, although not by his own choice, in making Suka's father look bad.

Attu called a halt when the sun was only halfway to its highest point in the sky. He passed word along that no one should unpack anything except for a bit of food and drink, and that they'd be stopping again at sun high. This was just an extra rest, a short one.

Attu smiled at the look of relief on the women's faces, and everyone dropped packs and sat, enjoying the unexpected rest. The people chattered among themselves, still in the initial excitement of beginning their journey again.

Attu was kneeling in front of his pack looking for an extra bit of padding for his carry strap as the hum of voices suddenly stopped. Suka was loping toward the front of Attu's group. He was not yelling for help, but his long legs ate up the distance between them. Attu stood as Suka reached him.

"We're being followed by an ice bear," Suka said. "I'm sure of it."

Chapter 15

"What did you see?" Attu asked, as Meavu, hearing the words, "ice bear," buried her head in her mother's parka. Everyone else looked on the edge of panic.

Careful now, Attu thought and he glanced to the sides, hoping Suka would get his message. The last thing the clan needed was to begin fleeing across this tricky ice, trying to run from an ice bear that might or might not be after them.

Suka took in a deep breath and let it out, apparently to calm himself before he spoke.

"I began thinking we were being followed shortly after you told us to guard the rear," Suka began. "The hair on the back of my neck kept rising, and I had this feeling…"

Attu knew that feeling well, like suddenly you were the prey, not the hunter. He nodded.

"So I let the others go ahead, and I stayed back. I lay flat upon my pack, very still, against that ice mound we passed a while ago."

"A good idea," Attu said.

Attu's father moved to stand by them as Suka paused, looking around the group. He seemed to choose his next words carefully.

"I saw a strange mound of ice off in the distance, back towards the land we'd come from. It hadn't been there before. I thought of how the ice bear had hidden behind the mounds before attacking the women, and how you said the bear you killed had pretended to be a mound, lying still, blending in with the surrounding mounds, before it attacked Meavu and Shunut."

Attu nodded.

"I waited. And the mound moved. After a long time, the ice bear raised its head as if it were sniffing in our direction, catching our scent on the winds blowing from the south, and it began to walk toward us."

Several women popped their lips in fear.

"It wasn't running," Suka said in a rush, looking around at the frightened faces of the clan. "Just following."

"Where is it now? Has it continued to follow us?" Ubantu asked.

Suka turned and looked back along the path they'd come. He pointed to a vague spot, a slight lifting of the edge of the horizon, barely discernible in the glare of the sun.

"It's there," Suka said.

"What do we do?" cried Meavu suddenly, running from her mother into her father's arms. He lifted her up, and she buried her face in his neck. "I'm afraid," she cried, "I'm afraid."

Ubantu looked at Attu.

"Tell the other hunters," Attu ordered Suka. "We'll meet here. Hurry, but don't panic."

"I'll take Meavu and the others over there to rest," Yural said, pointing to a spot on the path back the way they'd come.

The group shouldn't stand closely together on the ice, and Yural seemed to be using that excuse to allow Attu and the hunters a chance to talk without having to worry about scaring the women and children any more than they already were.

"Thank you, Mother," Attu said. He was grateful for Yural's wisdom in the face of danger.

The hunters gathered. Even Moolnik came. Attu tried not to be intimidated by the older man's sullen presence. He looked to his father, who gave a slight nod of encouragement.

Attu opened his mouth to speak but stopped when Yupik, the hunter who'd been injured while fighting off the ice bear, placed his hand, palm down in front of him. Surprised, Attu nodded, giving Yupik the chance to speak first.

"It's the bear that attacked Taunu," Yupik said, his voice trembling. "I feel it in my spirit."

"What do you mean?" Attu asked. Glancing around the group, Attu saw that the rest of the hunters looked as surprised as he was by Yupik's claim.

"He seeks revenge," Yupik answered. "He won't stop until he gets it."

The hunters popped their lips in dismay.

Could an ice bear be smart enough to seek revenge?

Attu looked closely at Yupik. Yupik had joined the other hunters in spite of Elder Nuanu's arguing that he wasn't well enough yet. Yupik's wounds were healing, but he still couldn't see out of his left eye, even though Elder Nuanu could find no injury.

Yupik's eyes looked wild as he stood there, his face feverish. Healing scratches laced his left cheek and forehead. Attu knew Yupik was plagued with headaches and sharp pains in his eye now, which caused him to tear at his face, especially in his sleep. Elder Nuanu had ordered his hands bound at night, to prevent him from hurting himself as he slept.

Perhaps there is a connection between Yupik and the ice bear now, even though the ice bear didn't die.

Attu decided to have Elder Nuanu begin working with Yupik's Remembering, just to be sure. He didn't want to lose a hunter.

"Whether or not it is the ice bear that attacked Taunu," Attu said, his thoughts returning to the group, "we're being followed. I trust that what Suka has seen with his keen eyes is true."

The other hunters nodded, and Suka stood taller.

"I don't see that we have any other choice except to continue, but we must circle the women and children with hunters to protect them," Attu added. "Do we agree to this?"

A few of the hunters nodded immediately, the older ones, who were used to the time when Ubantu was leader and they'd been asked their opinion on matters of such importance. Suka and Kinak looked surprised, then thoughtful. Suka nodded first, and Attu noticed he hadn't waited for his older brother to decide for him, as he'd done in the past. After a pause, Kinak nodded also, although Attu sensed he was reluctant to agree to Attu's decision in front of his father.

Moolnik was standing slightly apart from the group. Attu looked at Moolnik, holding his face calm, his voice steady.

"What say you, Moolnik?" Attu asked.

"I do what my sons do," was Moolnik's terse reply.

He agrees to his son's choice rather than to say he agrees with mine. Tooth fish Moolnik might be, but unlike that stupid fish, he is clever.

"Suka, since your eyes are sharp and you've already seen how the ice bear tries to fool us by lying down and blending in with its surroundings, are you willing to continue guarding the most dangerous part of the group, the back?"

"We will guard the back," Suka and Kinak said at once. Moolnik nodded his head. "I guard with them."

Starting out once again, Attu put the other hunters at points in the front and sides, leaving Moolnik and his sons to guard the rear of the group.

Moolnik would probably be useless to his sons in a fight, Attu reasoned. *But perhaps to save them he might step up to the task like a real hunter for once.*

As the clan set out again, silent as always to listen for cracks in the ice, they were also scanning the horizon for the ice bear. Twice, Attu thought he spotted something moving behind them, but it was so far in the distance he couldn't tell.

Perhaps my mind is playing tricks on me.

When no attack came, the initial rush of fear at exposing the whole clan to the ice bear receded, and Attu's thoughts began drifting. He wondered how far the Great Frozen Clan was ahead of them. If the two clans had been able to travel together earlier, the ice bear attack wouldn't have happened, Taunu would still be alive, Yupik wouldn't have been injured, and they'd probably not have an ice bear following them now. *And I would still be able to see Rika, even if she is promised to another.*

Attu's anger rose as he considered the consequences of Moolnik's stubbornness. *Did the man even begin to realize the harm he had caused?*

But there was nothing Attu could do about it now. Taunu was dead and Yupik injured. Rika was gone, and they were one small clan, fleeing on the ever-thinning ice with an ice bear on their heels, to the safety of the land Elder Tovut and the storytellers of Banek's clan had promised was there. Attu prayed they were right.

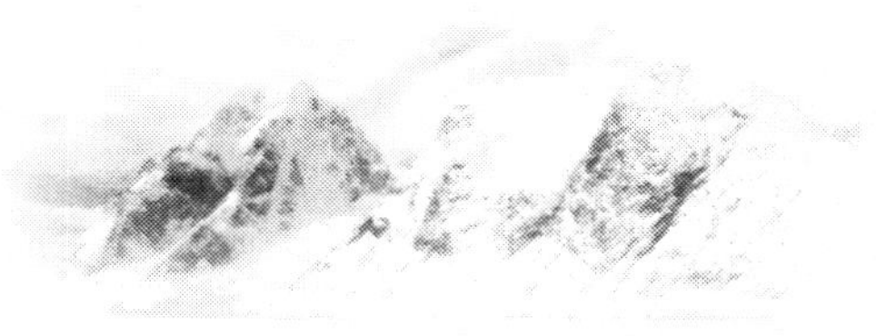

Chapter 16

A full moon bathed the clan in its white light as the people slept through the long Nuvikuan night, warm in the skin shelters they'd erected as the sun was setting.

Attu stood guard on the northwest corner of the camp, looking back in the direction they'd come, searching for signs of the ice bear. He saw nothing but a fine dust of snow, occasionally blown up into tufts of crystals, sparkling in the moonlight, circling in the air like trystas. Attu hoped they were trystas, the ones of protection. His people needed protection right now, as they lay huddled together in shelters placed as close to each other as the ice would allow. The hide of a tent was no defense against the teeth of a bear.

Attu turned to see Yupik, who was guarding the opposite side of the camp. Attu watched as he slowly moved his head back and forth, turning occasionally to see the Expanse with his good right eye. As he watched, Attu saw Yupik bring his mik up to his face, then apparently he remembered he needed to leave the painful eye alone and dropped his hand again.

Attu hadn't wanted to put Yupik on guard duty, but the man had insisted. Attu couldn't think of a reason to prevent him that wouldn't shame the hunter with his own weakness, so Attu had placed Yupik on the side furthest from where the bear had last been spotted. Kinak stood at the edge of the camp between Attu and Yupik, his broad shoulders casting a wide shadow in the bright moonlight. Looking to his left, Attu saw Moolnik guarding the other side. The watch had been divided into two, and this was the first, moon at its highest until almost set. Ubantu, with Suka and two other hunters, would take the last watch until the sun colored the sky to the south and east once again.

Attu turned when he saw movement behind him. He let out his breath slowly as he realized it was his mother. She held a pouch, steam coming from its neck.

"Here, my son," Yural said, handing Attu the warm blue algae drink.

"You shouldn't be out here," Attu gently chided Yural, but he eagerly reached for the hot beverage.

"All is well?"

"Yes. I've seen nothing but those snow swirls."

"Thank you, Yuralria," his mother whispered to the dancing trysta spirit for which she was named. The sparkling crystals twirled out over the Great Frozen. "Protect my son."

"Protect us all," Attu said.

His mother smiled at him, and the pride in her eyes made Attu feel as warm as the algae drink in his hands.

"Go back now, Mother," Attu urged her, and Yural touched his arm before hurrying back to the warmth of the shelter.

Attu watched as the moon slowly made its way across the sky. He kept moving, walking back and forth along the edge of the camp, keeping himself warm and his muscles ready in case he needed to fight. But there was no sign of the ice bear.

Attu wondered just how far they'd have to travel until they reached land again, and how they'd know if it was the land they were seeking, the huge expanse of rock that Elder Tovut had said was as big as the Great Expanse itself. That seemed impossible to Attu. Land was small places of rock sprinkled here and there on the ice. He'd never seen any land not small enough to walk across in a day, even if it was hilly.

Some land had ice mountains on it, large slabs of ice that rose almost straight up a good spear throw or so from the shoreline. They were very high and too steep to climb. His old home had been like that. But still, the land was not large. Not like Elder Tovut had said. Elder Tovut had said so many impossible things.

All Attu's life, he'd been hearing the stories. The stories of the land where huge plants colored green like the rock moss grew taller than a man. The plants changed every few moons. The green parts of some turned bright colors, red like blood, or faded to brown like fur, and fell off as it got colder. But the cold didn't last like it did on the Great Expanse. Soon it became warm again and new green grew on the plants.

There were so many different kinds of animals there as well, and the animals walked easily on four legs like snow otters climbing on the rocks near the land's edge. Some creatures had two feet and two flat arms and could push themselves up against the air and fly above the huge plants.

Attu had always thought of these places as places in the Between, or places in the imagination of storytellers like Elder Tovut. That's where the ice bear lived, and the skin boats Elder Nuanu had sung about. They were places of the spirit world, interesting to know about, but not of the Here and Now.

Yet ice bears had proven themselves real. And they walked the land on four feet, like the animals in Elder Tovut's tales. Unfrozen water with chunks in it as big as moving hills were real. A place that grew warm was beginning to seem like a real place to him. He knew it was to his father, also. *But,* he shook his head, trying to reason it out, *not just a place, but a time,* like Elder Tovut had said, a time in the Here and Now, when the Cold turned to the Warming and the whole world of Nuvikuan-na changed. If the Warming was real, and it was coming, his clan was going to die if they didn't make it to the great land before the ice melted.

Everything Elder Tovut had told Attu and the clan over the years began to make sense to him now in a way he could barely grasp but knew he needed desperately to understand. For the sake of his family and his clan, he needed to know everything he could about the cycles of Nuvikuan-na. Attu decided to ask Elder Nuanu to walk with him the next day. He had a lot of questions, and perhaps she'd have answers for him. And he needed to share his dreams with her as well. The ridges between which he walked in his dream were beginning to trouble him almost as much as seeing Rika across the open water. Night after night the dreams came to him, and he needed to know why.

Attu was jerked from his thoughts as a piercing cry split the night. *Yupik!*

Attu spun around and began running through the camp toward Yupik. Dodging the shelters and the people streaming out of them, Attu saw the silhouette of a huge ice bear, larger than the one that had attacked him, swiping its massive paws at Yupik, who was struggling to stay out of its reach, darting off first to one side, then another.

Kinak and Moolnik reached the pair first, and as Attu closed the gap between them, both men, spears raised, began stabbing at the air in front of the bear, crying out, calling to it, and daring it to come after them. This gave Yupik time to scramble backward a few more feet away from the bear's slashing claws.

Attu had a brief moment to be both surprised and pleased that Moolnik was in the thick of the fight before he looked at the bear and all other thoughts fled. The left side of the massive beast's face was torn and oozing. Its left eye was gone, leaving a weeping hole where the eye had once been. It looked like the bear had torn it out himself, leaving a bloody mess behind.

The same eye Yupik is now blind in, Attu realized. His stomach twisted into knots at the thought. The bear's other eye was bulging, the white showing all around, as if it were ready to explode at any moment.

It must be in excruciating pain, Attu thought as he moved around the bear, closing the remaining gap in the hunters' circle at the bear's back. He was relieved to concentrate on the bear's hindquarters rather than to have to look at that face as the four hunters began working together, screaming and jabbing at the bear, dodging massive claws as it swung its paws wildly at them, and forcing the bear to move away from camp.

Attu glanced back toward the shelters to see if they'd made much progress. He saw the other four hunters lined up in front of the women and children, who clustered behind them. It had been Ubantu's idea that only half the hunters attack the bear at once while the other half guarded the women and children. The other hunters would enter the fight only if the bear killed Attu's group and came for the clan.

It was right to not risk all the hunters at once, but it was eerie to see them all gathered to witness the attack, their faces pale in the moonlight. A few women also brandished spears, and Attu knew the women's knives were at the ready too, Meavu's included. The clan would fight to the last person to kill this bear, stop this enemy. Even Shunut, as terrified as he must be, held his small spear as he stood half-hidden behind his mother. Attu felt a rush of pride at the bravery of his people.

The four hunters continued to circle the ice bear, menacing it with their spears and cries. They were now at least two spear throws from camp.

Suddenly, Yupik struck on the bear's blind side. He lunged at the animal and stabbed it full in the chest with his spear. The bear roared in pain as Moolnik, seeing his chance, struck the bear in the neck with his spear as well. Attu struck the bear as high up as he could, in a bare spot on the bear's back, probably where Yupik's knife had penetrated before. His spear slid into the old wound easily, and he cringed, remembering his own painful wounds as the bear screamed in pain and spun to face him.

Attu felt sorry for beast, in such agony. Hunters killed cleanly, hunters showed mercy. This wasn't the Nuvik way. The bear must be killed, not only to protect his people, but to put it out of its misery, but how?

"For Taunu!" Yupik cried, and Attu watched in amazement as the hunter launched himself onto the bear's back, just like he'd done during the bear's last attack. The ice bear screamed again, and this time, apparently remembering the attack from before, it bolted.

Yupik hung on to the bear, riding it as it plunged out across the ice, yelling and stabbing at it like a madman.

Attu, Moolnik and Kinak stood, shocked into motionlessness for a few seconds before the three of them began running after Yupik and the bear. Attu realized after a few steps there was no way they'd be able to catch up with the giant strides of the fleeing bear with Yupik on its back. They kept running anyway, out across the Expanse, their feet in the dark tracks of blood the bear had left on the moonlit ice. Eventually, Yupik would fall off, and the bear might kill him if they couldn't reach him in time. They had to try.

Suddenly the bear stopped. The men raced toward it as Yupik continued to plunge his knife into the heaving sides of the bear. He left his own spear in the bear, but ripped out Moolnik's and Attu's spears, tossing them back toward the hunters.

"You are mine, mine!" Yupik screamed at the bear. "I will kill you! I alone!"

The bear was either too winded or had lost too much blood to rise to its feet again. It lay there, growling and slashing with its claws, trying to bite and tear at Yupik.

It was probably weakened already by the spirits of the fever in its wounds, Attu thought as he grabbed up his spear. Moolnik lunged for his. They both approached the bear again.

"Stay back!" Yupik screamed as the other hunters closed in on the pair, spears at the ready. "This is my kill, mine!" And he lunged at the bear's throat, his two knives slashing. Suddenly, the ice, apparently rotten in the area where they now stood, began to move.

"The ice!" Attu cried. "Yupik, the ice is breaking!"

"I don't care!" Yupik shouted. He continued stabbing at the bear, now weakened beyond fighting with its claws, but still trying to bite Yupik when he came too close.

The ice under Yupik growled. A gap of unfrozen water appeared at Attu's feet, cutting him off from Yupik and the bear. He stepped back, forced away from its edge.

"The ice!" Attu yelled. "It's cracking under your feet! Leave the bear. It's dying. Get out of there!"

"No!" Yupik yelled, and he continued avoiding the bear's teeth as he stabbed at it, ignoring the now moving ice and small patches of water beneath him.

"He's crazy," Moolnik muttered, and motioning for Kinak, the two of them began backing slowly away from the edge of the crack. There was no way of telling in which direction it might begin to open next. They had to be careful.

Suddenly, the ice crumbled under Yupik and the bear. Attu saw the shocked look on Yupik's face, saw him reach out as if to somehow regain his balance before both he and the ice bear disappeared into the blackness of the water.

Suddenly the ice groaned, and leaping back, the other hunters were thrown off their feet as the hole in the ice closed again, leaving ice where water had just been moments before, a slight buckling the only evidence it had ever been there. It was as if the Great Frozen had opened its mouth and swallowed Yupik and the ice bear whole.

Attu scrambled to his feet. He looked at the other two men, wondering if the fear on their faces mirrored his own. He was too terrified to move. He'd seen the ice swallow a man. If the great underwater spirit Attuanin could do that to Yupik and the bear, he could do it to him any time he wanted to.

Attu began shaking violently. The clan must get to safety, off the Great Frozen. But to do so meant to continue to travel on it for now, to risk death at every step, to risk sudden imprisonment under the ice where no man could help you. It was worse than falling into an opening chasm. At least then, someone might be able to throw you a spear rope, get you back out. But this? There was no escaping this.

"Attuanin, I never knew you were capable of such power over men," Attu whispered.

"If I hadn't seen it with my own eyes…" Moolnik began.

"Let us pray your great spirit, Attuanin, is satisfied for now with the mighty hunters, Yupik and the ice bear," Kinak said, his voice solemn. Turning, Kinak began walking slowly back toward camp, carefully testing the ice before him with every step.

Attu and Moolnik followed.

Chapter 17

"Attu, you are pushing our people too hard," Ubantu said.

Attu said nothing, but tried to slow his pace. It was the third time that day Ubantu had warned him to slow down. Several days had passed since Yupik and the bear had been swallowed by the ice.

"You're having nightmares about Yupik's death. I know because you've been calling out his name in your sleep, my son. But hurrying now won't help anyone. It's not your fault he was taken by Attuanin."

Attu remained silent and the two trudged on.

"It's been many suns since Yupik passed to the Between. He is a hunter for Attuanin now."

Attu said nothing, but slowed his pace to match his father's.

Elder Nuanu walked up beside Attu later that day and touched his elbow with her mik. "There was nothing you could do to save him."

"I know," Attu said. His mother or father must have told Elder Nuanu about the nightmares, but he didn't want to talk about how he felt. He just wanted to walk, to get closer to the land Elder Tovut had told them about. Any land, actually. Attu had thought it ironic that since they left the land Moolnik had been determined to stay on, there'd been no more solid ground, no more places upon which a man could stand and know he wouldn't be suddenly sucked down into the deep.

"Attu, what's wrong?" Elder Nuanu asked.

"I have been dreaming. I want to tell you about my dreams, Elder Nuanu. Will you promise me you will tell no one else?"

"Yes. You can trust me with this knowledge, Attu."

Attu told Elder Nuanu everything, about Rika across the open water, drifting away as he called to her, tried to reach her, and about the ridges between which he found himself walking, night after night. He even told her about the voice Rika had heard in her dreams, telling her to show mercy when judgment would be the Nuvik way instead, and how he knew he should not expect to see Rika again, but somehow felt that he must, that somehow their dreams must be linked, they must be linked in some way. Attu felt his face flush as he shared, but it felt good to tell someone.

"What does it all mean?" Attu asked.

"Let me ponder these dreams a while. We will speak again of them after I have thought about it. I, too, was surprised when our clans parted. It seemed to go against the spirits. I felt this as well. And look what tragedies have happened since."

Attu nodded.

"Is there anything else wrong?" Elder Nuanu asked, her face troubled.

I won't shame myself by exposing my fear of the ice swallowing me. "Tell me about the times of Warming, and the place we're headed."

"You know all about those, mighty hunter Attu; you've heard about them since you were a child."

"But I listened as a child to a tale for enjoyment. Tell me now, not to entertain me, but to teach me." Attu cleared his throat, realizing his emotions had thickened his voice. "Please," he added.

"Very well," Elder Nuanu said. "Where do I start?"

"Start with the stories of the New Green, after the Cold. Tell me everything you know about the land to the south when that time comes."

"Thank you, spirits of the protectors," Elder Nuanu whispered, raising her hands up to the sky. She lowered her arms and began her tale.

Toward dusk, Attu walked, this time at the back of the clan, guarding the rear and ruminating on Elder Nuanu's words.

Elder Nuanu had told the story of the New Green. She told of how the people had come first to the land because the Great Frozen was melting, and they could no longer hunt and live on the Expanse. When they reached the shore of this land, they saw that everything there was new and strange. There were large plants they called "evergreens" because they were green all the time. There were many small animals that lived in and near these plants. At first, they were able to live much like they had before, eating mostly fish and staying close to the rotting ice, where they felt safe.

But one day the good spirit of fire was tricked by a Moolnikuan spirit into burning the evergreens of this new land, and many animals and plants were destroyed. Elder Nuanu told how the spirit of the wind had come then, bringing water that fell unfrozen from the sky. It was called "rain," and it put out the great fire and saved the rest of the evergreens and animals. This was the beginning of the New Green, the Great Warm, for the fire had warmed Nuvikuan-na and melted the last of the rotten ice of the Great Frozen. It was now open water. It did not freeze again for a very long time.

But the rain had brought great wetness upon the land, and the people could no longer wear animal furs; they rotted. They had to learn to wear plants, woven into clothing. And some grew sick with the cold of the rain, for the plant clothing was not as warm as furs. There was no more nuknuk oil. The people grew desperate.

Then the spirit of Shuantuan took pity on them. She hurled a great spear of fire from the sky, striking a dead evergreen standing alone amongst some rocks. A bold woman among them all took the dead arm of another large plant, one that shed its leaves, called a "tree," and she brought the burning tree arm into their camp and hollowed a place in the ground for it to burn, along with other tree arms, in a depression in the ground like a soft stone bowl. The fire brought warmth and light to the people. They thanked Shuantuan and promised to always follow all ritual for this wonderful gift. Shuantuan was pleased, and ever since has chosen to dwell in a bold woman from amongst the clans who follow all ritual.

As he continued walking now, Attu thought of Elder Nuanu's words again, and he imagined the fire, and the open water, and the brave woman who brought Shuantuan's gift of the spirit of fire from trees to their people. Then he considered what clothing out of plants might look like. In his mind's eye he saw everyone dressed in rock moss, the only dry plant he had ever seen. He laughed in spite of his anxiety.

"What are you laughing at?" Meavu said. Meavu and Yural had been walking a few steps in front of Attu, but now they paused until he caught up with them.

"Elder Nuanu said that in the place where we're going, we will wear plants." Attu winked at her. "We'll all wear a little rock moss here," and he pointed to a spot below Meavu's parka, "and…" he grinned, "someday you will also wear a little rock moss here and here," Attu pointed to the left and right sides of his own chest.

"Oh, Attu," Meavu cried, and she ran ahead of the two of them, her cheeks flaming.

"Attu," his mother scolded him. "It's not for a brother to tease his sister about becoming a woman." She slapped his arm, and he stepped out of her reach as she tried to slap him again.

"Don't embarrass your sister like that, Attu," her mother scolded him. He knew she was serious when she added, "Or your belly will be growling for the rest of the journey."

~ • ~

As the clan traveled south over the next several suns, hunters went ahead and behind, some guarding and all hunting. Game was growing scarce, and Attu wondered if the Great Frozen clan had traveled this way, depleting the resources as they went. On the tenth day after the full moon, they found evidence that a group had passed that way, blocks of ice arranged in a circle upon the Expanse with signal strings attached indicating Paven's clan had come this way and stopped here on the night of the last full moon. *They had made it this far, at least, in safety and are ten days ahead of us.*

"Thank you," Attu whispered to the spirits and to Paven. "We're going the right way." *And Rika is still all right. At least she had been ten days ago.*

That night, Attu had the nightmare again where the chasm opened with Attu trapped on one side, and the beautiful light-eyed Rika out of reach on the other side. But this time, she spoke, and although she looked like Rika, her voice was deep, that of a man's.

"When you reach the other side of the rock mountain, we will be here waiting for you, people of the Expanse clans. We have not forgotten. We'll keep the promises of our elders, the people of long ago, written on the Rock for all to see and remember."

Attu was no longer on the ice now, but was standing on ground, filled with small growing green things as far as he could see. The green at his feet was thick, like countless green fur pelts laid across the land. Above him was a tall Rock with sheer sides, like the ice mountains. He saw a huge circle, as big as the floor of the large clan shelter, carved into its face, and he saw patterns carved into the rock, into the circle. He had no idea what they meant. Attu felt frustrated and confused, but he couldn't move, couldn't speak.

The man WAS speaking out of Rika' mouth, for she stood before him now, just a spear length in front of him. Attu reached for her, but somehow he was turned instead, away from Rika and toward a path, a natural cut between two large mountains of rock, taller than any ice mountains he'd ever seen. It was the path between two ridges of rock he had been dreaming about. But this time he could see it clearly all the way to the top, without the haze, and he was amazed at the height of the mountains above the ridges on either side he had seen before.

Attu heard the voice behind him say, "See the odd-shaped rock at the top of that mountain, the one on your left? The one that looks like a double-pointed spear?"

Attu felt himself nod in the dream.

"Find that rock, and follow the path through the mountains. Then you and your whole clan will be safe."

Attu struggled, trying to force himself to turn around in the dream. He needed to see Rika, HAD to see Rika. What did he care about a path through the mountains? She was right there behind him, if only he could turn around. Attu's heart pounded as he willed himself to turn back, to face her again, and suddenly, he was. Attu opened his mouth, fighting to get out his question, forming the words, "Rika, is that really you?" over and over again in his mind. But try as he might, no words came out. In the dream, the man-Rika smiled, an odd smile, and Attu saw two faces smiling at once, as if the man's true face had begun showing through Rika's. He saw Rika, and he saw an old man whose hair flowed freely from his head, white as snow falling across his shoulders. His eyes sparkled, and they were blue like the sky… which, of course, was impossible…

Attu suddenly awoke from the dream, and as he did, he thought he heard a whisper, soft and light, a whisper belonging to the dream still, to Rika, not the white-haired man. Just as he was jerked from the Between of sleep to the Here and Now, Attu heard Rika's voice. "Soon," she said. "Soon."

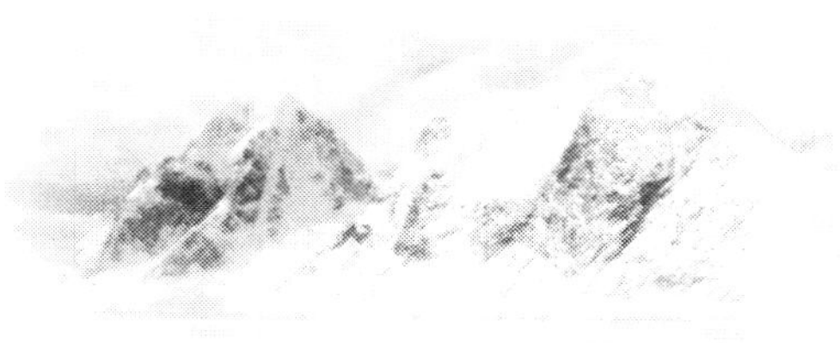

Chapter 18

Attu said nothing to Elder Nuanu about this new dream. He couldn't bring himself to try to explain what he knew he'd experienced in the Between of sleep, but which he didn't understand. He knew Elder Nuanu or his mother would listen to him if he chose to share what he'd seen, even his father would, especially after he'd dreamed about the ice bear and it had been proven real.

But Rika was mixed up in the dream again, and Attu couldn't even face Elder Nuanu with the truth about how much he still cared for the girl. He could barely face it himself. He knew that by now she'd be bound to Banek. Perhaps she was already expecting his child.

The thought of Rika with Banek made Attu's stomach twist, so he threw all thoughts of the dream aside, concentrating on getting his people to safety, off the ice.

~ • ~

Two suns later, the clan was walking along an unusual series of undulations. It was as if the wind had sculpted the ice as the people of the clan carved out the soft stone, making it into lamps for burning fat, dishes, bowls, and even small trinkets, toys, and amulets. The ice had been carved, it seemed, so that first they walked downhill, then through a concave valley much like a bowl before the ice rose up again, sometimes quite steeply.

It was difficult to traverse. The ice was slick, like nuknuk holes after they refroze and before snow covered the new ice.

"Wait, Attu," his father called from a spear throw to his left. "Tulnu has fallen."

Attu stopped his uphill climb and braced himself with his spear butt against the ice, turning to look back down at the clan.

Tulnu was sitting up, holding her ankle.

"Wait here, Father, I'll see what needs to be done," Attu called to Ubantu and half ran, half slid down the bowl of ice he had just climbed. He didn't want his father to have to climb this slippery stretch again.

"She's twisted her ankle," Moolnik said as he examined his woman's leg. He glanced up at Attu, and Attu saw a glimmer of fear flicker across Moolnik's face before he hid it with a scowl.

Does he think we'd leave them behind because his woman can't walk? Attu thought. *Perhaps, that's what HE might do in my place, but you, Moolnik, are not leader now. Father and I don't abandon our people.*

"I need three lamps lit to melt ice," Attu called to the others, and Yural, Elder Nuanu, and one of the other women reached into packs to get their lamps.

Moolnik sighed, relief evident in his voice. "I'll get the hide and rope," he said and began digging through the heavy pack of furs Kinak had been carrying.

Soon the clan had a large hide spread fur side down on the ground. The women took turns pouring small bowlfuls of water onto the hide, allowing it to freeze, building up a slippery coating of ice on it and stiffening it as well. The water seemed to take a long time to freeze, not like Attu remembered from when he was a child. Then, he had played games of spitting with the other boys and girls, watching their saliva freeze in the air as it fell, shattering onto the ice, or sometimes even bouncing like a hide ball. Like the clan children did now, he had used the old ruined hides from shelters and made small sleds to slide along the ground or down the hills around the clan's camps.

Ubantu had made his way back down the slope by now and suggested they combine the stop with the mid-sun meal, and so the men took over the task of freezing the hide while the women got the food ready and fed their families.

When the bottom of the new sled was coated with a thick layer of ice, spear rope was used to tie the ends of the hide, and a harness, complete with fur padding, was tied to the ropes, enabling a hunter or even a woman to pull Tulnu easily along. Sleds were rarely used on long journeys or for hunting trips unless much game was taken. They required constant re-coating of new ice every few hours, or the bare hide would begin to freeze to the surface ice, making it harder and harder to pull. Stopping to gather and melt snow, then coat the sled, then let it refreeze again used up a lot of time and more energy, most hunters thought, than simply carrying a pack. Besides, the constant freezing and rubbing ruined the hide after a few days, and it was difficult to keep enough good hides to shelter and clothe the clan without using them for sleds, too.

There was also the possibility of falling into a hole in the ice while wearing the sled harness. The weight of the sled would drag its wearer down so fast no one could save them. Most considered a sled too dangerous to use unless absolutely necessary, especially now, with such treacherous ice usually surrounding them.

Suka volunteered to pull his mother first as the clan started out once again.

Wanting to show his bravery, Attu thought.

Suka pulled his mother a few feet, quickly picking up speed, and then stopped. Tulnu and the hide kept sliding. They struck him in the heels, and Suka fell sideways hard to avoid falling backward and landing on Tulnu.

"Ow!" Suka cried as he hit the ice.

Everyone else drew in a breath, then laughed as they realized the two were in no danger.

"Stupid boy," Moolnik said. "You want to break through the ice and drown both yourself and your mother?"

"I'll try it," Kinak offered, while his new wife Suanu rushed up to Tulnu and arranged hides around her to keep her warm.

Moolnik growled at Suka. "Your brother will have his turn soon enough, Suka. Try again and do it right this time. And watch the ice ahead of you."

Kinak shrugged his broad shoulders at his younger brother and turned away with Suanu at his side.

"It's not as easy as it looks," Suka mumbled, and he stood up with difficulty and straightened the rope that ran up from one side of the sled, across his chest, and back down to the other side of the sled. He began pulling again, this time more slowly.

The smallest children followed the hide sled for the rest of that day. The ice was thick here, and no one objected to them taking turns riding on it with Tulnu. She didn't seem to be in too much pain, Attu noticed as they stopped for another break later in the day. She seemed to be enjoying the attention of the little ones as well as Suanu and the other women. They clustered around Tulnu whenever they stopped, talking and putting poultices on her ankle, covering her with furs to keep her warm.

Coming up over the final icy ridge late that day, Attu paused to catch his breath. Ubantu labored the last few feet and stood beside him.

"This last climb down isn't going to be easy," Attu said, looking down at the Expanse below them. When his father didn't answer, Attu looked in the direction his father was gazing.

"Is that what I think it is?" Attu asked. His mind reeled at the sight as his heart skipped one beat, then another.

"Unfrozen water," his father said. "See it gleam in the light of the late sun?"

Far into the distance, a band of dark water stretched across the horizon. It appeared to have no end.

"And look," Ubantu said. He pointed off to the right.

Attu, looking to where his father was pointing, saw a cluster of dark dots moving out across the Expanse, single file, in three lines, like tiny mussels hugging the shoreline of the great unfrozen water beside them.

"Rika's clan," Attu said. "I mean… Paven's clan."

Ubantu turned, and Attu could see his father was studying him. Attu felt his face flush. He looked away, but he knew his father was still watching him closely.

"Yes, my son, I think it is Paven's clan," his father replied finally.

Attu chanced a look at Ubantu. Sad understanding flashed across his father's face.

Pity. Attu didn't want anyone's pity, especially his father's. He was angry with himself for not guarding his feelings for Rika more carefully as a hunter should for a woman he could not have without a fight, one he would have surely lost against Banek. He would've had to fight Paven, as well, to get Rika. And he didn't believe in fighting for a woman or trying to take one from another hunter by trickery. He didn't even think Rika wanted him, anyway. But if Paven had tried to take Yural, both he and his father would have fought to the death to keep her. She was theirs to protect.

It was the Nuvik way to obtain what one desired through violence if necessary. Most hunters were like his father, able to wait beside a nuknuk hole or their fishing lines for hours at a time, unmoving. Only the most patient hunters and their families survived. Holding on to what was his, each hunter was also vigilant against possible theft, be it tools, game, or a woman. Among the Nuvik, dwelling in this harsh land where only a few could live, there was no room for mercy. And now, there was Rika before him again, and he had to pretend he didn't care about her or risk violence upon himself and his family. His father knew this, and Attu hated seeing the pain on his father's face, his understanding, his sympathy, his pity.

Attu pulled off his pack and threw himself down on it, overcome by what he saw before him, what his father now knew, and what he'd seen in the dream, what he'd heard, those whispered words, "Soon, soon." Rika's voice had called to him. Now, there she was, with her whole clan spread out before them. And there was the water, stretching off into the horizon as far as he could see, both ways, effectively trapping them on this treacherous ice. *And against all common sense, all I can think about is seeing Rika again.*

"What are we going to do?" Attu asked.

"They'll stop soon to make camp," Ubantu said. "Once we make the bottom of this last ridge, we should rest, too."

"But-" Attu began to protest.

"But not make camp," his father finished. "We rest and then move on, catch up with Paven's group while we know where they are."

"All right," Attu agreed.

Ubantu motioned to the others behind him. "Last one," he cried.

A few hunters gave a shout of triumph, and the group quickened their pace up the last rise.

"What?" *Why didn't Father tell the others?*

"Let them make it to the top of this last hard climb; then we'll all face the unfrozen water together," his father explained. "No need to discourage everyone just yet."

Ubantu pulled off his pack and the two of them sat, watching as Paven's clan continued to trek along the edge of the impossibly large body of unfrozen water. Attu couldn't even see any ice chunks floating in it.

Attu closed his eyes. *What if Moolnik had been right to believe they needed to stay on the land they'd found and not move on as Elder Tovut had said they must? What if it was already too late to get to the safety of the great land, the place of New Green Elder Nuanu spoke of in her stories?*

Attu tried to concentrate on the dream. They'd be joining Paven's clan soon. Rika's message in the dream had come true. They had met again and it had been "soon." The man's voice in the dream had said they'd make it to the land. Rika had been there in the dream. Did that mean she'd be with him when they made it to safety? *Or was she there simply because the old man, whoever or whatever he was, needed a person I would recognize to speak through? Why not my father, or mother, or Meavu?*

The man was obviously some sort of shaman, like Elder Tovut had been, like Elder Nuanu, a man of great wisdom, if he could somehow communicate with me through a dream. But how did he know about our clans on the Expanse? And of all the people to choose from, why reach out to me? It makes no sense.

And what about the other dream where I couldn't reach Rika, where the ice split and the water came between us, me on one side, Rika on the other? Was it this water, ahead of us? But we are both on the same side of it, so that can't be true. What does that dream mean?

Elder Nuanu had said Attu would save his people. Right now, it looked like he was walking them into a dead end if they couldn't find a way around the water. *Was that why Paven's clan was right here, instead of ten days' further journey onward? Had they been stuck here for that long, trying to find a way around? We'll find out soon enough,* Attu supposed. But whatever their reasons for losing so much time, it couldn't be good, that was for sure.

One by one the people of the Ice Mountain Clan reached the top of the ridge, and one by one they pulled off their packs and sat, looking out over the Expanse at Paven's clan, walking along the edge of seemingly endless water.

Moolnik took one look at what lay ahead and began swearing as he steadied his woman's sled on the top of the ridge of ice, while Suka and Kinak, with Suanu at his side, edged themselves away from Moolnik as if trying to avoid his biting words.

Attu and Suka exchanged glances. *Now what?* Suka's eyes seemed to say.

Elder Nuanu, one of the last to reach the top, took one look at the scene before her, and raising her arms to the sky, began a keening cry to Shuantuan.

Yural got up and began to cry out to her trysta as well. Soon every woman stood, their voices carrying eerily across the valley of ice and water before them. They called to their name spirits to protect them, called out their past obedience to ritual, telling how the Ice Mountain clan had never failed to follow all necessary ceremonies and observances.

Their keening grew louder and louder. Attu felt the hair on his arms rise and his spirit vibrating within him. He felt their pain; it was his own, and their women's cry gave voice to his own fear.

Looking around, he saw the same look of hopelessness on the other hunters. Tears streamed down Meavu's cheeks as she cried out to the spirits. Tears formed in Attu's eyes, but he bit them back. Hunters did not cry. Instead, he gave way to the crying of the women, felt his spirit lift with theirs. As he did, he knew what he must do.

Attu stood, and with him the other hunters rose. They began to shout, deep warlike shouts of challenge, challenges to the unfrozen water to come and fight them, challenges to the Expanse to try to thwart them. They shouted to the spirits of their strength, of their willingness to do the spirits' bidding, of their accomplishments as hunters, as protectors of their clan. Their voices rose to a crescendo carried with the wind across the Great Frozen.

"The spirits have heard us," Elder Nuanu said as their voices died away across the Expanse. She pointed off into the distance, towards Paven's clan. "And so has the Great Frozen Clan."

Attu's clan grew quiet, and as their own cries faded, the faint sound of returning cries from Paven's clan came drifting up to them where they stood.

"Then there is hope," Ubantu announced. "Let's go to them, my son," and Ubantu led the way down the steep slope towards Paven's clan. He walked slowly, careful of his leg on the slippery decline, but his steps were sure, his back straight. The clan followed. For once, even Moolnik obeyed without a fight.

Chapter 19

Attu's clan reached Paven's in the middle of the night. But instead of setting up camp and sleeping, Attu's people set up their hide tents together, forming a large covering under which most of the two clans gathered.

The two women who had been given at the bonding ceremony were reunited with their families, and their joy spilled over to the rest of the group, creating a mood of celebration amongst the two clans, even with the threat of the unfrozen water lurking in everyone's mind.

Attu looked around, studying the groups of people sitting around the many lamps. *Where was Rika?*

"Sit here, my son," Ubantu called, and Attu reluctantly walked over to where his father, Suka, Kinak, Paven and two other hunters from the Great Frozen clan gathered at a lamp, away from the women and children. Their shadows flickered on the walls of the hide tent as Attu sat down in the place his father made by his side. *Why wasn't Rika here, with the others?*

"We went as far as we dared travel to the east," Paven said, apparently continuing his story of what had transpired with his clan since the two clans had parted. "Then the ice became so rotten, we were forced to turn back. We lost much time in the attempt."

He shook his head.

"Now we're heading west. We must find a way around the chasm."

The two hunters of the Great Frozen Clan popped their lips in agreement.

"So tell me, Attu," Paven asked, "why do the other hunters come to you and your father now with their questions, instead of Moolnik? You seem to have gained great status in a short time with your clan. How is this so?"

Paven was speaking in a low voice to Attu, who was sitting directly across from him, but the others heard as well. They looked at Attu.

Attu stayed silent, not wanting to speak of Moolnik's shame in front of his sons.

"Attu and Ubantu have served our people well since we began our journey," Kinak answered for Attu. "We honor them for their bravery and their willingness to serve."

"And their willingness to allow a foolish hunter his mistakes," Suka added quietly.

Both Ubantu and Paven shot a glance at Suka, but Suka continued studying the flickering light of the lamp's flames as if he hadn't just spoken derisively of his father.

Attu met Kinak's eyes and gave him a quick nod of thanks. Suka, however, avoided looking at anyone. He continued to stare at the row of flames licking up from the long wick laid across the soft stone bowl filled with nuknuk fat. He studied it as if it held a secret only he could see.

In a quiet voice, Suka began telling of the attack on Taunu, of Yupik's bravery, of the second attack, and the ice swallowing up both the bear and the hunter. He left out the part about Elder Nuanu's fight with Moolnik and about his mother throwing a fit of grief to get her man to come with the rest of the clan. The women would carry those stories back to Paven, and his whole clan would know about it soon enough, if they didn't already.

Thankful that Suka had changed the subject, Attu relaxed and listened to Suka's telling of recent events. *Someday, Suka will tell the stories of the warming and cooling cycles like Elder Tovut,* Attu thought as he listened in growing wonder to Suka's version of the events of the last moons. He knew his cousin was a good storyteller, but tonight Suka made what had happened to their clan sound as good as Elder Tovut's stories of the Between. *But Moolnik will never let his son be a conduit for the spirits through his stories, as his own father had not let him be for his dreams. What a waste for both them and the clan.*

Suka looked up. Attu caught his gaze, and Suka smiled at him, never missing a beat in the storyline. For that moment, it felt like old times between them once again.

The conversation lasted until almost dawn, when one by one, the men, women, and children of both clans simply rolled up in the furs they'd carried with them to the large shelter and fell asleep.

Attu lay down, sick at heart that Rika had chosen not to see him, had hidden from him instead. Rika didn't have feelings for him. She belonged to another. He needed to call his heart back from her. But he didn't know how.

It was midday before the clans began their now combined trek to find a way around the open water. Attu walked with Ubantu and Paven, scouting ahead, amazed at the size of the chasm in the ice and trying not to lose all hope.

"Where is Elder Nuanu?" Attu asked his father. "She didn't do the ritual for the beginning of the journey day. Why?"

Ubantu shook his head. "I don't know."

"She's with Rika, helping with the new baby," Paven said. "Last night Umikuk had her first child, and it wasn't an easy coming into the world. Rika said it was the spirits' intervention that brought

Elder Nuanu just in time to save both mother and child. Both Umikuk and the baby live. And it's a boy!"

The look of pride on Paven's face was as fierce as if he had fathered the infant himself.

Attu felt both relief and pride rise up in him. *That's where Rika was last night.*

Rika came to Attu when the clans stopped for their first rest of the day, which on this day would be their only rest since they'd gotten such a late start.

"Would you like a drink, mighty hunter Attu, leader of the Ice Mountain clan?" Rika was suddenly at Attu's side, a hot bowl of blue algae drink in her hands.

Attu jumped, almost knocking the bowl aside. Rika pulled it back just in time.

How does she do that, sneak up on me like I'm a child? Attu thought. He wasn't frustrated by Rika's trick this time, but he was by what she'd said.

"Elder Nuanu is filling your head with stories. My father is the leader once again, not me." Attu took the bowl from Rika's hands and drained it in one long sip. When Rika frowned at him he added, "Thank you, Rika, healer and worker of miracles for the people of the Great Frozen clan." He flashed a teasing grin at her.

"Elder Nuanu saved Umikuk and her baby; I just followed her instructions." Rika moved to sit down beside him on his pack.

Too close.

Attu felt his stomach begin flopping like a tooth fish pulled out onto the ice. He grabbed Meavu's pack sitting next to his own with his free hand and plunked himself down on it just as Rika's backside came to rest on his own pack.

"More room," he said.

"Oh."

Attu turned to look at Rika. Her parka hood was thrown back and she was wearing her hair loose. Its black waves gleamed in the late sunlight. Attu knew his gaze was frankly admiring. He couldn't help himself. This time, Rika looked away first.

"The drink was good," Attu said. *What a stupid thing to say.*

"How's your back?" Rika asked.

"Healed," Attu answered. "I hardly notice it anymore."

"I should check it for you, just to be sure."

"No, it's fine." Attu leaned back, afraid Rika would try to pull his parka off right there to examine his new scars.

Rika's mouth thinned to a tight line across her face.

Attu could see dark circles under her eyes from lack of sleep. *She was up all night with the baby coming and must be exhausted.*

"How are Umikuk and the new baby?"

"Both are well. The baby will be named Yupik when he is grown, in honor of the hunter from your clan who died with no sons of his own. Elder Nuanu told Umikuk's man about Yupik, and both Umikuk and her man thought it a good idea. Right now, he is called Niverpok."

Attu laughed. "One who is 'backward'?"

"Yes, because he tried to come into the Here and Now backside first. The baby was coming the wrong way."

"What did Elder Nuanu do?" Attu asked.

"She gave Umikuk a drink to make her sleep then put her hand up inside Umikuk and had me put my hands on Umikuk's swollen belly, and together we turned the baby within her so it would come out as it should, head first."

"I don't believe it," Attu said, shaking his head. "If the baby can't come out the right way, the woman dies. Sometimes the baby can be saved, by cutting it out, but never both the mother and the baby."

"We did it," Rika said and smiled, her expression fading quickly to wistfulness. "Elder Nuanu said she wasn't going to lose another mother to a backward birth. She said putting Umikuk to sleep so we could attempt to turn the baby was worth the risk. It worked."

"Did you know that Suka's mother died having him?" Attu asked. "He was born backward and Elder Nuanu had to cut him out. His mother had already died. Tulnu is really Kinak and Suka's second mother. That is why Shunut, her son, is so much younger than his brothers."

"Is that why Moolnik hates Elder Nuanu so much, because she couldn't save his woman?"

"Partly. And it's one reason he's so mean to Suka all the time. I think he blames Suka for his first woman's death."

"That's crazy."

"That's Moolnik."

Attu shifted uncomfortably on his pack. He'd wanted to talk to Rika for such a long time, ever since she'd fled his shelter. He'd wanted to ask her why she'd run from him. It seemed like throwing salt water in his heart's wound to find out, but still, Attu had wanted to know if Rika had any feelings for him. But then she had left, and now it was too late. Paven had made his decision. She was Banek's.

Silence grew between them. "Please tell Umikuk and her man they honor us by planning to name their son after one of our hunters," Attu said after he could no longer stand the quiet between them.

"Anything for the new leader of the Ice Mountain Clan," Rika smirked.

"I don't seek to lead. That's just what Elder Nuanu wants."

"And what do you want, Attu, mighty hunter?" Rika's signal ornaments jangled on her parka as she shifted around on the pack so she was looking directly at him.

You, Attu thought. But he said nothing.

Rika pushed her hair back and studied him, a strange expression building on her face.

Attu stared back at her, looking for answers in her face to the questions he couldn't ask. If she were happy with Banek, wouldn't it show? But Rika didn't look happy. She looked sad, and confused, like something wasn't right…

No, I'm just wishing she cares when she doesn't. Who's the fool now?

Attu looked down at the bowl in his hands.

"Like I said, I don't seek to lead, but I'm helping my father lead, that's what I'm doing. That's what I want, Rika. That's all I want."

With those words, he stood up and handed Rika back the empty bowl.

"Thank you," Attu said in Rika's general direction. He couldn't look at her again. Attu started to walk away.

"Wait!" Rika jumped up from the pack and stepped in front of him.

Attu looked down at Rika's upturned face. She seemed so small, suddenly so much more like a child than a woman as he stood in front of her, his own body so much larger and stronger in comparison to her slight build.

Rika was smiling at him, reaching out her hand to him, like Meavu might, apparently to draw him back to sit with her awhile longer. *As if I'm her big brother. As if we're just friends. As if we could ever be just-*

"Wait," Rika said again, and tried to grasp his mik, to pull him back toward the packs.

Attu felt his anger rising like a sudden snowstorm over the ice. "Wait for what, Rika?" He glared at her. "Just what am I waiting for?"

Rika stepped back, her hand falling to her side, fear in her eyes.

He hadn't meant to scare her. "Rika," Attu said, his voice now an intense whisper. "You belong to Banek. Don't play games with me when you know I can't win. Don't be so foolish."

He turned from Rika and strode away, leaving his pack and the girl he loved behind.

Chapter 20

That evening, Attu sat in his family's shelter by himself, carefully repairing his spear. He needed to be alone. He needed time to think. Besides, one of the tips of his two-pronged spear had been split when the bear attacked, and he hadn't had time to fix it properly. Sitting here, studying the damaged weapon, Attu convinced himself it was time to try something entirely new for a spear instead of just repairing his old points.

"What are you doing?" Ubantu said as he entered the shelter and sat down next to Attu in front of the lamp.

Attu had a tough hide across his lap to protect himself from slips of his rock chisel. On the hide rested a massive back tooth from the ice bear he'd killed. He was studying it, considering how best to carve it into a new spear tip.

"I'm thinking to split the tooth, here," Attu pointed to the place where the tooth had a small vertical crack in it. "I'll shave it to look like this," and Attu took the edge of his rock chisel and scratched a crude drawing on the hide to show his father the basic shape he had in mind.

"The tip will be as long as a man's hand with his fingers extended," Attu held up his own hand to show his father. "It'll be sharpened the full length on both sides in notches, like the jagged teeth of the tooth fish, each notch as sharp as my bone knife."

Attu was getting excited now that he'd started explaining his idea to his father. "I want a spear that will plunge deeply into a large animal, such as an ice bear, but not stick like a nuknuk spear does because of its two curved prongs."

"This will work well to kill an ice bear," his father said as he studied Attu's design. "You must make it as thick as you can so it won't break off easily in an animal."

"It won't throw as well then. It will be too heavy."

"But you won't need to throw it far."

"That's true."

While his father watched, Attu slowly tapped the rock wedge into the crack with his bone hammer. After many taps, when it seemed firmly in place, he moved the tooth to rest on a large flat rock he'd placed on the ice floor of the shelter. Raising his bone hammer, Attu struck down on the rock chisel as hard as he could. The tooth split cleanly.

The two hunters grinned at each other. The edges of the tooth in the split were already as sharp as a rock tipped spear.

"This spear will kill other large animals, too," Attu added as he felt along the newly split half of the tooth.

"You believe Elder Nuanu's stories?" His father asked, picking up the other half of the tooth and examining it.

"Yes. And I want to be prepared the next time a mountain of snow turns into an attacking animal with teeth and claws."

"But how will you hunt nuknuks with that spear?" His father suddenly seemed concerned.

Attu laughed. "I'll make another for hunting nuknuks."

Ubantu shook his head. "Why can't a man have different spears for different game?" He asked the question out loud, but Attu knew he was reasoning it out for himself, much as Attu had.

"This is wise," Attu's father concluded, and he looked steadily at Attu. "As our people move off the ice to the land, we'll all have to learn new ways of hunting the new animals. It will take new tools, if Elder Nuanu's stories are to be believed."

"I believe them," Attu said. "And I'm going to be ready. If this works, I'll teach the other hunters how to make these new spear tips. I have plenty of ice bear teeth."

"I bring no evil," a voice called from the other side of the shelter's doorway.

Paven.

"You're welcome here," Ubantu answered and motioned for Paven to come and sit with them. "See what Attu is working on."

Paven studied the tooth and the drawing on the hide Ubantu showed him while Attu began to shave thin slivers off the bear's tooth. It was the hardest material he'd ever worked on, even harder than the male nuknuk's tusks.

"I've never seen a spear tip like that," Paven said. He frowned, making the furrows of his scars seem even deeper.

"It's to kill ice bears and other large game on land," Ubantu said.

"Other large game on land?" Paven looked confused. "There are no other large land animals besides the rock bears Banek speaks of."

"And ice bears only live in the Between," Attu snapped.

Both men looked at Attu, shocked into silence at his rudeness. Suddenly, Paven threw his head back and laughed. "You're right, Attu. I think like a child, like I know all there is to know. Then-"

"An ice bear attacks," Attu finished for him.

"True." Paven stopped laughing.

"You must have Elder Nuanu tell you the stories of the Warming," Ubantu urged Paven. "It's more than just ice bears and open water. She will tell you of the evergreens and the Great Fire and all the rest. Your clan needs to know these things."

"I will," Paven said. "We lost our storytelling elder, who was also our healer, just before Rika's naming ceremony. That's why she was named the new healer, even though she was so young. The old healer had taught her well, but she didn't have time to tell Rika everything, especially not stories, when there were sicknesses to be healed and spirits to be appeased."

"Rika has done well with the knowledge she was given," Ubantu said. "Attu's back is healed."

Attu nodded his agreement. He was glad he had to concentrate on the spear point in his hands. Paven and his father's talk of Rika made him feel uncomfortable.

"So, with Rika bound to Banek now, you'll be needing a new woman to prepare your game," Ubantu began, his face serious.

He's trying to find out if Paven still wants Mother, Attu realized.

"Oh, I have eyes on one, Ubantu," Paven said. He sounded as if he was teasing, but Attu couldn't tell for sure.

Attu felt Ubantu tense beside him, but he didn't speak.

Careful, Father.

Paven continued, "Her hunter was lost to Attuanin many moons back."

"Tenukik? She's a good choice," Ubantu said, relief evident in his voice. "Her front teeth are worn almost to the gums."

Both men nodded. It was a mark of great beauty in a woman of the clan to have her front teeth so worn down by chewing furs that when she smiled, they barely showed. It was a sign she was a hard worker, careful to chew the furs of her hunter until they were soft and desirable to be worn. This made her desirable, too, in the eyes of the men.

"She's willing to have me, scars and all," Paven said, his face macabre in the dim light. "But I'll have to wait awhile longer," Paven added. "Banek has yet to take Rika as his woman. We've been on the move, and I thought it wise to wait a little longer. We passed far south of Tooth Fish territory, and he has promised to stay with us once he is bonded, and not take Rika back to his own clan, but…" Paven's voice trailed off.

Attu felt the older hunter's eyes on him. His heart started hammering in his chest. *Rika wasn't bound to Banek yet? Why didn't she tell me? I didn't give her a chance to even hint at it.* He felt his cheeks reddening, but he held his gaze on the tools in front of him, willing himself to take steady slow breaths.

"Banek is throwing himself around like a lone male nuknuk, but he'll have to wait awhile longer for my daughter. As I will for Tenukik," Paven said, and chuckled to himself. Ubantu joined in, obviously relieved his woman was safe from Paven's schemes.

Attu's bone chisel slipped, cutting his finger. He sucked on the wound, turning away from the conversation while he thought about what the two men had said.

Paven's using Rika to keep Banek with his clan until they get safely off the ice. He knows Banek is an adventurer, and keeping Rika from him will keep another strong hunter with his clan, strengthening them. Doesn't he care about Rika's feelings in any of this? Is she just a tool in her father's hands to be manipulated like he manipulates everyone around him, to his own plan?

Will he hold Rika like bait until Banek tires of the game and simply disappears with her one night, shaming her by taking her away from her clan without the ritual of giving and taking being performed? What if Banek grows so frustrated he attacks Paven? But Paven thinks he is invincible. After all, he survived an ice bear attack, didn't he? The attack of the bear has made me more cautious. Has it made him arrogant? And Rika is caught in the middle...

~ • ~

Five suns later, the clans still hadn't found the end of the chasm of open water. Paven and Ubantu conferred with Attu and the other hunters late in the day and called an early halt. Doubling the size of the group had put a strain on their resources, and most of the hunters moved off to seek game while it was still light. The rest set up camp.

"Attu, Ubantu, stay with me," Paven said. "We need a few hunters here to guard."

Ubantu moved to follow Paven. Attu followed reluctantly. He'd rather be hunting. How quickly Ubantu had slipped into following Paven's every request. It rankled Attu, but he found himself going along with Paven also. *What else can I do if Father trusts him to lead?*

"Sit here," Paven said. Paven motioned to a seat beside him in front of his shelter on the edge of the encampment where they had a good view of the clans.

"So tell me, Attu, have you had any more dreams, lately? Any advice to give?"

Attu looked at Paven. *That same edge in his voice, that same leer. Is he teasing me, or is he serious?* "Everyone dreams," Attu replied. "I have no new knowledge to share." *Nothing I understand, and certainly nothing I'm going to tell you.*

"That's too bad," Paven replied. "We headed for the great land when I saw the signs in the weather and the ice and finally believed the stories of my childhood, but I, too, dreamed about the Warming, at least twenty moons ago. Did you know that?"

"What?" Attu was shocked. *Why hadn't Paven told us this?*

"I did nothing about them. If I had, we would be off the ice now. Still, I do not trust in dreams. Last night I dreamed Rika's mother was alive. It is as I said, we dream of what we wish for or what unsettles us. Dreams cannot be trusted."

Attu and Ubantu shared a look of disbelief at the hunter so sure of himself that he was ignorant of the ways of the Between with its many kinds of dreaming, and had ignored the warning of the spirits when the prophetic dreams had come. He had waited too long before setting out, putting his whole clan in danger, just like Moolnik had their own.

He plays with his whole clan regardless of the danger. Just like he's playing with Rika and Banek. The thought made Attu feel sick.

"We need to-" Paven began, but he was interrupted by a shout coming from across the Expanse.

Paven and Ubantu grabbed their spears and headed toward the sound. Attu hefted his new spear with its ice bear tooth point he'd finished just the sun before, and he ran with the older men toward the shouting.

Kinak and Banek came loping over the Expanse, their voices calling out to the clan in excitement.

"Clear ice ahead!" Banek cried as the two came close enough for the rest to hear him.

"And a great land of hills just beyond it!" Kinak yelled. "We saw it!"

The clan erupted into shouts and yells. A few women began dancing the hopping and spinning dances of thanksgiving as they called out to their name spirits. The smaller children began running about wildly, not understanding what the adults were so excited about, but knowing it was something very good.

Attu looked to Paven. "We go?"

"As soon as we can," Paven replied.

"Even if we must travel at night," Ubantu asserted. "We must take advantage of the ice reaching to the shore of this land before it, too, melts, like the ice did on the land from which we just came."

Attu and Paven popped their lips in agreement, and the clans' celebration turned immediately into preparation to travel again.

The clan traveled the rest of that day and into the night. Even though Banek and Kinak had seen the ice and land, it was still a far distance over the ice to reach it. Paven called a halt for a few hours of sleep when the moon set and it became too dangerous to walk ahead in the dark on untested ice.

People hastily erected their shelters. Attu rolled into his sleeping skins and tried to sleep with the others. He listened to Meavu's soft snoring and his father's more rough breathing as he tried to keep Rika and the dreams out of his mind. But he kept seeing her. First as the gap of open water moved her away from him, and again, standing by the stone wall with all the carvings on it, speaking with the man's voice.

Find the rock shaped like a nuknuk spearhead at the top of the mountain near the pass, and follow the path through the mountains. Then you and your whole clan will be safe.

Attu saw the rock, high above him, as if it were right in front of him, not something he'd seen in the Between. He saw its two points, like a nuknuk spear's tips, rising up and curving back. He heard the man's voice, over and over again. *Find that rock, that rock…*

Attu had heard of a person speaking to another in a dream. One of the Great Frozen storytellers had told of a clan healer of long ago who dreamed he spoke to the clan's leader, even though the leader and three of the other hunters were gone hunting. The clan leader had told the healer that one of the hunters with him had died. Two days later, the clan leader and his hunters had returned, without the man he'd spoken of in the dream, who had fallen through the ice and drowned the very day the healer had dreamed his death announcement.

Attu had marveled at that story. *But what of my dream?* If someone had spoken to him, it was from a great distance, and it was someone he didn't know. Yet they somehow knew him and had conveyed a crucial message, a plan for his clan's survival. Perhaps what he was hearing was the voice of a spirit, sounding and looking like a man.

He needed to talk with Elder Nuanu about these newer dreams, how they seemed to be developing into a plan he must follow. If it meant the survival of his clan, and Attu was becoming convinced it did, he needed to tell her, seek her advice. He would not be ignorant as Paven had been with his own dreams. He'd talk with Elder Nuanu first thing in the morning.

Attu rolled over, trying to get comfortable on his bed of furs, and he fell asleep thinking of the land ahead, the twin pointed rock, and the journey south they must make once they got to the shoreline. But when he fell asleep, Attu dreamed instead of the golden-eyed Rika, spinning off over the dark waters, gone forever.

Chapter 21

"Throw me that rope, Attu," Yural called from the other side of the shelter. She had the last hide down, and Attu threw her the rope to tie it together with the others into a pack bundle.

"Kinak saw land," Meavu repeated for the hundredth time as she scurried about picking up odds and ends of the few supplies still not packed. "We're almost there, Attu, almost there!"

Meavu, her cheeks flushed, paused a moment, grinning at Attu in delight before she turned back to her work.

"Tell your father we're ready," Yural said.

Attu walked to where Ubantu, Paven, and Banek were taking down Elder Nuanu's shelter. Moolnik stood off to one side, his family packed, watching Elder Nuanu rewrap his woman's ankle for travel. He didn't offer to help the men with the shelter, but scowled at the other hunters instead.

He thinks he's too good to help an old woman, Attu thought. *Even the one who was healing his woman Tulnu of her ankle injury.*

Attu hurried to grab the hide Ubantu was holding so he could help roll it. He'd talk with Elder Nuanu once Tulnu left.

Elder Nuanu finished wrapping Tulnu's ankle. Attu heard her say, "One more sun with the wrapping should be enough," as she patted Tulnu's leg.

"Attu, come here," Elder Nuanu called.

Attu turned away from the shelter and walked to where the two women were sitting. *Does she know I need to speak with her?* Attu wondered.

"Grab that small pouch dangling out of my potions pack," Elder Nuanu said.

Attu grabbed the small pouch from where it was hanging and brought it back to her.

Elder Nuanu took the small bundle from him, handing it to Tulnu. "Remember to keep drinking this in the tea I gave you, one bowl, every night. It will help keep down the swelling while the ankle finishes healing itself. You may begin walking the whole day now. No more need for the sled."

Attu heard Moolnik's satisfied "Humph," as he heard Elder Nuanu's words.

"Yes, Elder Nuanu," Tulnu said. She flashed a glance at her man then looked down at the ice in front of her. She seemed disappointed she no longer needed to ride for part of the day. Attu knew Tulnu had enjoyed traveling that way, especially when Moolnik pulled her. She'd smiled widely the whole time her man dragged her sled, while he grumbled with every step.

"Thank you," Tulnu said finally, standing up. Tulnu reached out her hands to help Elder Nuanu up as well.

"These old bones," Elder Nuanu groaned, as she leaned heavily on Tulnu. "I'm too old for this much walking."

Attu popped his lips at her statement. Who'd been keeping up with the strongest hunters these last several moons if not Elder Nuanu? She was tough meat, like his father said.

"We're almost there," Tulnu said. "Soon." She patted Elder Nuanu's arm as if Elder Nuanu were a child, and not the embodiment of Shuantuan, most powerful of all land spirits.

Tulnu turned and started walking toward Moolnik. Apparently seeing she was done, Moolnik strode away, leaving Tulnu to catch up with him.

Attu looked down at Elder Nuanu as she stared off into the distance, past where Moolnik and Tulnu had gone. He opened his mouth to begin telling her about his dreams, when he realized she was already speaking. Her voice was too low for Attu to hear, and she clutched the amulet she wore around her neck with her free hand. Elder Nuanu reached for Attu and grasped his arm fiercely. A shudder passed through her body.

"You must be first through the pass," Elder Nuanu said in a voice that Attu recognized. It was the white-haired man's voice, the voice of the man in the dream, the one with the blue eyes, the one who had spoken through Rika.

Attu tried to pull away from Elder Nuanu, but she grabbed his arm still tighter, her fingers like claws digging into him as she swayed on her feet. Her eyes were unfocused, staring out over the Expanse toward the way they must go. The voice came again, almost a whisper. "Before the others. You must travel first through the pass, along with the one who will bear your sons and daughters. Do not give up hope, Attu, even when things seem grim."

Attu was terrified. *What dark force of the spirits was this? What was happening to Elder Nuanu?*

Attu stared at her as Elder Nuanu released her amulet with her free hand, raising it as if to brush a few strands of grey hair away from her eyes. But Attu saw the look of pain on her face. For a brief moment, her face looked like that of Rika's in the dream, like it was both Elder Nuanu's face and the face of the man, someone powerful. Her grey braids seemed to change, to become white flowing hair, her face, the face of the old man, heavy white brows, impossibly blue eyes…

"Elder Nuanu?" Attu asked. "What's happening to you?"

"I need to sit down," Elder Nuanu said, and Attu was relieved to hear her own voice coming out of her mouth again. He helped her sit on the pack she'd used as a seat earlier. He studied her face. It looked normal, wrinkled with age, tanned by the sun.

Suddenly, however, Elder Nuanu began to shake violently. Her whole body pulsed, as tremors ran from her head to her feet.

"Get Rika," Elder Nuanu managed to say through gritted teeth. "Tell her to hurry." Elder Nuanu fell sideways off the pack.

"Father!" Attu cried as he grabbed Elder Nuanu up into his arms before she could hit the ice. She had passed out.

"I tell you, I don't know what's wrong with her," Rika said, as Paven, Banek, Ubantu, and Attu stood in Elder Nuanu's hastily re-erected shelter in which she now lay, still unconscious. Rika hovered over her, wringing her hands.

Attu wanted to tell Rika about Elder Nuanu talking in the man's voice before she convulsed and passed out, but he couldn't say it in front of everyone, so he just said Elder Nuanu had started trembling violently before she went into the Between of unconsciousness. He'd tell Rika the rest as soon as he could get her alone for a moment. Attu knew he should say more now, but he couldn't, not in front of Paven and Banek. He didn't want them to know about Rika and the dreams.

"She has no fever. She wasn't injured," Rika was saying. "I've examined her and found nothing wrong. I don't know what to do."

"We have to leave, daughter," Paven said, pacing back and forth in the small space. His scarred face looked even worse as he drew his brows together in thought. "We can't risk staying here until we can figure out what's wrong with Elder Nuanu. We have to move onto the land while we have the chance."

"I'll just have to stay behind with her," Rika said. "You can come back and get us once the clan is safely on land. Elder Nuanu will probably be-"

"No!" Paven, Banek, and Attu cut her off all at the same time. Apparently surprised, Paven stared first at Attu, then back at his daughter. Banek just stared at them both.

Attu studied Banek's face. But Banek just stood there, his bearded face impassive, his eyes cold, staring at Attu and Rika as if he were seeing them for the first time.

"I can't move her like this," Rika said, her voice stubborn.

Banek just stared at her. Paven moved closer to Banek, but said nothing.

"I won't let you stay behind," Attu said finally, when no one else spoke. He moved toward Rika, but his father put out a hand to stop him from reaching her.

"I WILL stay with Elder Nuanu if I want to," Rika said through gritted teeth. "It's my choice as healer of this clan."

Attu wanted to shake Rika. She was so stubborn. He opened his mouth to continue the argument, but Paven cut him off.

"It is NOT your choice, daughter," Paven said. His voice was low and full of a leader's power. "It's mine. Until you are given to BANEK," and he shot a glance at Attu, "I decide."

Realization struck Attu. What had he been thinking? He had no right to tell Rika what to do. He'd been so angry with her, he'd forgotten. Now, it was too late.

I have to get out of here.

Attu took a quick step backward toward the shelter door, but Ubantu put a firm hand on his shoulder, stopping him from rushing out.

"We're all going," Paven said, and he stepped between Banek and Attu. "Together."

Attu looked up. Both Paven and Ubantu were watching Banek. Banek had his spear raised, slightly, and as Attu looked at him, Banek glared back, first at him, then at Paven. Banek's face was a mask of hatred, and at that moment Attu didn't know which of them Banek might spear first, himself, or Paven.

Attu saw Paven's arm move, touching the knife at his belt. Paven's eyes locked with Banek's.

Banek lowered his spear again.

Attu let out his breath, slowly, and turned away from Banek, back toward Rika and Elder Nuanu. He tried to steady himself, but his knees were shaking.

" Elder Nuanu can't travel," Rika said, her voice now small. She had been staring down at her hands, but now she looked at Attu for help, tears streaming down her face.

Y*our father is using you and pushing Banek to his limit, and all you can see is that Elder Nuanu needs you.* "We can use the sled," Attu suggested. He carefully looked away from Rika again while avoiding looking at anyone else in the shelter. "Tulnu doesn't need it anymore. I heard Elder Nuanu tell her while she was wrapping her ankle."

And, a belligerent voice inside his head reminded him, *just before the man's voice spoke through her, just when you were going to ask her about the dreams... just before you made Banek furious with you and with Paven.*

Attu found a spot on the floor of the shelter and stared at it, trying to calm himself, to slow his heartbeat like he did while waiting over a nuknuk breathing hole.

The silence in the shelter was deafening.

After what seemed like forever, Paven turned to Banek. The older man waited until Banek lowered his spear to his side. Finally, Paven spoke. "Banek, get the sled from Moolnik. Have the women re-ice it, thick. We don't want to have to stop on the way to do it again. You'll be first puller, and when you're not pulling, I want you to stay with Rika in case she needs your help with Elder Nuanu."

At Paven's order, Banek glared at Rika. Rika looked away immediately, turning back to Elder Nuanu. Attu saw her shoulders sag.

Paven cleared his throat and glanced toward Rika before he spoke. "I want you to guard the rear of the clans, Attu, along with Moolnik."

Attu said nothing.

"This close to land, the chances we might be attacked by an ice bear are great. You may get to use that new spear sooner than we thought, Attu." Paven looked at Attu, his scarred face set.

"So, what are you waiting for, Banek?" Paven asked, turning again toward the bearded man. "Go!"

Attu felt Banek's eyes boring into him before Banek turned and stalked out of the shelter.

Ubantu let out a deep breath and limped to the shelter wall. He began dismantling Elder Nuanu's shelter again, stripping off the hides on the inside. Attu stepped up to help his father. The first hide he touched was brittle. It ripped in his hands. Looking to his father, Attu saw Ubantu touch his forehead then his lips. They were turned away from Paven and Rika so the others couldn't see Ubantu's signal.

Attu moved his head, the slight sideways motion of hunters. His father saw it and let out another long slow breath.

No, I won't endanger myself, or you, any more, Attu thought. *I'll use my head. I'll keep my mouth shut.* He continued working to take down the hides, more carefully this time.

Rika began packing the healer's tools and potions she'd brought with her to treat Elder Nuanu. The old woman didn't stir, not even when Rika, apparently deciding Elder Nuanu still wasn't wrapped warmly enough, rolled her on her side to place another large fur beneath her.

Ubantu turned from pulling hides off the shelter and said, "Paven and I will lead the clans across the last piece of ice."

Ubantu looked to Paven, who apparently lost in thought, had stopped giving orders and stood fingering the knife at his belt, his eyes still locked on the doorway.

"Yes. We will lead," Paven agreed, and he shook his head as if to clear it from what he'd been thinking. "We'll begin now. You follow as soon as you can," Paven added, catching Rika's eyes. She nodded.

"And you, Attu, go now to tell Moolnik to bring up the rear guard with you," Paven concluded. "I'll get others to finish taking down Elder Nuanu's shelter, then Ubantu and I will get the people moving out."

Attu grabbed his spear and left the shelter. He didn't even risk a last glance back at Rika or his father.

Chapter 22

What can I do? Attu thought as he walked toward the group of hunters standing near the front of the clans. Moolnik would probably be with them. Attu knew he'd be angry at being asked to guard the back of the clan with Attu, but Moolnik would come. Attu couldn't care less how Moolnik reacted. He almost hoped his uncle would yell at him. It was clear to Attu now that neither Paven nor Banek cared if their posturing hurt Rika; neither treated her with respect, but had he figured out a way to stand up for her himself? Get her out from between them? Fight for her? No, instead he'd made a fool of himself. *I deserve to be yelled at.*

Attu stepped behind one of the last shelters still standing, cutting across the now empty camp, when suddenly, a hand reached around his neck, his arms were pinned to his sides and a knife came to rest against his throat.

Banek.

Attu felt the sharpness of the knife pressing against him and fought back the urge to swallow. He felt the stiff hair of Banek's beard tickling the nape of his neck where his own hair was drawn aside in its braid.

"I AM Rika's man," Banek said into Attu's ear, his voice a menacing growl. "I have waited many moons for her, and YOU will not take her from me."

Attu felt the bone knife knick his throat and a trickle of blood, warm against his skin, began sliding down his neck and into his parka.

"Do you understand, boy-hunter who tries to take what is not his?"

"I have not-" Attu began to protest, but Banek pressed the knife further into his throat. Attu smelled the sweat of fear. His own.

"No excuses, boy," Banek hissed into his ear. "I asked you a question. Answer me. Do you understand?"

"Yes," Attu replied. He was terrified and furious at the same time. Part of him wanted to run, to flee across the ice and never return. Part of him wanted to turn and rip Banek's throat out with his bare hands. He could do neither. Banek was older than he was, stronger than he was, and he had the knife. Attu was helpless in Banek's grip.

"Good," Banek said. He slowly began lowering the knife from Attu's throat. Suddenly Banek punched him, hard, right in the old wound in his back, and pain shot through Attu. He fell to the ground face first as Banek spun away, his knife at the ready in case Attu tried to strike back.

But Attu didn't try. He landed on his chest and didn't move. Not even when Banek spat on the back of his head and kicked him in the side on his way past, walking around the shelter where he'd been laying in wait for Attu. Attu heard Banek start whistling as he headed toward the women's group to get the sled.

Still, Attu lay on the ice where he'd fallen. *One swipe of that knife and Banek could have left me bleeding out like a dying nuknuk.* It would've been that simple. He'd stepped over the line Banek had drawn around Rika, and if he did anything to make Banek think he'd stepped over it again, Banek would kill him.

Attu wished the ice would open up at that moment and swallow him. *How could I have been so stupid? There is nothing I can do to save Rika.* Pain radiated from his old wound across his whole back and around to his sides. The cold was beginning to numb his face and his chest where he lay.

Attu rolled over on his back and felt the cold begin to seep into the place Banek's fist had sunk just a short while before. His back pain lessened as it was replaced with the numbing cold. But the ice didn't lessen the pain Attu felt when he thought about how he'd spoken out in the shelter, allowing everyone to see him for the fool he was.

Rolling back onto his stomach, Attu pushed himself up, groaning a bit from the pain, and walked slowly toward the other hunters. He had to tell Moolnik what Paven had ordered. He'd have to face Banek when he and Moolnik walked past to guard the rear of the clans. He'd have to make sure he gave no indication to Rika, or his father, or Paven that anything had happened between himself and Banek. Banek had not murdered him. He was being given a second chance because Banek saw him as a boy and not a real threat. He must remain silent now until the clans reached land and Attu could convince his father to separate their clan from the Great Frozen Clan and head out on their own again. *There is nothing else I can do.* That thought felt like another kick in his ribs.

Attu sighed as he saw Moolnik up ahead. He worked to make sure his face was impassive as he approached Moolnik to tell him Paven's order. Moolnik complained, as Attu knew he would, but in the end he headed back to the rear of the group with Attu, spear at the ready. They passed Banek, pulling Elder Nuanu on the sled. Rika walked beside Banek, her face lowered. Attu carefully ignored them both as he and Moolnik headed to the back of the group.

"You take this side, I'll take the other," Moolnik said and walked off to Attu's right without waiting for an answer.

Attu trod carefully in the tracks of the two clans, the leading edge of the group almost out of sight ahead of them. He turned and scanned the way they had come, watching for anything unusual. Moolnik did the same on his side. They walked in silence until a call from the front echoed back to them. The clan was celebrating. They'd seen the end of the chasm and the land. Soon the nightmare of their journey across the Expanse would be over.

A while later, Attu watched with Moolnik as the clans slowly made their way, a few at a time, across the ice and onto a rocky stretch of shoreline in the distance. The people moved silently, as they always did on the ice, listening for the sound of cracking, the moaning warning that ice was about to give way under them.

As the first people crossed the last few feet to shore, Attu saw several break through the shoreline ice, falling into water, some knee deep, some chest deep. They scrambled out, or were pulled, and soon several lamps were lit, over which drying foot miks and other clothing dangled from some of the bone frame supports used for making shelters.

"Look, they've found a safer path," Moolnik said and pointed further south to where the new arrivals seemed to be heading.

"It's rougher; looks like jagged ice mounds where the ice meets land," Attu replied.

"But it'll be thicker there, too."

The line of people straggled across the ice. Now everyone was going towards the thicker ice, scrambling over the huge chunks near the shore. Once there, they turned to watch the rest coming, and soon most of the people were on the shoreline, with only a few remaining on the ice.

Attu looked and saw a person Meavu's size waving in his direction. He recognized his father's slight limping gait as he joined the smaller waving figure and a taller one, Yural. His family. They were safe. Attu sighed with relief and kept walking.

"I'm not waiting any longer, no matter what Paven told us to do," Moolnik decided. "I see Tulnu and Shunut on the land. I'm joining them." He trotted off, leaving Attu alone to guard the last few people, mostly from Paven's clan, including Rika, still walking beside Banek as he pulled Elder Nuanu's sled.

Attu was glad to see Moolnik go. There were obviously no ice bears on the Expanse behind them. Now that the clans had reached land, Attu should be with the other hunters there, too. Any threat to the clan would come from the surrounding hills just off the shoreline where they now stood. But nobody seemed to be thinking about that right now; they were too busy waiting to welcome the rest coming off the ice. Attu knew the women would be anxiously awaiting Elder Nuanu's arrival also, watching the sled as it moved across the ice.

Attu came up behind Banek, still pulling the sled with Rika at his side. Attu slowed down and concentrated at looking anywhere but the pair as he brought up the rear.

Banek apparently saw him out of the corner of his eye and turned. "Attu?"

Attu looked up. A slow smile spread across Banek's bushy face.

Attu's stomach clenched.

Rika jerked her head up from where she'd been studying the ice in front of her foot miks ever since they'd started walking. Her face was tear streaked, and a welt of bright red, the size and shape of a man's open hand, burned on her left cheek. Seeing it, Attu felt a surge of fury. *Had Banek struck Rika? Or had it been Paven?*

Rika jerked her chin toward Banek then turned away, apparently afraid Banek might catch her looking at Attu. *So, it HAD been Banek…*

"Attu, are you deaf?" Banek shouted.

"Yes?" Attu answered him this time, keeping his voice as calm as he could. He wanted to strangle the man, right there, right then, for hurting Rika. But he couldn't. Attu had to pretend everything was fine, for Rika's sake.

But Attu's anger was spinning him out of control. He almost didn't catch Banek's next words, but jerked his mind back to the Here and Now as he heard Banek speaking again.

"I said," Banek was obviously repeating something he'd just said and Attu had missed, "we're last off the ice and there's still quite a distance to go. Pull the sled now."

Banek smiled, dropped the rope, and stepped aside.

Attu gritted his teeth and moved over to pick up the sled rope, fastening the harness across his chest as Banek, grabbing Rika's arm, moved to walk in front of him.

Banek isn't tired of pulling the sled. He just wants to order me around in front of Rika because he knows he can get away with it and it will hurt her. He knows I'll do whatever he tells me to do to avoid causing her any more harm.

Attu had a sudden vision of what the future would hold if their clans stayed together. Not only would he have to watch Rika with Banek every day, Banek could make Attu work like a slave, doing everything for him he didn't want to do for himself. And Attu would do whatever Banek ordered him to do, not to protect himself, but to protect Rika.

And it won't stop there, Attu thought. *I saw how Banek looked at Paven in Elder Nuanu's shelter, and Paven's reaction afterward. Banek isn't going to leave with Rika once they're bonded. He's going to fight for leadership. And if our clans don't separate soon, our hunters will be drawn into the fight. How many of my people will die because of their lust for power?* It made Attu sick to think of leaving Rika behind with Banek and Paven, but he knew it was the choice he had to make. *To protect Rika, and to protect our clan, we have to get away from them.*

Who's the great leader now, Elder Nuanu? Attu's thoughts were bitter as he dragged the sled closer to the shoreline. *Why now, when I need you more than ever, have you fallen into the Between and can't seem to find your way out?*

Attu stopped a moment, and turning to look at Elder Nuanu, searched her face for any sign she might be about to wake up. But the old woman lay as still as death, her wrinkled face calm, her body still wrapped tightly in furs.

What would Elder Nuanu tell me to do if she were in the Here and Now with me? Attu thought. He remembered her words, back before they'd even begun their journey. *...The spirits do not call the man who is worthy in his own eyes, but the one who is willing to listen and to sacrifice for his clan...*

I'm definitely not worthy. Instead, I'm a fool.

But Elder Nuanu hated people who took pity on themselves. She would say, *Do what you can do, Attu.*

"Off the ice, just get off the ice," he whispered, trying to pull himself out of his self-pity. *Then worry about what to do next to protect your people. Do what you can do for now.*

His father would understand. He'd tell him about Banek's attack, and Ubantu had witnessed the exchange between Paven and Banek. His father would agree to separate from Paven's clan. Their clan would go south to the pass through the mountains alone.

Attu took a deep breath and tried to relax. Banek had frightened and angered him so much, hurting him, hurting Rika, that Attu's spirit had been in turmoil, and he hadn't been able to think clearly. Now, having had time to think and make his decision, Attu strode forward with the sled, catching up to Banek and Rika.

Attu began whistling the same tune Banek had whistled after leaving him on the ice. He'd prove to Banek he couldn't care less about being ordered around. Banek's shoulders stiffened at the sound, but he didn't turn or speak, just kept walking, pulling Rika along as if she were a sled, too.

After a few moments, Rika put her free arm behind her back, the one Banek did not have trapped in his, and waved her mik at Attu slowly, a teasing gesture the children used to taunt others into running after them in chasing games. Attu knew she was trying to make him feel better, but he stopped whistling as tears stung his eyes. It was going to be impossible to watch her walk away again. Proud Rika, who even now was asserting herself in the only way she could.

But he would leave her, Attu told himself. When it was time, he would. Rika wasn't the woman to bear his children. He'd been wrong. His dreams had been of his own making, his own desires.

But what of the man's words, somehow spoken through Elder Nuanu? "You must be first through the pass… along with the one who will bear your sons and daughters. Do not give up hope, Attu, even when things seem grim."

Wake up, Elder Nuanu, Attu pleaded with Elder Nuanu's spirit in his mind as he pulled the sled closer to the shoreline. *I need to talk with you about what happened, what was spoken through you. I need you. Don't go to the Between of Death just yet. Please.*

Chapter 23

Moolnik and Paven stood at the edge of the shoreline as Banek, Rika, and Attu approached with Elder Nuanu on the sled. One by one the two hunters were hauling people across the last bit of ice, which was jagged and tumbled looking as if it had broken apart, been tossed around, and then refrozen. The large pits and crevices in the ice made it difficult to traverse.

Paven must have ordered Moolnik to help him, Attu thought as he saw the scowl on Moolnik's face. The man was strong, and he was easily lifting the last few people over a deep crevice in the ice and into Paven's grasp. Paven lifted each person up again over the last sheer tumble of ice and let them slide down the other side, into the arms of the families waiting for them.

As Attu grew closer, he realized that getting Elder Nuanu's sled across this jagged ice was going to be difficult, if not impossible. Attu drew the sled as close as he could to the first crevice and butted it up against a large chunk of ice that had been thrown back from the tumbled shoreline and refrozen to the smoother surface. It was about the size of a man squatting, large enough to keep the sled from sliding into the gap if the ice shifted again. Attu took off the harness and draped the ends of the rope over it.

"Are we going to have to carry her?" Attu shouted to Paven.

"What do you think, Banek?" Paven asked.

So he's going to ignore me, too?

Rika brushed by Attu, going to stand beside Elder Nuanu on the sled. She rewrapped a fur that had come loose in the pulling, keeping her head down and her face hidden in the waves of her loose hair. Something about the way her shoulders were slumped now, how she carried herself, told Attu that Paven had spoken with her once Attu had left the shelter.

But Rika seemed to be hiding her face from her father as well.

She's probably ashamed, Attu thought. *She shouldn't be. No man has the right to hit a woman. Her father should know.* But Attu knew it was up to Rika to tell her father if she wanted Paven to know her future man was violent. He wondered if what Meavu had told him about Paven's own attitude toward women was true after all.

Attu clenched his teeth to stay quiet and stood beside the sled, waiting for what the men would decide to do with Elder Nuanu.

Rika sat on the edge of the sled with the old woman, her arms wrapped tightly around herself, looking down at nothing.

Attu's heart sank to see her so miserable.

"Moolnik and I are strong enough to carry Elder Nuanu, sled and all," Banek said, stepping up to the edge of the gap.

Banek looked at Attu, a fierce grin on his hairy face.

"You are no longer needed," Banek said, and pointed to the shoreline.

"We don't need HIM," Banek shouted this time to Paven, pointing at Attu.

Paven nodded his agreement, his scarred face stony.

I've had enough. Attu jumped the first ice chunk, and moving past Moolnik and Paven before they could even try to help him, leaped the crevices and slid down the last ice sheet. He landed on his feet and walked away.

Solid land, again. He thought. In spite of his anger toward Banek and the way Paven was now treating him, Attu felt a deep fear in him ease. Land couldn't suddenly open up and drop him in to his death. Here he was safe.

Attu turned to walk in the direction he'd seen his family, just ahead. Meavu, seeing Attu, rushed toward him, her arms outstretched. Attu picked her up, spinning her around before setting her down on the land again. Ubantu and Yural walked to meet him.

"Paven doesn't need your help with the sled?" Ubantu asked as the two men turned to see how Moolnik and Banek were going to get Elder Nuanu and the sled over the jumbled ice and crevices.

"Banek ordered me to leave it to him and Moolnik," Attu said.

Attu felt his father's eyes studying him. Attu had gotten hot pulling the sled, and he'd thrown back his hood and opened the top of his parka. He looked at his father just as Ubantu's eyes widened when he saw the knife knick on Attu's throat.

"What happened?" his father asked. He took a step closer to Attu.

"Banek," Attu whispered through gritted teeth. "He threatened to kill me when I left Elder Nuanu's shelter."

Ubantu grasped his son in a fierce hug, then apparently seeing Yural and Meavu moving closer as well, released his hold on Attu and motioned for him to close the front of his parka again, hiding the wound from his mother and sister.

"We'll figure out something," his father said. He placed a strong hand on Attu's shoulder as Meavu and Yural came to join them, and both hunters pretended nothing was wrong as they turned to watch Moolnik and Banek prepare to move the sled.

Rika had remained with Elder Nuanu, so apparently she was going to help steady the sled as it was lifted over the first crevice. The hunters could carry the sled over the other crevices to safety. Paven stood at the end to help them. Rika would be last off the ice.

It should be me, not Rika. Attu thought. *What are they thinking?*

Banek stood on one side of the sled and Rika on the other as Moolnik approached the crevice. Banek held out his hand for Moolnik to help him up, but Moolnik ignored it, and leaped up to the higher ice where the sled sat against the ice chunk.

A sharp crack, as loud as any Attu had ever heard, ripped through the air as Moolnik landed heavily on the ice shelf. The sound echoed off the hills behind them, and in their confusion, Attu saw some of his people turn to see what had made such a loud noise in the hills. But Attu knew. The ice at the shoreline was breaking.

Attu raced up the slick ice toward the men. Rika fell onto the sled on top of Elder Nuanu, and Banek tumbled forward into the crevice, his arm still outstretched. Moolnik lost his balance also, the sudden thrust of the ice away from the shoreline causing him to fall backward into the crevice where Banek had just disappeared. The ice moaned, and a large dark stain spread across the snow. Open water.

Attu, along with some of the other hunters, reached the edge of the rapidly expanding crack. A few feet below them, Moolnik and Banek struggled in the water, trying to stay afloat in their heavy fur clothes. They were losing the battle.

"Rika, the rope from the sled," Attu yelled across the chasm to Rika.

Rika pulled herself up from the sled and ran to the edge of the chasm.

"Throw the rope down on each side of the ice chunk," Attu motioned with his hands, showing Rika how to take the sled rope and dangle it but still keep the sled wedged against the chunk of ice.

"But what if it breaks off?" Rika screamed. "Elder Nuanu…"

"Roll her off the sled first."

Rika grabbed the furs under Elder Nuanu and hauled her off the sled as if she weighed nothing. Standing on the sled herself, Rika threw the long loop of rope over each side of the large ice chunk.

"The rope! Go for the rope!" Attu and the other hunters hollered down to the two men, who were struggling to keep their heads above the churning water. Large pieces of ice were dropping into the opening chasm around them, mostly from the shore side, and the water was roiling around the men like stew boiling in a soft stone bowl.

Banek must have heard Attu, or seen him point, because he pushed himself off from a floating ice hunk he'd been scrambling to climb on and reached the rope first, Moolnik right behind him.

Banek grabbed the rope. He began climbing, fighting against his own weight to pull himself up the side of the ice chasm, his miks slipping on the rope, slowing his progress.

Moolnik had somehow gotten his parka off, and he reached for the other rope and began climbing as well.

Suddenly, Banek began screaming at Moolnik, striking him on the side with one fist while he held onto the rope with the other. Moolnik turned. He'd made it halfway up the rope already, probably because he was lighter without the heavy fur parka weighing him down.

"One at a time or the rope will break!" Attu heard Banek shout. "Get off!"

Moolnik said nothing, but he raised his foot mik out of the water and stepped on Banek's head, using the other hunter to boost himself up further. Attu cringed at the sight.

Banek yelled in pain and grabbed Moolnik's foot mik. He began hauling himself up Moolnik's leg, then his back, as if Moolnik were another rope.

But Moolnik couldn't hold on with Banek's weight on him too, and with a cry, Moolnik let go of the rope and both men plunged back into the water.

"No!" Attu heard a voice cry out, and he realized that most of the clan were now behind him, balancing on the shoreline ice and watching the two men fight with each other to get out of the water.

Suddenly, Rika screamed.

"Attu!"

Rika was pointing behind her. Another crack had opened up in the ice, which left Rika and Elder Nuanu caught on what appeared to be a long peninsula of ice, at least a spear throw wide with the water of the edge of the chasm to the left of them and a narrow strip of jumbled pack ice to the right, extending off into the horizon. Unfrozen water lay in front and behind them.

The only means of escape to dry land now was that narrow strip of ice. It would take Attu half a sun's journey to reach the women, around the new chasm that was opening in front of them. There was no way Rika could get Elder Nuanu across the mess of tossed about ice hunks, some taller than Attu. If that last path to safety broke off the rest of the ice, the two women would be completely surrounded by water on a chunk of ice the size of a small encampment. It was large enough to be steady in the water, but they would be unreachable.

As the ice continued to move away, Attu had the sinking feeling they must already be surrounded by water. The end of the ice strip was just too far away for Attu to see if it was still connected to the land or floating free.

Attu stood at the chasm with the others, his heart in his throat. He couldn't make a leap across; it was far too wide.

Was this the dream coming to life before him?

He considered trying to jump to Rika anyway. Perhaps he could somehow make it across the water and climb the rope to save her. His muscles tensed at the thought, and his father's hand came down on his shoulder, holding him steady. Paven and Ubantu had climbed back up to the very edge of the chasm and now stood, one on each side of Attu.

"You can't make it," his father said. "Wait. One of the hunters might yet survive."

Moolnik and Banek continued to fight one another, flailing around in the water, oblivious to the clan watching them, oblivious to the danger they would still face if they made it up the rope. Like tooth fish, each fought to stay on a rope while trying to knock the other off. Over and over one of them would fall into the water, only to somehow scramble back up a rope again, knocking the other one off.

But both Moolnik and Banek were weakening; Attu could see that. They had been in the frigid water far too long, and the longer they remained in it, the more desperate they seemed to become.

The clan shouted at them. The other hunters yelled at both men, calling them fools, trying to anger them into helping each other. But it did no good.

Moolnik slipped off the rope again as Banek struck him from behind. Banek grabbed the rope and pulled himself up using each rope, wrapping them both around his arms, then lifting himself with one, grabbing the other one higher up and rewrapping it with a twist around his other arm. Attu winced at the thought of how painful the rope pressure must be on Banek's forearms, even through the man's parka, but Banek was making swift progress out of the water this way. Only his feet still dangled in the dark depths. All the while the entire ice chunk continued to move away from land.

Suddenly, Moolnik screamed, a cry that froze Attu's blood and silenced the clans. Moolnik launched himself out of the water where he had been struggling just moments before. Attu realized he had somehow gotten a foothold on a large ice chunk floating in the water behind him, and it had given him the leverage to push himself up out of the water again.

Moolnik began to climb up Banek's legs and onto his back. But, this time, he wasn't just climbing. He was stabbing Banek and climbing up the handholds his knives were making.

Just like Yupik had done up the back of the ice bear.

Attu shuddered.

Banek had twisted both arms into the ropes to hold himself, and now he was trapped. Moolnik stabbed and climbed, stabbed and climbed, while the dark water and the ice around it became stained with Banek's blood. Being a hunter, Moolnik knew just where to stab so the knives would hold his weight… above the knee joint, above the hip bone… Banek screamed.

Tulnu, Moolnik's woman, screamed as if in answer to Banek and buried her face in her son Kinak's parka. Suanu turned away, falling to the ground, her hands over her face. Women grabbed their children and turned them away from the grisly sight.

Still Moolnik stabbed and climbed. He threw his arms onto the lip of the ice chunk using Banek's dead or nearly dead dangling body to push himself up the rest of the way onto the ice's surface. Banek hung now from impossibly loose arms, his feet still in the water, his head lolling to the side. Moolnik knelt and made two quick slices with his knife, cutting the ropes. Banek's body slipped into the dark waters and disappeared.

Chapter 24

Rika, seeing the blood soaked Moolnik walking toward her, let out a cry and fell unconscious to the ice. Moolnik turned back to look at the clan. He raised both knives in triumph above his head.

"As if he were a warrior, not an abomination," Attu heard Paven whisper to himself as he stood beside him.

Attu realized that one of those knives must be Banek's. Moolnik had somehow grabbed it in their fighting over the rope, then used it, killing Banek with his own knife.

The knife Banek cut me with this very day.

Attu's hand slipped up to his throat of its own accord, and he shuddered. Now, Banek was dead. *And,* Attu thought, *as much as I hated the man, Banek did not deserve to die this way.*

Kinak climbed up to the chasm opening and stood beside Paven, above the rest of the clan. He held up his arm and shook his spear.

The clan grew quiet.

"The man Banek is dead!" Kinak shouted. "But the man Moolnik is also dead!"

Suka was standing on the shoreline below, one hand on his mother Tulnu's shoulder, the other on his brother Shunut's head. He nodded. "We no longer have a father," he said, his voice catching when he said, "father." Suka struggled to continue. He cleared his throat and looked to Attu and Ubantu. His eyes pleaded with theirs for understanding.

Ubantu nodded and said, "Moolnik is no longer of our lamp fire. And he is not of our clan," Ubantu added as he nodded at Suka. His strong voice carried far.

Attu knew if the men of his clan didn't cut off all ties with the murderer Moolnik right now, they faced immediate retribution from Paven's clan. That Paven's daughter had been promised to Banek made him as high in status as if he were Paven's own son. His murder at the hands of one of Attu's clan must be avenged. Only the shock of watching the horrific scene played out before them had given Moolnik's family and Ubantu the chance to speak before Paven's hunters attacked them.

A few hunters from Paven's clan brandished their spears, but when Paven raised his arm, all became quiet again.

Paven looked at the hunters of Attu's clan. He studied the two older brothers, Tulnu, and young Shunut. Then he spoke.

"Moolnik has murdered Banek and for this he must pay!"

"Revenge! Revenge!" Paven's hunters cried.

What did this mean? Attu thought. He looked to his father.

Ubantu jerked his head to the side.

Wait.

But what about Rika?

Attu was frantic as he watched the ice sheet move further and further from them. Rika still lay slumped to one side. Moolnik was over by the sled, rummaging through Elder Nuanu's furs, but when he heard the noise of the shouting, Moolnik looked up from where he had been pulling furs off of Elder Nuanu to dry and warm himself, to see the clans, spears up, yelling for revenge.

Moolnik stood and rushed to the side of the large moving ice. He began shouting obscenities back at Paven's clan from the safety of his ice across the chasm. He made lewd gestures with his hands, spinning on the ice and swearing at them all. The hunters beside Attu screamed back at him.

He's going to get us all killed.

Attu felt his whole body begin to tremble.

As if seeing it for the first time, Moolnik stopped his gyrations and looked behind him. He dropped to his knees as he saw the open water. As he did, the ice moaned again.

The noise of the shouting, even Moolnik's craziness, had not roused Rika. Attu feared the shock of seeing Moolnik murder Banek had made Rika's spirit flee from her body. He stood silently amongst the others, trying to stop shaking, to think. *What can I do?*

Paven raised his hand for silence, and as he did, another crack ripped through the air. The clans watched dumbstruck as the ice Rika, Elder Nuanu, and Moolnik were on broke away from the rest of the narrow strip.

The air ripped again with another crack, this time from further north. Attu gasped as a sheet of ice in the distance, the size of a small piece of land the clan might camp on, simply upended. The women screamed and grabbed the children, running back from the shoreline as the mass towered in the air, its shadow almost reaching them even though it was quite far away. The ice hovered like a giant sea creature leaping out of the water before falling again, flipping completely upside down, crashing the ice around it to splinters.

A gigantic wave of water rose up as the ice crashed. It was too late for them to try to get down off the top of the chasm. The men fell to the ice, and Attu clung to a frozen hunk near him, hoping they were high enough to avoid being washed away in the great wall of water that was now rushing toward them.

A fierce rush of wind hit the shoreline as everyone else ran for the hills close behind them. Seconds later, a mammoth wave swept across the ice, the shoreline, and the open water.

Attu watched in horrified fascination as it hit the ice sheet where Rika, Moolnik, and Elder Nuanu were. The ice slowly spun away as the huge wave pushed it up and up before it slipped down the other side, carried forward with the wave. Attu saw Rika, awake now, struggling to hold onto the sled and Elder Nuanu. He saw Moolnik using the cut ends of the rope to keep himself and the sled from slipping off. *He must have wrapped the rest of the rope attached to the sled around the protuberance of ice near the edge again, like I did to keep it steady before,* Attu realized. *In saving himself, it would also help Rika and Elder Nuanu.*

The ice sheet seemed to be moving away fast for its size as the wave carried it south. Miraculously, the water had not raised high enough to reach the hunters, but the lower ice behind them was now sheeted with water.

"Rika," Attu shouted.

I can't lose her.

He leaped over the other crevice and slid on the watery ice onto the rocky beach, tumbling when he hit the land. He leaped back to his feet and began running after the now disappearing chunk of ice, slipping and sliding on the drenched shoreline.

"Attu," his mother cried, but Attu didn't stop running.

Suddenly Kinak was at his side, running with him, carrying Attu's pack and his new spear.

"Your father says you'll need this," he said, and passed the spear off to Attu as they ran. He kept the pack.

Suka raced up to Attu on the other side, his own pack still on his back. They ran along the shoreline, dodging hunks of ice and rocks, trying to catch up with the ice that was still moving, even though the wave had passed.

"The water is flowing, carrying them," Suka said between breaths.

"But slower now," Kinak added. Indeed, they were catching up with the floating ice.

"Look, ahead… do you see that higher piece of land… jutting out over the water?" Suka asked.

Attu saw a high point of land just a short distance ahead, sticking far out into the unfrozen water.

If I run just a bit faster...

"Yes!" Kinak said. "The chunk... when it comes close... jump down to Rika. Too high for her... to leap up." Kinak could barely speak as they ran flat out down the shoreline.

"But fath..." Suka hesitated, "that man... he might..." Suka gave up trying to say anything.

Attu saw the tears streaming down Suka's face. Having denounced his father from their lamp fire and clan, Moolnik was no longer anything to Suka and Kinak but an evil stranger. *The pain for them both must be almost unbearable.*

"That man... might try... to kill you, too," Suka finally managed to say.

"I'm sorry... cousin," Kinak added.

"I have to... try to... save her," Attu gasped. "I just... have to."

Suka and Kinak nodded their understanding.

The three young hunters ran up the slope to the crest of land and stopped. The ice chunk was coming fast.

"Wait until the ice... is at its closest to us," Kinak said, catching his breath. "I'll throw your pack across to Rika. Suka, throw mine. It has a lamp and oil in it."

Suka nodded.

"Thank you," Attu said.

"If we aim true... perhaps both packs will make the ice. You aim true also," Suka said, his sides still heaving from the run. He grabbed Attu and pounded him twice on the back. Kinak took his turn at grabbing Attu into a hunter's fierce grasp. He released Attu as suddenly the ice was upon them. The point had somehow deflected it, and it began spinning as it flowed, further out from the land than they'd anticipated.

"Rika!" Suka called first, and he flung the pack with all his strength. Moolnik saw it coming and grabbed it just before it hit. He looked up to smile at his son, but Suka turned away, refusing to look at his father.

Kinak threw his pack next. The ice chunk was closer now, and he easily made the throw. His pack landed neatly beside Elder Nuanu's sled.

But a pack is not a person, Attu thought as his eyes measured the expanse of water over which he must jump. *I'll never make it.*

Attu looked up to see Rika's face. Almost half a spear throw away, now closer, a bit closer. Suddenly, Attu's spirit spun from his body, up over the ice and rocks of the point. He looked down on himself as he had before, when the ice bear attacked. He saw the distance he must jump and knew he would have to have a running start to make the leap.

Somewhere, mid-leap, Attu's spirit slammed back into his body. He didn't remember running a few feet back down the slope. He didn't remember turning and pushing with his legs, driving himself up to the crest of the hill again in a few bounds, and he didn't remember leaping toward Rika over the moving water, his feet still running as he launched himself into the air, as if he could run on the very spirits who inhabited it. His spirit fell back into his body, and he was Attu again, flying through the air, and all he could see was Rika.

It was Rika, the Rika of his dream, reaching out to him, calling to him, as if her desire for his safety could reel him in like a tooth fish, land him like a nuknuk onto the ice. He felt her spirit pull him the rest of the way, and Attu crashed, one leg on the moving ice, one dangling in the air. Rika pulled him to her, and Attu fell on top of her as she fell backward onto the ice.

Attu could feel himself grinning wildly, his heart racing from the leap. Rika grinned back at him and opened her mouth to speak. But Attu kissed her, instead.

Chapter 25

"What in the name of the lying trystas did you do that for?" Moolnik swore as he hauled Attu off Rika by his parka hood. Attu pulled back from Moolnik, making him let go of his parka and spinning to face the man.

Moolnik was furious, his whole body trembling with anger and fatigue from battling in the icy water for so long.

"I just threw myself down across open water to try and save you," Attu yelled. "And you glare at me like you're going to knife me next and drop my body into the water like you did Banek's?"

Rika gasped.

"Why, you son of a tooth fish and a trysta!" Moolnik swore, and he tried to pull his knife and lunge at Attu, but he seemed to have lost the ability to move quickly. "You've been sent to kill me! Paven sent you, or was it Ubantu?"

Attu stepped out of Moolnik's way as Moolnik stabbed the air clumsily.

Attu turned to face him again. "Moolnik, you don't have to do this," Attu began, but Moolnik lunged again, even slower this time, roaring and trying to cut Attu, but succeeding in only cutting the air and sending himself careening off balance across the ice.

Attu turned to face Moolnik yet again, but instead of attacking, Moolnik's eyes suddenly rolled up in his head and he collapsed on his face, his knife hand flung out above his head. He lay unmoving on the ice.

Rika walked over to Moolnik and knelt to examine him.

"Is he dead?" Attu asked, hopeful.

"He's gone Between to dream," Rika said. "He's not dead, yet. Help me roll him on his back."

"Why bother?" Attu said, but he moved over and taking a moment to put a large fur next to Moolnik, the two of them rolled him onto his back on the fur.

"Are you going to kill him?" Rika asked her voice tense. "Is that why they sent you?"

"I wasn't sent," Attu said. His eyes searched her face, and he felt sick as he studied the red mark on her cheek. "I came on my own."

Rika looked away. "But we're supposed to kill him."

"And you don't want to? Even after he killed Banek?"

Rika cringed at the mention of Banek, but she said, "I think… I think this is the time, like the voice keeps saying in my dreams, when I'm supposed to show mercy, rather than justice."

"Are you sure?"

"No. But what if it is and I don't heed the dream?"

"I've seen enough killing today," Attu said, "enough violence. Let's just wait and see what happens. He's weak, no threat to us right now. He might even die on his own if the trystas don't kill him first for profaning the spirits."

"All right, we'll wait. And thank you. For everything."

The pair sat silent for a while, Attu trying to wrap his mind around their situation. It had all happened so fast.

"What now?" Attu finally asked as he looked around. They were a few spear throws from shore, and the ice sheet was moving quickly. It seemed stable enough. He'd leaped on it, and there was plenty of room to walk around on it. The ice surface was as big as three large snow houses, the ones that had held his whole clan.

"It's going to grow dark soon," Rika said. "Let's look through the packs and see what we've got."

“This one’s mine,” Attu said. “It has dried meat, extra furs, my bear teeth, my old foot miks, and my drinking pouch.”

Rika was rummaging through the other pack.

“Kinak said that one has a lamp and oil.”

“Thank the spirits,” Rika said. “We won’t freeze tonight.”

“I won’t let you freeze,” Attu said, and looking up, he met Rika’s eyes. Banek’s hand print on her cheek was darkening from red to the bruise it would become by next sun.

“I know you won’t,” Rika said softly. Suddenly, her body began trembling. “It was horrible, seeing Moolnik…” she began, and tears flowed down her cheeks as she clutched her hands to her stomach.

Attu reached for her, but Rika jumped up and ran to the other edge of the ice chunk where she threw up. She walked rather unsteadily back to where Attu was still sitting, watching her.

“I’m sorry, Rika. No one should have to die that way. Banek was going to be your man.”

“I don’t want to talk about it right now,” Rika interrupted, her voice weary. She closed her eyes and leaned back on her own pack near Elder Nuanu, who lay, still unmoving, wrapped in the furs near the sled where Rika had pulled her off.

Attu got up, grabbing a fur from his own pack. He spread it over Rika. “Rest now,” he said. “I’ll set up a shelter for us. Whenever either of these two awake, they’re going to need your skills. You need to be ready.”

Rika nodded.

Attu smiled as Rika began snoring softly just moments later.

Using the two pack frames and part of the sled that had been reinforced with a bone framework after its initial construction, Attu was able to construct a small shelter. It would hold the four of them, barely, and it would keep in the warmth of the nuknuk oil lamp. Kinak had a full pouch of oil, enough for a few nights if they were careful.

It didn't seem that cold, which worried Attu, but he'd other things to think about and he pushed the thought of warmer temperatures and melting moving ice sheets aside and concentrated on making a camp as comfortable for Rika as possible.

Once he was set up, Attu began to pull Elder Nuanu towards the shelter.

Rika awoke as he was moving past her, dragging Elder Nuanu on the large fur. Rika jumped up to help.

Moolnik was next. Elder Nuanu was cold, and seemed to be barely breathing. Moolnik, however, was hot. Too hot, and Attu knew that fever spirits were already attacking him because he had gotten so cold and exhausted in the water. *Perhaps the trystas would let the evil fever spirits kill him quickly, since he was a murderer...*

"Put him right next to Elder Nuanu," Rika said, "I'll take their clothing off, make their bodies touch." "You want to do what?" Attu asked, incredulous.

What was Rika thinking? Attu wanted to push Moolnik off into the water, not lay him naked next to the clan's beloved Elder Nuanu. It was disgusting.

"If Moolnik is going to die of spirit fever, at least we can use his warmth to help warm Elder Nuanu," Rika said, as she started unwrapping Moolnik's body. He stirred but then fell back into a deep place in Between.

"Just one thing, first," Attu said and carefully removed Banek's knife from Moolnik's belt, placing it with Moolnik's own knife Attu had retrieved when Moolnik had passed out.

Rika turned her head away when she realized what Attu was doing. The knife, as well as most of Moolnik's clothing, was stained with Banek's blood.

Attu's hands shook as he picked up the bloodstained garments and took them outside. He had no idea what ritual needed to be performed to take the curse off the knife and the clothing. He wasn't sure there even was one. Moolnik's actions were unforgivable.

"Thank you," Rika said as Attu re-entered the shelter. Rika had lighted the oil lamp, and it gave off much warmth in the small shelter. Moolnik was sweating under the furs he and Elder Nuanu shared, and Elder Nuanu's cheeks began to regain some color.

Attu grabbed a couple of dried meat chunks out of his pack, and the two of them chewed in silence.

"I don't know what to do," Attu admitted after a time. "I don't know if this ice sheet will remain solid or break up suddenly."

Rika shivered at the thought. "I've been thinking the same thing. We've got to get off of here as soon as we can, but how?"

Rika looked at the two bodies in front of them, both deep in the Between of Sleep. "How can we get Elder Nuanu to safety? And what about him?" Rika jabbed her finger at Moolnik.

"Both our clans have sworn to kill Moolnik," Attu said.

"He deserves to die." Rika took in a shaky breath. "But right now, his fever is helping Elder Nuanu warm. Perhaps that's why we need to allow him to live, to save her." She closed her eyes.

"If revenge must be sought later, I'll do it." Attu looked at Rika in the light of the lamp. "I'll have no problem working justice for Banek, even though I hated the man."

"You hated-" Rika stopped. She looked away from Attu's face.

"What is that?" Rika whispered.

Attu realized he had let his parka hood slide back in the warmth and it was undone at the top. Rika's eyes were fastened on his neck. She'd seen the slit in Attu's throat, and the now dried blood trail down his chest.

"Banek threatened to kill me," Attu said.

"He tried to dishonor me," Rika whispered, touching her hand to her bruised face, then lowering her eyes. "I fought back, and my father heard the struggle and stopped him."

Rika's voice lowered even further. "Afterward, Father said it was my fault, all my fault for speaking to you, for letting you think-"

"No, Rika. No." Attu reached for her, and this time Rika came to him. He wrapped his arms around her, and she tucked her head into his chest. He could feel her sobs as she cried quietly into his parka.

Attu held her until she fell asleep.

Attu awoke in the night. Moolnik was thrashing.

"Rika!" he yelled and Rika, roused from sleep, grabbed Moolnik's legs while Attu tried to stop Moolnik's hands from hitting Elder Nuanu. After a few moments, Moolnik grew still again.

"Tie him," Rika said. "I'll not let him hurt Elder Nuanu."

Rika warmed some liquid from her healer's bag over the lamp and drizzled a few drops into Moolnik's mouth.

"That should quiet him, and if the spirits are willing, bring down his fever," she said. "You heard him, Attu; he cursed the spirits. He murdered Banek, then he cursed the spirits. There's not much hope for him at this point." She shook her head.

As the sky began to lighten, Attu left the shelter to relieve himself near where Rika had been sick the day before. He was shocked to see the ice sheet they were on had gotten much smaller in the night, and Attu had to admit to himself it was melting.

Rika came out of the shelter. They both looked at the land they were moving past. It was close enough so they could make out the details of the rocky hills and stretches of shoreline, bare of ice in places. The safety of land stretched out before their eyes, yet it could've been a lifetime's journey away, the water stretching between them impossible to cross.

Rika lifted her hand to her forehead to throw back her parka hood. She opened her jacket. "It's so warm," she said. "I'm sweating in all these furs."

"I've never felt so warm outside of a shelter or snow house," Attu agreed, and they both took off their parkas and miks, standing in the breeze coming off the hills towards them. For a moment, Attu felt the freedom of wearing just one layer of furs, his forearms bare, then his heart sank again as he gazed out over the water that trapped them on this floating ice. He bent to grab his knife sling from his parka.

"Look!" Rika exclaimed.

Rising up from the edges of the hills just coming into view, he saw first one, then another, then suddenly whole groups of large green plants, with green arms, many of them, waving in the breeze.

"Trystas?" Rika asked. She looked terrified.

"No," Attu answered her. "I think they're called 'trees'."

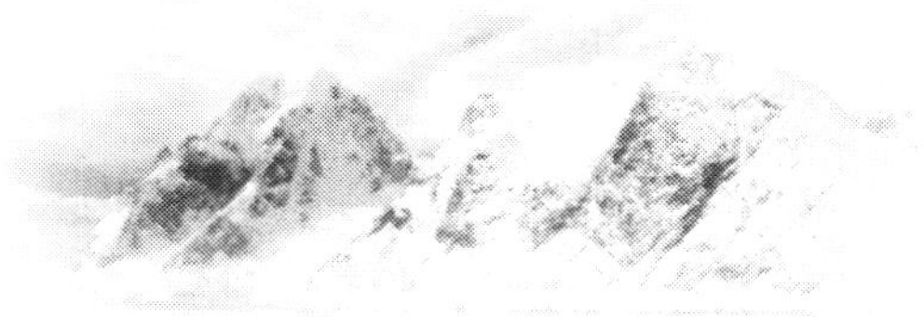

Chapter 26

All that day, Rika tended Elder Nuanu, rolling her up first on one side, then the other, and again to her back, "to stop the spirits of sickness from entering her body through the ice and causing sores," she explained to Attu. Elder Nuanu would swallow if Rika carefully dripped warmed water into her mouth, and toward evening of that first full day on the ice, Elder Nuanu stirred a few times.

"I think she may come back from the Between," Rika said.

But Moolnik grew worse. Rika rolled him also and adjusted the ties on his arms and legs, but he wouldn't drink and alternated mumbling and sometimes swearing as he fought the spirits of fever.

In the few moments of calm, Rika and Attu sat outside the shelter and watched the amazing landscape moving past them. As the day progressed, the green plants, the "trees" they saw, had grown larger and larger, until Attu and Rika realized the first ones had to have been stunted somehow; perhaps they were at the edge of where it had became too cold for them to grow. Now, the hills were covered with huge trees, and the smell in the air was spicy, like the potion Rika had used on Attu's back.

"I've been thinking about how at first there were no trees then the trees became larger," Attu said. "The Nuvik have spent so many generations on the ice; is it possible our people forgot that far to the south of us, here in this land, it is perhaps always warmer, at least enough to grow such large plants? And if that is true, why would our people have gone north, instead of south, when life in the north is so hard?"

"I don't know," Rika said.

"I think we have come much farther south than we thought to come. The ice is just starting to be unsafe where we came from; here it is breaking up, in some places almost gone. Perhaps it was never that thick to begin with, here in this warmer place."

This is all so new, so confusing.

"I'd love to walk this land," Rika breathed, looking with longing at the strange new world passing in front of their eyes. "It is beautiful."

"You will, Rika, you will," Attu said.

"How do you know?" Rika asked. "Look at this ice sheet. It's becoming smaller as we sit here. In another two or three days it will melt to nothing…" Rika's voice trailed off.

Attu shuddered to think of them all, this close to land, this close to reaching the end of their journey only to drown. "I'll think of something," he reassured Rika.

Moolnik moaned, and Rika sighed and went back into the shelter.

Attu paced the small distance back and forth across their ice chunk. He couldn't understand why they continued to travel south, as if a giant hand pushed them along. Other ice sheets and chunks, some of them rising high out of the water, some flat like theirs, were traveling south too. It felt like their ice sheet was moving in the water faster than a person would walk on land, but it was hard to tell.

Attu knew his parents and Meavu must be frantic for him, and also for Elder Nuanu, although some would've assumed she'd passed to the Between of Death by now. Attu wondered if Paven was just as worried about Rika, or if he somehow thought she deserved this for angering Banek. It was hard to know. Paven was a complicated man.

Attu turned as he reached the edge of the ice sheet and noticed how the rottenness of the ice seemed to be eating at the rest of the surface even more quickly now. Glancing down, Attu could see where the ice had melted leaving only half a footprint from one of his earlier walks to the edge.

We have to get off this ice before it's too late. But how?

Attu looked up and saw a large ice chunk floating between them and the shore. As he watched, Attu began to notice that once in a while large chunks were beginning to move in toward the shoreline. The water seemed to be pushing them closer as well. *Perhaps...*

"Attu!" Rika hollered as Moolnik came staggering out of the shelter. He was naked, his hands still bound, his feet now freed.

"You do not kill me, but you keep me prisoner?" Moolnik shouted at Attu. "Where are my clothes? Where are my weapons?"

"He jumped up as I was untying his bonds to roll him," Rika said. "I'm sorry."

"You're sorry?" Moolnik screamed. "I'll make you sorry you didn't kill me while I was Between," and he turned and raised his tied arms to strike Rika.

Attu reached Moolnik just as he threw himself at Rika, who dodged out of his way. Moolnik fell and began to writhe on the ground, having some sort of fit, as steam rose off his fevered body wherever the snowy surface of the ice came in touch with his burning skin. His eyes were wild, his cheeks sunk in from lack of water combined with fever.

Attu reached out to grab him, but Rika stopped him.

"Let him roll on the ice," Rika said. "It'll cool his body."

Rika curled her lips at Moolnik's naked form on the snow and stomped back into the shelter.

Attu dragged Moolnik into the shelter a short while later. He had passed out again.

"He does feel cooler," Attu said as he rolled Moolnik back onto the furs.

"Elder Nuanu is plenty warm enough without him, so keep him on that side of the shelter," Rika pointed to the spot remaining, as far away from Elder Nuanu as Moolnik could be yet still be under some cover.

Attu dragged Moolnik where Rika had pointed, carefully retying his legs. He covered the man's nakedness with a fur, leaving his upper body and legs bare to the cold to help with his fever.

"Rika?" A crackled voice whispered from the pile of furs.

"Elder Nuanu," Rika cried, and she dove for the old woman, unwrapping her arms and hands from the furs as Elder Nuanu looked up at her.

"I knew you'd be able to help me," Elder Nuanu said, but her mouth and lips were so dry, she could barely move them to speak.

"Here," Rika said and spooned some warmed water into Elder Nuanu's mouth. The old woman drank a few spoonfuls before motioning for Rika to hand her the bowl. Elder Nuanu took it in her trembling hands, and Rika helped her lift her head enough to drink. The old woman drank all the water, slowly, one sip at a time, wetting her cracked lips with the last few mouthfuls.

"I'll need to drink again, soon," she said, as she looked around the shelter, trying to focus on the Here and Now.

"Where are we?" Elder Nuanu asked. "This isn't my shelter. Help me sit up."

"Are you sure?" Rika asked, but as Elder Nuanu was struggling to sit up without her help, Rika put her hands behind the old healer's back and helped her into a sitting position.

"Well, look at that," Elder Nuanu said, noticing Moolnik, mostly naked, lying there tied hand and foot. "Moolnik, trussed up like a snow otter to be carried on a hunter's back. Now that's an interesting sight. I'm sure you have a very good explanation for it," and she paused, looking at both Rika and Attu, her eyes gleaming with new strength and mischief. "Although, as far as I'm concerned, Moolnik should've been tied up and thrown into the corner of the shelter a long time ago."

Elder Nuanu chuckled to herself, ending her laughter with a cough. "Now, tell me everything that's happened," she added. "I don't have much time before I go to the Between of the Spirits, this time for good."

"Elder Nuanu, don't say that," Rika protested.

Attu looked at Elder Nuanu, and for a moment, he thought he saw the man's face looking out at him again, flowing white hair, on either side of Elder Nuanu's face. Attu shuddered. *It was just a trick of the light in the shelter,* he told himself, *because Elder Nuanu's braids have come loose.* She settled herself back down on the furs.

"Tell me," Elder Nuanu repeated.

Rika told her everything that had taken place since Elder Nuanu had slipped into the Between, finishing with Moolnik rolling in the snow and Elder Nuanu waking up.

"Why didn't you kill him, Attu?" Elder Nuanu asked.

"I asked him not to," Rika answered for him. "I'll explain later."

"How long before the ice melts?" Elder Nuanu asked, looking at Attu, curiosity evident in her eyes at Rika's words.

"I think we have only another day, maybe two," Attu said.

"And your clans are behind you, you think?"

"Yes."

"And Moolnik is dying of the fever?" Elder Nuanu asked the question as she studied Moolnik. "Yes," she said, almost to herself, but loud enough for Rika and Attu to hear her. The old healer nodded her head. "He'll rage with another fever this very night," she said to Rika. "Nothing you can do will help him. He'll be dead before morning." Elder Nuanu coughed again.

"The Spirits of the Between are coming for my breath," she said. "My chest is fighting them."

Elder Nuanu looked to Rika. "Help me lay back, Rika," she said, "I need to talk to you. Alone."

Elder Nuanu looked at Attu.

"I need to speak with you as well, Elder Nuanu," Attu protested.

"Most important things first," Elder Nuanu said. Her voice suddenly sounded stronger, determined.

"But-"

"Trust me, mighty hunter Attu, leader of the clan this giant ice chunk is carrying you away from. There will be time." Elder Nuanu smiled at him and shooed him out with one arm. She coughed again.

Attu left the shelter.

"And no listening from behind the furs," Elder Nuanu added.

Rika giggled.

Women.

Attu walked to the other edge of the ice chunk and watched the trees as they passed by. Once, he thought he saw a large shape moving along the edge of a bare cliff. But it was too far away to be sure.

Chapter 27

Rika spoke with Elder Nuanu for a long time. When she finally came out of the shelter, she called to Attu, turning away from him before he could see her face clearly. She walked to the other end of the shrinking ice chunk, her arms folded tightly across her chest. As Attu entered the shelter, the sun was disappearing behind the open water and the Great Expanse that lay beyond it. Rika had lit the lamp, and the shelter was bright and warm.

"Come close, Attu," Elder Nuanu said. He sat down near her.

"Do you need anything?"

"No, Rika has taken care of all my needs, and I've slept a long time, Rika says, almost two days, so don't worry. I'm not too tired to speak with you now."

"You can see my thoughts," Attu admitted.

"Tell me what happened before I went to the Between of the edge of the Spirit world, for I was indeed almost gone Between forever," Elder Nuanu said.

Attu told her about the white-haired man's voice, how he seemed to speak first through Rika in the dream, then through Elder Nuanu. Elder Nuanu started when Attu told her about the man's blue eyes, but growing thoughtful, she nodded her head.

"This would be so," she said, "And now? What do you think about it all now?"

"The chasm was real, the ice bears were real, Rika calling to me from the moving ice was real," Attu said. "So, I must believe there'll be a rock formation like the old man showed me by speaking through Rika in the dream, and we need to be first through the pass, Rika and me."

Attu shook his head. "But how are we to get off this ice chunk before we all drown? Nothing else can happen if we die before we can get to the rock."

"Somehow you will, Attu. This much you must believe. Remember, you were told not to give up hope." Elder Nuanu touched his cheek. "Now, about the most important thing-"

"What? What is more important than getting off this ice sheet and finding the pass?" Attu heard his voice rising in agitation, but he couldn't stop it.

"Oh, Mighty Hunter, Attu," Elder Nuanu said. Her voice was as gentle as if he were a poolik and she were singing him to sleep. "You don't understand the most important part of the prophecy is that you do these things, 'with the one who will bear your sons and daughters.' Your woman."

"Rika," Attu whispered. His cheeks burned.

"Yes, my lovesick hunter who didn't wait for the spirits to make the way possible for him, but who declared himself too early and almost got killed for it." Elder Nuanu winked at him.

Attu looked down. *How embarrassing. Rika must have told Elder Nuanu about my foolishness.*

"Do you love her?" Elder Nuanu asked, breaking into Attu's thoughts.

"Yes," Attu admitted, "but she must think me the biggest of fools." He shrugged and looked away.

"No, she doesn't," Elder Nuanu said. "Rika has told me of her dreams as well, and that you honored her wishes, showing mercy to Moolnik. She has told me many things."

Attu looked at Elder Nuanu's face again, studying her expression. She seemed to be telling the truth. *Was it possible?*

Elder Nuanu continued, "Now, go to Rika and tell her, before we run out of time. We only have until the next sun."

"What? Will the ice sheet be melted by then?" Attu felt his heart begin to race. He couldn't tell if it was from Elder Nuanu's warning about how much time they had left, or because she'd told him to leave the shelter and tell Rika he wanted her for his woman. Right now, both seemed equally perilous…

"Just go, boy, just go!" Elder Nuanu laughed. She began coughing. Attu helped her to lie back on the furs. "I'll rest now," Elder Nuanu shooed him out. "Go."

Attu went.

I don't know what to do, what to say, Attu thought as he slowly walked over to where Rika was still standing, looking out over the water. *What if Rika tells me no? I'll die.*

No, another part of him, a more practical part, said. *You won't die. You'll just wish you could.*

Thanks, he told that part. *So much for the mighty hunter reaching in and finding his inner strength.*

Attu approached Rika, standing near the edge. Rather than watching the shoreline with its trees now turning dark as evening approached, she was facing west, watching the sunset over the open water. She looked beautiful in the light of the red sky. Attu knew what he wanted to say, but he simply could not say those words.

"Rika?"

Rika turned.

Attu held out his arms, holding them as if he had something very large and very weighty in them.

"I have returned from the hunt," he said.

"Your hands are empty, Mighty Hunter, Attu," Rika said. A hint of a smile was playing about her cheeks, and curiosity lit her eyes.

Good, Attu thought. *That's my Rika. I hope.*

"Look again, Rika, Healer of the Great Frozen Clan, my hands are not empty."

"What is in them, Attu?" Rika looked at him now, confused, hopeful.

"My heart."

Rika drew in a sharp breath. Her voice grew positively mischievous. "And yet you live, hunter without a heart in his body." She looked at Attu, tears and a smile both springing from her simultaneously.

"It is a mighty wonder."

Still Rika stood, her arms at her sides, looking at Attu. He saw compassion, and something else…

"Will you accept it?" Attu asked. "A bad hunter, who has no patience, did not wait beside the nuknuk hole, but threw his spear too soon. He almost lost all. He almost lost his own life. Then another would have surely provided for the woman he loves. Can you forgive this hunter's foolishness?"

"He loves?" Rika's voice was a mere whisper as she seemed to breathe in those words.

"He loves."

Abruptly, Rika bowed. "May the spirits be thanked for the offering of this heart, mighty hunter of the Nuvikuan-na," Rika said, slipping into her woman's role. She smiled.

Attu inclined his head to Rika and said, "Indeed may they be thanked, because they have brought us together when it seemed impossible, and our people are to be saved because of our union."

"What? I don't understand."

"I'll explain that part, later. But for now…" Attu smiled slightly, as he carefully pretended to hand over his heart into Rika's upturned palms.

"I will protect it with my life," Rika said, and then the ritual dropped away and Rika and Attu were holding each other.

I don't know how this can work, for neither of us has the permission of our families... Attu thought. He held Rika tighter, feeling how well her slight body snuggled against his.

But she'll be mine, now. Attu thought. *No one will take her from me.*

"Now, I must go prepare," Rika said, squirming out of Attu's grip.

"Prepare?" Attu said.

"Yes," Rika said. "Didn't Elder Nuanu tell you? She'll perform the ceremony of giving and taking as soon as the moon rises. It's a full moon tonight."

Attu felt his real heart start hammering in his chest.

"As elder of your clan, Elder Nuanu has the right to give you away to me. And I have the right to accept you because I saved your life," Rika looked away, suddenly shy. "I protected you from the spirits of fever and of the ice bear taking over your body by telling my father you needed the Remembering rituals. So, I actually saved your life twice."

Rika grinned up at Attu. "Elder Nuanu helped me to see that this is when I..." and she paused, her cheeks reddening. She turned her face away for a moment, exposing the bruise on her cheek.

Attu noticed it was beginning to turn the color of new hide. *No one will ever be allowed to hit you, again,* Attu swore to himself. Rika was looking at him again.

"That's when you..." Attu prompted. He reached out and took her hand in his.

Rika smiled at him.

Proud, fiery Rika, one minute so bold, the next so shy. Attu smiled his encouragement.

"That's when I..." Rika paused again, then rushed out with the rest, "...gave my heart to you."

Rika whirled away from Attu and flew back into the shelter.

Chapter 28

Elder Nuanu insisted on being helped out of the shelter onto the ice to perform the giving and taking ceremony. She sat on a pile of furs near the shelter, Rika and Attu standing before her holding hands and the full moon lighting the moving ice sheet as if it were daylight. All around them the water sparkled. *A beautiful setting for the joining,* Attu thought, *if we weren't trapped here with impending drowning on our minds.*

The ceremony was also punctuated by Moolnik's loud snoring. Elder Nuanu had insisted Rika give Moolnik an extra dose of sleeping potion.

"The last thing we need is for him to start thrashing around right in the middle of the ritual," Elder Nuanu said.

Attu and Rika stood as Elder Nuanu spoke the words over them both. They had to bend when she wrapped both Rika's hands together in a strip of hide, placing Attu's hands over Rika's, one on each side, wrapping them together. Attu's large hands enfolded Rika's completely. When he looked up, Rika was smiling at him, her heart in her eyes. Attu's heart lurched.

"This is to symbolize the protection Attu will give you, Rika, for the rest of your life," Elder Nuanu said.

Elder Nuanu untied them, and the hide strip was given to Rika.

"You will keep this safe, Rika, until one day, upon bearing a child, you will stand again, and your hands will be wrapped around the newborn's body, and your hands, Attu, will once again be wrapped over Rika's and your child. You will both promise to accept the responsibility for the new life the spirits have given into your care."

Elder Nuanu motioned for Attu to strip to the waist. He smiled as Rika suddenly looked shy again, even though she'd treated his back and seen him often without his parka and inner vest.

Since there was no fresh meat available to obtain blood, Rika smeared a wet paste of dried nuknuk from Attu's last kill on her hand and placed it over Attu's chest.

"You are now Rika's hunter until the spirits call you to the Between of death," Elder Nuanu said.

"I will bring you the game," Attu promised.

Rika scratched the spark stones over the nuknuk lamp Kinak had given them in his pack. The wick of the lamp lit with the ease of long practice.

Rika picked up the lit lamp, careful not to spill any of the oil.

"I will bring you the light," Rika promised, and Attu took the lamp from her.

"May each of your name spirits and the name spirits of all those who have gone before you in your clans, those who have followed the rituals and now inhabit the Between, guard and guide you both, until you join them in the Great Beyond. May you bear many sons and daughters, Rika, and may the spirits of the game animals find you a hunter worthy of the sacrifice of their bodies, Attu. May your lamp burn brightly and your shelter always be full of laughter."

Elder Nuanu attempted to lift the largest hide they had on the ice chunk, to wrap Rika and Attu in, but it was far too heavy for her.

"I cannot toss you," she grinned, "but this will work just as well."

Rika and Attu laughed as Elder Nuanu made them lie, each on their sides, facing each other, arms around each other, and roll themselves up in the hide, until only the tops of their faces showed enough to breathe.

"You must stay together so, the rest of the night," Elder Nuanu ordered with a grin before she slowly made her way back to the shelter and the still snoring Moolnik.

Attu and Rika lay, wrapped in the warmth of the furs, the moon above, the sparkling water all around, and for a short while forgot about anything else but this time, and the wonder of becoming one in the giving and the taking.

~ • ~

In the morning, Moolnik's fever was gone, and Elder Nuanu lay dying.

"The Moolnikuan spirit in him has tricked us yet again," Elder Nuanu said, as she glanced over toward where Moolnik slept peacefully. "It must have almost complete control of him now. If not, he would have died in the night as I predicted."

"So he is the embodiment of a Moolnikuan? Is that possible?" Attu asked.

"Perhaps his father naming him so cursed him in some way. I do not know. But it seems to have made Moolnik amazingly strong against the trystas. Do not worry. Once I am Between, I will be stronger than any Moolnikuan spirit. I will protect you."

"Oh, don't say that, Elder Nuanu. You can still recover," Rika said.

"It's all right, child."

Rika continued to fuss over the old woman, trying to convince her to take this potion or to let Rika put on a poultice, to draw out the evil spirits trying to take Elder Nuanu's breath.

"I'm ready to go, to join the spirits, to see my man Tovut again, now a star I can visit, for I'll be free in the spirit world of Between." Elder Nuanu smiled and patted Rika's tear-streaked face.

"Take this amulet," Elder Nuanu said, "and when the clans try to shame you for being alone on the ice with Attu without being joined, you show this to any of the older women and you tell them this," and Elder Nuanu whispered a few words to Rika.

Rika's eyes widened. "Why?"

"Because only a woman who has been joined to a man is ever told these words," Elder Nuanu said. "It'll be proof you are telling the truth and the joining ceremony was performed by me."

"I understand."

"Thank you," Attu said from where he was sitting on one of the packs.

Elder Nuanu studied Moolnik's sleeping form again. "He should have died in the water, should have died of the fever, should have died when the revenging trystas came after him for murdering Banek."

Elder Nuanu looked at Attu. "What are you going to do about this Moolnikuan, if he continues to recover?"

"I don't know."

"He needs to be pushed off this ice into the water without a rope to climb back up on."

"I know," Attu said. "But, I can't seem to-"

"You will do… what… you can," Elder Nuanu said, her voice growing weaker and punctuated with wheezing to catch her breath.

"Yes, I will," Attu promised.

"And I… will… also…" Elder Nuanu said. Her voice was now a mere whisper. "I will be protecting you both, remember that."

Elder Nuanu shuddered, then grew still. Attu felt her spirit leave her frail body, slipping out into the Between. The hairs on his arms stood up as an invisible power enveloped them.

Rika looked at him, wonder in her eyes. "Surely, Elder Nuanu is much stronger in death than she was in life, even as the embodiment of Shuantuan."

A gust of warm air blew through the shelter, warm and full of the spicy smell of the pine trees along the shoreline. It was as if the air itself was full of life, and the power Attu and Rika were feeling drifted out of the shelter on the fragrant air. Elder Nuanu was gone.

"Thank you, Elder Nuanu, for your promise of protection," Rika said. "I know your spirit will be watchful of us as we continue our journey. We are honored."

Tears streamed down Rika's face as she knelt to prepare Elder Nuanu's body.

Attu stepped outside the shelter. He wiped away his own tears as he stood looking off into the distance again, out across the water. More and more ice sheets and tall chunks were floating past now, many of them closer to the shoreline, some even bumping it as they floated or became stuck against jagged rocks or other ice along the land.

A warm breeze blew across their ice sheet from the land beyond. *We don't have much time,* Attu thought. The ice sheet they were on was now less than half the size it had been. They had another day, maybe, before enough would melt so their weight as they moved on it would make it so unstable it would flip.

Attu continued to watch the moving ice, like stepping stones across the water to the land. He knew they couldn't just step from one ice piece to another, even if they could reach them. If anyone moved too close to the edge, the entire ice sheet dipped down on that side. It was no longer large enough to be stable near the edges. If he tried to help Rika from one to another, surely one or the other would fall into the water.

Attu cringed as he remembered Moolnik and Banek, their panic and their violence, each trying to save himself from the icy water's depth.

Still, there had to be something Attu could do, some way to use the ice chunks floating past them…

Why couldn't I spear ice chunks and use them to drag us closer to shore? Attu thought. He chuckled to think of hunting ice sheets, stalking them and stabbing them like nuknuks. *Biggest prey I've ever gone after,* he thought. *Most dangerous, too,* he realized, for their lives hung in the balance. *But I've got to try.*

Attu readied his spear by tying all the rope he could find to its shaft, in the manner of the hunt, so when he threw the spear, it would fly, unrolling the rope as it went, one end tied securely to the spear, the other in his hands.

Attu sensed it would be difficult and maybe even dangerous to pull their ice chunk against the flow of the water, and he feared the spear wouldn't hold well because of its point. He could use the weight of the point to his advantage, however. He needed a large enough ice chunk, close enough for an easy throw, and a bit further down the shoreline than they were.

There were so many ice chunks in the water; it didn't take long to spot one to try.

Attu lofted the spear in a high arc towards the ice chunk. There was a possibility it would stick and he wouldn't be able to pull their chunk over to it. Attu knew he could lose his spear by such an attempt.

But what good is a spear to a drowning person? He reasoned, and called upon the spirits to make his weapon fly true. It did. Attu's spear sank straight down into the middle of the ice chunk he had been aiming for. Attu let out a whoop of satisfaction.

"What are you doing?" Rika asked as she bolted out of the shelter at the sound of his cry.

"Spearing ice chunks," Attu said with a grin.

"What?" Rika asked. Looking toward shore at all the chunks of floating ice now between them and the land, Rika nodded. "It might work."

Attu began to pull, taking up the slack in the rope. As it tightened, he pulled slower, feeling the line for unusual movement as he would when hunting, watching his spear point to make sure it was holding.

"Are we getting closer, or is it coming toward us?"

"I think a bit of both." Rika looked north and south. "If those ice chunks are moving with us, we are definitely getting closer to land, because they're now further out."

"That makes sense. We move toward it, and it moves toward us." Attu continued pulling. "Is Elder Nuanu's body-"

"Yes." Rika interrupted him, "it's ready for burial. But it's too soon. I don't want to do it just-"

"I know. Just keep Moolnik asleep with the potion for now. We have to try to get as close to shore as we can, while the ice chunks are here. Who knows when they might stop floating by? See how many there-"

A sudden shuddering passed through the ice, throwing both Rika and Attu down onto its surface.

"What was that?" Attu asked, quickly jumping up. He hadn't let go of the rope. "I didn't do anything."

"That ice chunk hit us," Rika said, pointing to a small one, now breaking up to the left of them, behind the shelter. A piece of their own ice fell into the water as they watched.

Rika and Attu looked at each other. The moving ice that might save them could also kill them. They were surrounded by pieces, some moving faster, some slower.

Looking to the north, Attu saw two enormous ice sheets in the distance, coming toward them. If one of these huge masses hit theirs, they would be the ones breaking into bits. Attu had to work fast.

"Take down the shelter, ready the packs and pile everything in the center of the ice," Attu said.

Rika nodded and turned back toward the shelter.

Attu pulled the ice piece closer and closer to theirs. When it was still several spear lengths away, he stopped pulling and noticed the two continued to move toward each other for a while, even without him pulling. Attu marveled at what it must mean, this floating, and for a moment he thought of the skin boats Elder Nuanu had spoken of.

How wonderful it would be to be able to move among the ice sheets, skimming across the water, dry, knowing I could go back to shore whenever I wanted to. That would indeed be like magic, Attu decided.

But he needed to get his spear back. Attu sent a silent plea to the spirits before he snapped the rope, a quick motion, designed to slice the spear out of the ice by its sharp point. It worked.

Attu sent up another shout. Behind him, Rika laughed. For a moment it almost seemed like it should be, the day after their joining, all celebration. But Attu had many more ice targets to spear if they were going to have a real reason to celebrate.

Chapter 29

Attu continued to spear ice and by mid-sun, both he and Rika could see they'd made over half the distance to land.

"I've never felt such deep sadness and such hope at the same time," Rika said as she stood next to Attu, who was waiting for the next ice piece to come within reach.

"Me too," Attu said. "Elder Nuanu brought me into our old world. I wanted her to see this new one with us. She would have loved that opportunity."

They both stood in silence for a while as Attu continued to watch for the next ice chunk to spear.

"And yet…" Attu hesitated. He wasn't sure Rika would understand him, but he wanted her to know how he felt, anyway.

"She's still here with us," Rika said, finishing Attu's thought. She smiled up at Attu. "That's what you were going to say, isn't it?"

"Yes. You feel her, too?"

Rika nodded, her face lighting up with a smile that turned to a frown as Moolnik moaned. She walked back to check on him.

Attu continued watching for an ice chunk to spear. "Got it!" he called out as his spear landed in the center of the ice he was aiming for. He began hauling in the rope.

"You son of a trysta and an ice bear!" Rika swore, a few moments later.

Attu spun around, almost dropping the rope he was holding. "What's wrong?"

"Moolnik is feverish again. He was flailing around just now, and he knocked the sleeping potion out of my hands. It spilled in the snow." Rika looked at the dark stain spreading across the ice in front of her.

Attu's stomach fell. "Is that all you had?"

"Yes. I'm sorry." Rika brushed away fresh tears of frustration. "Help me!" she cried as Moolnik began thrashing again.

"I can't let go of the rope!"

Moolnik rolled onto his back and suddenly stopped thrashing and started snoring loudly instead, punctuated with nasal grunts. Attu started laughing at the ridiculousness of their situation with Moolnik, but one look at Rika stopped him. She'd sat down next to Moolnik again, and her face was a mask as she stared off at some distant horizon only she could see. Her tears sparkled as they fell.

"Come here," Attu called to her. "Please?"

Rika looked up when he called. Attu could see she was trying to come back to him, trying to stop crying.

"Please?" Attu asked again, more softly this time.

Rika sighed, and slowly rising, she walked to stand beside Attu.

Attu bunched the rope he was reeling in into one hand and reached up with the other to wipe the tears off her face.

At his touch, Rika flinched away.

"It's all right to cry, Rika," Attu said. He didn't try to touch her again.

"I'm sorry." Rika scrubbed at her own face. "It's my fault the potion got spilled. What will we do now?"

"Do you have anything else you can give Moolnik to keep him in the Between of dreaming?"

"I have one other potion, but it's dangerous."

"How?"

"It's tricky to give the right amount. Just the slightest bit too much and it can make a person's spirit flee out of his body."

"Well," Attu said, his voice as gentle as he could make it. "I think it's better than the alternative for Moolnik, don't you?"

Rika looked at him. He saw her fear. He thought about how when he'd first met Rika, she had sat, the hair across her face, as if trying to hide herself from others. He knew Banek had struck her and Paven had apparently been satisfied with Rika being given to such a harsh man. Meavu had warned Attu about Paven not respecting women. Paven had hinted he might be ruthless to acquire one, even Attu's own mother if he'd chosen to fight Ubantu for her. It made sense that Paven had also been cruel to Rika, his own daughter.

Was Rika scared of him because he was a man? Attu needed to let her see he wouldn't hurt her, that theirs was an equal partnership. He believed in the true way of the Nuvikuan-na, not the way some hunters behaved. But he knew his words alone wouldn't calm her fear. He would have to earn her trust.

What should I do?

What you can... Attu suddenly heard Elder Nuanu's voice as if she were next to him, whispering in his ear on the breeze. It startled him so much that he jumped, and looked at Elder Nuanu's body, checking to make sure she truly was dead.

Attu looked back to see Rika studying him.

"I trust you to give Moolnik just what you need to keep him asleep, no more."

Rika exhaled, and Attu realized she must have been afraid he would tell her to kill Moolnik with the potion.

"I would never ask you to go against what the spirits in your dreams have told you to do," Attu said.

Rika studied him. The fear was fading from her eyes. She turned and walked to her pack, pulling out her bag of potions. She began rummaging through them.

Attu continued to haul on the rope. His back and legs were aching, but he had to get them as close to shore as he could while they still had so many ice chunks floating by.

Twice more that sun, ice hit them as they traveled south. Once, Attu almost fell into the water, and after that he tried to stand further back from the edge. It made the pulling harder, but the ice upon which they floated was growing increasingly unstable and by late in the day, they were standing on ice only about the size of a large gathering snow house. Attu didn't think they'd make it through the night without either being broken up by another ice chunk or by simply melting. And they still had half the distance to go. Each time he threw the spear, they only gained a few spear lengths toward the shoreline, and sometimes it seemed the water flowing along pulled them back out almost as fast as he could pull them in. They could see the land more clearly now, though; if a person had been standing on the shoreline, Attu thought he might have been able to tell who it was, but of course there was no one but them as far as they could see, and the icy water still held them trapped.

Attu began to take chances, throwing the spear further, dragging them toward the ice chunks faster, causing theirs to rock. Rika stood by him, pulling when she could, then going back to check on Moolnik, who continued to moan and thrash occasionally, although Rika said his fever had subsided.

Late in the day, they were approaching a large peninsula, not high like the one he had jumped off to reach Rika, but flat, curving out like a bent finger far into the water. Attu scanned the water for another ice piece to spear. Judging the distance they had to go and the speed they were traveling along the shore, it looked like they wouldn't be able to reach the peninsula, but would float by it. Attu ignored the pain in his arm and shoulder muscles as he raised the spear and took aim at the next available floating ice. He had to try to get them to that peninsula.

Rika screamed.

Attu whirled around, spear in hand, to see the largest animal of the Nuvikuan-na rising out of the water behind them.

Attu ran to Rika, and she clung to him as the huge beast continued to rise up, up, and up out of the water, its body seeming to have no end. Attu saw its hide was sleek, a grey color not unlike some older nuknuks, but that was where the resemblance ended. This animal was like the landmass that had upended, sweeping away the ice chunks, and it was so close it blocked out the whole western sky. The late afternoon sun behind it made the huge animal seem to glow.

A whale fish!

Once the whale fish had surfaced, it seemed to rest, allowing the water's movement to carry it along like a huge ice sheet. It was moving a bit faster than they were. *Will it hit us with its side as it floats by, crushing us, ice and all?*

Drawing alongside them, the animal paused. One snow house-sized eye looked at them. Attu saw intelligence in its eye, and suddenly he was no longer afraid. This animal was the most amazing thing he'd ever seen, even more amazing than a land with trees or water where there should have been the Great Frozen.

Attu loosened his grip on Rika and stood, stepping closer to the animal on the ice.

"No," Rika whispered.

"It's all right," Attu said. He bowed to the whale fish and spoke. "Mightiest of all hunters, ruler in the Here and Now of Attuanin's Kingdom and of the whole world of water below, I am Attu, poor hunter of the above ice, and I give you honor."

Attu struck his spear shaft across his chest three times. "I have always thought of you as ruler only in the Between. Please accept my apology. I was ignorant." Attu dropped his head, as one shamed.

The whale fish seemed to dip his massive head as well before plunging back into the water. Attu had a moment of wonder as the sleek body disappeared into the deep before he saw the huge flippered tail above him.

"Rika!" Attu warned, and fell to the ice.

He heard Rika's answering yell as the whale fish's tail flippers hit the water. It missed the ice chunk, but sent them careening through the water on a wave at least three spear lengths in height. The salt water of the Great Deep sprayed over their heads, and they were pushed toward the shore at a tremendous rate.

Attu tried to stand up, but the swirling ice chunk was rocking back and forth in the water. He fell down and stayed there, afraid he might be thrown off the ice if he didn't. As they continued to speed toward shore, Attu realized if they didn't break up, the wave made by the whale fish's tail might carry them all the way to the peninsula.

"Rika, are you all right?" Attu hollered.

Nothing.

"Rika!" Attu tried to stand up again, but fell. He spun in circles on his stomach, searching, but he couldn't see Rika anywhere on the ice.

Oh no, Attu thought. *Attuanin, is this how you treat your namesake, by hitting him with a whale fish and drowning his woman?*

"Rika," Attu yelled again, this time out over the water back the way they had come. *She can't have fallen off...*

Then he heard something, a noise coming from behind Elder Nuanu's body.

"Rika?" Attu cried, scrambling toward the sound on all fours as the ice continued to spin toward shore.

"I'm…" she said, but her voice cut off.

"Hang on!" Attu said. "I'm coming." He saw Rika sitting up near Elder Nuanu's body, and relief poured through him at the sight of her. He began crawling even faster toward her, but a sudden jolt dropped him flat again, and he looked to his left to see them ricocheting off another ice chunk. An arm's length of ice fell off the side. *If we get hit again,* Attu thought, it might be the end…

Their ice slowed, and with a few back and forth movements and some slight tipping, it was once again riding on the smoother water.

"Attu," Rika said.

Attu scrambled to his feet again and looked to where Rika was sitting, just in front of him.

"Rika, are you all…" Attu began.

"She will be fine, as long as you do exactly what I tell you to do."

Moolnik was kneeling behind Rika, half-hidden in some furs and crouching low. One arm was around Rika's neck, Banek's knife at her throat.

"Moolnik!" Attu yelled. "What are you doing? That's Rika. She's been taking care of you ever since you got out of the water."

"Drugging me, you mean," Moolnik snarled. "But I've been more in the Here and Now than she thought. I've tricked you all into thinking I was still Between, when I have seen you throwing your spear and dragging us to land. I will hold her here, so she can't give me any more of her foul potions, and you're going to get us the rest of the way."

Attu looked past Moolnik. They WERE within a spear's throw of the peninsula. Ahead of them lay a large icy shoreline. If Attu could spear it, he could pull them to land.

Attu took in a deep breath, trying to calm himself. This was their chance. But he needed to know what Moolnik's plan was, so he could think of some way to get Rika away from him before he hurt her.

"Then what, Moolnik?" Attu asked. "We just go our separate ways, like nothing happened? I give you some supplies, and Rika and I head south while you go wherever it is you want to go?"

"You don't get it, do you, you fool?" Moolnik spat off to the side. A look of smug satisfaction crossed Moolnik's sunken face. "You pull us to land and I will let you live. I take the supplies and the woman. That's the way it's going to be."

Rika started to struggle at Moolnik's words, but Moolnik twisted her arm behind her back with his free one until she screamed.

"Stop that!" Attu yelled. *Why didn't I kill him earlier? I know what kind of man he is. Why did I allow Rika to convince me to show mercy?*

"Get us off this spirit forsaken hunk of rotting ice right now, or I'll hurt her again." Moolnik smiled. He looked like he hoped Attu would continue to protest, just so he could make Rika scream again.

Elder Nuanu was right. Even Moolnik was never this cruel before. The Moolnikuan spirit must be controlling him.

Attu looked at Rika. Her face was pale, her eyes hard. He saw that glint of fire in their golden depths. *She is not beaten, not yet.*

"I'll do what I can," Attu said, and hoped the tone of his voice would convey his message to Rika. He wouldn't let Moolnik take her, would not let him live to see another sun rise. But first, he had to get them off the water onto solid ground.

Attu turned and picked up his spear. He'd have impaled Moolnik with it in a second, if Moolnik wasn't holding Rika's back up against his chest, using her as a shield.

Coward.

Attu gathered up the rope in readiness and hurled the spear to the closest point of the ice-covered land. It stuck firmly. He began pulling what little remained of their ice sheet to shore.

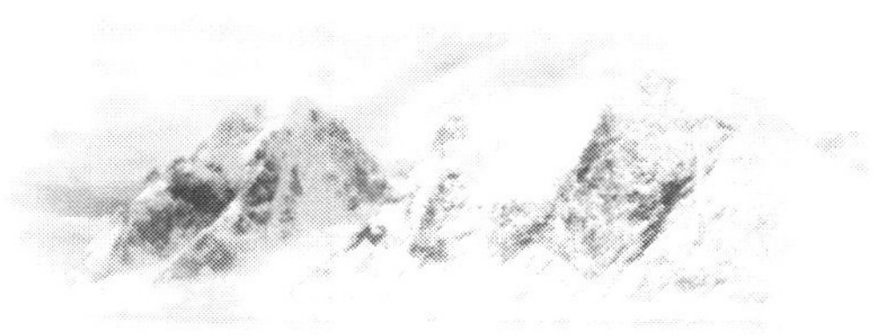

Chapter 30

Attu was exhausted from the day's throws and pulls across the ice, but his fury at Moolnik and his fear for Rika fueled his muscles to pull them all toward the shoreline, even though it was harder this time with the land being stationary. Something tore deep in his back muscles as Attu pulled, and he bit his lip to keep from crying out from the pain. He kept on pulling, the taste of blood in his mouth.

The whale fish had probably saved their lives, pushing them almost to shore, past where any other ice chunks had been floating, but all Attu could think about now was Rika, with Moolnik holding Banek's knife at her throat.

Attu pulled as more pieces fell away. He glanced back to see Moolnik watching him as he dragged Rika around in front of himself, using a free hand to pull on his old fur leggings and inner vest and gathering up items to carry off the ice. Once he was ready, Moolnik moved with Rika toward Elder Nuanu's body, instructing her to push it off to the side, away from the rest of the supplies.

Rika was silent the whole time she worked, doing what Moolnik told her to do, not even protesting when Moolnik made her unwrap the large fur from around Elder Nuanu's body, leaving her laying on the ice just in her own clothes, marked with the signs of the dead Rika had painted on her face.

If I pull hard enough at the end so the ice chunk slams into the shore ice, it will knock Moolnik off his feet. That will give me a chance to get the knife away from him. My spear will still be stuck in the shore ice, so I'll have to go after Moolnik with just my own knife.

However, this proved impossible. The ice underneath them started scraping the ice under the water at the tip of the peninsula, preventing Attu from pulling them any closer. Instead, they were going to have to jump across more than a spear length of water to reach the shore.

Attu gathered up the rope, but left the spear in the shore ice, tethering them to the land. The water was already tugging at them, urging their ice chunk around the peninsula and back out into open water. Attu couldn't risk taking the spear out. The water was deep here, and if they drifted only a few more feet away from shore they would pass the peninsula. Without more ice chunks to throw to, the distance would become as impossible to cross as what they had just traveled, just as deadly. Moolnik pulled Rika over to where Attu stood, Banek's knife stuck against her back. She was struggling to carry the three loaded packs.

"Hold the rope," he ordered Rika.

Rika let the packs fall and took the rope from Attu, her eyes downcast.

"Throw the packs and supplies across first," he told Attu.

Attu grabbed two of the three packs and walked to the edge of the ice sheet. As he did, the ice chunk sank towards the water. With a cry, Attu leaped back, and the ice bobbed the other way.

"You fool, the ice bottom is almost melted," Moolnik said. "Be more careful."

Attu threw the packs from well back on the ice, one at a time. His movement as he hurled them to shore caused their ice to bob again, but not as badly.

How are we ever going to jump off? Attu thought.

He tried to catch Rika's eye, to tell her to be ready, to watch for the one chance, maybe when the ice moved again when someone jumped, something that might give her a chance to escape Moolnik, but Rika was busy looking off into the distance, as if deep in thought.

"The woman next," Moolnik said. "Throw her over, too, but give me your knife first."

So that was it, Attu thought. *Moolnik will jump after Rika, taking the rope with him. When he jumps the ice will move far enough out from the shore to strand me, or if I jump in and struggle to shore, he'll be waiting there, knife in hand, to kill me.*

Reluctantly, Attu handed over his knife. Moolnik stuck it in the belt of his leggings. Attu wouldn't have attacked Moolnik until Rika was safely on land, but Moolnik didn't know that. To him, the woman was a prize, nothing more. If their roles were reversed, Moolnik wouldn't let endangering Rika stop him from attacking Attu.

Moolnik grabbed the rope from Rika and she lost her footing, falling hard against him. Moolnik swore and shoved her in Attu's direction. She fell into Attu, and they both landed on the ice, almost sliding off as it tilted under their combined weight.

Attu grabbed the rope that was stretched between the shore and the land with one hand, and Rika with the other, pulling them back from the edge just before they both tumbled into the water.

Moolnik laughed.

Rika got her feet back under her and stood up again. She straightened her parka, then without warning, Rika wrapped her arms around Attu and kissed him, hard. He stared at her wide-eyed as she pulled away.

"When I land, I'm going to scream," she quickly whispered. "Don't look to see if I'm safe, Attu. Attack. That's your chance."

Rika turned, and before Attu could help her, she took three quick steps toward the edge and leaped. Her lighter frame hardly tipped the ice at all as she flew over the gap towards shore. Attu forced his eyes off Rika's jump and concentrated on Moolnik instead, watching for his chance to attack.

A look of wonder changing quickly to desire crossed Moolnik's face as Rika soared across the open water to the shoreline on the other side. Attu had never hated him more. He heard Rika land behind him and fall.

"My leg, my leg, I broke my leg," Rika screamed.

Moolnik took a step forward, his eyes still locked on Rika.

Attu was on Moolnik in a heartbeat, knocking Banek's knife out of the older man's hand before Moolnik even saw him coming. The knife skittered across the ice, coming to rest against Elder Nuanu's body.

Moolnik struck Attu in the face with his forehead. Attu fell back, blood flowing from his nose, his head spinning. Moolnik reached for Attu's knife, the one he had wedged in his belt, but his hand came away empty.

"You!" Moolnik roared at Rika as he realized she had taken Attu's knife from him when she'd fallen against Moolnik, just before she kissed Attu and jumped. "You will pay with a beating for that," he yelled as he turned and launched himself toward Elder Nuanu's body and Banek's knife.

Where was Moolnik's own knife?

Attu watched as Moolnik grabbed for the knife. The ice tilted down and Attu thought Elder Nuanu's body would slide off into the water, taking the knife with it, but her body remained motionless. *How could it be holding fast on the ice?*

Moolnik grabbed the knife laying against Elder Nuanu's body and leaped up, scrambling uphill against the ice tilt, back to the center.

A grin lit up Moolnik's sunken cheeks and wild eyes as he circled Attu again. Moolnik slashed out, missed, and slashed again, his knife nicking Attu's parka sleeve.

Moolnik continued circling, at first slowly but increasing his speed as Attu dodged strike after strike. He seemed unnaturally strong for someone who'd been fighting a fever and had been drugged. The ice began to tilt, first towards the shoreline, then away, as the two continued their macabre strike and dodge dance.

Attu leaped aside again, and water washed up over the ice chunk behind Moolnik and over Elder Nuanu's body. No one was holding the rope, and it uncoiled as the ice chunk drifted out, their movements drenching its surface.

Attu dodged again and fell on the now water-coated ice as Moolnik lunged for him. Attu rolled away, perilously close to the edge now. He scrambled furiously to get back to the center of the ice, his miks wet and stiffening.

"Attu!" Rika screamed, and Attu heard, rather than saw, his knife hit the ice beside him. He grabbed for it, but his icy mik was too stiff and he couldn't close his hand on it. Instead, his mik pushed it forward, past Moolnik and toward where the body of Elder Nuanu still lay.

Attu couldn't believe the old woman's body hadn't rolled off the ice yet, as much as it had been tipping and swaying, but there it was, and Attu's knife, just like Banek's had before, lay wedged in front of it.

"Oh, no you don't!" Moolnik yelled and turned to leap for the knife.

But Elder Nuanu's body HAD slid while they were fighting. It was now dangerously close to the edge. Moolnik, thinking to grab the knife as he had the other one, pushed himself off in the direction of the knife and body just as he had before. But Moolnik slid on the slick surface into Elder Nuanu, and her body slipped off the ice as easily as if it had been waiting for this moment: Moolnik was reaching for the knife, then he was sliding with the body, and then both disappeared over the edge and into the icy water.

Attu saw his chance. The ice chunk was still elevated on this side from Moolnik and Elder Nuanu's body weighing it down on the other side. Attu slid, fell, got up, and fell again, scrambling up to the apex of the ice. Just as he reached the edge, still elevated at least half a spear length in the air, Attu leaped and landed on the shore ice, next to Rika. He grabbed the rope, now dangling loose in the water, and reeled it in as fast as he could, afraid Moolnik might somehow be able to get to it and pull himself ashore. The ice crashed down again – the water was still deep close to the shore – and broke into pieces. As Attu and Rika watched, the ruins of their ice sheet began drifting back into the even deeper water.

"Where's Moolnik?" Attu asked searching the water in front of him, spear in hand.

"I saw his head come up out of the water, and then one of the ice chunks crashed down on him. That one," Rika pointed to one of the larger pieces, now drifting out from the shore.

Attu thought he saw movement behind it, but as he watched, a snow otter chirruped in agitation and swam away. It dove into the water, out of sight. Had that movement he'd seen been Moolnik, or the snow otter? Could Moolnik be hiding in the water, behind the ice chunk?

If Moolnik was alive, wouldn't he be trying to get to shore?

"If the ice chunk knocked him out, would he float or sink?"

"Elder Nuanu's body sank," Rika said. "I guess Moolnik would, too."

Attu and Rika stood on the shoreline until it was almost dark, watching and waiting. The ice pieces continued to float away to the south, and the water grew unusually calm as the sun set and the wind died down, but there was no further sign of Moolnik.

"He must have drowned," Rika said. She shivered.

"We need to set up camp before dark," Attu said.

They turned and walked up the peninsula toward the main shoreline.

Chapter 31

Rika looked toward the line of trees where the peninsula met the land. It was dark in the gloom of evening.

"Let's stay here," Rika said, her voice small. The peninsula was rocky, but from where they stood, Attu and Rika could see out over the water on both sides of the land and it would be difficult for someone, or something, to sneak up on them. They moved back a bit from the shore and set up the shelter next to the largest rock, out of the wind, which had picked up again. Once in the shelter, they didn't even need the oil light for warmth. Attu left the flap open, gazing out over the water where Moolnik had fallen in. Just in case. He still couldn't believe Moolnik had drowned.

Rika took the last of the dried meat and divided it between them. They ate silently. Neither seemed to want to talk.

"I'll have to hunt tomorrow," Attu said after the silence began to wear on him. "For what, I don't know."

"If you kill it, we'll eat it," Rika said. She yawned.

Attu patted the hide beside him, and Rika snuggled up to him. She fell asleep after a few more yawns.

But Attu lay awake far into the night, haunted by the sight of Moolnik and Elder Nuanu's body disappearing over the edge of the ice into the water. The rocky beach was hard underneath his furs, and even in the shelter, Attu felt vulnerable. They were off the floating ice and alive, but he was anxious again. He didn't know this new world, didn't know its dangers or how to protect himself or

Rika, and he knew he'd have to learn fast. They were out of food now and almost out of fresh water.

When he finally slept, Attu dreamed of the white-haired, blue-eyed man who had spoken through the body of Rika, the wheel on the rock wall, and the spearhead shaped rock they needed to find. As he slept, the images jumbled together with the sound of trees moving in the wind, warning him of danger. But no matter how hard he listened to their whispering in his dreams, he couldn't tell what they were saying.

~ • ~

"We should get moving, I suppose," Attu said the next morning. He felt stiff and still tired. It'd been days since he'd been able to sleep free from thoughts of imminent death or impending danger.

Attu studied Rika. Dark circles marred her cheeks.

She looked up to see him staring at her and tried to smile. It didn't reach her eyes. "Yes," she said. "Let's go."

"We should be curious about what's in there, what it's like, don't you think?" Rika asked as she studied the gloom of the pine forest. She looked anything but curious.

Attu took her hand, and they walked slowly to the edge of the trees. Rika put her hand out first, touching the long greenness that grew from the tree arms in clusters.

"Ouch," she said as one of the needle-like pieces poked her.

"They're sharp at the ends," Attu agreed, running his fingers along the edges.

"The smell is strong," Rika said, touching her hand to her nose. "It's on me, just from the contact. I don't know if I like the smell or not. I can almost taste it, strong and sharp."

Attu studied the ground in front of him. It was brown and covered with dead tree arms and dead needle pieces. "It's so full somehow, almost like a crowded clan tent, so many trees, so close together. It makes me feel trapped." Attu shook his head. It was all so strange; it didn't seem real.

"Did you hear that?" Rika said as a shrill call, almost like a whistle, but not quite human, came from deep within the trees. "What was that?"

"Your guess is as good as mine," Attu replied. He stepped away from the pines. "For now, let's stay close to shore."

"All right," Rika agreed. She looked relieved.

After glancing at the forbidding trees once more, they turned and walked back to grab their packs. Rika picked her pack up, then began looking around the gravel surrounding her.

"What is it?" Attu asked as he saw her searching.

"I had two small knives slid into my pack where I could reach them if I needed them quickly. One's missing."

"Did it fall out when I threw the packs from the ice chunk to land?" Attu asked.

"No. I was sure I saw it afterward. It was there…" Rika slid her hand along the two small pockets she had sewn into the side of her pack. One held a bone ullik knife. The other was empty.

Attu and Rika scoured the camp, and Attu walked back to the area where he'd thrown the packs, but they found nothing.

"I lost my own knife in the fight when Moolnik fell…" Attu didn't finish. He caught the look on Rika's face and added, "It's a good thing Suka had an extra in the pack he gave me."

"I guess I must have been mistaken, with everything that happened and all," Rika concluded. "I was pretty upset." She wiped her hand across her face. "Let's go."

They gathered up their packs again and walked south. Air as warm as the inside of a shelter flowed down from the forest, and soon their miks and parkas joined the other items in their packs. Both of them were sweating.

They walked a long time in silence, small rocks crunching under their feet, water on their right side, forest on their left, as they traveled the sometimes narrow, sometimes wide and curving gravel beach in between.

Ahead, the rocks gave way to a long patch of yellow in the early morning light.

Another one of Elder Tovut's stories coming true, Attu thought. Attu stopped and looked at the strange ground before he took a step into it. His foot sank down to his ankle.

"Watch out!" he yelled and fell back, causing Rika to fall as well, landing on her backside and scraping her bare hands on the sharp rocks behind her as she tried to catch herself.

"What did you do that for?" Rika asked, frowning and wiping her injured hands on her fur pants as she stood up.

"It's not solid," Attu said. He grabbed his spear and began testing the ground ahead, pushing his spear butt into the yellow granules that flowed away from it as he pushed.

"What is it?" Rika said, fascinated. She knelt and picked up some of the yellow material, and it slipped through her fingers, flowing like water. "I think this is sand, like Elder Nuanu told me about."

"But they didn't say anything about it being like rotted ice," Attu grumbled.

"Look," Rika said. She scraped away the sand in front of her, revealing a harder surface of more sand below it.

"I think it's just flowing on top, but gets harder underneath. It has to be rock further down, if you dig deep enough, don't you think?"

"I don't know."

Attu had a sudden thought of being caught in this sand, pulled down, drowning in the yellowness of it, having it pour like scratching water into his eyes, his mouth… he shuddered.

"I think it's fine to walk on, just loose on top," Rika decided and took a few quick steps out onto the sand before Attu could stop her.

"No!" Attu protested, but Rika was now jumping up and down in the sand.

"See, it's fine," she said, "except it's getting into my foot miks."

Rika plopped down in the sand and pulled off her foot miks and unwrapped her fur foot linings. As she stood up, Attu saw the much paler skin of her feet and ankles sticking out below her fur pants. Sand squished between Rika's toes, and she giggled.

She is crazy, Attu thought, *and braver than I am.*

"Try it," Rika said.

Attu took a step, then another. The sand felt solid enough under him, down just a spear point length or so.

"Take your miks off," Rika said as she moved around him. "It's easier to walk without them."

Attu took off his own miks and foot wraps, marveling at how warm the sand felt and laughing at his own pale feet. They were sensitive to the sand slipping through his toes, and he tried not to laugh at the feel of it.

"See?" Rika asked.

"Feels good."

Tying their foot miks together with their foot wrappings, Rika and Attu added them to their packs and walked across the sandy beach.

Rika kept sprinting ahead, *almost like Meavu,* Attu thought. Attu's heart clenched at the thought of his little sister and his parents. *They must be devastated, thinking we are dead. They'll be traveling south, too. Once we go through the pass, we'll go back for them. They'll be overjoyed to see us still alive.*

Rika seemed to grow tired of the sand after a while and came to walk beside Attu. She was sweating, her hair damp around her face, curling tighter wherever it was wet.

"Let's rest a bit," Attu said.

Rika plopped down on her pack. "I'm thirsty."

Attu grabbed the last water pouch from under his parka and handed it to Rika. "We'll have to melt more snow when we make camp tonight, and the farther south we've traveled the less snow there has been." He looked around. The only snow he saw nearby was a few dirty clumps in the shadows of the pines. The floating ice chunks were mostly fresh water, but the only ones he'd seen all day were far from shore. *What will we do for water once the rest of the snow melts?*

"It's warm," Rika remarked about the water. "Almost as warm as our bodies."

She took another drink and passed the water pouch to Attu. He gulped a few mouthfuls and wished the water were colder; he was so hot. "I've never needed water to cool me before. Everything about this place is strange."

They rested awhile in silence, looking around them at the trees and sand and growing expanse of open water, now truly a sea with ice chunks floating in it near the horizon.

"I know we started out without talking or planning-"

"I just wanted to get away from that place," Rika said. "Away from where Moolnik drowned and where Elder Nuanu's body fell into the water."

Rika brushed her hand across her face, dashing away a sudden rush of tears. "We didn't say the proper words over Elder Nuanu's body." She slumped down on the sand again.

"I think Elder Nuanu will understand," Attu said, "and tonight, when we make camp, we'll speak the burial words for her." *And I'll thank her for somehow using her body to trick Moolnik into falling off the ice,* Attu thought. *Would Elder Nuanu truly prove more powerful in death than she was in life?*

Attu felt the hair on his arms rise at that thought, for as the embodiment of Shuantuan, Elder Nuanu had been a potent force in the clan.

The sun had been growing even warmer as the day progressed. When he breathed, he couldn't see his breath.

Attu stood up and slipped off his fur vest, shivering as the slight wind evaporated the sweat from his chest and back, now exposed. It felt strange to be warm enough without layers of heavy clothing.

Attu reached out, taking Rika's hand in his own and lifting her onto her feet. "Your turn."

"What?" Rika asked. She was staring at Attu's chest.

Attu grinned at her.

Rika looked up at him, flushed, and looked away.

Attu pulled at her arm again. "I was just wondering how this warm air might feel on the rest of your skin. If it gets any warmer, you're going to have to take off your vest or die sweating," Attu teased.

"I should," Rika said, her boldness suddenly returning, and Attu's mouth dropped open as she turned away from him, whipped her short-sleeved inner vest over her head and grabbing one of her foot wraps, quickly tied it around herself, covering her chest and leaving the rest of her upper body exposed to the sun and breeze.

"Wonderful," Rika said, lifting her arms and letting the wind blow across her bare skin. Turning back to Attu, she grinned wickedly up at him.

"Yes, wonderful," Attu said and reached for her.

"Time for that later." Rika stepped out of his reach, picked up her pack, and started walking across the sand again. "Let's walk and plan."

Attu grudgingly picked up his own pack, and they headed south again. But he couldn't help watching Rika, seeing how her hair brushed over her bare shoulders and how the wrapping stretched over the curves of her body.

Growing tired of walking through loose sand, Attu and Rika moved closer to the water. The sand, where it had gotten wet, was firmer and much easier to walk on. An occasional wave touched their feet, and the water was freezing, but used to the frigid temperatures of The Expanse, neither of them grew cold.

"We're far enough away from where Moolnik…" Rika paused. "Why don't we just wait here until the rest of the clans catch up with us?"

She stopped and dropped her pack for a moment. Taking a string of hide from her parka front and turning into the wind coming off the hills, she slicked her hair back, re-braided it over her shoulder, and tied the string on the ends.

Beautiful, Attu thought.

"Better," Rika said. "So why don't we just wait?" She asked her question again.

Attu cleared his throat, working to focus himself back on their conversation. "I think we need to find the place first, because-"

"Attu, what's that?" Rika interrupted, her voice a fierce whisper. She pointed a trembling finger toward the edge of the trees.

A huge brown creature had detached itself from the pines and was moving slowly along the edge of the tree line. As Attu watched, it stopped, raised its head, and looked in their direction.

Chapter 32

"It's as tall as a large shelter," Attu whispered. "Higher than I could reach."

"Do you think it sees us?"

"It should, but it doesn't look alarmed."

Attu saw and felt no immediate threat from the beast, and as they watched, the creature started walking again, its head down, tearing and chewing at the knee-high plants that grew in a boggy area between the open water and the trees. When it raised its head again, water and green plants dribbled from its fat lips, and it made slurping sounds as it turned its head slowly toward them while it chewed.

"It sees us," Attu breathed. "Don't move."

The beast stared at them for a long time before it ambled toward the trees again, walking with an awkward gait, feet sucking in the wet sand, short tail flapping side to side as it walked. Its ears dangled off both sides of its elongated head, flicking first forward, then back.

"It's so ugly," Attu breathed.

"I'd laugh if I wasn't so scared," Rika agreed. "It doesn't seem to know how to walk using four legs."

The creature lifted its head high, sniffed the wind, and pierced the air with a shrill call. Attu's whole body trembled at the eerie sound.

An answering high-pitched cry came from the north, back the way they had come. *Another one.*

The creature spun around.

Attu gasped as it leaped out of the low area and began running toward the sound of the other creature, a shelter-sized wall of fur flying above the plants and disappearing into the trees.

"Well, I guess it knows how to use its legs well enough," Attu said. He added, "Do you think we could eat it?"

"You kill it, and I'll tan its hide and cook its meat. An animal that big would feed our whole clan for several days."

"It wouldn't be easy to kill."

Attu turned from the place where the huge creature had disappeared into the trees. The animal had been so large, and it ran so fast. *How am I going to feed and protect Rika here?* He felt like a child in this place, ignorant and afraid of what he didn't understand.

Rika touched Attu's bare upper arm, sending new shivers down it.

Attu shifted his own pack and readied his spear in his hand, and trying not to think of how much Rika's touch affected him, he said, "I think there's a lot about this world our elders never told us."

"I don't think they knew. All they had were stories of the spirits and the ancient people. What was remembered and passed down."

"Let's hope something doesn't kill us before we figure out how to kill it."

Rika nodded her agreement before changing the subject. "As you were saying before that crazy brown creature came by-"

"We need to keep moving," Attu said. "I've been waiting to tell you, because we were, well, kind of busy trying to save ourselves and all…" he paused.

"Tell me what?" Rika looked at him, curious.

"There is a pass we must find through the mountains before the rest of the clans catch up with us. We must be the first two to go through the pass."

"How do you know this?" Rika asked.

"I saw it in a dream. The one I told you I couldn't talk about. And there's more."

"What?"

"I think the reason Elder Nuanu passed into the Between of unconsciousness just before we made it to land was because, somehow, someone else spoke through her. It was her, but a man's voice. And her face changed… it was… a man. He said the same thing he'd said in the dream. We must go through this pass first."

"Why didn't you tell me someone spoke through Elder Nuanu before she passed into the Between of sleep and couldn't get out?" Rika stopped walking and turned to face Attu. She looked angry.

"Because the others were there and you had been in the dreams, too, and-"

"Me?"

"Yes."

"And just when were you going to tell me all this?"

"I'm telling you."

"And before? On the ice sheet? With Elder Nuanu?"

"I was trying to save us. I'm telling you now, aren't I?" Attu could hear his voice rising in frustration. *I'm trying. Can't you see that?*

"I dreamed of the bear before it attacked. You know about that."

Rika nodded.

"But what I didn't tell you is I also dreamed of you being separated from me by a crack in the ice, before we even met. I didn't know it was you, at first…" Attu rushed to explain, then paused when he saw the look of disbelief on Rika's face.

"Before we even met?" She asked.

"Yes, and when I thought I would never see you again, I thought I was wrong, I thought I was just dreaming like your father said, what I desired and could not have, not what was prophetic. But then, it happened. We are together, and-"

"How do you know it's me who goes through the pass with you?" Rika pulled Attu down beside her so they were sitting, facing the water.

"Because the white-haired man said I must go through the pass with the one who will bear my sons and daughters." Attu looked down then, his cheeks reddening.

"Oh," Rika said, then again, "Oh… I will have sons…and daughters…?" She looked at him in amazement.

Attu suddenly realized he had never considered what the man had said in his dream past the fact that he must be bonded to a woman before he went through the pass. *Sons and daughters?* He thought. *Rika is right. We will have sons and daughters. How could that be? At least four children? It was unheard of amongst his people. A miracle…*

They sat in silence for a while. Then Attu took Rika's hand. "In the dream of the pass," he explained, "we head south until we come to a rock shaped like a nuknuk spearhead. The pass is there."

"And you saw that, too?"

"Yes."

"Do you have any idea how far it is?"

"No."

"Or how far ahead of the clans we might be?"

"Not for sure."

"I need you to tell me more. Tell me exactly what you dreamed."

Attu did his best to explain to Rika about the dreams, about the white-haired blue-eyed man, about the need to go through the pass together, alone, before the others. He explained how he believed that what he'd learned in the dream was true, that if they didn't do this, everyone would die, even though he had not been told how those deaths would occur.

Rika listened.

"Whenever Paven is with us, he takes over," Attu said. "And right now, I don't think your father's too happy with me."

"True."

Rika studied the rock-strewn beach in front of them. "He doesn't even know we're still alive, we're bonded." Rika looked at him then, her face soft.

"I don't think once we rejoin the clans that Paven will agree to us going by ourselves through the pass first."

"And you don't want to have to argue your way into convincing the clans to let us pass through first. But in your dream, you weren't told why you have to be first, we have to be first," she corrected herself, "just that we do. And if we don't, everyone dies."

Attu glanced at Rika. Her forehead was creased in thought.

"Do you think me needing to come with you could have anything to do with the voice in my dreams?"

"I don't know. I thought showing mercy to Moolnik on the ice fulfilled your dream. But I thought warning my clan when the ice cracked fulfilled mine at first; still, it has turned out to be so much more."

"Yes. Tell me more about this pass."

"In my dreams, the pass isn't too long, a day's journey at most."

Rika nodded. "You know it's too dangerous to go alone, just the two of us."

"How could anything be more dangerous than what we've already been through? We've survived being trapped on an ice chunk, Moolnik's attacks, and I've survived two ice bear attacks. Nothing has been able to kill us yet."

"I'm not saying we shouldn't go," Rika continued. "I'm just saying it's dangerous."

"I know. I feel it in my spirit, too."

"Then let's get going. Who knows how far behind us the others are?"

They quickened their pace, loping along the beach, their long strides eating the distance, covering in one afternoon what would have normally taken them an entire day to travel. When the sun was nearing the western horizon and the sea was sparkling in the evening light, they halted, both exhausted.

"I need to find us snow to melt and something to eat," he said. "Can you set up the shelter?"

Attu dropped his pack on the rocky beach and began readying his hunting equipment. He grabbed the skin pouch with the large mouth for packing snow into it and turned to walk toward the trees.

"Be careful," Rika said.

Attu turned back. Rika looked so small against the background of the restless unfrozen water and ice chunks glimmering in the late sun. "Keep your knife out."

"I will."

Attu approached the dark line of the pines with their whispering limbs. He felt dread seep into his bones. Forcing himself to keep walking into the strangeness of the pine-scented darkness, he soon found himself surrounded by the green spicy trees with their brown needle-like castoffs. They littered the ground, cushioning it like furs on a sleeping platform. He took a few steps into the trees and turned around. Suddenly everything looked the same.

Attu's breath caught in his throat. He listened for the sound of the water rolling up onto the rock beach. Confident he knew where it was coming from, he turned his back to it, drew a line with his spear butt deep into the brown-needled ground, and put a sideways mark across it to show in which direction he'd come. Satisfied it would work to help him find his way, he walked a few more steps. Turning back, he could no longer see the line. His heart began pounding. He tried tying a signal string onto a tree arm a few feet ahead. Walking a few more feet, he turned. The signal string was designed to show up against snow. With its hide colored string and grey rock, it was now hidden in the swaying branches of the trees he had just passed.

How can I walk in this place without getting lost?

Then he had an idea. Attu touched one of the trees. Fascinated, he felt the life force in the pine as it moved in the wind. It was old, the tree, old and somehow wise, in a way he'd never experienced before. Asking the tree's spirit for forgiveness, Attu pulled out his bone knife and at shoulder height, cut a few strokes into the rough skin of the tree. Inside, its meat was white, and Attu saw that its blood was almost clear, thick and very sticky as it moved slowly into the wound he'd made. Attu walked a few more steps into the trees and turned back again. The blaze of white was clearly visible against the dark skin of the tree.

Good.

Attu continued to walk into the trees, at a slight angle to the shore, making more cuts in the trees as he went. He was looking for snow. Attu was hungry, but both he and Rika were used to going days without food. Everyone did when the hunting was poor. They'd survive without food for a while, but not without fresh water.

Off to Attu's left, he heard a sound that grew louder as he walked in that direction. Curious, he followed the sound and came upon an area of thick moss. The trees were even bigger here than near the shoreline. Attu walked across the moss a few steps and looking toward the rocks, he saw water, flowing from uphill, down along sand and rocks and moss. *How could that much water be here? It wasn't part of the sea...*

Attu knelt by the flowing water and touched his finger to it. *Cold.* He wet his finger again and licked it. *Fresh.*

Attu had been walking uphill, and this water was flowing downhill, toward the sea. It was cold, like snow when first melted.

Attu had seen a few drops of melting snow dripping from the rocks on the last land they'd stayed on, but never more than a tiny amount. *If great areas of snow melted when the air of Nuvikuan-na warmed, then that snow would become water and it would run downhill to the Great Frozen. No, that wasn't quite right. It would flow to the Great Sea, which is what the Great Frozen was becoming...*

Attu quickly filled the snow skin with water, and his own water pouch as well. The snow skin was much heavier filled with water rather than snow, and Attu worried it might split. He'd have to move slowly back to camp. He set it down on the soft moss and turned to adjust his smaller pouch so he could carry both. As he did so, something caught his eye.

A small bundle of fur hopped along the edge of the water. As he watched, it hopped again and stopped. Ridiculously long ears moved first this way, then that. It took two more hops and stopped. *Did all creatures of this place have huge ears?* Attu wondered. Ears like that on the Expanse would freeze in a few moments.

Attu saw an eye on the side of the fur ball's head, large for its face, and a nose, with whiskers like a nuknuk's, twitching as it smelled for danger. It was close. If it would just hold still long enough...

Attu shifted his spear into his throwing hand and raised it slowly. The little animal didn't move. Attu drew his arm back and aimed at the center of its body.

Attu's spear hurtled through the air. It pierced the animal clean through and pinned it to the ground. Attu ran to the creature. It was still alive, its back legs kicking the ground helplessly, trying to escape the spear. Attu pulled it off the spear point by its ears and twisted its neck quickly to kill it.

"Little furry one, whose name I do not know," Attu said, his voice solemn, "forgive my ignorance. Thank you for giving your body for us to eat. May your spirit soar wherever your kind desires to be in the Between, and may you be born into another body like this one, when you are ready. See, I have killed you quickly and with mercy. Please tell the rest of your kind, so they won't be afraid to die at my hand and avoid me when I hunt."

Attu took the small creature and went back to pick up the water skin. He retraced his steps using the blazes he had made in the trees as he walked. He was almost to the beach, watching the last sunlight fading through the trees as he neared the shoreline, when he saw the fire.

Something large and yellow, like a thousand nuknuk lamps, was burning near the hide shelter. It lit up the shelter and the rocks in a wide circle, as well as Rika, who was hunched down next to the snapping brightness.

"Rika, run!" Attu yelled.

Chapter 33

"We'll be walking into the trees, through the mountain pass. I believe it will be like the passes through the hills back on the land we knew, but the hills here are mountains like the ice mountains, only even taller."

Attu was trying again to explain to Rika what he'd seen in his dream about the pass. He was still embarrassed about dashing madly across the beach and throwing Rika off to the side to protect her from the roaring spirit of flame, only to discover that it was only a fire she herself had made from dead tree bodies.

"Wood," Rika explained. "Elder Nuanu told me about it."

"Oh, like in the story of the New Green. I didn't know," Attu said. He knew he sounded like a whining child, but he didn't care. He'd thought Rika had been in danger.

"Because women are keepers of the fire."

"I know that, but this..." *keeping of the fire meant the small nuknuk lamps,* Attu thought, *not some mighty conflagration that roared, an inferno of heat and light with acrid smoke that rose up like trystas spinning off into the night.*

How was I to know it wasn't attacking Rika? This fire was too powerful a thing for a woman to handle...

But Attu knew he'd better keep that thought to himself. So instead, he sat and glared at the fire as if it were his enemy. It didn't help that Rika had commented, "Saving me seems to end up with me bruised and scraped and you in a bad mood."

He changed the subject and began outlining his plan. They'd leave a cairn of rocks at the pass when they found it, and three strands of hide lacings with time stones tied to a pole, cut to the right lengths and identified with Rika and Attu's patterns. The clans would see them and know Attu and Rika were alive and that the people needed to wait three days before they attempted to go through the pass. That should give Rika and Attu plenty of time to go through and back, with an extra day for whatever they might encounter along the way.

"You know it's likely my father will not wait one day, let alone three," Rika said.

"And we have no idea why we have to go through first, what we do to save everyone. I know, it's frustrating," Attu agreed. *And it doesn't help that I haven't dreamed since Elder Nuanu spoke in the man's voice. It makes all of this seem unreal, like we could just go on, find the pass, wait for the clans, and move forward as if I never dreamed at all.*

Rika poked at the fire with a tree arm, sending a shower of sparks into the air.

Attu slid farther away from the heat. He knew he was being unreasonable, but he felt uneasy around this fire made from tree skeletons. He didn't think it right to burn tree bodies. What if the spirits of the trees grew angry with them for doing it? They were surrounded by trees, countless trees…

"When I see the pass in my dreams, it's just a day's journey across, not too steep a climb up or out of, and most of it is pine trees, with rocks rising up on both sides. I can't sense any reason we must be first through it, just the two of us. Still, everything else I've seen in my dreams has come true. Why should I doubt them now?"

"Who knows what we might encounter in that pass? We have no idea what kinds of people or animals might live here," Rika said, motioning with her head towards the forest behind them. "We both know the way of things. Bigger animals eat smaller ones. The tooth fish eats the smaller fish, and the snow otter eats the tooth fish. The ice bear eats the snow otter and the nuknuk. So just think how big an animal must be to eat one of those big-as-a-shelter plant eaters we saw."

Rika cringed as she spoke and reached out with the tree arm to stir the fire again, raising another shower of sparks. Attu moved away from the fire even further. Rika, however, seemed to draw comfort from the blaze and slid herself closer, increasing the distance between them. Attu didn't like it.

"And how would you ever kill such a predator if we were alone?" Rika added as she stared at the flames. "It might be the size of a hill, and it would certainly eat us if it eats those animals."

Rika set the tree arm on the ground beside her, pulled her knees up to her chest, and wrapped her arms around herself.

Attu hadn't stopped to think about the possibility of a monster predator, big enough to kill the shelter-sized creature. No wonder Rika was scared. *How can I protect Rika from some monster like an ice bear only ten times bigger? But we have to go. We have to fulfill the prophecy, or everyone will die. That's what the white-haired man in the dream said through Rika, and through Elder Nuanu. We can't back down now.* Attu didn't know why, but as they spoke of it, it was like some power rose up in him, compelling him to continue. He had to do this.

"It will be all right." Attu moved over to Rika. She leaned against him, and he folded her in his arms.

"I'm afraid," she whispered.

Attu took in a deep breath. "So am I," Attu whispered into her ear.

Rika drew back from him.

"I'd be a fool not to be scared, wouldn't I?" Attu challenged.

Rika looked at him, confused.

"I'm tired of all the lying between hunters and their women, Rika. We get scared, too. You must know that. Can't I be my real self with you? Isn't that what you want? Or do you want the lies, Rika?" He paused.

Rika continued to watch him. He couldn't tell what she was thinking.

"I just wanted you to know the truth," Attu finished, his voice now barely above a whisper.

Rika nodded her head.

"Look at all the things that have happened so far, as the prophecy has been fulfilled, piece by piece," he said. "We're heading into something awful. I feel it in my spirit, but we must go alone."

"I feel it, too." Rika said, her voice soft as the gentle breeze blowing through the pines. "In my dreams, and I thought I was just being silly, but ever since I met you, it's like voices in my mind, calling me to this place I've never been, never seen… I thought it was just… I don't know what I thought. It frightens me. And it compels me… to follow you…"

Rika looked up at him, her eyes begging him to hear what she could not explain.

"I understand," Attu said. He smiled at her in the firelight. "I feel it, too."

Rika sighed and leaned back into him, and he held her as if she might break at his touch.

"We're going to make it." Attu knew he spoke to reassure himself as well as Rika. In the glow of the strange dancing firelight, Rika had never seemed more beautiful. He drew her into his arms and held her close in the light of the fire until the wood burned down to embers and she slept, nestled in the fur of his parka.

But Attu couldn't sleep. He was concerned about their planning making them forget to say the words of burial for Elder Nuanu this night, and it was too late to wake Rika now. She needed her sleep. He hoped waiting one more night would do no harm. Thoughts raced around in Attu's head as he tried to rest but also remain alert for anything unusual at the same time. *It's so hard, when I don't even know what the danger might be until it could be too late.*

Attu jumped at a snapping sound coming from behind them. He eased himself away from Rika and walked over to where the packs and other supplies were neatly laid out. The rest of the meat from the animal he'd killed, along with its pelt, was gone. It looked as if something had dragged it away, but Attu couldn't see any tracks in the small light of the stars and waning moon. *Stupid.* He hadn't stopped to think there were other animals on land that would steal food from humans.

"See, Elder Nuanu," Attu whispered, "we need your help more than ever before. We'll say the words of ritual over you tomorrow, but until then, can you keep us safe anyway?"

Attu searched the perimeter of the camp for any signs of an animal. Nothing. *We needed that hide and meat. I have to be more careful.*

Attu spent the rest of the night walking around the edge of the camp, occasionally sitting and dozing in his exhaustion. Would he be able to keep Rika safe from whatever danger lay ahead? Attu knew he had bravely spoken of trusting in the prophecies but now, after not even being able to hold on to the leftovers of his own kill, he wasn't so sure.

Chapter 34

"I didn't protect the meat," Rika said the next morning, as she examined the now empty rock slab where the little hopping animal's pelt and bit of meat and bones had lain the night before. She crossed her arms in front of her and began to kneel before Attu.

"No, Rika," Attu said. He grabbed her shoulders, lifting her back up. "Stand up. It's my fault for not realizing other animals must roam this new land, looking for food."

"The meat was mine once you gave it to me," Rika reminded him. "It was my responsibility." She raised her face to look at him. She seemed determined to take the blame.

"We'll share the responsibility for the loss of this meat, and…" Attu said, careful of his words now, "every mistake we make in this new world because we are ignorant of this place. We are bonded. We make mistakes together. We learn, together."

"But the way of our people, the Nuvikuan-" Rika began.

"Is NOT the way of this place," Attu interrupted. "So, we'll keep what is good from our people and leave behind the rest. Do you agree?"

"I don't know the proper way to keep this new fire or how to keep us safe from the evil spirits of this land that do not exist on The Expanse," Rika whispered. Her face paled.

"I don't know how to keep us safe, either," Attu said. "We both have to learn new ways. Together."

Rika grew thoughtful. "When we speak the words over Elder Nuanu this night, we'll ask her if this is a good way to proceed. She'll tell us if she can."

"Good idea," Attu said, and they quickly gathered up their belongings and began walking south again.

As they walked, the hills behind the trees became higher and higher. Soon, they were so high Attu had to tip his head back to see the tops. After they'd been walking awhile, the heights of the mountains began to disappear, then reappear, lost in a swirling whiteness, like the tree's fire, only whiter. *Are those clouds? Are the mountains as high as the clouds?*

"What if we miss the rock formation because it's lost in the whiteness?" Attu asked.

"We both looked ahead while the sky was still clear and saw nothing like a nuknuk spear tip," Rika answered. "I think we can walk awhile longer, but then we'll have to wait until we can see the tops."

"I agree. We can't risk missing it."

They kept walking, slower now, avoiding looking too long at the swirling whiteness of the mountain tops, lest it anger the air spirits who dwelled in the clouds.

The rocky beach began narrowing until there was only a strip as wide as a spear throw between the sheer rock cliffs and the sea. Attu had noticed earlier that the Great Sea seemed to rise and lower about twice during the waking hours. It made no sense that water would rise and fall that way, but he began to worry they might come to a place where the water was high and there was no more beach. *What will we do then?*

A wind picked up from the unfrozen water as the beach narrowed even further. It blew warm and strong across the sea, well above freezing and buffeting them as they walked. Rika tied her hair back, and they stopped to secure their packs. Both of them wore only their fur pants and Rika her top made of foot wraps, but still they sweated as they walked. Their bodies were used to such cold weather, anything above freezing seemed hot.

"Look at the ice chunks," Rika said.

"I've been watching them."

Huge ice chunks were floating towards the shore in the wind, and several crashed against the beach ahead. Above them, the air had cleared as soon as the winds began, and the mountain tops showed stark and grey against the blue of the sky above them, with patches of bright white as the sun reflected off the snow near the top.

"We could never climb those," Rika said.

"We won't have to. Look!" Attu shouted, above the now almost storm-force wind. "There it is!"

They had rounded a bend in the beach, and off in the distance, the clear outline of the nuknuk spear point's two prongs jutted up from one of the mountains, as if a giant had carved it. It rose above the mountains around it, each point curved slightly inward, exactly like the people's spears.

"We can make it by nightfall if we don't stop again for a rest," Attu said. He had been plodding along, exhausted from lack of sleep the night before, but now he felt energized. He glanced toward Rika.

"Let's go," she said and began the slow lope that would eat up the distance they had yet to travel.

Attu and Rika made it to the foot of the spearhead mountain just as the sun touched the edge of the sea. It was too late to search for the passage through the mountains that evening. The beach had widened, and a thick stand of trees now blocked their view of the base of the rock, which seemed to rise almost vertically from the ground. Attu was anxious to find the passage, but he knew this was a time when the patience of the hunter must prevail. Besides, he was starving. The only fresh meat they'd had in days had been the hopping animal, and it had been small.

Rika began gathering pieces of dead trees, which lay scattered about the beach, and soon she had a fire going. Attu pulled out his fishing gear and quickly caught two large fish. They resembled tooth fish except for their jaws, which were smaller and had only a few teeth. They were fat fish, with much meat on them, and their bellies were the color of the sky in the evening. Attu chanted his thanks to them, and decided he would call them sunset fish. He hoped the fish would like the name.

"The meat is provided," Attu said as he handed the fish to Rika. "Sunset fish."

"The meat is most welcome, mighty hunter," Rika replied. She smiled at his name for the fish, but Attu heard her call them sunset fish as she dribbled a few drops of water into the mouths of each one, to give their spirits a drink before they departed for the Between. He sat by the fire and closed his eyes.

"Wake up, Attu, you need to eat," Rika said.

Attu jerked awake. He should have been guarding the camp, and instead he'd fallen asleep so soundly he hadn't heard Rika approach.

She handed him a large portion of the fish, crispy from the fire.

"Good," he said through a mouthful of the tasty flesh. "Best fish I've ever eaten."

"It is good," Rika said, and together they devoured almost all of the meat of one fish. Rika had covered the other with some wet green plants she gathered from the shoreline. "I think those will keep it fresh, and we'll cook it tomorrow and eat it before we go. The rest of this first one I'll dry over the fire tonight. We can take it with us. They're rich with fish fat and will give us energy for the journey through the pass."

Once they were done eating, Rika built the fire up again. They stood, side by side, looking out over the Great Sea, which now, after the wind from earlier, was almost free of ice. Attu marveled at the expanse of dark water, lit by the moon and stars.

"I would never grow tired of watching how it moves," Rika said. "I'm glad to speak the words of burial over Elder Nuanu here. I think she'll like it."

As if in answer, a small swirl of sparks rose up out of the fire as a burning wood piece snapped.

Together, Attu and Rika performed the burial ritual. They didn't have a body or large stones to place over a grave, so each of them took small wood pieces and threw them on the fire as they took turns speaking the words of protection. Elder Nuanu's body was gone, but her spirit still needed their words.

The end of the ritual came, the part reserved for the personal things one wished to communicate to a clan member now gone. Since Elder Nuanu was the embodiment of Shuantuan, this part of the ritual needed to be done with extreme care.

"Oh, Elder Nuanu, Shuantuan in human form, may your spirit rest back with the Shuantuan of the Between, until another chooses to be born to our people," Rika began.

"We are thankful you have chosen to reside with us for a time, and welcome your arrival again in another clan or ours again, whenever you may choose to come to us." Attu said.

Back and forth they recited, thanking Elder Nuanu for the blessings of allowing a Shuantuan to live amongst Attu's clan. It was a great honor, and they must express this with both sincerity and longing for another opportunity to have her among them in the future. This was easy, because both had loved Elder Nuanu. They were true in their hearts, which was most important. The spirits knew the thoughts of humans and when they were being deceitful. Still, both of them breathed a sigh of relief as that part of the ritual was spoken without a mistake.

They stood for a while, silent in the darkness, lit by the fire. Rika began to sing. Her voice was high, and Attu swelled with pride at the beauty of it. He hadn't known his woman had such a pleasing voice. She sang the ancient words of their people, the words to send Elder Nuanu into the spirit world with power, the words to elicit her help when needed, her protection always.

She finished, and it was Attu's turn. Stripped to the waist, he danced the dance of the hunter, his movements showing his attention to ritual, his calling upon the spirits for a good hunt, his thanking of the game, his understanding that it was Elder Nuanu and the women of the people, now residing in the spirit world, who protected the hunt and brought game to the hunter. The dance was hard, and Attu had only learned the last few moves when they'd buried Taunu. He was glad to be able to dance for Elder Nuanu and was surprised, as he finished his last leap and twirl, to find tears flowing down his face.

Sweating before the heat of the fire, he reached for Rika's hand. He puffed as he stood, catching his breath.

"Elder Nuanu, we stand bonded before you," Rika began speaking again.

"Do you want me to ask?" She whispered to Attu, suddenly shy of what they had decided earlier.

"Yes."

"This is a new place, and we believe we must learn new ways," Rika continued. "We wish to keep all ritual we need to keep, and learn all new ways we must learn, all new rituals. We will learn some from the one Attu has told me waits for us on the other side of the pass, but the pass is dangerous, and I am afraid to go through it without the proper rituals being performed."

Rika glanced at Attu. She hadn't said that before, but Attu nodded his head. He trusted Rika to ask for what she needed, what they both needed.

"Please show us what to do."

They stood in silence for a long time. Attu began to fall asleep on his feet, but he shook himself awake and tried not to stare at the mesmerizing flames of the fire. So much more entrancing than mere nuknuk lamp flames… he felt heavy somehow, like he couldn't stand up any longer. He felt his body go limp, realized he was falling, saw Rika reach out for him, heard her cry, then, nothing…

Attu awoke, his head cradled in Rika's lap, a wet hide on his forehead.

"What happened?" He asked.

"Elder Nuanu spoke through you," Rika whispered. Her hands were trembling as they stroked the hair away from his face.

"She what?" Attu tried to sit up.

"No, don't," Rika said, pushing him back down.

Attu looked up into her eyes. They were filled with tears.

"I was afraid you'd die, like Elder Nuanu," she said.

"I'm awake. I'm all right."

His head was pounding and he felt weak, but he wasn't going to tell Rika that. She looked terrified. "What did she say?" Attu asked, as a shiver traveled the length of his body. *Do I want to know?*

"She said she will protect us as we go through the pass, and once we save our clans and travel to the other side of the mountains together, the people there will teach us what we need to know to fulfill our rituals in this new place."

Attu couldn't believe what he was hearing. Elder Nuanu had spoken to them, had assured them of her protection. He shook his head, trying to clear it, but the movement made him dizzy.

Rika was watching him. She looked odd. Was there something she wasn't telling him?

"Is that all?" Attu asked.

"No." Rika smoothed the wet cloth over his forehead.

"What else did she say?" Attu asked when Rika didn't continue.

"It doesn't matter. I can tell you later. You need to rest now." Rika moved as if to jump up and tend the fire.

"Rika," Attu said as he grasped her hand, trying not to scare her by grabbing her too hard. "No lies between us, remember? Tell me."

Rika ran her fingers through her hair, as if to calm herself. "She said that when the time comes, I have to let you go." She looked at him, her face a mask of pain.

"Let me go?"

"Yes. And I don't know what that means. Where will you go without me?" Rika began to cry.

Attu reached out for her, and Rika fell across him where he was still lying and buried her face in his chest.

"We won't know what Elder Nuanu's words meant until we're there, in the moment when it's happening," Attu reassured her. "She might mean something totally different from what you think. I'm not going anywhere without you."

Despite Rika's protests, Attu sat up and wrapped Rika in a fierce embrace. "Listen to me," he said. "I mean it. I will not leave you."

"But Elder Nuanu said."

"Like I explained, what is said through someone else, or in dreams, it isn't like us talking in the Here and Now. It's different. Like the ice bears looked like snow mountains with teeth, and seeing you across the gap of unfrozen water turned out to be you on the ice sheet. And you weren't alone, like I dreamed. We will just have to trust and see."

Rika nodded, but Attu could tell she hadn't believed him.

They sat in silence for a while. Attu's head was clearing and he realized he felt rested, as if he'd slept a long time, even though he could tell it was still the middle of the night. He hadn't been in the Between of sleep that long.

Slowly, Rika pulled away from him and wiped her tear-stained cheeks with the back of her hand. Attu studied her face. She was biting her lower lip. “What else?” he asked. “I can tell something else is troubling you, too.”

Rika shook her head.

“Tell me,” Attu teased, “or I will haunt you.” And taking a piece of Rika’s long hair in his hand, he put it over his lip, screwing up his eyes to look like a spirit mask.

Rika laughed, but her face grew serious again. “I didn’t believe you before,” she admitted. “And I’m ashamed of that.”

“You didn’t believe me about the dreams, the visions?”

“I believed that; I’ve dreamed, too. I didn’t believe someone else spoke through Elder Nuanu to you. It just seemed impossible.”

“Oh, Rika…” Attu began.

Rika interrupted him. “But now, after Elder Nuanu talked through you to me… well… now I believe.” She looked at him, her face filled with regret. “I’m sorry I didn’t before.”

Rika lowered her gaze, letting her loose hair hide her face.

“It’s OK, Rika. I knew you agreed to go with me because you love and trust me, not because you believed in everything I told you, especially about Elder Nuanu speaking in the white-haired man’s voice.”

Rika looked up, her face confused. “Really? You knew? And you said nothing? I was feeling so bad…”

Suddenly, Rika smacked his shoulder with her hand. Her voice rose. “You knew? And you went along with my apology just now as if… as if…” She slapped his arm. “You tooth fish!”

Rika began pummeling him on the chest. “You knew all along…”

She pushed him back to the ground.

Attu fought back, tickling Rika as he dodged her small fists pounding on him. Soon they were both tickling each other, laughing until Attu couldn't breathe.

"Stop," he cried, coming up for air.

Rika grinned at him, and Attu had the feeling that kissing was going to replace tickling, and soon.

Attu took in a deep breath and called out to the night sky, "Thank you, Elder Nuanu! For everything!"

Chapter 35

"Fog," Rika said, looking up at the mountains disappearing into the whiteness. "Elder Nuanu told me about fog. She said it was the breath of the spirits and usually evil ones."

Attu and Rika were standing on the edge of a small ridge, overlooking the pass through the mountains. They could see up to a bend in the pass, and nothing beyond that. The pass had been easy to find, just a couple of spear throws distance into the trees, marked by a cairn of rocks and with deep scratches dug into the side of the rock face at its entrance, some sort of symbols that neither Attu nor Rika recognized for sure, except for the signs for both their clans, the Ice Mountains and the Great Frozen Clan. These markings were the same as the tattoos all the men were given at their final naming ritual.

Attu thought he recognized the Tooth Fish clan symbol he had seen on Banek, but he wasn't sure. The others must be clan symbols as well, Attu decided. Whoever carved them all into the rock had gone to great lengths to communicate to them that this was the way to safety, the way they must travel when the Warming time came.

Attu and Rika had built a waist-high cairn of rocks on the beach, above the high water mark, in a place it would be easily spotted, a clear flat area with no plants or hills to block the view of their marker. The clans would see it from far off.

They buried a long piece of tree arm in the rocks so it stuck out the top. To this, they tied three time stones, using both their parka strings. The message to the others would be clear. They were alive, and the clan needed to wait three days before it was safe to go through the pass.

Both Attu and Rika prayed to their name spirits as they headed into the pass, a narrow opening in the rocks, only wide enough for two people to walk, quickly growing wider until it became a path several could travel on at once. The mountains rose up on either side of them, a few twisted pines clinging to the rock, but mostly bare, and steep. When Attu tilted his head back and looked straight up, he could see the tops of the mountains, still white with snow.

The ground along the path they were walking was covered with small round stones, and their smoothness reminded Attu of the little rocks he'd sometimes found along the edge of the land he had lived on as a child. He picked one up, his fingers caressing its smooth blackness. He thought about the stream he had seen the day before. The rocks in that were rounded as well. Attu slid the rock into the pocket of his parka as he thought about his mother telling him about the rocks that grew round along the edge of their land. She said it was from the constant movement of the water under the ice. She'd held them up for him, and he'd collected a few while she gathered the mussels. *They bounce across the ice when you throw them.*

But there was no water here, although the rocks were wet. Attu felt a sense of unease in his stomach, and it grew as they traveled along the path.

"I feel like the mountains will fall down on top of us at any moment," Rika said. "I don't like it."

"We're so used to being able to see to the horizon. I feel the same way. Let's climb up here," Attu suggested to Rika, pointing to a place where the mountain on his right seemed to ease back a bit, giving them a hard but accessible climb to a ridge high above the path.

They stood there now, looking down at the pass and up at the fog-covered mountains. The fog had snuck in when they were climbing the ridge, and the hair on the back of Attu's neck prickled at Rika's comment about Elder Nuanu and the fog spirits. Something was wrong. He recognized that feeling of suddenly being the hunted instead of the hunter.

"Do you hear that?" Rika whispered. "Across the pass and up on the other side. Look!"

Attu saw a pine tree's green movement. There was no wind.

"Something is following us," Rika said.

"Whatever it is, let's keep distance between it and us. Let's see how far we can walk along this ridge," Attu said. "It will be safer up here on this side where at least we can see if it comes at us. It has to go across the pass, and there's no place to hide at the bottom. We'll see it coming."

"All right," Rika agreed, and they continued walking the edge of the ridge, climbing higher and higher as they traveled along the pass.

"Do you think we'll be able to get down?" Rika asked.

"We may have to go back the way we came, but I'm not walking down there, not with something hiding on the other side."

Twice more, Attu and Rika saw movement on the ridge opposite the pass. Rocks slid, making a clattering noise that echoed along the stony bottom of the pass. A while later, Rika thought she saw a shadow darting from one rock to the next. Attu didn't see it, but Rika's eyes were keener than his.

"I think there's some sort of path over there," Rika said, squinting to look across the pass. "It's narrow, like this one. Do you think there are animals that walk along these ridges? Why would they do that, instead of walking the pass?"

"Same reason we are. Too visible down there. It's like a trap."

"When we come through here with our people, you will set hunters as guards," Rika said.

"Yes."

They walked on, climbing higher and higher along the ridge path. Soon they were walking in snow, large areas swept clean by what appeared to be places where the ice of generations had loosened from the rock in the Warming and tumbled down, bringing rocks and trees with it. The ridge path was scraped clean in places, in other places the path had been obliterated and Attu and Rika had to climb over dead trees and around large boulders in their path.

The way began to clear again, covered in snow but no more debris.

"This area doesn't seem to have been affected by the Warming," Rika said.

"Not yet," Attu replied and looked above him at the wall of snow and ice, barely clinging to the edge of the mountain. He grew even more wary, wondering what it would take to send the whole mass down the side, on top of them.

Coming around the next bend in the ridge, Rika stopped. Their way ahead was blocked by a tumbled mass of trees and rocks.

"What to we do now?" Rika asked.

Attu walked to the side of the ridge. It was steep here, but not as steep as in some places. "I think we can climb back down."

"Attu, look!"

Attu turned and looked back the way they had come. They were far enough above the ravine's floor to see the entrance of the pass with the sea behind it. Attu saw smudges of movement against the stillness of the rocks and occasionally a flash of color. People were coming through the pass.

"They didn't wait."

"No, and look." Rika pointed upward where a dark mist was swirling above the trees and rocks of the blocked ridge. "The fog spirits are gathering. Something awful is about to happen, Attu, I feel it deep in my spirit. I think Elder Nuanu is trying to warn us."

"Hurry," Attu said, and the two of them scrambled down to the floor of the ravine. "We've got to make it through the pass first. It feels like a trap down here, but there's no other way."

Neither spoke as they hurried along in the shadows of the mountains on either side.

As they rounded yet another sharp bend in the pass, Rika stopped. Attu ran into her.

"What?" Attu asked.

"Look!" Rika said, bringing her hand up to her mouth. "Moolnik," she whispered as she stared at the figure in the pass ahead. Attu reached for her and felt her begin to tremble under his hand. "It's the ghost of Moolnik."

Attu stared ahead. "No!" It looked like Moolnik, dressed in a parka and fur leggings and carrying a tree arm, long, like a spear. He was running along the bottom of the ravine near the ridge, looking up. He apparently hadn't seen them yet.

"It can't be…" Attu said.

"But, he drowned," Rika said, her voice small and filled with disbelief.

"I should have known Moolnik wouldn't die that easily," Attu muttered as he drew himself closer to Rika and readied his spear. "I'm tired of this devil, this Moolnikuan," he said, more to himself than to Rika. He lifted his spear and leaped ahead with a cry.

Moolnik saw him and ducked, but continued running as if to run past them.

"Wait!" Rika yelled. "Stop, Attu. Don't kill him."

"Why?" Attu asked, but he lowered his spear. Instead he rushed Moolnik, cutting him off. Moolnik's speed caused them both to tumble to the ground. Attu grabbed Moolnik by the back of his parka, jabbing his knife into the man's side.

"I'm going to kill you, like I should have the last time I had the chance, on the ice sheet."

"No!" Rika begged.

"Why not?" Attu asked. He wanted to kill Moolnik. He'd had a taste of what it was like to live thinking the man was dead. *Life is better without madmen like Moolnik lurking in the shadows waiting to strike.* "I'll make sure you die for good this time. It's clan law."

But he glanced at Rika. She was studying Moolnik.

"No, Attu. There's something very wrong here. Look, Moolnik is wearing one of my father's old parkas; I recognize the pattern, and look," she jabbed with her foot. "That's my missing knife."

"You've been following us all along," Rika accused Moolnik. "You took my knife, and you must have sneaked up on the clans' camp and stolen that parka."

"More reason to kill him. He's a murderer and a thief." Attu pushed the knife harder into Moolnik's side, but the man was strangely silent, his face impassive, although he was sweating. He didn't even struggle.

"No. Don't you see?" Rika asked. "This is all wrong. How did Moolnik find the pass before we did? What is he doing here? Look at his hands, and the front of his parka, and that tree branch he was holding." Rika motioned to the broken piece of branch that Moolnik had been holding before Attu tackled him. "They're covered in mud. What has he been doing to get so dirty? And why?"

"Who cares? He won't be able to do any more harm once he's dead." Attu grabbed Moolnik more firmly with his free hand and dragged the man into a standing position as if to get a better position for stabbing him.

A smile spread across Moolnik's face at Attu's words. "You may kill me, but that won't stop me. It's too late to stop me from killing all of you." Then Moolnik chuckled. Attu's stomach twisted at the sound.

"I'm through playing games with you, Moolnik," Attu said. He slid his knife up to Moolnik's throat.

"No," Rika said, her voice firm, unyielding. "This is the time. We will show mercy, at least long enough to find out if this is another one of Moolnik's lies." She turned to Moolnik. "So you think you've done something that will kill us all? I don't believe you. Prove it. Prove you are not just a coward trying to buy a few more breaths with your ranting."

"I'm not lying, girl. You know nothing. You are very stupid for one who is supposed to be a healer."

"Watch your tongue, Moolnik," Attu hissed. "Or did you forget my knife is at your throat?" He pressed the knife blade into Moolnik's skin. A trickle of blood oozed from the edge.

"You may have the knife, boy," Moolnik said, his voice a harsh whisper in an effort not to move his throat, "but you are not the only one to have dreamed. Did you think you were the only one to know of the pass?"

Attu released the pressure on his knife, slightly. *What was Moolnik talking about?*

"I have dreamed of the pass, and more, boy, and I have moved with the spirits to seek my revenge on this clan, and yours too, girl." Moolnik suddenly twisted his arm, trying to pull free of Attu's grip, grabbing for the knife at his own side, but Attu held firm.

"You dreamed of the pass?" Rika asked.

"Yes, and I knew I must be the first one through it. Once the clans vowed to kill me, I vowed to kill you all. And I have succeeded." Moolnik started looking around now, his eyes wild, his forehead dripping sweat.

"He's crazy," Attu said. "I'm finishing this."

"Go ahead. It will make no difference now," Moolnik said. "You're all dead, anyway." He twisted again, as if trying to look behind him. He was becoming increasingly agitated, and it seemed to have nothing to do with Attu holding a knife to his throat, which made no sense.

"What were you doing?" Rika asked. "Why are you so filthy?"

"Just making sure you all die, and soon." Moolnik grinned.

She leaned forward to look more closely at Moolnik's clothing.

"But not me!" Moolnik shouted, startling them both. He slumped forward and down, slipping under the knife, twisting, and pushed past Rika. Instead of running back down the pass, he ran for the edge of the ravine.

Rika recovered her balance, and both of them chased after Moolnik. They saw the rope at the same time, hanging hidden against some trees and tied far up the side of the ravine on the ridge.

"Oh, no you don't," Attu yelled and for the second time crashed himself into Moolnik, who hit hard on his chest and face in the dirt. He came up struggling and pulled away from Attu. Attu stood in front of the rope, blocking Moolnik's escape. Moolnik grabbed inside his parka and pulled out two knives.

"You think you can stop me, boy?" Moolnik leered. "I think it's time you knew the truth. What difference does it make if I tell you now, since you'll be dead before sunset?"

A deep rumbling noise made them all stop and listen. The ground underneath them trembled. "Sooner, I think," Moolnik added.

"What was that?" Rika asked.

Moolnik leered at her. "Your death sentence, girl. Serves you right for drugging me on the ice, for stealing my knife, for preferring this boy over me."

Another rumble echoed down the pass.

The hair on Attu's neck stood.

"I have dreamed since I was a child," Moolnik said. "And while you were dreaming of ice bears and chasms of open water, I dreamed of the pass. I saw it, too. But I certainly wasn't going to tell anyone of my dreams. Dreams are for children."

Suddenly Moolnik sounded far away, as if he were speaking with someone from the past, someone long gone. His voice became bitter. "You taught me well, Father, to pay no heed to dreams. But I dreamed of the pass, Attu, the pass I heard you tell Rika about as you two sat by the fire, and I dreamed of the blockage in the pass, which you did not!" Moolnik looked at them both in triumph.

"There is a wall of rocks and trees and ice, a new avalanche, which has stopped the flow of water along this ravine. Behind it the water is rising, waiting to rush through this pass when it is finally freed. I was going to be the hero of the clans, save you all, by telling you of this blockage once we got here, showing you how to break it, let the water flow, stay high above the rushing torrent until it was safe to travel through." Moolnik shook his head, and his voice grew hard. "But no, once again my brother must be the one all look to, and his son, and all listen to his dreams, even Elder Nuanu. All look to Ubantu and to Paven. And then even Banek thinks he is better than me, pushing me off the rope, willing to let me die so that he might live. But I showed him."

Moolnik clutched his knives in his hands, raising them up, as if remembering how he had stabbed Banek.

Rika blanched, but she did not move.

"What have you done, Moolnik?" Attu asked.

"I have killed you all," Moolnik said. "I moved a few rocks, dug out a bit of ice here and there, slid a tree or two from the blocked pass, just like I was told to do in the dream…" He looked back the way he had come, smiling. "The water will soon break over what remains, and everyone in its path will be swept away. Everyone will die. But not me!" And Moolnik leaped for the rope. Attu hit him from the side, pushing him into the rocks, and one of Moolnik's knives was knocked from his hand. Attu pulled his own knife.

"Climb!" He yelled to Rika. "Climb to the top of the ridge and run. The clans are coming. Our families will all be killed. Run to warn them!"

Rika stood for a moment longer, her face blank with shock.

"I'll hold him off as long as I can! Climb, Rika! You've got to get back to the clans and warn them."

"But..."

"Just climb!"

"I'm not leaving without you," Rika said, but she leaped for the rope and began hauling herself up it, quickly gaining height.

"No!" Moolnik shouted and as he looked up at Rika, Attu took advantage of his distraction and hit him in the side of the head with his fist. Moolnik fell in a slump.

Attu grabbed the rope and began to climb. Rika had reached the top. She threw her leg over the ridge and then turned and grabbed the rope.

"Go!" he yelled. "Don't wait for me!"

"The rope is coming loose," Rika shouted down to him. "I need to hold it for you."

Attu was about to answer her, tell her he'd take his chances on the loose rope, when he felt the rope below him jerk.

Rika screamed.

Moolnik was climbing the rope. He had one knife in his mouth, the other in his hand, and his leg was wrapped around the rope as Banek had done with his arms. Attu had a sudden vision of Moolnik climbing up his body, one knife strike after another while he dangled as Banek had, trapped on the rope, bleeding to death.

"Release the rope!" Attu yelled. "You have to let me go!"

"No!" Rika yelled.

Attu reached out for a scrubby tree, growing from the side of the ravine. "I'll hang on to this and drop to that narrow ledge below. From there I can climb down. You've got to let me go, Rika. This is what Elder Nuanu prophesied when she spoke through me. Let me go, and run to save the others."

Moolnik was gaining on him. Attu could almost feel himself being stabbed…

"Let go!" he yelled.

"I love you," Rika said.

Attu grabbed the tree branch and let go of the rope. The branch held.

Rika dropped the rope.

Moolnik screamed. Attu looked down to see Moolnik land face down on the rocks below. He didn't move.

"Are you all right?" Rika called. She was on her hands and knees, peering over the side of the ridge at him. "I think Moolnik's dead."

"Yes, now go, Rika. Run. Warn the others, before it's too late."

As if on cue, a deep rumble and the sound of falling rocks echoed through the pass.

Rika's head disappeared. Attu hung from the tree branch a few moments longer, working out how best to drop to the ledge below. He looked down, judging how far he would need to climb, and that's when he saw Moolnik's body was gone.

How could Moolnik have possibly survived that fall?

Attu felt the hair on his arms and neck rise at the thought of what kind of spirit controlled Moolnik. What evil power was in him to make Moolnik seek vengeance, even to the point where he no longer cared if his own woman and sons were killed? Surely, Moolnik must be more than a mere man; he must have become the embodiment of a Moolnikuan. Attu prayed it was not too late, and Rika would reach the clans in time, before Moolnik caught up with her. For surely that must be what he would try to do? Attu shuddered at the thought. He had to get down from this ridge and help Rika.

Attu decided to push himself out from the edge a bit before dropping. He pushed out with his legs as a rumbling sound rose up from the opposite side of the ravine. Attu looked out across the ridge to see snow spraying in all directions on the other side and debris flying. A small branch hit his face, and a roaring sound rushed at him. The tree he was hanging on to broke away from the side of the mountain, and Attu had just enough time to swing himself out, once, then in, and he fell onto the narrow ledge below, the tree toppling past him, tearing at him, almost ripping him off the side of the mountain, also. But Attu saw a narrow opening at the base of the ledge where the rock was still attached to the mountain, and he shoved himself into it, squeezing his body as far under its protection as possible. A rain of ice and rocks and tree debris came pouring down on him.

Had the avalanche trapped Rika? Or had she made it far enough down the ridge before the ice and debris began to fall? Attu poked his head out from under the crevice and at that very moment, a rock loosened from the avalanche fell off the side of the mountain and cracked Attu on the back of the head. He was unconscious before his face slammed onto the ledge.

Chapter 36

It was growing dark when Attu awoke from the Between of sleep, rubbing his hand on the back of his head where he felt a lump the size of the hide balls he used to play with as a child. His head pounded in rhythm with his heart. He tried to stand, but waves of dizziness crashed down on him and pain seared across the back of his head.

Slowly, Attu managed to slip into a sitting position on the ledge. He wiped his eyes clear with his hands, flinching at even this slight movement.

Across the pass, the entire side of the snowy mountain had been swept off as if with a giant ice bear's paw. Bare rock now showed where before had been deep ice and snow and a few straggly trees. It had fallen with such force, bumping and crashing down the mountain, that the rain of snow and ice had spread out over the pass and much had hit Attu's side of the mountain pass.

Below Attu, a rushing body of deep water coursed over the path of rounded stones he and Rika had walked earlier. It was moving fast through the pass to the sea.

"Rika!" Attu shouted, wincing as pain shot through his head. Some snow had stuck on the ledge, and he made a loose ball of it and placed it on the injury. His head was excruciating to the touch, but Attu held the snow there, anyway. Soon the pain began to ebb slightly. Attu tried to think.

Rika couldn't have gotten far before the snow slide had begun flinging debris at them from across the pass. There was a bend in the path, so it was possible she escaped the worst of it. *But when had the blockage broken and the waters begun to flow? He had no way of telling. Had Rika made it in time to warn the others? Or had she been caught in the avalanche backlash, hit by a rock or ice hunk? Was she lying injured right now, needing him?*

The thought made Attu try to stand again, but the pain in his head made his stomach clench and he threw up over the side of the ledge instead. Sitting again, Attu forced himself to take a drink from his water pouch, which was still inside his parka where he always carried it. The water seemed to clear his head and ease the pain a bit, so Attu sat for a while longer, taking drinks and putting fresh snow on his head. Then he tried again to stand.

This time he managed to get upright without throwing up. But as soon as he removed the snow from the back of his head, it began to throb painfully, making him feel sick to his stomach. Attu rigged a wide strip of hide around his head, resting a mixture of ice and snow against the lump on his head, and forcing it to stay there by tying the band tightly around his forehead. It was awkward and freezing on the back of his neck as the ice and snow melted and dripped down into his parka, but at least with it on, he could walk without his head feeling like it was going to burst.

Attu labored up onto the ridge, slipping on the loose rocks. He headed back down the path toward the opening of the pass.

"Rika," Attu called every few steps, wincing at the pain that erupted in his head every time he shouted. He listened and looked around for any sign of her. He saw and heard nothing. It soon grew dark, and there was a moon, but the ridge was filled with rocks and other debris. Attu forced himself to move slowly, even though he longed to hurl himself down the mountain like the water roaring below him, screaming Rika's name. *I can't risk another fall; I can't risk missing Rika, injured on the side of the path somewhere. I have to search carefully.*

There was also the matter of Moolnik. *Could the man have gotten to Rika? Could he now be waiting for an opportunity to kill me? All I've got is my knife.* Attu was in no shape to fight anyone, let alone a Moolnikuan spirit. He should be sneaking along, watching for Moolnik. But he couldn't. He needed to make sure Rika wasn't hurt somewhere along the path. He had to take the risk. And so he continued calling for her, knowing it made him a target every time he cried her name.

It had taken them half a day to journey as far into the pass as they had come. It took Attu most of that night to walk back. He searched along the path and called until he was walking just a few feet above where the water flowed. He knew from his height on the path that the water was still very deep, much deeper than a man was tall, and it seemed to be moving fast. Attu tried not to think of what had happened to the clans if they'd been caught in what must have been a torrent of water and debris when the blockage first broke through. Instead he walked faster, calling Rika's name more often.

Attu had abandoned the ice wrap on his head once the snow had melted, and his head felt hot now and hugely swollen. His eyesight seemed blurry also, but he couldn't tell if it was from his injury or because it was darker here where the moonlight didn't reach the base of the pass.

Looking ahead, Attu saw the path was blocked by water. He could go no further. The ridge ended at the water's edge, and there was no way up or out from here. Frustrated, he sat down and held his pounding head in his hands. Rika hadn't been trapped here. He'd hoped to find her at some point on the path, but she must have moved along farther. And that meant she might have been caught in the water as it raced down the path. She would've tried to make it, to warn the others, that Attu knew. *She is that brave.*

Stuck at the edge of the moving water with no way to go further, Attu spent the rest of the night curled in a ball to keep warm, his head causing him to sleep fitfully and dream of Rika, at first running to the clans in time to warn them, and then Rika riding the waves like the whale fish, looking at him with eyes of terror, finally Rika disappearing into the water like Banek, never to be seen again…

~ • ~

Someone was shaking him. "Don't, my head," Attu mumbled and put his hands up to hold his throbbing head. Hands grabbed his. "Rika?" he asked, struggling to open his eyes.

He couldn't see.

"Rika!" Attu began screaming, and he pushed the hands away from him and tried to stand up, but the hands held him down.

"Attu, it's me, your father," the voice said. Attu felt arms around him, holding him, lifting him.

"Father?" Attu asked. "Is everyone, is Rika…"

"Rika is fine, we are all fine," Ubantu said as he held on to Attu, steadying him. As Attu stood there, Ubantu's shape began to form before his eyes, dark, out-of-focus, but he could see the light and shadows around him.

"How did you reach me?" Attu asked.

"The water has receded enough for us to walk along the edge of the pass. It's narrow and you must be careful, but we can make it back."

"Did the water strike the clans?"

"No," Ubantu said, turning to steady Attu, who was wobbling on his feet. "Are you hurt?" He asked as Attu almost fell.

"My head." Attu pointed to the back of his head.

Ubantu let out a low whistle as he saw the lump. "Let's get you back to the clan."

Attu began walking, stumbling every few steps because he couldn't see anything except outlines, light and dark in front of him.

He said nothing to his father, however, letting him think it was from weakness instead and allowing Ubantu to support him, to lead him along the path.

"That must have been some rock that hit you," Ubantu murmured.

"Tell me what happened, Father. Did Rika make it in time to warn you?" Attu asked.

"Rika made it. She warned us and everyone turned and ran, just like we did over the ice. No one panicked as we reached the narrow opening and we made it far enough away from the opening just as the waters began flowing."

Ubantu looked at Attu. He added, "And Paven killed Moolnik."

"What?" Attu couldn't believe what his father was saying.

"Paven and I were the last ones out of the pass. Or at least we thought we were. Then Paven heard someone running hard along the stones of the ravine toward us. It was Moolnik. Paven saw him first and when he recognized him, he grabbed his spear and threw it, killing my brother instantly." Ubantu looked away, his face inscrutable. "It had to be done. It was clan law to kill the man immediately. We left the body where it lay, and Moolnik's body was swept out to sea on the first wall of water rushing down the pass."

"I am sorry you lost your brother," Attu said.

"I lost him a long time ago, my son. I realize that, now. A long time ago."

They walked on for a time in silence before Ubantu spoke again.

"We made it to safety just as a wall of water crashed out of the pass. If you look now as we go through it, the pass is wider than it was by at least a spear's throw. The water broke through the rocks like they were made of thin ice and crashed into the sea. The sea rose up in a huge wave, and it pounded down on the beach. But we had made it far enough away from the opening. No lives were lost."

"How is Rika?" Attu asked.

"She's sleeping. Her foot miks had torn, and her feet were bloody from running across the sharp rocks in them. She kept crying out for you, so your mother gave her something to make her sleep."

Ubantu stopped then, and turned Attu to face him. Attu could see the shadow of his father's face, a little clearer than before.

"Moolnik dreamed, too, did you know, Father?"

"No."

"He knew the pass was blocked and would be about to break as the clans came through. He dreamed it all. He was going to save the clans by telling everyone when the time was right. But after the clans swore to kill him, he decided to take revenge on us all." Attu explained about Moolnik setting his trap, including the rope he had rigged for his own escape.

"But son, how did you know these things?" Ubantu asked, confused. "Why did you allow him to speak at all? Why didn't you kill him like Paven did when he saw him, instantly?"

"Because of Rika."

"Rika?"

"Yes, Father. Rika had dreamed she must show mercy when judgment was called for, and that somehow this would save the clans. I dreamed we must go through the pass together, first." Attu ducked his head and flinched as his head throbbed. "I was hesitant to tell you because Rika was in the dream. She was the 'one who will bear my sons and daughters'."

That statement took a little more explaining, but Ubantu quickly understood why Attu hadn't told them about the dream. How could he, when Rika was promised to another? No one would have believed him.

"And only you and Rika could have saved the clans," Ubantu said, as he considered all that had happened, "once Moolnik turned to the evil spirits, letting them control him instead of using what he knew to help us all. Only you would listen to Rika, believe in her need to show mercy, let Moolnik live long enough to tell you what you needed to know to save us. Only you, who had dreamed also, would believe him, as Moolnik believed you. Only you and Rika could have done this thing."

"I know." Attu shook his head in wonder at the way of the spirits, the dreaming and the white-haired, blue-eyed man who seemed to be behind it all. Somehow, he had even known Moolnik would betray his people.

"I wonder why I did not dream of the blocked pass?"

Neither of them had an answer to that question.

Attu filled his father in on the rest of what he had been told as they continued walking toward camp.

"Elder Nuanu is dead?" Ubantu asked when Attu mentioned how she had helped them.

"Yes."

"Paven is very angry, because-"

"Do not worry, father," Attu said, and he told his father how Elder Nuanu had bonded them before she died.

"Rika knows the words of protection for a woman?" Ubantu asked.

"Yes, she does."

"Good," Ubantu said, and Attu could hear the relief in his voice. Then Ubantu smiled broadly as he considered what else Attu had said about Rika. "And she will bear you sons… and daughters?" Ubantu smacked his thigh with his palm and laughed. "I will be a grandfather to many." He grabbed Attu more firmly by the shoulder.

Attu smiled, glad to see his father pleased. And, Attu noticed as they walked along, his father no longer limped at all.

The two traveled in silence for a while. Attu was exhausted. He wanted to get back to his family's shelter and let his mother feed him and treat his head wound. He wanted to curl up beside Rika and sleep, leave everything else behind him. He was so tired, he thought he could sleep forever.

They rounded the last bend in the pass, and Attu saw the torn opening where the water had rushed through. He popped his lips in amazement at the damage. *Who knew water on the move could be so powerful?* He shook his head, then regretted it as new stabs of pain encircled his skull. Ubantu reached out and grabbed Attu's shoulder, steadying him. Then his father's grip tightened.

"Remain quiet," his father whispered.

Attu looked ahead. He could just make out the shape of a large man striding toward him.

"He is mine," growled Paven. "He will pay for dishonoring my daughter."

Attu imagined the man's scarred face twisting in anger as he stared at Paven, seeing only his outline against the sky. *So this is what I get for saving Rika's life?* Attu thought. It all seemed so remote, so unreal, all this posturing about hunter's honor and women's honor and all the rest. They'd fought Moolnik and escaped drowning and discovered a whole new world. Yet all Paven could see were the old ways.

His father had told him to stay quiet. Attu had been quiet and obedient his whole life. No longer. He was a hunter and had a woman and was equal to or better than Paven. He and Rika had saved the entire clan, no two clans, more than once. His time of silence was over.

"Rika is no longer yours, Paven; she is bonded to me," Attu said. "We will go back to camp and settle this like men. And you're welcome, by the way, for saving your daughter's life and your own, as well as everyone else."

Attu broke away from his father and strode past Paven as if he were not there, standing to block Attu's way. Attu kept walking toward the opening to the beach and Rika. He didn't once look back.

Chapter 37

"Rika spoke the words of protection!" Yural shouted. "She is my daughter by bonding now, not yours. You will not take her!"

Yural faced Paven squarely, her eyes flashing anger, her hands clenched. Other women of both clans began moving behind her, reinforcing her position against Paven, who'd been yelling at Attu's mother just moments before, demanding she release Rika back to him.

"We have the words of protection," one of Paven's older women spoke up. "They are ours, to protect our honor, to ensure everyone, even you," and the woman curled her lips into a sneer at Paven, "that your daughter has followed all ritual. Elder Nuanu had every right to bond the hunter and his woman. She spoke the words over them and gave Rika both her own sacred amulet and the words of protection. It is the way of our people, Paven. The deed is done and you cannot undo it or you dishonor Rika and bring shame to us all."

Paven swore and turned away, pushing himself through the others to his shelter. He stalked in, pulling the hide door closed behind him.

"It's safe now," Yural called back to their family's shelter. Rika slipped out from behind the shelter's hide flap, with Attu beside her.

"You should have let me handle it, Mother," Attu said, as the pair reached Yural. He kept his voice low so the others couldn't hear. "I felt like a child, lurking behind the hides out of sight."

"Some things are a woman's job, a woman's right," his mother replied. "It isn't about you anymore, but about Rika and the way of the women."

Yural pulled herself up to her full height, and even though the top of her head barely came to Attu's shoulder, Attu felt the power emanating from her. *Will she become the next Elder Nuanu?* He wondered. He stepped back, deferring to her judgment.

"Come on," Rika said, grabbing at Attu's sleeve and pulling him away from the women. "I want to start through the pass ahead of everyone else, so we can get our packs and make sure the rest of the way is clear. The women will deal with my father, and I'm not going to worry about how he feels anymore."

Had it only been a day since he'd stumbled into his family's shelter, falling beside Rika, and reaching for her as he slipped into unconsciousness again? His mother had treated his head wound. Rika had made him a potion that eased the pain. The two women had worked to make him comfortable, to feed him, and as they did, they chattered as if they'd known each other all their lives. Attu watched as Yural beamed at her new daughter.

Meavu and Ubantu had been given a chance to visit with Attu, but just briefly. Then they'd been told to give him some time to rest. It had been so good to have Meavu hugging him and pestering him again. He'd promised her he would tell her all about his adventures on the floating ice chunk after he was feeling better. His eyesight was back to normal, but his head still hurt whenever he moved.

Attu realized Rika had stopped in the path, and he felt the tug of her hand in his as she looked up at him.

"I belong to your family now, and I trust in your mother's strength," Rika said. She grinned up at him. "Your father's too, of course." Then she began walking toward the opening to the pass, even more quickly than before. "Let's go!"

"My head hurts," Attu complained. Walking made it worse. He didn't think one day of rest was enough, but the clans were eager to move through the pass now, and he and Rika did want to be first, even if they no longer needed to be.

"We can take the ridge trail, backtrack to the path beside the moving water, and be almost through the pass before the clans get halfway," Rika said. "We'll be first to the place you told me about, the place of the symbols, and the wise man who could talk to you in your dreams."

Attu tried to hurry in spite of his headache. He was as eager as Rika to get through the pass.

There was no place where the ridge disappeared on the side where Attu and Rika walked, and it didn't take long for them to round the last bend in the pass. There before them lay a green expanse of plants, stretching out to the horizon. Large shapes moved along, gathered together in groups. They were a long way away, but still Attu could see these huge animals had long fur that hung on them like hair, and a few had long curved tusks, one on each side of their face, like male nuknuks.

"They seem to be plant eaters," Rika said. "I'm glad."

"Me, too."

Attu and Rika walked down the ridge as the pass opened up toward what seemed to be a stand of trees, where mountains met the flat land.

"This way, I think," Attu said. "I've seen this before, in my dream."

It was farther than they'd first thought. Distances from above were deceptive, Attu decided, but it was still light when they reached the trees. Within their tall branches, people moved, fires were lit, and shelters made out of plants instead of hides could be seen here and there in a small cleared space against the large black rock of the mountain.

Suddenly shy, Attu and Rika moved slowly through the trees, Attu careful to hold his spear in the position of friendliness, over his shoulder, even though it kept catching on low tree arms. When they came into the clearing, Rika stopped, her eyes large in her face.

Before them, a huge wall of rock rose up toward the sky, with a circle of symbols carved into it, each one taller than a man. Attu saw the symbols for the Ice Mountain Clan and the Great Frozen Clan, among other symbols, and across the bottom much smaller close carvings and symbols that meant nothing to him.

Attu caught movement to his right and turned. Out of the shadow of the rock he saw the old man he'd seen in the dream, white hair flowing over smooth plant clothing, decorated all over with rich and strange patterns. Behind him stood several other men and women, all robed in unusual plant fibers and carrying tree arms. The man strode toward them, spear upright in his hand. It was carved like bone and decorated with strange ornaments that jangled as he walked.

"Attu," Rika grabbed his hand. Hers was trembling.

"It's him," Attu whispered. Rika nodded her head. Neither of them moved as the man approached. He stopped directly in front of them. Attu felt shivers run up and down his body as the man searched his face with those eyes Attu had seen before, eyes impossibly blue.

"You are here, Attu and Rika; you have answered the call to come to The Rock of the Ancients, and in doing so, have saved your clans," the man said in a voice full of power. "The Great Spirit has brought you here at last."

Attu felt as if he had been lifted up on a mighty wave in some long forgotten time past and had now been set down again, unharmed, in this strange new place and time. He felt light-headed. He tightened his grip on Rika's hand. She squeezed his in return.

"That's the voice I heard," she whispered to Attu. "The voice in my dreams."

The old man smiled. He reached out his arms as if to enfold them both, as well as the men and women who now surrounded them.

"Welcome to your new world," the man said. "Welcome home."

32698503R00175

Made in the USA
Middletown, DE
14 June 2016